This book is unique. Contained within are QR codes. Simply scan them with your barcode scanner app on your smartphone. Any barcode scanner app can be used on your phone. If you do not have a smartphone or scanner app, when you see the website address next to the QR code, enter it into your c

D0890498

LOVE…

THE ILLUSION

Ann Marie Graf

www.lovetheillusion.com/01.htm

To everyone that made this book possible…

Thank you

PREFACE

Naked he stood...the one I loved...a complete disgrace, unlike any other. At the door of the bedroom, I made my grand entrance, unannounced. Jasmine clutched the scarlet sheets, a portrait of deceit I pain to envision, alarming my inner senses that everything I once thought true was now revealed to be a lie.

Agony spread, like wildfire, my perception of love left in ashes, leaving me alone to wonder... Is love worth the risk of getting burned?

Maggie

www.lovetheillusion.com/00.htm

Chapter 1

TWENTY-ONE stories high, fashion designer Maggie White overlooked the busy streets of Manhattan from her hotel suite. It seemed only yesterday when she was just a small girl and first took hold of the sewing scissors to cut that favorite piece of rose printed fabric. "Don't cut yourself," her mother had warned.

Maggie now knew that no physical pain could compare to a wounded heart. Six years had passed since her mother's death, and she would always remember that dress. She wore it on her first day of school. It was special and one of a kind—both the dress and the love they shared. And with the last thread sewn, her mother spoke the words that she would never forget: "Someday, Maggie dear, you will design clothes for other people to wear."

Her biggest fan had always been her mother, even when others had their doubts. "What is that?" her father would ask when Maggie would sew something. But her mother would always defend her, proudly announcing *her* belief that one day Maggie would be a fashion designer.

After losing her mother, Maggie understood heartache. But she had no experience on how to handle her latest grief—the loss of her fiancé whom she thought was her very soul mate. And losing him was not only painful, it was humiliating as well. How did Phillip think he could pull off a one night stand with Jasmine while engaged to her? And how could such a friend betray her trust? Could she ever forgive them? At least she found out. But now she could no longer say, "I do."

Staring out into the big city, she suddenly felt small—too small to deal with her latest rival, Jasmine. It seemed only prudent to find her life's fulfillment in her career. She adjusted her watch to the new hour while gazing upon a stone clock embedded within her view. Soon she would meet with her new boss, the highly acclaimed Francis Louis, to prepare for the flaunting of Magnetic Threads, his latest dress line.

It had been a long day—a seven hour flight from London, misplaced luggage guaranteed to "arrive shortly," a pair of red swollen feet in a pair of tan patent stilettos, and a stomach that wondered why she had not eaten for hours.

With briefcase in hand, she entered the elevator while adjusting her pencil skirt which, after the long flight, felt glued to her buttocks. Sharply dressed in her charcoal grey suit and starchy baby blue blouse, she had just enough time to find something to eat. A caterer, tending to a cart of food, nodded with a friendly smile.

"Hello, madam."

"Could you please tell me where the closest restaurant is?" The pleasant aroma of braised beef and potatoes filled the air.

"Uh, that would be Atrium Cafe, next to the main entrance on the first floor," he informed.

"Thanks!" Maggie smiled while fixing her chignon.

The elevator came to the first floor where hotel guests were swarming the premises, a child in a stroller was screaming, and bellboys scurried about.

"Excuse me!" She flagged down another member of the hotel staff. "I'm looking for Atrium Cafe."

"Oh... no..." he said apologetically, speaking broken English, "No here, that in *north* wing."

"Oh," Maggie deliberated, exhausted. "Then where's the closest restaurant? I'm completely famished."

"Long trip?" He showed concern.

"Yes, from England—here for the spring fashion show."

"Ah, you European, I show you Biagio's! You like, excellente Italiano."

Where she ate was not a concern. She followed him down a hall to a secluded back entrance where he opened the door and motioned for her to go into the bar area. Immediately, the stress from the day's events melted away as she stepped into the dim, cozy atmosphere. Classy, inviting, but where was everyone?

The bartender peered over his shoulder, aware of her entrance. He wore heavy black rimmed glasses. She took a seat when he asked, "What can I get for you?" His playful demeanor suggested that he needed a drink to pour.

Why not, Maggie decided.

"I'll have red wine. What do you recommend?"
He spoke quickly. "We have Antinori Solaia Cabernet, beautifully crafted from Italy—bold, richer, and darker than the Tignanello with textural richness to match an expressive core of blackberry jam, smoke, scorched earth, crushed rocks and cassis, and notably intense fruit driven aromas of ripe cherries and blackberries without excessive hints of—"

"That sounds great." Maggie thought he was quite the salesman. "And can I get a burger and fries?" she requested without even a menu. She decided to pass on her typical weight watching salad while hoping to have the energy to make it through her longwinded meeting with Francis and his associates.

The bartender acknowledged her request. "We aren't open for lunch, but I'll have it sent from The Atrium." He picked up the phone to place her order. Maggie was grateful for the exceptional service.

Peering over her glass of red wine, she suddenly noticed the other patron, an attractive man, sitting to her right. She wondered who he was. He was now speaking to the bartender, and they seemed to know each other quite well. Strangely, it was just the three of them. The bartender glanced over at her, and then their conversation continued. Were they discussing her? *The lack of tact!* Maggie swerved her barstool in their direction while crossing her legs and kicking her heel into the side of the bar. "So...Where is everyone today?" she asked with her eyes curiously fixed on the other patron.

"Not sure," he spoke confidently, betraying a slight accent. Hearing him speak, she could not help but take further notice. Dressed in a fitted black shirt and a pair of belted, black tailored dress pants, he wore his jet dark hair with a bit of wave, at a carefree, medium length, accentuating his dark eyes and tan complexion. He appeared smug and aware of his appeal. Then he leaned back in his barstool to make eye contact with her, and when he did, she blushed and felt her stomach drop.

Well, look at that! Maggie assessed. *A hot, ego-immersed bad-boy from top to bottom!*

The bartender disrupted her thoughts. "We open for dinner in two hours—right now, just happy hour."

"Not a lot of happy people in New York?" she asked the bartender, while the man in black gave a short laugh as his glass of what appeared to be water hit the counter with a soft clank. She instantly fell captive to his energetic smile while contemplating her first assumption. She quickly turned away to watch the bartender methodically rearranging the liquor stationed in an elaborate display on mirrored shelving above the marble countertop. Without even realizing, she soon held an empty glass as the bartender moved to pour her more wine.

"Oh, no," Maggie declared, raising her eyebrows to meet his. "I didn't purchase the bottle."

"It's on the house!" He waved his hand to indicate the insignificance.

Maggie considered his generosity.

"Oh! Don't tell me! I'm the only woman in the house, so you're trying to get me drunk?" she teased.

"Don't be silly." He chuckled. "Your food's just going to take a bit longer than we thought. By the way, I'm Stanley...Stanley Watson and this is... ah..."

"Chad." The man in black gave her a flirtatious smile and then sent a message on his cell phone.

"Well, nice to meet the both of you. I'm Maggie...Maggie White." She stared at Chad, eager to determine what promoted his confidence. "So, Chad..." she humorously probed, hoping to get another glimpse of his engaging smile, "What brings you to this lonely pub for happy hour?"

"I'm...working," he spoke mysteriously, making brief eye contact. "Just on a quick break."

"Me too..." She studied him. "I have a meeting pretty soon, with Francis Louis. We're here for the fashion show." She wondered what sort of women he dated.

"You work for Francis?" Chad sounded alert. "That's interesting." He turned over his undivided attention. "Are you from the UK?" His eyes circled her face, acknowledging her beauty.

"Yes, all the way from London." She stared back at him, wondering how he knew Francis.

"That's a long flight!" He grinned, assuming she was intrigued by him.

"Feels like a day and a half!" She grinned back, absorbed by his interest in her.

"Well, welcome to New York!" He spoke carefree.

Now a man, dressed in a black tuxedo, arrived to speak with Chad, and after a private conversation—much too vague for Maggie to pick up on—left the room on a mission.

"Don't worry, your food will be here soon," Stanley explained.

Shortly afterwards, the man in the tuxedo returned, set Maggie's food in front of Chad, tapped him on the shoulder, and left. Maggie stood, realizing he mistakenly received her food. Watching to see her next move, he pushed the dinner plate a couple spaces over, inviting her to sit next to him. She hesitated, but then decided to accept his offer.

Now up close, his dark eyes and brow seemed to pull her in to his very soul, and although she found him attractive, she remained cautious of his intentions.

www.lovetheillusion.com/08.htm

"So, are you a waiter...here early?" she asked him.

His eyes immediately shifted as his mouth curled on one side in a grin. He appeared deep in thought while processing her assumption and then gave a quick nod. "Yeah." He looked at her, and she blushed again. Then he smiled. His confidence was intimidating. She decided to keep the conversation minimal. She did not need another man taking advantage of her.

"You better order something before you have to spend the whole night watching everyone else eat," she told him, feeling a bit nervous.

He seemed amused. "Is it good?"

"You should know. You work here." She hoped he couldn't sense her attraction.

Chad signaled to Stanley, as his face broke out in a smile. "Yeah, can I get what she's having?"

Stanley and Chad exchanged a smirk, and then Stanley issued his guarantee. "Coming right up...*Chad.*" He shook his head, letting out a snicker of laughter.

"Oh..." Maggie alleged, "So, not your real name? *That's* really charming." She rolled her eyes. Now it was obvious; he belonged on a list with all the others! Chad bit his bottom lip, shifting his eyes in her direction, indicating he was guilty as charged.

Maggie lowered her eyebrows in disgust while letting out a huff. "So typical," she said in a repulsed tone. "What exactly *are* you doing here anyways? Oh, let me guess! You're a waiter, arrived early for lack of better things to do, waiting for the crowds to come pouring through the door, but meanwhile you just can't help but satisfy your childish sense of humor!"

"Ouch! That was mean!" Chad let out a laugh under his breath as he addressed Stanley, hoping for condolences. Maggie glanced over Chad, wondering why she still found him so intriguing.

Then he announced her worst nightmare. "You got ketchup on your collar!" He wore a grin. Immediately grabbing for her napkin, she tried to wipe it clean, but it smeared into a bigger mess. "That's not going to look good for your appointment," he reminded her.

Maggie stood up in a panic, looking at her half eaten food and grabbing her briefcase, when she felt Chad's hand on her arm. Her eyes followed his hand to his face. "Aren't you going to eat with me?" he asked with his eyes staring into hers. And in an instant, she watched his sweet side emerge from the egotistical bad-boy image that he flaunted about. Her next assumption? He knew how to seduce any woman before she would ever know what happened!

Maggie recomposed herself.

"Well, in the fashion world, a stain is a dreadful sight and a huge embarrassment, so…" She paused, landing her forehead in the palm of her hand. "Crap! I can't even—my luggage isn't here yet. It got…Shit, shit, shit!" She paced about, flustered.

"They got one hour dry cleaning at the front desk," Chad said lightheartedly.

"That's cutting it too close! Francis is expecting me in exactly one hour! And he *hates* my tardiness!" She shrugged off his deliberate attempt to minimize her disaster.

Maggie saw that Chad was looking at her.

"I bet Stanley could get your blouse back in...less than an hour!" Chad volunteered. "He's got connections."

She looked to Stanley, awaiting his reply.

"Uh, yeah, sure," Stanley said comically, as if told to bungee jump from the first floor. Then he changed his demeanor. "Seriously, we can, but I need your blouse!"

Maggie opened her mouth in shock to calculate, then looking at her watch, pursed her lips, lowering her brow to debate a quick shopping trip versus their ridiculous hospitalities. Her feet were in too much pain for shopping. Were these jokers trustworthy for a favor? Her face transformed to an excruciated state.

"Where's the ladies' room?" She finally capitulated.

Stanley nodded straight ahead, and Maggie turned around to where he looked, ready to face her next dilemma.

Having removed her blouse, she put her blazer back on, glad to see a modest covering over her black bra. Facing the mirror, she shifted about, removing a hint of ketchup that left a smear on her cheek as well. Her soft brown eyes and small rounded features stared back at her, while the vanity lighting captured the golden highlights in her dark brown hair. *I am such an awful mess*, she thought, while attempting to fix her hair back to its original.

On her way back into the bar, Chad seemed to be eagerly awaiting her return as he eyed up her revised ensemble, but she no longer wished to speak to him.

www.lovetheillusion.com/11.htm

Stanley grabbed the blouse from across the bar.

"So, I'm in charge of this disaster?"

"Sure…and thank you." She sat down as she watched his stroll as he made his way out from behind the bar, with her blouse in tow. *Hopefully, it would be considered a priority.*

When Stanley returned, he happened to bring Chad's food and Maggie took notice, checking her watch.

"Are you timing the one hour service?" Chad asked her.

"Should I be?" She looked at him, concerned.

"Stanley, pour the lady some more wine." He sat amused.

"That's quite alright. I already had two glasses. I can't afford to be sloshed on the job." She laughed off his suggestion. "I would have coffee?"

"So demanding!" Chad teased her.

Maggie dropped her jaw while absorbing his presentation. *Attractive, witty, and bored!* She let out a huff, refusing to satisfy him with a reply.

"Coffee…" Stanley verified her request.

"Yes, please, what I should have had in the first place…cream and sugar too, please."

"Cream and sugar...coming right up!" Stanley set down the cup of coffee and rummaged through a drawer on a mission to find a couple of creamers and packets of sugar. "Not too many people drinking coffee at a bar." He laughed quietly.

"Thanks." She inhaled the refreshing aroma as she took a sip of her coffee.

"You better not spill that." Chad enjoyed teasing her again.

"Aren't you funny." She praised his humor while glaring at him. She hated to admit, she still found him appealing.

Maggie sipped her coffee, trying not to look at Chad. She focused on her upcoming meeting with Francis. He was probably already waiting for her, and she could already predict their meeting—a mind-numbing overview of the upcoming event. Today was Friday, and he insisted that everyone arrive nearly a week before the scheduled fashion show. And spending time in New York City would surely bring back memories of a family vacation taken when her mother was still alive. If only her mother could share in the excitement of her new job.

"Did you know that wine that you drank is from Italy?" Chad disrupted her daydream.

"It was good."

She couldn't help but feel flattered by his friendly attempts. But why did it matter that the wine was from Italy?

Then he told her. "The Americans can't make food and wine like the Italians, but the coffee's okay here, as long as it keeps you awake."

"You must be...Italian?" She laughed.

"Of course!" He grinned.

She managed to exchange several glances with him, and while he kept a steady grin, she hesitated but then finally let go of a smile.

And in less than a half hour, her blouse arrived on a hanger in a clear plastic bag, delivered by the same man in the tuxedo.

"Thank you so much!" Maggie's face lit up as she reached for her blouse.

After returning from another trip to the ladies' room, she reached inside her briefcase and pulled out her wallet, realizing she forgot to pay for the blouse.

"That's okay. We'll take care of the blouse. It's on Stanley," Chad grinned in amusement while Maggie's eyes jetted back and forth at the two of them—both very strange, as was the bar that no one else hung out in.

She held out her hand in Stanley's direction.

"Check please, for the food."

"Oh..." He turned and faced the both of them. "*That* is on Chad!" He seemed anxious for her response.

"It's a company write-off, really, but I need the bill," Maggie insisted.

"Too bad, you won't get one," Chad insisted.

She had to smile and take one last look at him.

"Fine, I don't have time for debates, so, thank you, that's awfully sweet of the both of you and...thanks for a fun afternoon."

What would they entertain themselves with next, after she left? Next for her, of course, was the meeting.

Maggie had finally gotten her big break. A graduate of Istituto Marangoni, she now worked for Francis Louis, a prominent designer in Europe. Fresh out of school, it was a struggle to make ends meet, but now she felt fortunate to receive a decent salary. Her mother, who encouraged her dream from the time that she designed her own clothing at a young age, had passed away from cancer only a week before Maggie had graduated high school, requesting on her deathbed that Maggie use the insurance money to go to school in London. She had been living there since, and wanted to make her mother proud.

Sitting in a taxi on her way to see Francis, Maggie remorsefully recalled her latest tragedy — terminating her engagement to a guy that she thought she knew. How could she have been so blind to misinterpret his character? And they had not spoken since, although he wished to offer an explanation. Certainly, there was none worthy of reconciliation. And although she missed him, she also despised him, and tried to let go of any sweet lingering memories.

Her mind drifted onto Chad...*another liar...couldn't even get his name right.* She knew his type, always a thrill ride to a huge disappointment. *And hot guys with an ego? ...Always a problem.* Surely, he was waiting tables by now and busy charming all of his customers. Now she contemplated his mystery. Was he even a waiter? She wondered. Who lies about their name? Unless, maybe, he was undercover with the CIA, in which case it would be boring for him to run into her. There was not even a speeding ticket on her record. Or, was he with the Mafia? He was Italian. In which case, he had a list she would not want to read. All would remain a mystery, because absolutely no way would she see him again, in such a big city.

The meeting adjourned — well, almost. *He's been talking for over two hours!* Maggie sat on the edge of her chair, listening to Francis tediously ramble out the details of his latest dress lines as he deliberated from the photos which models presented the best. The fashion show was Thursday, and the models would soon be adorned in all the latest eye-popping threads that she and Francis "co-designed." *Interpretation:* He designed it, she praised his new creation, and on a rare occasion he would incorporate one of her ideas. Frustration lingered. However, Maggie capitalized on every opportunity to step ahead in the industry and appreciated her mini moments of creative success.

Early the next morning, Maggie enjoyed a leisurely jog through Central Park, when her cell phone went off. It was her roommate from London.

"Hey! Dana! What's up?"

"Where are you?"

"I'm in New York, remember?"

"You're there now? That's brill. Sorry to bother you. I thought that was next week." There was a long pause. "We got engaged! Shane proposed last night at dinner and guess where my ring was? In the bottom of my glass of white wine! Good thing I didn't swallow it because it is a huge rock!"

"That's great! Congratulations! Ha! I was drinking wine too yesterday, but no ring in my glass! Well, the two of you are definitely meant to be. I knew the first time I saw you together, and I'm so happy for you!"

"Will you be my maid of honor, and design my wedding dress and the bridesmaid dresses, and when you get back, we can talk all about it, in detail!?"

"Yes, yes and yes!" Maggie accepted.

"It's in eight months, so I'll be moving out then."

Maggie realized Dana was now getting married before her.

"No!" Maggie pretended to cry. "I'm just thinking how you are the sister I never had, and now I'm going to miss you like crazy, and I'm not going to get a better flat mate!"

"Well, then you need to find your Prince Charming, and then you will!"

"Yeah, right...You know all too well that all my princes have turned into toads."

"Right, but I bet your prince is sitting right under your nose, and you just haven't figured it out yet."

Maggie thought about how disgusted she was with men.

"Okay, Dana, just keep reminding me how I live off your optimism. I really should go, but I will see you Friday?"

"Friday, see you then, and did I tell you to try to have fun while you are there? Why land in New York and be a stick in the mud!?"

After her jog, Maggie sat in a café, with a coffee roll and mocha, thinking about Dana's latest revelation. She felt happiness for her, but sadness overwhelmed her as she wondered whether or not she would ever follow in Dana's shoes and walk down the aisle. She feared love and with good reason.

Now on the way back to her room, she had a strange suspicion that she was being followed. A big, polished, Mike Tyson–type figure, also sitting in the café, now stood a foot behind her. She recognized his familiar black patent wing-tipped Prada's. She sure seemed to be running into all of the weirdoes in New York City.

Maggie entered her hotel room, relieved to be back safe in her own headquarters. But then she stood startled. She gazed at a bottle of red wine sitting on a table next to the chair where she had left her suit. *How did that get in here?* She could not help but feel a bit creepy. She walked over to it, picked it up, and ran her thumb across the label. It appeared to be the same wine that she drank at the bar, yesterday.

It was time to call the front desk.

"Hello? I'm in room 2116, and there's a bottle of red wine in here, possibly by mistake."

"Can you hold on? I will check."

Maggie waited. Surely this would not be a business write-off.

"No, we don't know anything about that."

"Has there been anything charged to my room?"

"Just a minute." The lady put her on hold, again. Seconds later, she informed, "No. No charges."

Certainly, it came as a gift? What an unusual display of interest, but from Chad or Stanley? Maggie felt those well-known butterflies, thinking it could be from Chad. It was time to visit the bar and find out.

Is it even open?

She pushed on the door to the bar, but it was locked. Perhaps it was too early. She didn't really know him. *What if he's a creep?* Best to let it go! There was no point in adding to her list of life's greatest regrets.

Now on the way back to her room, a wine display in the gift shop caught her attention, as it took up the entire back wall. Her curiosity led her to enter the shop, and she soon found the wine with its familiar label. She reached up to remove it from the rack, when a grey-haired gentleman with a Dutch accent said, "You like that Italian wine? You are an expensive lady!"

Overcome with embarrassment, Maggie wished he would mind his own business. But then she saw the price—297 dollars? ...*Really?* Quite the romantic stunt and she had seen plenty.

Later that afternoon, on an early dinner break away from Francis, Maggie contemplated her independence from the male species. As much as she wanted to find love, she now feared reliving its painful ending. While her friends found love at the drop of a hat, she seemed to be her own pilot, magnetizing to the guys that were nothing but trouble. First crush, at age twelve, over the boy that every other girl liked—*not worth the bother.* First love at age thirteen, a cute fifteen year old boy on the soccer team hung out with her for two months and then wanted her to lose her virginity on the soccer field one night. And when she refused, he told her, *he* had *needs*! Junior year of high school, her to-be prom date videotaped the girls' volleyball team showering after a game. *Don't ask how.* College guys came and went faster than the last, until her recent engagement to Phillip. That ended last month, after he slept with her friend Jasmine, *end of story.* The last dinner date, coming to her aid after the break-up, was with a client that bashfully admitted he was married. She may as well have a sign on her back reading, "I love assholes."

After she finished her spaghetti, Maggie observed the other clientele seated nearby. There were several other people dining alone. And of course, there were the couples that appeared madly in love. She contemplated her dilemma, once again, but then reached for the bill, sandwiched between the covers of a black book.

She opened the book to find there was no bill at all, but rather a note. Maggie felt her eyes bulge almost out of their sockets. *No Way!*

www.lovetheillusion.com/18.htm

A rush of heat left her feeling flush. Her eyes wandered around the room to make sense of where the note had descended from. She motioned for the waiter who immediately attended to her table.

"Uh, yeah," Maggie panicked, "I need the bill, and I seem to have gotten this note instead, maybe by accident."

"Oh, no, that's not an accident," the waiter said, shaking his head. "Your bill is on the house," he explained and then walked away.

"Wait! Come back!" Maggie raised her voice, holding the black book in the air.

Now, she had caught the attention of a few people at the tables next to her. She cupped her other hand over her face to hide her embarrassment, while watching the waiter return, only to instruct, "Now, please leave quietly, and do not make a scene."

Maggie got up, baffled, leaving the note on the table.

"Make a scene?" She chuckled quietly to herself. "You can't be serious."

She stepped outside the restaurant, in haste, but then bumped into a familiar looking guy wearing the black patent wing-tipped Prada's. She darted off quickly, believing it was no longer a coincidence. As for Chad, she could not visit his room—talk about mistakes. *He would be trouble!*

Maggie rummaged through her purse for her cell phone, while keeping a quick step back to the safe headquarters—her hotel room. She needed to call Dana.

www.lovetheillusion.com/19.htm

"Maggie! You are calling me back, already?"

Maggie was glad to hear her voice.

"I hope I'm not calling you too late, London time, but I'm just freakin' out over here! Yesterday, I chat in a bar with a couple of men who I'm not even sure if they are using their real names! They tell me my food, wine, dry cleaning—never mind—are all on the house. And then you know what shows up in my hotel room?"

"Both of them, naked?" Dana teased with hysterical laugh.

"No, Dana. Save the humor. A bottle of red wine that I was drinking at the bar that, get this, costs nearly three hundred dollars!"

"I'm so excited! You have my wedding present already?" Dana joked again.

"Dana! How can you be funny at a time like this? I am a nervous wreck. Now, let me finish. So, I go to dinner, right? And after I'm done eating, someone has paid my bill, and I get a note saying that Chad—if that's even really his name—wants to see me, and he's in room 460! He just happens to be the Italian waiter I sat next to, at the bar! Now there's a man who's been following me and…Who is he? No idea."

"Right, you are having a blindin' time! All the men in New York City noticing the beautiful fashion queen from London!"

"Are you joking?" Maggie challenged. "I should be cautious of any man, especially here!"

"Maggie, you sound completely paranoid. I think you should look them up. They're probably just a couple of chaps that want to drink that wine with you," Dana suggested calmly.

"Seriously, Dana, why don't you fly out here and join them."

"I'm sure they're harmless," Dana reassured her. "Maybe, the chap following you isn't even related. I'd be more worried about him than that wine. That wine is awesome! It's sweet whoever sent it."

"You think?"

"Yes, Maggie! If you're so worried, just call the front desk and change rooms. By the time they figure it out, you'll be gone!" Dana concluded.

"Yeah, maybe…" Maggie thought it over. "Actually, that's a good idea—almost genius! Thanks." She sighed. "So, what are you doing tonight?"

"Shane and I just sat down in the lounge to watch a film. We're staying in, so that we can save money for the wedding. Ah, and don't be angry, but Shane ate your last biscuit! You know he eats anything sweet."

Maggie chuckled. "Well, you can just tell him, he owes me a jaffa cake."

"I will. And about your situation, how do you think they even know what room you're in?" Dana inquired.

"Because, when I introduced myself, I gave my last name," Maggie said, completely aggravated. "But why would the front desk give out room information? Isn't it confidential?"

"I don't know, but Shane's nudging me now, so I have to go. But if you need any more advice from a blonde, give me a ring, alright? Bye."

Maggie stood at the front desk.

"May I help you?"

"Uh, yeah, I'm in room 2116, and I'm having a problem sleeping, due to some disturbances in the room next door, and I was just wondering if I can move to a different room?"

"Oh, I'm really sorry, but we are booked solid for the weekend, but we might be able to arrange it for Monday."

"Monday, um, well, alright," she reluctantly agreed.

"We will give you a call when something becomes available," the hotel desk clerk assured her.

The next morning, the phone rang during Maggie's shower. She hurried out of the stall, nearly slipping on the tile, while holding her towel and dripping wet as she picked up the phone.

"Hello?"

"This is guest services at the front desk. We were able to find a room for you, if you still wanted a switch."

"That was quick! I'll come at four, after—"

"Actually, we need your room ready for a twelve o'clock check-in. Can you come to the front lobby, now?"

"Sure," Maggie decided, trying to sound grateful.

She would now be late for her meeting. Yes, Francis had everyone busy on a Sunday! She looked at the bed where she had just started to assemble her outfit of the day. Various mismatched pieces lay, and she wished that she had not packed in such a hurry, at the last minute. What would she wear? *That would have to wait!*

She rushed back into the bathroom and quickly threw on her t-shirt and pajama pants, now wet from the bathroom floor, and hurried to gather her belongings back into her suitcase. Her hair still dripping wet, she had only twenty minutes before her meeting with the fashion show coordinators. Francis would have to cover for her until she got there. His extreme punctuality always made up for her tardiness.

The elevator took her to the main lobby entrance where people appeared well-suited for a work day, despite the fact that it was the weekend. She quickly paced over to the check-in counter.

"I'm here to change rooms…Maggie White."

"Oh, sorry, we're booked solid. It's a busy weekend. We've got that magic show and the Broadway musical," the clerk explained.

"But someone just called and said—" Maggie stopped, as another clerk from just several feet away started to approach them.

"No, she's right, everything's ready to go!" The woman placed a receipt and new room card on the desk in front of her.

"Thank you, so much!"

Maggie took off, new room card in hand, and dragged her luggage behind at a fast speed when she noticed one of the wheels was now broken.

"Would you like some help with that miss?" she heard a bellboy call out.

"No, I'm fine," she called back while managing to maneuver her luggage into the crowded elevator.

She waited until it came to the fourth floor and then stepped off in haste, dragging her luggage down the hall to her new room. She made a quick dart around the corner and scanned the room numbers in order as she passed.

She stopped.

Standing in front of her new room, it only took moments to draw her conclusion.

"Just my luck," Maggie muttered under her breath, her eyes on the number: 468.

Suddenly, she heard someone calling out her name.

And the voice came from down the hall.

Chapter 2

"Maggie! Is that you?"

Is that him?

Standing in a self-conscious display of wet hair and pajamas, she wanted to wave a wand and disappear. But instead, she stood in a state of shock as she stared down the hall at Chad, the guy from the bar, dressed in a shirt and tie.

"You're on my floor!" he called out.

His… floor…? She pondered. *How strange.*

www.lovetheillusion.com/24.htm

"Hey…" She suddenly felt irritated as she saw him approaching and decided to meet him halfway. "So! You think you're clever …leaving wine in my room, having me stalked, delivering notes to my table, and telling me to meet you in your room? I finally decide to switch rooms, to avoid your plague, and now I am—Ha! Right next to you, on *your* floor! Well, to what do I owe this great honor, *Chad*?" Her eyes were piercing through his as he just stood there with his hands in his pockets.

There was a long pause as he stared back until he finally opened his mouth slowly to speak. "Are you done?"

He tried not to smile.

"No! The question is...Are *you* done?" Maggie sneered. "This whole thing...it is...just freaking me out!"

Chad grabbed the back of his neck and shifted his eyes to the floor as if he acknowledged her embarrassment, as she stood in her pajamas.

"Gee, I'm really sorry. It's not...what you think." He spoke in a relaxed, quiet tone, and then let go of a grin.

Maggie suddenly felt foolish. Perhaps he was harmless.

She tried to back up her words. "No, I'm sorry, I mean...the wine...you shouldn't have."

"I just...wanted to see you again?" Chad raised his eyebrows and tilted his head to one side, revealing his sweetness.

"Mmm, well, I guess you did," Maggie said, raising her eyebrows in return.

"My apologies?" Chad reached out for a handshake. He wore a soft smile. Maggie moved her hand slowly into his.

He's not only harmless...He's really cute.

"Hey!" A shout came from down the hall. "Bob's on the phone and said the shipment didn't come in yet, and he left two messages on your voicemail."

"Yep, be right there." Chad let go of her hand. "Talk to you later," he spoke in his accent. And it seemed that his mind had completely switched gears.

"When?" She heard herself speak—a shot into her ears— as if someone had spoken it for her, and she could no longer retrieve the question, or her desire to see him again.

"When what?" he asked.

"When will I see you?" She felt stupid. But there was something about him that left her curious.

He paused, looking at her for a few moments, as if he was thinking.

"Meet me for coffee…or dinner…at Bouley," he decided, as he took a few steps backwards. "Six, tomorrow night," he finalized the details.

Maggie sat in her room on her laptop, researching Bouley. It was an elegant five-star French restaurant located twenty minutes away from the hotel. What would she wear there?

The multi-colored rhinestone Louboutin shoes—worth nearly a thousand pounds—were a perfect match! They went with the light blue shimmering dress with the shoulder strap and brooch. It was one of the dresses that she designed for the teen formal events line that Francis graciously put her in charge of. He had told her to bring a few of her designs along to show one of the buyers that sold formal wear for teens. The dress and the shoes were supposed to be displayed on a mannequin at the fashion show. But now she needed to wear them!

Maggie stared into the full length mirror, after finally deciding to wear the stunning ensemble. She could not believe that she was going out with him. She hoped that she did not look like she was going to prom. Tonight, she would put an end to her *crazy* intrigue with Chad. After peeling the layers, she would lose interest and have a clear head when returning to London.

www.lovetheillusion.com/27.htm

A taxi was waiting.

"Hello, I need to go to Bouley."

"Bouley? Okay..." the driver restated, "We're goin' to Bouley. Must be a special occasion?"

"Ah, just dinner, you know."

Maggie's mind raced back to her last dinner date with the man that ended up being married. Who knew the frightful course of events that tonight would bring? Hopefully, her simple curiosity would end her ridiculous infatuation, and she would discover why she was right about Chad in the first place. Then with every emotional nerve in her body, she would pronounce her well-thought conclusion about men—*such a painful addition to the earth!*

Noticing her stomach tied in knots, she wondered how she would eat as the cab pulled up to the elegant French restaurant.

"Bill us," she heard someone speak as she stepped out of the cab. And with that, the cab drove away and someone familiar approached. "You are Maggie White?"

She felt a chill run through her as he spoke.

"Yes," she said timidly.

"You're very pretty. Follow me."

She walked alongside him, peering down at his wing-tipped Prada's. He wore a tailored suit and seemed friendly.

"By the way, I'm Bradley Davis, and I'm flattered to meet you, Maggie."

"You know, you look *so* familiar!" Her words spilled out. "And, I can't imagine why I keep running into you!"

"Well, I'm security," he told her. "You know, it can be very dangerous for a lady like yourself to be just wandering around, alone in a big city."

"Well, I'm not afraid," she lied. "What can happen in a big crowd of people, anyways?"

Bradley let out a bit of laughter under his breath.

"Well, let me at least get you safely to your table."

"You mean, to Chad?"

"Chad?" he repeated. "Oh, okay, yes, to Chad." He wore a strange look on his face, as he opened the door. "After you."

Maggie stepped inside, feeling like a princess arriving at a castle. A crystal chandelier hung at the entrance, over velvety green carpeting surrounding the hostess station. As they entered the dining room, she noticed that it was busy for a Monday night, everyone in elegant attire. Crystal wine glasses and white china placed on yellow chargers adorned the tables draped with white linens, and bright yellow and white tulips sat in Lenox vases made for centerpieces.

She followed Bradley's lead into a private room, away from the crowds. Then she saw him. Chad stood, wearing a European cut suit, a purple shirt, no tie.

www.lovetheillusion.com/28.htm

"Bonsoir." He greeted her. "Have a seat."

Bradley had disappeared. They sat in a room off of the main dining area and had it all to themselves. The room was traditionally exquisite with a fireplace and windows that reached from the ceiling to the floor. Outside, there was a patio with a fountain and village style street lights. They were seated next to one of the tall windows, but all she wanted to do was look at Chad. Their eyes met, and she knew she was in trouble.

"You look good," he said.

Maggie repositioned herself on her chair as the lead brick in her stomach got replaced with a Mayan pyramid. Chad watched her as she shifted about.

"Are you nervous?" he asked with an involuntary smile.

Unbelievable!

"Are you the king of awkward moments?" She shot back in defense, ready to shatter his attempt to make her feel even more uncomfortable.

"So, that would be a 'yes'?" He wore a grin.

"Sorry I was late." She changed the subject, passing him a stern look.

Chad was leaned back in his chair just enough to indicate that he was not the least bit nervous.

"So, will we have service out here, or do we need to move to a table in there?" she asked, loosening up just a bit.

"Don't worry, I got us covered," he said, reaching down to gather up a couple menus which were lodged between the window and his chair. When he handed one to her, he looked into her eyes until she blushed.

"Thanks." Maggie took the menu from him, trying to shake the effects he had on her. She opened it up, only to realize it was in French. Her eyes scanned the entrees, trying to recall the bit of French she knew—not a lot. Over the top of her menu, she could see Chad tapping a pen against the back of his. She wondered what he was up to as he seemed to be enjoying every minute.

"So, Chad, do you read French?"

"Um, just enough…So, do you know what you want?" He passed her a sweet look.

She tried to avoid eye contact. He was definitely getting to her. She gave an exasperated sigh.

"Well, that would be 'no,' because I can't read a thing on this menu!" She started to laugh.

"That's too bad." He offered sarcastic apologies.

She studied his face that seemed to depict an agenda. It left her puzzled.

"I'll just have what you're having." She set her menu down, hoping it was not a mistake to be having dinner with him.

"So, you trust me?" He wore a curious grin.

Maggie was startled by his question.

"Well, if I organize all the facts, there are definitely some things that don't add up, but then again, you haven't done anything to make me think that you'd be someone I should be afraid of, either. Am I right?"

"You would be," he informed, "but I was only talking about the food." He tried not to smile.

"Oh." She felt embarrassed, breaking their eye contact again. She found his humor intimidating. "Well, then just order something, and I'll have the same, provided there are no eyeballs on my plate staring up at me."

Chad laughed quietly to himself, tucked the menus aside, and picked up his phone to send a text.

Now she had to wonder.

"Are you seriously texting people while you eat with me?" She gave him a dirty look.

Chad sounded defensive. "I just ordered coffee!" He grinned in amusement.

Before she could ask questions, Bradley arrived with two cups of coffee and a spare canister. He set it down and then gave Chad a wink. She watched him leave and then looked at Chad.

"What makes you think I want coffee? Are you trying to keep me up all night?" She stared at him, inquisitively.

"You said you'd have whatever I was having, and if I would have ordered wine, you might accuse me of trying to get you drunk and..." He gave her an inviting look. "I don't *need* to get my women drunk."

Maggie felt her stomach curl into a frenzy. He was quite the smooth one. She decided to put him in his place.

"Nice ego! Exactly how old are you that you have all this experience on how to entangle women?" She spoke in a hostile tone.

"Twenty-eight… And what are you? Like eighteen?" he teased. "Just kidding, I won't ask."

"Twenty-four." She gave him a curt look, realizing she wore the teen dress.

"So, how long are you here?" he asked defensively, yet leaving her enticed by his eyes on her.

"Just until Friday…The fashion show is Thursday, but we are here early to set up. Francis is a meticulous perfectionist! And working for him? He never stops short of keeping me busy." She let go of a smile.

"That doesn't sound very exciting."

He chuckled, wearing a grin.

"It beats waiting tables!" Maggie returned his look. "How was your shift last night?"

"I'm not a waiter. Sorry to disappoint you. I work for AD Enterprises—an entertainment industry—so I'm in New York a lot, but travel everywhere. I'm from Italy," he vaguely explained.

She contemplated his mystery and then revealed, "I grew up here, in Boston, but went to London for fashion design school, and have been there since. I live in Greenwich."

His cell phone went off, interrupting their conversation. He reached for his phone and took the call.

"Yep, okay…tell them, there's still one more load coming. No, he's so… not in charge. Tell him I said he's done for the night!"

She listened to him give orders as if he controlled the world he lived in. He then excused himself from the table, signaling to her that he would be right back.

Maggie watched him having his private conversation. He was quite the package. She considered whether or not he could be tamed. *Probably not. That would be a hopeless chase for any woman!*

"Sorry about that." Chad returned to the table.

"So, Chad, can I ask how you got a bottle of wine into my room?" She decided to play the game and send him a flirtatious look.

"Why is that so fascinating?" He laughed. "You're Maggie White...Stanley delivered it to the front desk and said to drop it off in your room next time they were cleaning."

"Really?" Maggie thought about it. "And speaking of rooms..." she asked, "Do you want to tell me how, in a hotel with so many rooms, I end up next to you?"

He seemed deep in thought, and then finally admitted, "Well, that was an entertainment for all of us. You claimed a disturbance, so Bradley had to investigate. There wasn't anyone but an elderly lady next to you, by the way, with a hearing aid, who claimed she hadn't fallen or anything and had no idea what the disturbance was about!"

Maggie felt embarrassed as he went on to explain, "Bradley noticed your name on the complaint list and asked me if he should tell the front desk to put you on my company floor, because we had several rooms unoccupied and everything else was booked. I said they could."

"Your company takes up an entire floor?"

She thought it strange.

"Yes, I'm here working, like I said," he reminded her, as he showed off his smile.

Maggie realized that she was not losing interest.

"So, this Bradley dude, you know him?"

"Of course, I know Bradley."

Chad found her questions amusing.

"So..." She tried to uncover more mystery. "You had him following me, the night that you had a note delivered to my table and paid for my food?" she asked, as he leaned back in his chair.

"I just wanted to see you again. Is that a crime?" He issued back a flirtatious stare. "Bradley works for hotel security, but when we stay here, the company hires him on the side. Trust me. He's completely harmless. We have that in common...Anything else?" His voice carried concern, hoping to have answered all her questions.

A waitress brought over some bread and soup.

"Baguette and bouillabaisse," she informed.

Maggie made an immediate approval of the bread, but the soup had a strange smell. She leaned over her bowl, trying not to signal any hesitation.

"It's fish," Chad explained.

"Oh, that's what it is?" She picked through it with her spoon.

"If you don't like it, don't eat it. It won't bother me. I didn't cook it." He laughed under his breath.

"No, I'm in for the adventure of whatever you ordered us." Maggie picked up her coffee cup to toast and Chad met his cup halfway, and when his eyes and smile met hers, she felt herself blush, again.

"Not so bad?" Chad wanted to know.

"It's good. I'm just not a risk taker, especially when it comes to food," she explained.

"I'd say you are a huge risk taker, just because you're sitting here, eating dinner with me."

He waited anxiously for her response.

She wondered what he meant to imply.

"So, are you saying I'm going to regret this evening?"

She lowered her brow.

"Well," he chuckled quietly, "I don't know, but I hope not. I'm having fun."

She wondered who else he dated.

"So, is that what you do for fun, Chad? Entertain ladies that you barely know?" She sounded skeptical.

"I'm trying to change that."

"Which would be...entertaining strangers or...?" She wanted to know his intentions!

"No, what I mean is that I'm trying to get to know you."

"So, why me?" She raised her brow.

"Now, why would you ask me *that*?" He gave her a sweet look.

Her heart melted, and she knew better than to continue that conversation. She had properly assessed his sweet side.

"Ratatouille," Chad explained when the main dish arrived.

While eating her dinner, she had to wonder. Why did Chad want to date her? What was the point? Did he like random adventures, random women? *One night stands?* Surely his "list" ran a mile long. And could the English language even rightfully define his ego? Yet, something about him made her crazy. She should know better than to sit here, getting emotionally tattered by all his clever maneuvers.

"Excuse me, I'll be right back," Maggie told Chad.

She got up from the table and darted off to the nearest ladies' room, closing herself into a stall, where she could think.

This date was a disaster. She had not lost interest in him. On the contrary, the chemistry between them sent her head spinning out of control, entertaining the thought of what it would be like to be alone with him! She needed to leave. *A one night stand with him? No way!* She could never shake that off after returning to London. A streak of bad luck with men led her to conclude that surely he would be no exception. And although he was a dynamite distraction from her self-pity after her failed engagement, mingling with him definitely carried a huge risk. He lived here…she lived there…and she was bleeding from a broken heart already, and he looked like a major heartbreaker. *Surely he must date a ton of women. Who wouldn't want to date him?* She reached her decision. Her date with him was done!

Maggie quickly left the stall, approaching the table without sitting back down.

"I'm sorry, Chad. I appreciate your invitation to dinner, but I leave Friday and there's no point to this. I have to go."

The surprised look in his eyes told her that perhaps she bruised his ego for the first time. But then he spoke confidently. "I just ordered dessert. I think you'll like it."

"What is it?"

"Chocolate mousse!"

She hesitated, but then sat back down.

"And now you're glad to stay?" he assumed.

"Aren't you manipulative," she told him.

"No, but I'm not sure why you want to leave. Let me guess. You hate adventure, you don't like taking chances, and you're afraid to step out of your *box?*"

Maggie held her breath as he diagnosed her love stricken soul. She missed his smile that had been replaced by a more serious look. And she could not shake her intrigue.

After the chocolate mousse arrived, Chad sent a text on his phone while explaining, "You can leave right after the mousse. Your ride will be here in just ten minutes."

Maggie tried to fight her disappointment.

"Thanks for dinner, Chad." She did not wish to be rude. "We could wait by the waterfall fountain for my ride."

"Sure, whatever you want," he agreed.

After finishing dessert, Chad took the lead and went out the back door to the stone walkway that encircled the waterfall. He sat down on the stone ledge, and she decided to sit a comfortable distance from where he was.

"Those are some interesting shoes," Chad pointed out, looking down at her feet.

"Christian Louboutin, a bit tight, but they are worth the fashion statement," she admitted, reaching for the back straps to remove the shoes. She placed them neatly, side by side, next to her, on the stone ledge.

"Can I see you tomorrow?"

His suggestion sent a shock of excitement through her veins. But despite her crazy interest in him, she knew it was a bad idea.

"I don't know." Maggie reached behind her, placing her hands on the ledge. She immediately heard the sound that could only mean one thing. Yep! One of the rhinestone Louboutins had fallen into the pool of water, surrounding the waterfall. She could feel the weight of her jaw drop, as she tried to see Chad's response out of the corner of her eye.

It was a terrible sight!

www.lovetheillusion.com/37.htm

"Oh no…" Chad laughed. "…Say good-bye to that!"

Maggie stared into the water.

"I think you should get it, just… I need that shoe!"

"Ehhh, I think it might be more fun watching you try to get it." He sounded amused. "Come on! The water looks so warm and inviting."

She stood, thinking… *That shoe is supposed to be exhibited at the fashion show! And NOW look at it!*

"Pleeaase…! You get it!" She grabbed hold of his arm to convince him.

"If I do, you will see me tomorrow night?" He looked into her eyes.

Maggie felt her insides tighten as she stood in front of him. She gave him a blank stare, letting go of his arm. She watched as he pushed up his sleeve in a hopeless effort to stay dry. Then he leaned over the edge as far as he could. But when he reached in to get the shoe, his sleeve got drenched.

He pulled the wet shoe out of the water and set it onto the ledge.

"Thanks!" Maggie smiled, thinking that she should have gotten it since she wore a sleeveless dress. But now reaching into his coat pocket, Chad handed her a ticket and said,

"Meet me at the magic show, tomorrow night." He spoke, assuming that she would.

"You like magic?" She tried to fight her feelings.

Chad's eyes sparkled and his face lit up. "I *love* magic!"

Maggie looked down to the bottom of her glass, after drinking a Long Island Iced Tea within five minutes of her arrival. She needed to drink *something* before her next date with Chad. The bartender raised his brow, indicating his shock, but she did not notice. Her eyes were glued to the flat screen, behind the bar. "...AND LIVE, TONIGHT, IN NEW YORK CITY, LIKE YOU HAVE NEVER SEEN HIM BEFORE! ARE THE FANS READY? THE SHOW IS SOLD OUT ONCE AGAIN AND RADIO CITY HAS ANNOUNCED AN AFTER PARTY FOR THE FIRST HUNDRED PEOPLE THROUGH THE DOORS. MEET, IN PERSON, THE ALL AMAZING, WORLD-RENOWNED MAGICIAN, ANTONIO DELUCA, HIMSELF! AND HE WON'T BE WEARING HIS MASK! GET READY LADIES, 'CUZ WE KNOW YOU ARE JUST *DYING TO* MEET HIM..."

Maggie heard her phone go off.

"Dana, what's up?"

"I should be asking you! Did you lose the Chaps?"

"Actually, I'm going to the Antonio DeLuca magic show."

"Really? It's wicked!" Dana sounded excited. "I saw it in Canada. I hope you have front row seats. That Antonio is really fit! So, is Francis splurging for a big night, or what?"

Maggie tried not to think about Francis.

"I'm going with Chad. We had dinner last night and unfortunately I like him. Now I leave Friday and—it's a huge mistake—I'm going out with him again, tonight."

"You worry too much! Just have fun. You're in New York City!"

"Right, easy for you to say. At least we'll just be watching a show. I won't have him staring in my eyes, making me crazy, or talking to me in his sensual way with that accent of his. And if I don't want, I don't even have to look at him!"

"You know, Maggie, you might as well become a nun."

"That's mean! You should be proud of me. I know his type, and I'm *not* going to let him mess with me. He knows just what he's doing and could care less that I leave in a few days. It's so depressing. I have to go."

Maggie put her phone away. Hopefully, after tonight, she could walk away with no regrets.

Unfamiliar with the theater, Maggie was grateful when an usher offered to assist her in finding her seat. He handed her a program. On it, Antonio wore a black and white facemask and stood holding a ring of fire, his arms up in the air, his cape blowing behind him.

Maggie sat behind a row of kids with their gift shop gadgets already flying dangerously through the air. She could bet this would intensify once the show started.

The place was packed. It was a huge event as people crowded to get in their seats. She combed the isles with her eyes. Where was Chad? *Did he find a better opportunity?*

The lights went out completely. The red curtain lifted off the stage floor, and smoke replaced its view. The crowd went wild, screaming and shouting, and as the smoke cleared, she could see Antonio, low to the stage, tucked under his black cape. A fan blew the cape as he rose to his feet while the lights changed his appearance from blue, to red, to purple, and suddenly to bright white. And then she could see his black and white face mask. Pop music played while large pieces of gold glitter blew in the air before descending to the stage floor.

Maggie watched the show, deciding it was unlike anything she had ever seen before. Music, dancers, and circus performers accompanied the stage, while Antonio shocked the audience with his magic acts.

A cheetah stood center stage. She watched as Antonio jumped onto its back and then rode it up a staircase leading to a balcony above the dancers and acrobatic performers. The lights flashed out. When they came back on, everyone was gone except for the cheetah that stood center stage. She wondered where Antonio and his crew went and how the cheetah got back down onto the stage from the balcony. Suddenly, Antonio popped up from behind the cheetah, as fire shot up in blazes around the stage floor. The crowd started screaming, as confetti flew into the audience. The lights went out again, and when they came back on, the cheetah was gone, and Antonio was standing with his arms folded, facing the audience.

The color purple popped out everywhere on fans that wore their souvenir shirts decorated in white confetti from the last stunt.

And for a moment, she forgot about Chad's absence until she got elbowed by a goofy girl dancing to the music.

Antonio came to the front of the stage and stared into his sea of fans. "I need someone from the audience that would like to learn a magic trick that they can show to all their friends."

The row of kids, in front of her, went bananas and Maggie covered her head for protection as a couple plastic swords jetted aimlessly about.

A young boy beamed in the spotlight, as he stood next to Antonio who was shuffling the cards onto the stage floor and instantaneously back into his hand. Now the crowd whistled and hollered for Jimmy who tried to duplicate the trick, but with little success. Then Antonio grabbed onto his hand, and in an instant, all the cards flew up from the stage floor and back into the boy's hand. The boy wore a huge smile as he left the stage with the magical cards.

Afterwards, Antonio threw the deck he had in his own hand out to the audience. Everyone scuffled to pick up the cards when Maggie noticed that one had landed right next to her boot. She stooped down to pick it up. It was an ace of hearts.

Several acts later, Antonio came to the front of the stage, holding a ring of fire.

"I need a pretty lady from the audience that's not afraid of fire!"

Maggie's eyes focused on the flames that burned around the ring while the girl next to her screamed in a loud shrill, "This is where he takes his mask off! And he's so hot!"

Maggie observed the multitude of volunteers. Suddenly, she felt someone grab her arm. Her eyes followed the stranger's hand up to his face. He wore a white, screen printed t-shirt with "security" in large blue block letters.

"You, miss, come with me."

She immediately felt her stage fright kick in.

He brought her over to the bottom of the steps by the stage.

I hate being in front of crowds.

"I didn't volunteer!" she yelled up at him. A full head taller, he did not hear her over the noise. An exit sign caught her view, but the security guard issued her up on stage.

Maggie stepped carefully onto each step that led up to the stage, but she did not see Antonio anywhere. Just about the time she wondered how to keep the audience busy, he descended from the air.

The mask now gone, he wore a gold tie and a white satin shirt tucked into a pair of black pants. The lights were extremely bright, causing her to squint.

"What's your name?" he asked, holding the ring of fire.

"Maggie?" She seemed to have forgotten.

He approached her, and as he reached for her hand, she recognized a familiar smile. *Chad?!* She thought her knees were going to completely buckle, landing her face down onto the stage. But instead, she stood in shock and disbelief.

"It's Maggie!" he announced, facing the audience, before turning to her. "So you're not afraid of fire, but are you afraid of heights?" he asked as she stared back at him, lost in confusion. "I think Maggie's afraid to talk to me!" He faced the audience again, with a big smile. The crowd laughed, and she heard Antonio repeating the question of whether or not she was afraid of heights.

"I think so." She finally responded. A dead expression covered her face, but Antonio shined in the spotlight.

"Okay, Maggie. We have not lost a pretty lady yet, so...I'm going to make you float... inside the ring of fire!"

She could feel the heat from the flame as Antonio turned to face the crowd.

"Do you think she should trust me?"

The crowd started screaming.

Holding hands, he led her to a table where he positioned her horizontally. The lights became dim, and the table ascended in the air. She wanted to scream but held onto the sides of the platform, instead. The hoop, blazing with fire, passed over her. She closed her eyes and waited for it to be over.

Soon the table returned to the floor, and when Antonio reached for her hand to help her off the table, the audience cheered while he wore a big smile. He led her to the front of the stage, brought their hands up in the air, and then took a bow. She drove her thumb nail into the palm of his hand, indicating her disapproval of his stunt, but he remained completely oblivious to her gesture. He brought her back to the security guard who then helped her down the steps and back to her seat.

Two girls, in red satin dresses, danced out onto the stage. She wondered how close he was to his crew as she focused in on one of the dancers, admiring her rhythm.

www.lovetheillusion.com/42.htm

Antonio stood center stage as they danced around him, removing his cape. She felt a shiver of jealously. They handcuffed him behind his back, and a skinny, clown-like figure appeared with a string of white fabric, which he gave to the girls. The clown proceeded to do acrobatics while the girls wrapped Antonio up like a mummy. The lights went out, and seconds later when they came back on, he was out of the mummy tape and facing the audience in a victorious stance.

Maggie knew she would be a complete idiot to pursue him, even before this, and now? More risk...more strange. More complicated...*more tempting.*

After the final curtain closed, Maggie followed into the crowded aisle as people were trying to make their exit when she felt someone tap her on the shoulder.

"Maggie...Right?"

She turned around to the familiar t-shirt which spelled out "security."

"Yeah, that's right." She looked up at him.

"I've got something for you."

What could that possibly be...a souvenir photo from the most embarrassing moment of my life?

"Follow me." He made a request.

She followed him in the opposite direction of the crowd. When they got to a secluded area, he explained, "Look! Antonio told me to get an after the show party pass for you, but they get handed out to the first hundred people through the door, and when I went to get one, they were gone. You can't get in without one. They rented out Night Owls, just a few blocks from here, and he wants you there. He told me to give you this, and the security people outside the bar would let you in. Oh, and don't lose it!" He placed it in her hand. "Make sure you go!" And with that, he turned around and walked away.

Maggie opened up her hand and stared down onto a gold ring that had letters, formed from diamonds, in the shape of a rectangle. "DELUCA," it read. She beheld all the diamonds and immediately realized the shocking value. *This is insane! What next?*

www.lovetheillusion.com/43.htm

"Now I suppose I will *have* to meet him to give this...this *thing* back to him!" she mumbled quietly to herself. It was definitely expensive, and she thought back to the words, "Don't lose it!" Certainly, it could not be left at the hotel lobby desk for him to pick up. He would be worried sick if she did not make an appearance with it soon. Of course, she wanted to see him again. But first, she needed to go back to her room to change. She had not perspired this much in her entire life!

Chapter 3

There was no doubt. Her new dress designs were certainly coming in handy. Now that she knew who Chad really was, she wanted to look good. Flaunting her figure, she wore the black knit dress with a lace hemline and ruching. It was flattering with her favorite western boots. And the DeLuca ring fit perfectly on her thumb and flashed brilliantly, reflecting in the mirror.

www.lovetheillusion.com/45.htm

She followed her heart on a long leash, while her brain had turned to mush.

When she stepped out of the cab, she felt uneasy as she walked up to the entrance of Night Owls. There were two young security guys standing outside the glass, double door entrance where she could see into a crowded room of people screaming and shouting.

"You got a pass?"

"A pass…? No, but Antonio said—"

Maggie suddenly realized his celebrity.

"You gotta have a pass...purple ticket with—"

"I have *this*," she emphasized proudly, flashing her thumb at him.

"Oh!" they both sneered in almost a unison taunt. "Then I guess you're in," proclaimed the chubby bald one.

She glared at them while lending a sarcastic smile.

"Ouch, he's got his hands full with that one!" she heard the other one comment in a feminine tone as she walked through the doors.

People were dancing to loud music in a room decorated in Vegas style glitz. Maggie shuffled through the crowd alongside the bar that stood against the wall to her right. Then she spotted him, his back turned, and she could feel people staring as she approached him.

Antonio turned to acknowledge her, and she felt her insides slipping when he declared, "You look...lovely."

She scooted in between him and a bar chair, hoping to remain discreet.

"What do you want?" he asked her, casually looking to the bartender. But her mind was racing from the day's events. "To drink?" he added, thinking he left her confused.

"I don't know." She stared at him, finding it hard to make even the simplest of decisions.

Antonio stood up straighter and called to the bartender who attended quickly. He ordered her a drink, with his hand cupped at his mouth to conceal his request. She watched with concern, as he tried to hold back a smile.

"What? You trust me, don't you?" Antonio teased.

"Sure." She shrugged, thinking she would rather be in his company drunk than by herself and sober.

"And I trust you!" he informed, looking at the ring that weighted down her thumb.

"Oh, yeah." She made eyes at him. "And I suppose you were happy that I showed up so that you could get this back!" She started to remove it.

"No, you can wear that. You can wear this too." He placed his hat on her head.

Maggie blushed, feeling like a spectacle. But she felt flattered to be in his company.

The bartender handed Antonio her drink, and he moved it in front of her. It appeared to be a cherry vodka martini.

Now a brunette with long straight hair and lots of pink lip gloss approached, wearing a souvenir t-shirt that had to be at least two sizes too small. Behind her stood a group of her friends that were too shy to approach.

"Can you sign the front of my shirt?" she asked, holding onto his arm.

Maggie watched him as he signed her sleeve. The girl flashed a flirtatious smile as she stared into his face. Antonio waved to her friends, and they giggled and took off. He turned back to Maggie.

"So, what is this?" she asked, holding up her martini glass.

Antonio whispered back in her ear, "*That* is a kiddy cocktail."

Maggie's eyes popped open, as did her mouth.

"What? You ordered me a kiddy cocktail?"

"I'd hate to get you drunk!" He wore a confident grin.

She started laughing.

"Please! I wish you would! After everything I've been through tonight, you have me drinking a kiddy cocktail?"

"What do you mean? You were only on stage for five minutes!"

"Yes, but that was the longest five minutes of my life, *Chad*...or am I supposed to call you Antonio now?"

Their conversation was interrupted by a young girl.

"Mommy, there he is!"

"I'm sorry. Can I bother you for a picture?" the mother asked. Her son was an arm's length behind his sister, prodding his sword into her back. "Stop with that, Devon, or I will take it away!" the mother threatened as her daughter came and stood next to Antonio.

"Sure," Antonio agreed, bending down to the young girl who innocently draped her arm around his neck, grabbing the ends of his hair. Maggie watched her fingers entangled in his mane, and she wondered what his hair felt like.

"Hey! Isn't that your hat?" Devon asked pointing at the hat that Maggie wore. Maggie quickly removed it and put it back on Antonio's head, feeling embarrassed by the attention.

"There, is that better?" Maggie muttered while watching the ensemble.

The mother took a picture, and then Antonio signed the sword, first making Devon promise not to hit his sister with it anymore. The mother smiled a silent thank you, and then they were on their way. Maggie admired how natural he was with his fans.

"They were so cute!" Maggie said, preferring them to the girl in the tight shirt.

"Yeah, but I think they drank a lot of soda." Antonio laughed.

"Speaking of..." she motioned for the bartender, "I'll have a vodka martini straight up with an olive."

"Do you want the hat back?" Antonio asked in a sensual tone.

"No, that's okay, I think it looks better on you," she remarked flippantly, wishing to dilute his intimate gesture.

"I don't think so." Antonio placed it back onto her head as he peered into her eyes. She stared back into his, her eyes wandering to his lips, and then back to his eyes. She wondered what it would be like to kiss him. *Heavenly.* She really wanted to, but she knew she couldn't. There were too many cameras and too many fans. Already, she could feel her heart pounding in her chest just from the thought.

"Your drink, Maggie," Antonio said, breaking her out of her daydream.

Maggie wondered how long she should stay.

This can only end in disaster.

She watched as an arm wrestling competition took up the space at the bar to her right, and the next thing she knew, an entire glass of beer spilled over her black dress. She jumped back, on a quick impulse, landing on Antonio's lap!

www.lovetheillusion.com/49.htm

Maggie stood up and ran her hands down the front of her dress, saturated in beer. She turned her head around slowly to look back at Antonio who was entertained by the whole event.

"Black, that's a good color!" he teased.

"Yes!" She made a loose fist and lightly punched him in the arm. "Better than the blue blouse."

"Hey, what's that for?" Antonio protested defensively. "I didn't spill that on you!"

"No, but you just can't help but think it's funny!" Maggie wondered why every time she was with him, her fashion statement became a disaster. She decided to put the hat back on his head.

"Sorry about that!" She received an apology from the arm wrestling duo.

"Yeah, knock it off with the spills over there, would ya'!" Antonio laughed. "Or I'll have to cut you off." She watched him tease a member of his crew.

"Hey man, the show is over, and I don't have to listen to you anymore," his crewman explained.

Now, two fans were grabbing Antonio's arms and trying to pull him off his chair to dance with them. The girls were giggling, and they looked maybe twenty at best. Antonio reluctantly followed them, and Maggie tried to keep track of them. And while she did, the twin show dancers with the red dresses approached.

"Hey, are you Maggie?" the one with the freckles asked.

"Yes," Maggie verified, trying to tell them apart. She recalled them dancing around Antonio.

"Oh! Well, I'm Amber and this is Angela. Antonio was bragging about how he was going to bring you up on stage, and we were all like, she is just going to die when she figures you out!" they shouted over the loud music.

"Yeah, well that was quite a stunt he pulled."

Maggie thought they seemed nice.

"So, do you guys have a thing?"

"I guess." Maggie shrugged. She noticed their short hair and thought perhaps they wore matching wigs on stage. They looked like identical twins, and she had trouble telling them apart.

"You have his...that ring?" the one with a nose stud questioned, looking down while grabbing at her hand. Maggie felt embarrassed as they gawked at her hand.

"Just to get in tonight, since they were out of passes," Maggie informed them.

"Yeah, right," the one with the freckles said in a doubtful tone. "Well, you have a fun night. Nice meeting you!"

She watched them impishly converse as they walked away.

Maggie had lost track of Antonio. To be honest, she had lost track of herself. She could not compare the events of the past few days to anything she had ever experienced before. The whole situation was insane, as was the delusional world he lived in.

She felt vulnerable and emotionally trapped as she tried to sort everything out. How did she manage to get herself into this situation in the first place?

She needed a quiet place to think. *Where's the closest utopia?* She headed for the ladies' room, retreated into a stall, slammed the door behind her, and leaned against it. *It's just an anxiety attack!* She stared into the toilet. Her brain seemed to be on vacation, while she stood at her wits end, pondering her dilemma. Was this an extreme case of opposite attraction? Of course! He lived here, she lived there. He loved attention, thrill, and adventure, and she loved privacy and reading books. He was famous, she was nobody. He used money like water, and she worked for Francis. Women chased him and he chased them, and she was running scared. Although infatuated with his interest in her, she knew that she left on Friday and the more time she spent with him, the more difficult it would be to leave. She still felt stricken by her past engagement coupled by the loss of her mother, and she could not combine those losses with another. Besides, what she did not know about him would most likely make her head spin. Nonetheless, he seemed to know all the right moves to make her fall in love, just like magic! How ironic. Just what he did best...*create magic, intrigue, and then surprise—poof!*

Maggie found her thoughts completely aggravating and exhausting. She could never tolerate a distant affair. Besides, she saw how the other women admired him—and what would make him loyal? It ripped her apart to let go, but greater pain would be hers the longer it lingered. She simply could not fall for him, and although she tried to put her head above her heart, her heart ached at the thought of never seeing him again.

When she finally exited the stall, she saw a woman facing the vanity, washing her hands. Maggie approached the other sink and began to do the same. The woman gave her a quick glance.

"Hey, I think your man needs a rescue out there."

Maggie tried to appear unalarmed.

"I'm sure he doesn't." She laughed, loosely.

"I'm Rainelle, by the way. I'm the make-up artist for Antonio's crew."

Maggie thought she was pretty.

"Nice to meet you, Rainelle, I'm Maggie!"

"I know. I saw you standing by Antonio, and I put two and two together."

What two and two was that? She wondered.

When Maggie stepped out of the bathroom, she saw strobe lights beaming in various hues, and those two girls, *still* by Antonio, attempting to both dance with him at the same time. Antonio sent her a "help me" look, but she just kept walking. Why would he need her help to free him from his entrapment? After all, he was the magician.

"Maggie! Come here and dance with me! Let's shake this place up a bit!" She saw Bradley motioning to her. She was no longer afraid of him.

"Sure!" She grabbed his arm.

He was a big guy and she felt physically safe in his arms, if not emotionally. He led her over to where Antonio danced with his two rapacious fans. Maggie tried not to look at them as they clung to Antonio like he was their crazy fantasy.

Bradley held her tight and secure, but it did not compare to the clinging that Antonio was dealing with. She could not help but stare. When she saw that she finally had Antonio's attention, she waved and smiled at him as if she could not be having any more fun. Now she thought she could smell Bradley's cologne—*a nice distraction*—but her eyes still followed Antonio.

www.lovetheillusion.com/53.htm

A slow song started playing, and Maggie thought that her stomach was going to tie itself into another double knot if she had to watch the scene much longer. One of the girls was trying to kiss him, but he turned his head to dodge the kiss onto his cheek. The girl wore black spandex pants, Converse tennis shoes, and the purple t-shirt worn over a red long sleeve shirt. And her long blonde hair was swaying to the music, while another friend took pictures of them dancing.

Bradley looked down at Maggie and then glanced over to Antonio. "Ah man! Look at those two little mamas!"

Maggie observed Bradley who appeared ready to take action.

"Watch this!" He spoke in an amusing tone. He flung Maggie out and spun her around, disengaging the blonde from Antonio's arms and shouted, "Hey sister! She's gonna dance with him now!"

They both darted off and disappeared in the crowd. And Maggie was face to face with Antonio.

Antonio placed his hat back onto Maggie's head and then grabbed her waist, bringing her close to him. Maggie dangled her arms on his shoulders and danced strategically, hoping to distance any intimacy. But instead, she could barely breathe. She felt herself melting away with each beat of the music, wondering what Antonio was thinking. The ends of his hair brushed against the top of her hands, and against her better judgment, she sifted her fingers through the waves that fell against his neck. She could feel his hands on her back as he stepped closer to her. Intermittently, she felt him against her chest as they continued dancing. She tried to escape the effects he had on her.

Maggie saw Bradley out of the corner of her eye, who was now dancing with Rainelle. Perhaps, they were a couple. Next to them, the tomboy twins were dancing more of a fast style with several guys in a group. They danced as if they knew that they were professionals. Everyone seemed to be having fun. *That's good.*

Antonio suddenly became aware of her distraction while she clung to her inner resolution to distance her emotions. With a single jolt, he pressed her up firmly against his chest, and placing his right leg between hers, tilted her back until their eyes met, indorsing his control. Maggie, completely aware of his maneuver, fell limp against his tight body, her heart pounding. She felt dreamy in his presence.

The song ended and Antonio held onto her, as if the song was still playing. When he finally let go of her, he took her hand to his lips and kissed it. His eyes penetrated through hers while she stood mesmerized, leaving her emotions all over him. She loved being in his arms.

"Another martini please," Maggie requested as the bartender set out random sample shots on the counter. She thought she needed a few of those, also.

"Having fun?" Antonio wanted to know.

Maggie thought about it. *Fun? I don't think so!* She considered the sick feeling in the pit of her stomach. She wasn't sure what she was feeling, but it did not make the "fun" list. The whole situation was unnerving.

"So, Antonio, is your magic better on stage or off?" The guy that spilled the beer wanted to know as he raised his glass in a toast.

"Since when do you get to ask me loaded questions? You sound like a reporter," Antonio dished back.

Maggie looked at Antonio and suddenly realized she was unable to control her emotions when she was with him.

"Chad...or, I suppose I should call you Antonio now," Maggie fussed. "I have to go." She tried to be strong; she could not afford the risk.

"Why's that?" He seemed surprised.

"Because, I'm emotionally stripped of my sanity right now," Maggie confessed, reluctantly. She felt torn, as her feelings for him left her in disarray. She needed to keep a clear head, so she could focus on work. Or was it already too late for that?

"What's that supposed to mean?" Antonio looked confused.

"I leave at the end of the week!" Maggie wondered why she should have to explain. "Or don't you think that far ahead?"

Antonio took one step closer to her, standing within inches of her as he spoke his mind. "Just relax...and have a good night—sweetheart." His last word seemed to cling to her heart.

"I need to go!" Maggie tried to sweep away his comment, as she turned to leave.

"You don't want to ride back in my limo with me?" Antonio looked into her eyes, enamored by their mutual attraction.

Maggie could feel an adrenaline rush that she had never felt before. Her feelings for him were overwhelming, and they frightened her. She did not want to let her guard down.

The longer I spend with him, the harder it will be to leave.

"I need to go—and here's your ring, by the way." She tugged the ring off her thumb, placing it in his hand, but he held onto her arm.

"Come on, it's a fun ride—a little bit of chase if there's paparazzi—otherwise I chase you in my limo," he teased.

"Sounds...dangerous!" Maggie glared at him, trying to resist him, but wondering how she kept slipping under his spell. Determined to keep her head on straight, she headed for the door.

She stepped outside, attempting to hail a cab, when she felt Bradley grab her arm.

"Maggie, Antonio sent me after you."

She turned to look at his friendly face.

"Well, tell him, I am not interested in any more of his *magic* tricks!" She crossed her arms.

He seemed concerned.

"It's not like that," he revealed, speaking in a soothing tone. "Let me tell you a secret, but you have to promise not to tell him that I told you." She waited for the bomb to drop. *What could he possibly say that would make everything okay?* "Seriously," Bradley continued, "he told me that when Jose let you into the bar—as a practical joke, by the way—he felt so lucky to meet someone that didn't recognize him and fall all over him just because of his celebrity. Then Antonio said, and I quote, 'and she's absolutely beautiful!' Now please come back in there, before he fires me!"

Maggie rubbed her hands on the leather seated interior to rid the sweat she could feel on her palms. She could not believe that she was now sitting in his limo. *Idiot!* Her brain was wide awake, making an announcement.

"You don't have to sit way over there!" Antonio grumbled, looking down at the space between them. Her thoughts flooded with caution, but she slowly inched her way into the space next to his.

"So, you are here only 'til Friday?" he asked.

"Yep, plane leaves at noon." She wondered why he cared.

"I wish you could stay." His words seemed to melt out of his mouth.

"Why?" Maggie asked, wishing to get inside his mind.

"Why? Why not? I like you, Maggie."

She noticed he had his arm around her.

"You seem to have plenty of girls willing to keep you busy."

Antonio started laughing. "It's not what you think, Maggie."

www.lovetheillusion.com/57.htm

"And what's that *Chad*?"

"That I can just fall in love with any crazy fan out there. That's not appealing to me. We started out different. I don't care that you know what I do, but I don't want that to be the reason you like me."

"Believe me, it's not," she confessed.

The limo driver sped up, and took a quick corner. "They're gone," he announced.

"Damn paparazzi, got nothin' better to do," Antonio fumed.

"They really get to you?" She pondered his strange life-style.

"You have no idea." He seemed distracted.

She confirmed with silence what he said while she tried to imagine what encompassed his celebrity. She recalled the private dining room where they had dinner, and concluded that he must have paid to rent out that space, allowing them privacy. Now it all made sense. His hotel floor obviously belonged to the show crew and other employees. Bradley was either his body guard or security personnel…*Stanley…not sure.*

"Who's Stanley?" Maggie asked.

"Stanley?" Antonio repeated, wearing a grin. "Oh, he's one bad dude. You'd better run if you see him coming. And he thinks you're cute!"

"Knock it off," Maggie interrupted him, finding his humor aggravating.

"I'm just kidding!" Antonio shot back his playful smile, which had originally captivated her at their first meeting. "He's our company financial executive. He books our tours, keeps track of our ticket sales, and coordinates events. He's top dog."

Maggie remembered him pouring her wine.

"You must have thought it funny when I questioned the vacancy?"

Antonio looked on her in amusement.

"Stanley says to me, 'Hey! Any minute now she's going to come over here and ask you to sign her briefcase.'"

Maggie laughed as she recalled their intimate discussion when she was sure they were talking about her.

"Sorry to make you sit on your ego, but I've been out of the U.S. for six years now, and you're not as popular among the Brits. Although, my roommate, Dana, saw you in Canada, and she will just split a seam when I tell her—" Maggie stopped herself in the middle of her ramble. What she would tell Dana, Antonio could leave to his imagination.

"She just got engaged!" Maggie changed the subject. "Now, I get to design all the dresses."

"I bet you're good at that." Antonio flattered her.

There was a love song playing on the oldies station, and they both stopped to listen. Maggie could feel the weight of Antonio's stare, and she reluctantly dared to look up and meet his eyes beaming right through her, making her feel as if she was about to fall through the seat.

"Come here," he instructed as he leaned against the back of the limo and motioned for her to lean against his chest.

Fighting him off was a vain pursuit.

She slowly maneuvered herself closer to him and leaned against him. Her nerves remained unsteady. She slipped her hand on the seat between them. She hesitated, but then she slowly placed her other hand on his chest, swallowing hard as she did so and wondering... *How can I feel so many conflicting emotions all at once?*

Antonio placed his hand over hers, confirming her decision. Now she could smell his scent—a rich scented musk—lingering in the air. *One more thing to drive me crazy.*

"We'll be there in a couple minutes," Salvador, the limo driver, announced.

"No. We're still driving around," she heard Antonio say.

Maggie knew he wanted to spend more time with her, but she did not think she could afford the risk. The longer she spent with him, the more she felt her sanity vanishing. She wondered who else he dated, and the thought of it made her cringe. Maggie bit her bottom lip as she started wondering what tricks were up his sleeve. She shuddered at her thought of being unable to resist his next move. She could tell he felt the same flush. She could feel every breath he took, as she leaned against his chest. Her lips were within inches of his neck. She envisioned kissing him. He still had his hand locked over hers, and his other hand was now in her hair. The clock in the limo said it was nearly four. She started to count the hours of sleep she would get. *Not good.*

Maggie was taking a detailed inventory on her feelings for Antonio. *One, he is really cute. Two, he is funny. Three, he is entertaining to be around. Four, I love his accent. Five, there's definite chemistry. Six, he didn't lie. Well, maybe he did. Seven, I have never felt like this before. Eight, he is reciprocating. Nine, I could stay in this position forever. Ten, I am leaving in two days. That is a problem!*

Maggie sat up.

"Chad, I have to be somewhere at ten."

"Where's that?"

"Umm, well, I have to set up for the fashion show. I need to get some sleep." Maggie's eyes burned with regret.

"Okay, then." He indicated concern. And in that moment, it seemed he could see into her broken heart. "We need to get back," Antonio told his driver.

They pulled up to a space in underground parking. Antonio grabbed Maggie's hand to help her out of the limo. "Catch ya' later," he told his driver, who sat and waited until they were out of view. He had her hand in tow, as he took the lead.

They entered a secret elevator and rode it to the fourth floor. And before the door opened, he looked in her eyes, still determined to break down her walls, and said, "See ya'...tomorrow."

When Maggie got back to her room, she tried to shake off the evening's events, but they kept flashing in her memory. And she could not forget dancing with Antonio.

www.lovetheillusion.com/61.htm

Chapter 4

Kneeling next to boxes lined up against the wall, Maggie proceeded to set up the clothes for the models. A runway emerged from a grey curtain that hung in a curved backdrop. The flowers were already delivered, which consisted of tall greens and mixed assortments of white daylilies, hydrangeas, and azaleas. Matt and Sally, assistant coordinators for the fashion show events, were at a table with a box of pastries and coffee for the three of them.

"Maggie!" Matt called out in his silly tone. "It's donut time! We brought caffeine and sugar!"

Maggie looked up, feeling almost dizzy, remembering that she had not taken the time to eat. But now she was busy arranging the clothes for each model. They only had four models, which left for a pretty tight rotation, but they were incredibly fast. Maggie did not think that she had ever changed clothes that quickly in her entire lifetime.

"Matt!" Sally yelled over to him. "Greta's on the phone, and wants to know if she can use the money in your underwear drawer to get some soda and snacks, because Ben and his friends ate everything last night!"

"What's she doing in my underwear drawer? Tell her fine, but she can only take fifty." He looked over toward Maggie. "Those kids, always making a pipeline from your wallet to the sewer," Matt said with a chuckle.

Maggie enjoyed his humor. And she needed to keep a sense of humor, working for Francis. He was never about "lightening the mood." And she knew that she had better get busy.

www.lovetheillusion.com/62.htm

Maggie, still bent over boxes, saw Francis fast approaching. He began to speak in his expediting tone. "That box over there, it's got the tablecloths and candelabras, and Oliver's catering service will be here two hours before the show with caviar, a cheese tray, and—oh! Can you call and maybe see if they can add a veggie tray? It's sort of last minute, but also double-check that the little mini-cupcakes have buttercream icing. I *abhor* the cool-whip kind, and they aren't supposed to forget to add those tiny little plastic fashion shoes that I sent FedEx last week—and be sure to let them know if there are any problems at all, we will *not* use them in the future! Bar will be set up over there. Now, let me see what we have set up for the models." He walked over to the racks and then viewed all the boxes. Maggie felt her insides tighten as he approached her, ready to make his assessment. Her head was already spinning from all his stupendous announcements.

"Not everything's out of the boxes yet," Maggie explained. "But I put our white palazzos with the sequined tank and this scarf..." She thumbed through the sets of clothing, hoping for his approval.

"No!" he corrected. "That cashmere scarf is for the double-layered chemise, and don't forget it goes with the Hot Flash shoes."

Maggie picked up the shoes, wishing she had gotten more sleep. "No!" Francis alarmed. "The tan ones, not the red ones, they go with the cream satin dress emblazoned with red ruby accents—don't be silly. We need that dress to pop! I have to get the music to the sound tech, and I will be back in a couple hours."

Maggie looked forward to his departure when he called out, "Oh! Make sure you embellish that purple lace dress with that scarf but remove the pin—it's a pitiful sight. And in case you didn't know, the beaded wedge slide came in eight and a half, instead of nine and a half, so tell Elle she'll have to deal with it."

That is just wrong!

Maggie could not believe that he expected the models to wear shoes that were too small! She shouted at him on his way out, "Elle doesn't even want to walk in anything over four inches! And now they're too small?" She watched him...quickly return...*Please...no!*

"That Elle is such a nitpicker. I've yet to see her happy about anything! Move that outfit over to Cassandra's rack. I think they're about the same size, and she wears a nine. Now Kensal said Latasha said that she still needed alterations on the formal palazzos that were way too big in the waist! It's too late for that now, but we don't want them falling down. It's a futile attempt, but I found these clips that they'll have to use discreetly, hopefully in the back with a wrap or sweater hanging over. Hope we brought some!"

"Which pants are those?" Maggie felt exhausted after only three hours of sleep. "They were supposed to have all their fittings done last week," she tried to sound pleasant.

"Yes, but they're a bunch of dieting twigs," he said as he picked up his cell phone to get a call. Maggie noticed his newspaper rolled up under his arm. *Antonio's show made front page news?* She strained her tired eyes, trying to read the details.

"See you later!" Francis said, on his way out.

Finally!

"Just when you thought you weren't busy!" Matt laughed, looking at Maggie.

"And don't you think when he starts with all his orders," Sally added, "that you need some Post-it pads to start labeling all his requests?"

"He's more demanding than our two teens put together!" Matt concluded.

Maggie appreciated their condolences, always in abundance.

"Hey!" Sally changed the subject. "Did you know that Antonio DeLuca did a show here last night? I would love to see that!"

Hearing Antonio's name sent Maggie into a shockwave of the past evening's events. She tried not to look like the cat that ate the canary. "Really," she finally said.

"And I heard that he interviewed with Bridgette Hansen this morning," Sally informed. "Greta thinks he's so hot. You know, dark and handsome, mysterious, Italian. I tell her, 'Greta, he's way too old for you,' but she has his posters up in her room anyways...one with the mask, one without, one with his cheetah..."

Maggie tried to picture her room.

"Yeah, and we can only hope she used poster putty and not the scotch tape for that display!" Matt said.

Maggie bit her tongue from joining the conversation. Surely, there were many fans that would be raving in jealously if they only knew that she had his attention for the past couple days. And that brought her to a final conclusion: *I would be a fool to pursue him!*

With her head in a cloud, she did her best to finish out the day, and at four o'clock, everything was finally done. She was relieved that she did not have a splitting headache by now. Other than the pizza delivery at noon, she was on her feet all day.

Now, on her way back to the hotel, she thought about Antonio's interview. Her curiosity was officially piqued.

And there it is! Downloaded on my laptop!

(Bridgette Hansen sat in a tan suit with a fuchsia blouse).

BRIDGETTE: "Antonio, thank you for taking the time to meet with me. Now you had a sold-out performance last night here in New York City, and I had the privilege of attending myself, and it was simply amazing! I even got a t-shirt, and I was so hoping you would sign it for me, later? (She gave him a flirtatious smile.) But now, I have just a few questions for you, and we need to move this along quickly, because we only have a few minutes. Now, we had heard, and let me know if it's true, that you had a fire backstage last night?"

ANTONIO: (He seemed surprised that she knew.) "Well, it was very small, and put out right away. One of our props—that metal ring with the fire—hit the inside of the curtain."

BRIDGETTE: "I see! (She giggled.) Has that ever happened before? Do we have to worry when we are watching, that something is going to...blow up that's not supposed to?" (She smiled.)

ANTONIO: "Well, we haven't lost a theater yet!" (He returned her smile.)

BRIDGETTE: "I see that you brought two of your performers with you, and you two are twins? How did it come about that you both got to be in the show?" (She turned her attention to them, as the camera also focused on them.)

(Amber and Angela exchanged glances and then...)

AMBER: "Well, we both auditioned together, and Antonio didn't want to hire just one of us, since we were sisters and twins, so...I auditioned first, and after that, she auditioned, and we have been with the company for five years, since it started."

(Amber smiled at Antonio, indicating she was done.)

BRIDGETTE: "So, are you signed to secrecy, as to how the magic is done?"

ANTONIO: (quietly laughed) "They have to sign a contract. It's our company policy for all of the performers—all the dancers, everybody."

BRIDGETTE: "So, Antonio, you have been performing for five years? And nobody knows your secrets, yet?"

ANTONIO: (grinned) "Yes, it's been almost six."

BRIDGETTE: "Now, Antonio, you started performing small-scale shows back in Italy when you were fifteen, but you came to the U.S. when your family moved here. Was it for your father's job?"

ANTONIO: "Yes."

BRIDGETTE: "But now, they have both moved back to Italy, and you are still here. How is that?"

ANTONIO: (looked frustrated) "Well, I still love to go back to Italy, but I have been in

New York now for several years, so it feels like home too, and my work is here and I love my work."

BRIDGETTE: "And why did they move back after coming here?"

ANTONIO: (frowned) "Uh, well...it was difficult for them to be in another country."

BRIDGETTE: "I see. Well, we have just a couple more questions. During the show, you bring people up from the audience, and is it true that those people are part of your crew, so that they won't blow the cover on how the magic is done?"

ANTONIO: "No. That's not true. The people chosen from the audience are completely random. I don't know them."

Liar!

BRIDGETTE: "And one final question. I know you just turned twenty-eight, and we want to know if there is any special lady in your life. Do you have plans to get married and have a family? Or do you just prefer to go out with a lot of women?" (She gave him a curious smile.)

ANTONIO: (raised his eyebrows, grinned and put on 'bashful') "Eventually, I want to get married, but I'm not dating anyone right now."

Maggie huffed. *Right...*

BRIDGETTE: "Okay, well there's a rumor—and let me know if it's true or not— that you've been dating French model Arianna Berkeley."

Maggie's mouth dropped open, as she squinted. *He's such a player!*

ANTONIO: "Uh..." (Antonio glanced down quickly, and shifted his position and then looked back into the camera) "That's just a rumor!" (He grinned.)

BRIDGETTE: "Well, there is supposedly a recent photo of the two of you taken in L.A."

ANTONIO: (appeared confused) "I was in L.A. two weeks ago. She came to my show."

BRIDGETTE: "So, you were together?"

ANTONIO: "Well yeah, but we're just friends." (Antonio gave a short laugh, and then smiled.)

BRIDGETTE: "Well, thank you so much, Antonio. I see our time is up. We will be looking forward to your next performance, in Canada, right?"

ANTONIO: "Right, and then Sweden. That will be our first time in Sweden."

BRIDGETTE: "Okay, well those folks have a lot to look forward to."

Maggie was puzzled by his interview. Who was Arianna Berkeley? *His friend...? Yeah, right.* She tapped her fingers on the keys of her computer...Arianna Berkeley, she typed in. There they were... photos of her, in various modeling poses, all disgustingly, perfectly beautiful! She had long dark hair and a captivating smile. *Why wouldn't he date her?* She wondered.

www.lovetheillusion.com/69.htm

Maggie closed her computer and then lay down on her bed to contemplate the latest information. He had said he was not dating anyone. That would mean Arianna and herself included. She wondered if they had ridden in a limo together and dined in private settings. She eagerly opened up her computer again, and typed in a search for Antonio DeLuca and Arianna Berkeley. She clicked on the heading: Report News magazine reports the magician and model…

She read,

> "Antonio DeLuca, world-renowned magician, was spotted with French model, Arianna Berkeley, two weeks ago in L.A. Even though the model was in the area doing a photo shoot, and DeLuca was busy performing…"

She stared at the photo. Sure enough, he was dressed to the nines, and she had on a white trench coat. *Where were they going?* They looked awfully cozy hanging out by his limo.

www.lovetheillusion.com/70.htm

Maggie closed up her computer again. *Time to end the torture. And time to call Dana.* She needed an outsider's opinion. Dana loved giving advice, and Maggie was always in need.

"Maggie White! I have gone mad, trying to call you. Where on earth have you been? You are now officially listed on Missing Persons. I don't know your timetable, and you weren't answering your phone. So, what's going on?"

"Okay, well, I got back at five a.m. this morning. It's been... uh...Where do I even start?"

"Let me guess. You bonked the waiter."

"No, Dana, seriously, you will never believe what happened! I got to the show, and I'm waiting for Chad to arrive, but the show starts, and he's still not there. So, I figured he stood me up."

"Ah, that's sad." Dana interrupted with a bout of pity.

"But listen! As I'm watching the show, thinking, 'Wow, this is so incredible, who cares if I'm alone,' the next thing I know, Antonio asks for a volunteer to float inside the ring of fire. Well, you know me. There's no way I would volunteer to be on stage, but everyone around me is waving to go up. That's when a security guard grabs my arm and starts dragging me towards the stage."

"Shut up! You can't be serious!" Dana let out a scream. "You were on stage with Antonio?"

Maggie ignored her, realizing that was a small detail of her telling. She continued to explain, "Yes, first, I'm up there thinking, where the heck is he...then he descends from the black curtain, and as he gets closer, I see that it's Chad!"

"What...?! I can't believe it!" Dana had trouble digesting her tale.

"I am totally serious!"

Dana screamed again, only louder.

"Come on Dana, you're making me deaf!" Maggie scolded her, annoyed.

"Sorry, I can't help it!"

"So after that," Maggie continued, "I'm watching the rest of the show in this complete mystical trance, and then, as if I'm not already blown away, the security guard says I'm invited to the after party, and I used his crazy, flashy, mega-karat ring to get in. We danced, all steamy, and he brought me back in his limo." There was a long pause. "Dana? Are you still there?"

"I think I just fell off my chair. So…is he pretty amazing up close?" Dana recalled seeing his show in Canada.

"Worse than that—I think I'm going to break out in a sweat just looking at him," Maggie admitted. "I'm so annoyed."

"I don't think so," Dana assessed. "You're getting it off with him, and now you don't want to leave New York! Are you getting any work done at all? Or just trying to get sacked, so that you can shag in his limo?"

"Today was awful. I had to work all day on three hours of sleep, and to make it worse, he had some stupid interview, which I watched later on YouTube. Now, after that, I don't know what to think, as if it's not already pointless the way it is! I leave Friday. Who knows if I will ever see him again?" Maggie felt her insides aching at the thought.

"It's strange that he does not have a lady friend already," Dana questioned.

"That's just it. I'm wondering how many he has! You should see his interview," Maggie said with disgust.

"I could watch it, right?" Dana suggested.

"You could."

"I'll call you right back," Dana agreed. "Hang in there."

Maggie lay down on the bed, looking up at the ceiling, waiting for Dana to call back. Five minutes passed. She sat up. *This is ridiculous!* She grabbed the TV remote. She could not keep drowning herself in thoughts of Antonio. He was so far out of the question, and she did not want to get caught up in the moment. She needed to face up to the truth—that he was going to cause her nothing but trouble, the more time she spent with him.

The news was on, with a weather update, predicting an ice storm which was not typical for New York this time of year—*possibly Friday? You have got to be joking!* Maggie slumped onto the bed to watch. "...AND COMING UP, BRIDGETTE HANSEN'S INTERVIEW WITH ANTONIO DELUCA..."

"Crap!" Maggie threw the remote onto the floor. She quickly leaned over the bed to see if it was broken. Her eyes shifted onto her romance novel. How would she concentrate enough to read anything right now? She was doomed, doomed to the frustration that only a man could bring into her life. She would date when she got back home. She had to somehow forget him. If only she would have gone to the Atrium Cafe, in the first place.

Maybe that is where I will have dinner tonight, by myself!

"...AND HERE IS A CLIP FROM BRIDGETTE HANSEN'S INTERVIEW..."

Maggie sat up in her bed and watched Antonio explain how the fire was small, and that they had not lost a theater yet.

Ha, ha, ha, ha. Isn't he so funny! At least, they did not show the question about Arianna. Maggie thought back to the photo, when the phone rang. She placed the phone to her ear.

"Sorry that took me so long Maggie, but after I watched the interview, I got nosy and looked up that Arianna girl and the picture of them together, and I can't imagine what you are thinking!"

"Ha! Well you aren't the only nosey one. I looked up her lovely pictures too, and the photo...all of it...just so wonderful." Maggie felt frustrated.

"Maggie! You need to talk to him. Call him and ask him!" Dana came to her rescue with advice.

"I don't even know where he is right now." Maggie sighed. "And I don't have his *phone* number. For all I know, he could be with her right now! He said that he would see me today, but when? He didn't say! I'm just supposed to sit in anticipation of the next thrill ride! I swear he gets his kicks just like that—surprises! That's what I just can't take any more of…his surprises."

"Well, he is a magician! Maybe he just can't separate his professional work from his personal life!" Dana attempted to diagnose his personality.

"Yeah, well if that's the case, he needs to make himself disappear!" Maggie pouted.

"Oh, come on Maggie. You don't really mean that. This is just what you need to forget Phillip—a short term affair with a hot celebrity!"

"Are you out of your mind?" Maggie could not stomach her suggestion.

"Do what you want, but he's awfully cute," Dana professed, egging her on. "I can't believe you're hanging out with him."

"Oh!" Maggie let out another sigh. "And did you know that now there's some wretched ice storm coming, and it's coming on— guess what? Friday of all days! Watch me get stuck here and prolong my *misery.*"

"I have an idea," Dana stated in a brilliant, Einstein tone. "I will ask Shane what he thinks! He's a man. Maybe he has an idea."

Maggie already felt lost in confusion.

"You *are* out of your mind!" Maggie discarded her idea. "What's he gonna do? Look into some crystal ball and verify, 'Yep!

He sounds like a player!?' Please don't even tell him, Dana. He's going to laugh his head off every time he looks at me, and then he'll tell everyone! And *that* will be completely embarrassing. Please Dana, you have to promise me."

"Fine, but it's gonna be really hard to keep my mouth shut. I mean, you went out with Antonio DeLuca!"

Dana screamed again.

"Dana! Cut with the drama," Maggie griped, completely aggravated.

"Shane just got here, so I should probably go."

Maggie realized she was on her own to make sense of everything.

"Okay, well, I promise when I get home, my bizarre adventure will be history, and we'll start planning your wedding."

Chapter 5

The Atrium Cafe was the perfect place to celebrate a clean slate. It was the restaurant she had originally meant to go to, instead of Biagio's. Maggie took off her work clothes and dug through her suitcase for...something special? Yes, it was a special occasion— *Time to break free from Antonio's magical spell!*

Maggie stared back at her reflection, struggling to retain a positive outlook on staying single. *One positive thing!* It did not matter how she looked! But the jean shorts and sweater still needed an accessory. Maggie grabbed a scarf, printed with a red rose floral design, and tied it around her neck. She slipped on her favorite boots, and, without using a comb, braided her messy hair, leaving it to hang on one side. *No reason to worry about hair.* She was celebrating independence!

www.lovetheillusion.com/76.htm

She grabbed her bag and headed out the door.

When she arrived at the Atrium Cafe, she concluded that everyone in the hotel must have decided to eat at the same time. There was a two hour wait.

After finally getting seated, she reviewed the menu. And after making her selection, she suddenly felt very alone. Francis had invited her to dinner, but she declined. She needed a break from him. Matt and Sally were enjoying their time away from their teenagers, and she did not want to intrude. She tried not to think about Antonio. She noticed an elderly couple sitting a few tables away. They hardly spoke a word to each other, but when the man smiled at his wife, Maggie thought *that must be what love would look like if you could see it.*

After ordering fettuccini, she noticed a couple of women sitting together, hovered over their table and cackling, enjoying their private conversation. *Probably discussing men.* Maggie laughed to herself, wondering why they had to be so difficult and why love had to be so complicated.

When her food arrived, she was reminded how much she liked Italian food. Funny thing, Antonio was Italian. She forked through her fettuccini, suddenly realizing that she had not spent much time thinking about Phillip, lately. He was not who she thought he was, which made it easier for her to dissolve her feelings for him. Her mind raced back to Antonio. She tried to clear him out of her head, but she could not. She wondered about Arianna. The thought of them together made her nauseous, not to mention the other girlfriends he probably had. After Friday, she would never see him again, and surely he would have no problem keeping busy without her.

Maggie suddenly lost her appetite and pushed her plate away.

When the bill arrived, she signed her name after writing down her room number. She thought about putting Antonio's room number on the bill, but then she stopped herself in her silly thoughts.

She darted her eyes across the room while making her exit.

No Bradley tonight. No notes delivered to the table, either.

Antonio must have forgotten about her as he spent time with Arianna or whoever else he could be entertaining tonight.

Just as she stepped out of the restaurant, a lady she had never met before came up to her and made conversation. "Excuse me miss, but were you with Antonio DeLuca at the Night Owl last night?"

Maggie suddenly felt invaded.

"Why do you ask?"

"Just tell me your name," the lady probed.

"Uh...Maggie," she hesitated, hoping she would not regret talking to strangers.

"Maggie, are you the one that went up on stage with Antonio, at the show last night?"

"Why?" Maggie questioned. "Who are you?"

"I just want to know. Was it you?" the lady asked in a pleasant tone.

"Why does it matter?" Maggie recalled Antonio's sea of fans.

"Well, yes or no?!" The lady sounded determined as if she owned the rights to know.

"Well...yeah, I was up there. What's the big deal?" Maggie finally gave in.

"And were you also at the Night Owl?" the lady asked, with needle-pricking suspicion.

"I gotta go!" Maggie broke free from the conversation and paced quickly down the hall to get back to the east wing. *Oh, no! That was probably some stupid reporter!* She looked behind her, but the lady was gone. She let out a breath of relief, keeping a steady pace until she got back to her room.

Maggie looked around. Everything appeared as she had left it. *No additional wine and nothing out of place.* The clock on the night stand told her it was already eight o'clock. She worried, thinking about the reporter. She did not want people concerned or even interested in her life! She wondered what Antonio would say about it. Should she be concerned? Now she needed to find out. She would go to his room one more time—*for closure*—mention the reporter, and catch him with that Arianna girl, or whoever else he'd be entertaining, confirming her suspicions that he was indeed a major player. Then, once and for all, she would have no problem getting him out of her head. *Perfect!*

She stood outside his room, hesitating to knock. She waited in toil, allowing five minutes to pass before finally knocking.

The noise of the door opening caused her to take a step back. She felt edgy.

"Maggie. Hi!" Antonio sounded surprised. He had the door opened just a crack, so she thought for sure Arianna must be in there, somewhere. But to her surprise, he pushed the door wide open and invited her, "Come in."

Her eyes combed the room from left to right and top to bottom. The room, three times the size of hers and furnished with a personal touch, triggered her curiosity. He decorated with older, vintage pieces of furniture, and a unique mahogany dresser and paintings that looked like the originals. The room gleamed—*exceptionally spotless*—and she thought he must have maid service twice a day to keep it that way. He was alone except for his food delivery. She pondered his living arrangements.

"I see you had dinner," she commented in order to make conversation.

"Actually, breakfast," Antonio informed her. "Pancakes and eggs again, but not as good as this morning…kind of soggy."

"Mmm, I see." She tried to avoid eye contact with him. "Well, I just got back from the Atrium Cafe. I got there at five but had to wait two hours to get in."

"Oh, you were done with work, already?" He sounded interested.

"We got done earlier than I thought." She spoke in a stiff tone. "But I came by to tell you that I think I spoke to a reporter this evening."

"You did?" Antonio raised his brow, surprised.

"Yes," Maggie explained, "a woman approached me as I was leaving the restaurant and where she came from, I have no idea. She wanted to know if I was at the Night Owl—after she asked what my name was—*and* if I was on stage with you. Now, why would she care?"

Antonio listened intently, but with little expression.

"So what did you say?" he finally asked, with his eyes glued to hers.

"As little as possible." She glanced at him, hoping he would indicate whether or not she should be concerned. "It felt kind of creepy and she caught me completely off guard. I told her my name was Maggie, and that I was up on stage with you, but I didn't tell her whether or not I was at the Night Owl."

Antonio stood completely stationary, except for his eyes which shifted to his left, then up and then back to Maggie.

"I just thought you should know," she concluded, forgetting her concern.

"Thanks. Is that all?" He looked as if he might smile.

"Yep." Maggie, still puzzled, turned to leave, but Antonio followed her and when she got to the door to leave, she heard him speak.

"Can you stay?" His voice sounded smooth.

"In here...with you?" Maggie imagined. "I would be better off finishing my novel." She spoke, facing the door.

"Wow...must be a good one." He spoke in an even tone.

"It's okay," she responded with little enthusiasm.

"Do you read a lot?"

"Sometimes," Maggie informed curtly, as she remembered the latest thing she had read was online about Arianna and him.

"I have something for you," Antonio said in a soft gentleman-like tone.

Maggie turned around squinting at him.

What could that be? Whatever it is, I don't want it!

She watched him walk over to a somewhat large cardboard box that was situated next to the wall by a Victorian style chair.

Seconds later, he held up a purple t-shirt from the show.

"It might be too big," he explained. "But we just have the extra-large left over." He held it up to her. She quickly grabbed it out of his hands.

"Thanks," she said, turning back towards the door.

"Don't you want me to sign it for you?" he asked with a perk of enthusiasm.

Maggie's mouth opened, but she was speechless. She turned around slowly to acknowledge his confidence, assuming she would. She wanted to kick his ego. And she was not in the mood for his favors. Now he was grinning at her.

"Sure," she finally agreed, letting sarcasm rule the moment. She could just as well choke on his ego. She watched him, with her eyelids drooped in disgust, as he seemed proud to take out a permanent marker and sign her shirt.

He held it back up for her to see. It now said, "To Maggie, Love Chad XO," written super large across the front right bottom corner of the t-shirt.

Maggie grabbed the shirt, making brief eye contact. "See ya'."

She had just turned to the door, once again, when she felt Antonio grab her arm. Her thoughts flashed back to the bar, when they first met, and he grabbed her arm and asked her to eat with him—when he was Chad. Now all she could think about was how to smother the chemistry between them.

"Do you have to go?" he asked with a sweet look, as if he was moments away from a smile.

Maggie felt swarms of butterflies swimming in her stomach as she stood close to him.

"Why, what do you have in mind?" She dared to look into his eyes that were glued to hers.

Antonio tilted his head. He seemed deep in thought, but then spoke intimately. "Hmm, whatever you want to do."

Maggie felt a shockwave of emotions hit her like a ton of bricks.

"I have to go!" She gave him an exasperated look, thinking the conversation had to be almost over. With the shirt draped over her arm, she reached for the doorknob. Antonio stood with his hands behind his back, watching her leave.

"Come with me! I have to show you something," he said.

She turned around, finding his enthusiasm hard to resist. She watched as he went over to a cabinet and pulled out a brown bag, the size of a lunch bag. When her eyes followed him across the room, she noticed his bedspread was made of a unique faux fur, resembling a zebra print. She watched Antonio who now held the bag in the air, as if he had just caught a fish. He proceeded towards the door, presuming she had agreed. And once again, she felt a victim to his persistence.

Hopefully, I will not regret spending more time with him.

"Should I drop this off in my room first?" She held up the shirt.

"Sure," he agreed, following her down to her room.

He waited at the door, until Maggie initiated, "You can come in but don't look at the mess." She walked over to the chair by the TV and dropped the t-shirt atop a pile of clothes that were already draped over it in a disorderly fashion. She thought her room must look like a messy disaster compared to his.

Antonio picked up her novel that had been sitting under the TV remote. "Is this the book you're reading?" he asked.

"Yes, that's it." She watched as he turned it over and read the back cover. "Do I need my purse?"

Antonio gave a quick glance up at the ceiling and then slowly shook his head. "You don't need any money, so it depends what you keep in your purse." He grinned, wishing to flatter her, and then placed her book back under the remote.

"Fine." She dumped her purse down on the end of the bed.

They walked towards the end of the hall together in silence. Maggie still had her mind on his interview.

Is he genuinely sweet...buried under his ego? Or is he just a major player? Not sure...

"So, did you have a bad day?" Antonio finally broke the silence as they stepped into the elevator. She remained silent, watching him press the G button to go to the ground level. "Maggie!" He circled her face with his eyes.

"Why would you think that?" She spoke in a stubborn tone.

"I don't know. You seem mad, or crabby, or irritated." He indicated his assumption.

Maggie felt as if she was going to explode.

"Alright, Antonio, I saw your interview. There! Are you happy now?" she blurted out.

Antonio appeared amused. "I thought you had to work."

"Convenient?" She wondered. "Well, I got curious and watched it online."

"Oh..." Antonio seemed flattered and humored at the same time, "So... you're wondering who Arianna is?"

"No, Antonio. I'm not! It's not my business since I just met you, I hardly know you, and what you do in your spare time is your own business. You can forget the so-called explanation." Maggie looked at him, surrounded by her protective walls.

"Is that really how you feel?" He tried not to smile.

The elevator came to a stop, and Maggie followed Antonio out. She walked with her arms folded as she stared down at the floor.

"Hey!" he began, setting the bag down and grabbing her arms to unfold them. He slipped his fingers through hers while staring into her eyes. "Go ahead, ask me... ask me who she is."

Maggie was too annoyed to appreciate his affectionate gestures. "Who is she?" Maggie mocked.

"She's a lady living in the fast lane. She came to my show in L.A. and afterwards says we should go hang out." Antonio looked into her eyes when he spoke. "So, I suggest coffee. We don't have after parties in L.A.—too risky—only in New York where our security is tighter. Once, we were in Phoenix and there were a hundred passes given out, and pretty soon the whole town came in, and we had to close down early. It was a nightmare!" He laughed, in recollection.

"So, you had coffee?" she reiterated. "And then you rolled around in your limo together? Yeah, don't worry, I understand men, and that includes you—out for a good time, new girl every night, and *you*? Why would you be any different? Look at you...just a busy womanizer! Well, I am pleased to be the first that is *not* interested."

"Is that right?" he challenged. "So, you read me like an open book? You don't even know me." Antonio lowered his eyebrows at her, slightly aggravated. "Now let me finish. I know what you're thinking...She's a beautiful girl so I just can't refuse, but honestly, the truth? She's an aggressive flirt like you've never seen before! When we got into my limo after leaving the coffee shop, she was all over me! And she has a new guy every week. She was out to use *me*! I would never date her."

Maggie considered his explanation. She was not sure what to think.

"So, what is it you want to show me?" Her face broke into a half smile, attempting to hide her embarrassment.

"This way!" Antonio picked up the bag and took her hand to lead the way. They walked down an underground hallway until they arrived at an entrance. He reached into his pocket and pulled out a key. She watched him intently as he unlocked a steel door. He turned to watch her face as if he was about to perform one of his magic tricks—and then she saw it! Maggie peered into a spacious concrete room as her mouth opened in amazement.

"It's your cheetah? That's amazing. He's so cool!"

Antonio seemed pleased with her reaction.

"Yeah, he's really cool, and he's completely tame! We rescued him from the wild, a couple years ago, in Africa. The ESO called me and asked if I wanted him for my show. Of course, I said yes, and now he's my buddy. He was stranded, and they thought his mom was killed, so he was too small to survive in the wild by himself. I named him 'Cheetos.'"

"Wow!" Maggie stared at Cheetos in amazement. He stood looking fierce, gated in an area fenced up with stainless heavy weight bars.

"Should I let him out?" Antonio sensed her fear.

"I don't know. Does he bite, ever?" Maggie hesitated.

"No. Not ever. Not yet, anyways."

She watched Antonio open the door to the cage.

"Here, you can feed him if you want." Antonio stuck his hand into the brown bag and pulled out a huge chunk of dried meat.

"Oh, I don't know..." She felt a bit squeamish as Cheetos took a step closer to her.

"Come on. I'm right here to protect you." He gave her an encouraging look. She glanced up into his eyes that were darting back at hers. She took a deep breath, trying to recalculate her emotions.

"How do you make him disappear when he's on stage with you?" Maggie wondered if he would share his secrets.

"Huh?" Antonio laughed, pouring out a smile on her. "I won't tell you that! Why would you ask me that? You know that's a secret." He gazed on her in amusement.

"Can I pet him?"

"Sure, but let me pet him first." He moved closer to the cheetah. "Heeeeey, Cheetos." Antonio rubbed his hand back and forth over his head, proud to show him off. Maggie's eyes opened wide as she wore her biggest smile. "Go ahead, pet him," Antonio encouraged, gently nudging her arm. She cautiously reached out her hand and skittishly ran her middle three fingers along the top of Cheetos' head. Her face brightened.

www.lovetheillusion.com/87.htm

"He seems friendly," Maggie concluded. "Now I want to feed him!" she requested in excitement.

"Are you sure?" Antonio teased in a suspenseful tone.

"Yes. Yes! I really do!" She held her hands together in a clapping position, resting under her nose.

"Okay, but don't say I didn't warn you!" he teased again, placing Cheetos' treat in her hand.

Maggie reached out her hand, offering Cheetos the meat as he took it with his teeth. She drew in a quick breath, but then let it out as Cheetos walked away, just like a cat with a mouse. Maggie looked at Antonio, and they both started laughing.

"How long will it take him to eat that?" she asked.

"That?" Antonio shook his head. "Not long."

"So, you take care of him yourself?" Maggie analyzed his love for animals.

"Yep, I'm his daddy." Antonio laughed at his own joke, and Maggie laughed back. And in an instant, their laughter ceased, landing them on a serious note. Antonio noticed she was warming up to him. It seemed to catch him off guard.

"Do you want to get something to eat?" he asked her, as she looked on him with hesitation. "Don't worry. We'll get ourselves something better than what Cheetos just had. I could go for some ice cream right now. Do you want to come?"

"You want ice cream after pancakes?"

She could not deny she liked his company.

"Sure, why not?" He smiled.

She shoved aside her previous concerns that she was leaving in a few days. "Ice cream's good," she decided. "Are we going back to Biagio's?" She gave him a sweet look, remembering where they met.

"No, you have bad memories there! Two strangers introducing you to that expensive Italian wine, trying to creep on you..." Antonio played upon the humor of the situation.

"I never *said* that!" she snapped back, letting go of a smile.

"But that's what you were thinking...what a creep I was! I'm still wondering if I should forgive you." Antonio's face turned sour.

"Maybe I was wrong," she admitted.

"Good, then we have that out of the way," he finished with a grin, and Maggie blushed, feeling overcome by his interest in her. "Tonight, we will have a new adventure."

She was pondering what exactly that would entail when he quickly informed, "We're going to have to wait a minute."

She watched him send a text on his phone as she deliberated his strange life-style, thinking it was a rare adventure to be out with him. He motioned for her to follow, as he headed back to the elevator.

They reached the first floor where he led her to an exit door.

He put his phone away and placed his hands in his pockets while they stood next to the window, waiting for their ride. Maggie looked up at him. He seemed to know just how to look at her with his dark mysterious eyes. And once again, she tried to brace her emotions.

Now she noticed his attire. He had on black pleated pants with a white t-shirt that fit snug and a flannel shirt that he wore open. She observed his penny loafers, and decided he did not match. Antonio picked up quickly on her assessment and grinned. "I know I look ridiculous, but you didn't tell me you were coming. So what's this?" He brought his hand around her loose braid of hair that hung down on the side and was starting to come apart.

"That," she paused, "is a lame solution to a wet updo that finally dried and came out looking like a mess! Late night, remember?"

"I'll make sure no one sees us!" Antonio suggested, still grinning. Maggie laughed under her breath, and the next thing she knew, Antonio was grabbing her hand and running with her to the limo. "Get in, quick," he said. His words signaled an alarm that he knew that people on the outside took interest in his life.

She watched him get in. He sat close to her. She felt their arms touching while she looked straight ahead, frozen to her emotions.

"To Fancy Franny's," Antonio ordered the driver.

Maggie looked up at him out of the corner of her eye.

"That sounds like a strip club!"

"What? I said Fancy Franny's, not Fancy Fannies!" Antonio laughed.

"Oh." She elbowed him for his smart return.

"But if you'd rather go to the strip clubs…" he added, to irritate her.

Maggie could tell he liked to cause trouble.

"Quit, before I smack you!" she warned.

"You wouldn't!" He played his game.

"I might!"

"Well then, I'll be ready to fight back!"

"I'm not scared of you."

"You…should be!" Antonio said, thinking he had the last word.

Maggie heard the driver chuckling.

"Is he always trouble?" Maggie wanted to know.

"Yep." He stared back in the rear view mirror. "You have yourself a real troublemaker."

"Do you want some gum?" Antonio asked, changing the subject.

"Aren't we having ice cream soon?" She found his spontaneous behavior amusing.

"Yeah, but not for a while—here, chew a piece with me."

Maggie looked at him, as though he was half out of his mind.

"It's magical gum," he explained. "You can blow these huge enormous bubbles that are bigger than your face!"

"How 'bout I just watch you?" Maggie decided he was unlike anyone she had ever dated.

"No Maggie, that's no fun." He gave her a look of suspense. "Come on, I bet I can blow a bigger bubble!"

"Alright, fine," she finally agreed.

Maggie unwrapped the gum, and just as she was putting it in her mouth, she noticed Antonio had already chewed his into a super huge bubble. He moved across from her, so that she could see him in full view. And Maggie now saw a childlike side of him that she had never seen before. She laughed, trying to pop his enormous bubble. Antonio grabbed both of her hands and held them down to prevent her. She chewed her gum as fast as she could and proceeded to blow a bubble herself. Antonio's bubble looked about the size of his head. She blew and blew, but it popped when it was not even half the size of his. He quickly sucked in his bubble and proclaimed, "See, I win!"

"You should be so proud." Maggie snickered.

"Fine, maybe I just had beginner's luck," Antonio suggested. "Let's try one more time."

"Beginner's luck?" Maggie laughed. "Yeah, right!"

They both started blowing their bubbles again, and Antonio once again had her hands held down to prevent her from cheating. Maggie watched Antonio blow an even bigger bubble this time. She felt proud of her own bubble, managing better this time, until it popped all over her face. Antonio sucked in his bubble and let go of her hands. "I win again!" he stated victoriously. He sat back down next to her and proclaimed, "Oh, no, look at you. You can't eat ice cream like that!"

Maggie elbowed him again, when he offered, "Here, let me help you." He attempted to remove the gum from her face.

"Antonio, I think I'm going to have to cut short your fun," she lectured.

The limo pulled up to the employee entrance of Fancy Franny's. Antonio grabbed her hand to help her out of the limo as he instructed his driver, "Wait here, just in case."

Just in case what?

She followed him in through the employee entrance.

When they got in, they sat down in a booth near the back door. Maggie darted her eyes around the ice cream parlor that was seated to capacity. Everyone was turning around to look at them. She tried to absorb the shock, while listening to the whispers:

"Is that Antonio DeLuca?

"Who's that girl with him?"

"Didn't he do a show here last night?"

"Wow, it's him!"

Maggie tried to dissect each phrase that flooded into her ears, finally concluding that her face was surely blushing—beet red.

Is he used to this?

"Maggie!" Antonio whispered at her, from across their booth, breaking her concentration. She leaned over and met him halfway, reading the concern in his eyes. She waited quietly for him to tell her that they were going to make a quick exit, but instead he informed, "I think you still have gum on your face."

She stared back in silence, as he brought his hand up to her face and brushed off the gum that was still there.

Maggie still felt embarrassed when the waitress approached.

"Oh look! It *is* you! Now, I will wait on you, but you have to promise to sign the guest check." She smiled, looking at the two of them. "Now, what can I get you?"

The menus were attached to the salt and pepper display, but before Maggie could grab one, Antonio ordered. "We will have a triple-decker brownie with mint chocolate chip, butter pecan, and strawberry ice cream, with slices of bananas, two spoons."

That sounds disgusting.

"Okay, coming right up!" The waitress wrote down his order and then glanced over Maggie before leaving.

Maggie slouched in the booth, wishing to escape the attention.

"So, your ice cream order sounds...interesting," she said.

Antonio frowned, able to read her mind, and motioned for the waitress to return.

"Yes?" She came back with a smile.

"You never took her order," Antonio informed.

"Oh, I'm so sorry dear. I thought when he asked for two spoons...What can I get for you?"

Maggie thought she must look like she'd seen a ghost by now. The waitress was staring her down while people were still whispering, but Antonio was completely oblivious. She took a deep breath, feeling overwhelmed.

"The extra spoon is because she's going to want to try mine," Antonio announced.

"I'll just have a strawberry sundae...small. Thank you." Maggie smiled at the waitress, trying to fit in to his world.

A small boy came and stood by the edge of their booth.

"Can I get your sigitor?" He only looked about three years old and was holding a stuffed cheetah. It reminded Maggie of Cheetos.

Antonio smiled pleasantly and proceeded to sign the napkin that had the Fancy Franny's logo on it.

"There you go." Antonio looked pleased, and Maggie had to admit he was nice to his fans. She watched the boy walk back to his table where he was seated with his parents and his older sister who reached out to grab the napkin and look at it.

By the time the ice cream arrived, Maggie thought some of the whispering had finally subsided. She stared in disbelief at his dessert. She thought it was funny that he had ordered such an enormous portion.

He is really harmless, she thought.

"Aren't you going to try my dessert?" Antonio asked, as he dished another scoop into his mouth.

Maggie did not know whether to look at him or his ice cream. She found him intriguing—*mysterious, funny, and extremely hot.* And unlike any guy she had ever met.

"No, mine's good." She wished she did not like him so much.

"That doesn't look that exciting. You just got strawberry." He sounded disappointed.

"Well, there's no way I'd be able to eat all that!" She eyed up his mound of ice cream, already half gone.

"Go ahead, try some." He pushed the other long spoon over to her. Maggie noticed she ate with a shorter spoon.

"Fine," she agreed, reaching for the spoon. "I'll try your ice cream concoction."

"Okay, now you have to make sure that you get some of each flavor." He sounded excited.

Maggie dug her spoon in the enormous dish, carefully gathering herself a bite.

"Interesting...it's actually kind of good," she decided while looking at Antonio, who smiled triumphantly back at her, as if he had just won the best dessert contest.

Before she knew it, the waitress had brought the check, but Antonio motioned for a pen.

"Oh, of course, silly me, I forgot you need a pen to sign the check!" the waitress said in her bubbly mannerism.

Maggie watched as he signed, "Antonio D."

After the waitress left, he stood up and put a fifty on the table. Now she contemplated his generosity.

"Let's go." Antonio grabbed Maggie's hand and led her out the door to where the limo was still waiting.

The limo clock revealed the time: *11:30, already?* She had to admit, she had fun every time she was with him. But tomorrow was the big day, and she could not afford to droop through the events.

"Antonio?" She dared to look at him.

"Yes?" His eyes emanated a warm glow.

"I had a lot of fun. Thanks."

"So this was better than your book?" Antonio gave her a sly look. Maggie returned a look to imitate his as he grabbed her hand, resting it on his knee. She wanted to jump on top of him and kiss him passionately, but instead she looked out the dark tinted window. She traced the events of the past few days. How was she going to bring herself to leave on Friday? As much as she wanted to deny her feelings, she knew there was no way to erase them, as they clung tightly to her insides. She wondered why Antonio had pursued her, and if he dated a lot of women. She still struggled to make sense of it all. Everything had happened so suddenly, and before she knew it, she was falling victim to yet another man's discretion.

Reality hit, and she quickly assessed, "I have to get up early tomorrow. It's the big day. You know, vendors, buyers crawling and brawling all over the convention center. And I have to make sure everyone stays happy. It stands nothing short of a complete miracle."

"When are you done?" Antonio cut through her distraction.

Maggie sighed, exasperated. "I have no idea...but late—very late." She worried as her emotions were spinning at no control of her own.

"We could have a late dinner," Antonio suggested while gazing in her eyes. She gazed back in his, wishing for strength. She had none. "Unless, you are...busy." He grinned while offering an out.

"No, we can." She could not refuse.

"Okay, I'll figure something out," Antonio promised, still holding her hand in his.

That night, Maggie lay wide awake in bed wondering what Antonio would plan for them tomorrow night. Would he finally kiss her? *What if he wanted more?* Was she even able to resist him? It would be their last night together. Soon, she would step out of his magical kingdom for good. Would she ever see him again? His company was stationed in New York, and she lived in England. She never had any luck with local relationships, much less a distant affair. She could never afford to quit her job and just hang out in New York City. *Does he even care that I am leaving?* Maggie felt her mind racing. She was so on edge about everything. How would she sleep? Then she noticed his t-shirt, still draped over a chair, where she had left it.

With her eyes closed, she held his shirt up to her face, breathing in a light trace of his scent. She removed her clothes and slipped it on. She crawled back into bed, closed her eyes, and dreamed of dancing with him.

Chapter 6

Maggie was wide awake before the alarm even went off. She studied Antonio's signature. "XO..." *Does he write that on all the girls' t-shirts?* At the Night Owl, she had been too engrossed with the girl's shiny lip gloss to notice how he had signed her sleeve. Obviously, he did not typically sign, "Chad."

Maggie thought about the cheetah stuffed animal, and how it reminded her of Cheetos. She recalled how sweetly Antonio had responded to his little fan. Her mind danced with pictures of him blowing his gum and later eating his ice cream. She could not remember the last time she had so much fun. But time was passing quickly, and soon she would be back in London.

She really needed to focus on work. She would get there early, and hopefully forget the miserable reality that she could never be with Antonio. It was *just an illusion.*

I need to quit thinking about him.

Maggie stood, in front of the mirror, looking a bit tired from the late nights, but nonetheless, today was the big, anticipated event—the fashion show. She wore a new, short sleeve dress made of a poly knit, hosting an overstated design in cream and red rectangular stripes running at various complicated diagonals. The dress had a v-neckline that gathered into the waistline covered by a belt—classy, sophisticated and one of Francis' designs.

www.lovetheillusion.com/98.htm

The convention center sparkled, dashing in extravagance, a beautiful sight to behold, until she saw Francis Louis hunched over his computer, sitting at a round table in the center of the room. Everything looked remarkable and perfectly arranged, *except for him.*

"Maggie! I didn't expect you until 9 o'clock." His eyes followed her as she approached.

"I decided to come early." Maggie wore her tattered emotions on her sleeve.

"Well, that's great, there's plenty to do! Did you eat breakfast, at least coffee?"

"Yeah, I had a bagel and an apple from the deli." Maggie stood for a moment, trying to clear her thoughts of Antonio.

"You look tired," Francis commented as if he was in charge of her appearance.

"I, uh, haven't been sleeping well. You know how it is when you're traveling."

He observed her, with his beady eyes, just over the top rim of his glasses. "Perhaps, you need coffee! We have a fresh pot right here." He fidgeted with the newspaper to move it out of the way, clearing a spot for her to join him.

"Thanks." She proceeded to pour herself a cup. She wished she could take a nap.

"Sorry, no cream and sugar," he added.

"It's fine, Francis. So, is everything ready to go? It all looks wonderful...far better than the last show we did." She tried to look energetic.

"Well," he said stiffly, in his usual quick pace, "that's not saying much, after we had to use those cut-rate cheesy blue tablecloths and cheap ugly vases with the poor excuse of dandelion looking floral displays, not to mention the caterers left us with food that must have been imported from one of China's street vendors!"

She remembered his detailed recollection.

"I know, it was awful," she gave way to laughter, "but this time I didn't give them a chance to screw up. I picked everything out myself."

He grunted while opening up the newspaper to read. "Well if it isn't Antonio DeLuca making the news, *again.* He plans to expand his show to include Sweden now? Well, la tea da!"

"So do you think we should go over the list of buyers?" Maggie changed the subject. "How many are we expecting?"

I cannot believe he mentioned Antonio!

"What?" Francis looked up from the newspaper as if he had barely heard a word she said. "You should double check the models' clothing rack and make sure nothing is missing. Cassandra came in and thought that a slip went missing that belonged with the sheer, layered organza formal she claims is way too transparent. It's the one we put with that necklace that we imported from Spain that we couldn't buy elsewhere. Perhaps it got misplaced under that floral silk dress that went with the nude silk leggings. And speaking of those, Elle said there was a run in them. I hope not! Now perhaps some of the stuff isn't even on the right hangers."

Maggie tried to focus, but her head was in a cloud when she heard him say, "Oh! And Latasha called to say she was feeling ill, but I told her, she'd better recover quickly. She was probably out too late last night, partying. Give me a break! Did I mention that we need to organize a packet of information for each buyer?" he reminded her. Maggie wished he would slow down as she listened to him ramble a mile a minute. "We have a catalogue and a separate price list that explains cost per quantity ordered. But now! I have a special flier printed on bright green laminated paper suggesting time frame! That's when we need to *receive* the orders! That way, they don't think that they can place some huge order at the last minute. That seems to be their favorite time to order...you know, last minute! Now, we have discount incentives for quantity orders and those are indicated on the orange flyers over there that just arrived in that box this morning." Francis turned around and pointed at it, pausing for a second. *Is he finally done?* "Instead of leaving it all on a table for them to selectively pick through..." *guess not!* "I picked up these colorful custom envelopes with our Louis logo across the mid-section. I have to admit they are truly marvelous!" *He must have said everything there is to say by now!* "...But! Let me tell you, it was no picnic getting these done last minute! I walked into a print shop yesterday, and they told me they were backlogged with orders, and it would take a wretched three weeks to get them back. I told them, 'nonsense, I need them today!' So then I had to pay a three hundred dollar upcharge for rush production. And then it was no problem. They decided all of a sudden, they could print the envelopes in a day! These businesses in the U.S. are so scandalous!"

Will he ever shut up? Maggie wondered if he had any idea how demanding the U.S. businesses he dealt with must think the European fashion designers were.

He reached down next to his briefcase and proudly handed one to her. "All the information can go in these...Now the buyers can't play the memory loss game—'Oh, I never knew the order had to be in by'—sort of a last minute thought on my part."

Maggie looked down at the envelope, signaling her approval. She felt dizzy from his energy. She removed herself from the table and began to get busy. The fashion show did not start until three, and she mentally prepared for a long day.

"Sally, Matt!" Maggie smiled, looking up. She was glad to see them. They always brightened the mood.

"We ate at the breakfast buffet today," Matt articulated, waltzing in with his usual enthusiasm, *"and* without standing in line! What a miracle! And now we are early. Another miracle!"

Sally darted over to help Maggie disassemble the boxes of fliers and catalogues, sorting them into the envelopes. But soon they were interrupted by Sally's cell phone. Maggie could hear the ringtone as Sally headed over to her purse to pick up the call.

"Oh...*Nooooo!*" Sally shrieked as if it was the coming of Armageddon. "Matt! Greta just called, and she's locked out of the house and thinks Ben locked her out when he left for work!"

"What? What was she doing outside?" Matt sounded out his pretentious fatherly concern. "I pictured her inside, in her usual spot on the sofa, with the Mountain Dew and Doritos bag."

"She was sunbathing!" Sally explained in an exasperated tone.

"Is that right? Is it even warm enough for that?" Matt questioned. "Guess she'll get to use her new cell phone and call a locksmith," he concluded.

"Oh dear, I don't know if that's a good idea." Sally still sounded concerned. "She's probably in that white, thong style bikini. She's a young girl, and we don't want some strange man coming over to let her in, especially—"

"Well, what do you suggest," Matt interrupted, "Batman or Superman?" He laughed off her worries.

Maggie smiled at the two of them.

After several hours, Maggie had reorganized the clothing racks and found the nude leggings with a run in them. Sally was quite the genius, using them as an excuse to leave for a quick lunch break and some shopping. They both needed a break from Francis.

When they returned, it was half past noon and shortly afterwards, the models started arriving. Maggie listened to the latest drama as they wandered in.

"I wish I wasn't here," Latasha whined, holding her stomach. "I think I must have food poisoning from one of the fast food restaurants I ate at last night."

"That'll teach you to eat fast food." Francis spoke into his newspaper.

"Well, I had a salad, and I feel fine." Kensal bounced alongside Latasha, with a tote bag over her shoulders.

"Hey! I received a text last night from some chick I don't know!" Matt announced with a low laugh, ready to entertain the staff with his "teenager drama." Sally listened as he told the story. "'Are you coming over tonight or what?' And I see it's from Hannah. And I'm thinking, who's Hannah? So I type back 'IDK,' and she types back a sad face. So, I send a happy face, and I'm waiting for her to call me or text me back, when Sally informs me that Ben had used my cell phone a few days ago, when he couldn't find his! Good thing! He doesn't need to respond to that chick anyways. He was probably driving around all night and just couldn't find her house!"

Maggie was entertained by his tales.

"Yeah, there sure is a lot to worry about when it comes to teenagers," Sally added in her sweet, concerned tone.

Maggie looked over at Francis who was completely disengaged from any conversation around him. She guessed he was in his late forties, but he had a full head of sandy brown hair tinted with just a bit of silver-grey. He looked thin and fit, and knew how to dress, and she thought that perhaps women found him attractive. He had been divorced ten years ago, but he had not, to the best of her knowledge, made any serious efforts to pursue any women since then. He was callous and bitter, and often times, she thought his traumatic personal life had driven him to persevere in his career, and become the success he was. Perhaps they had that one thing in common. They found emotional safety in their career.

Elle came in and interrupted her thoughts.

"Are we ready to do this or what?"

Cassandra followed behind her in a graceful stroll. "Hi everybody." She waved. "Looks like we're all here!"

Cassandra was her favorite. She possessed a personality as delicate and as sweet as they came. Elle was nice, but very much a tomboy and rough, and not that conversational. Latasha personified the perfect drama queen and had everyone spinning their wheels wondering what would happen to her next. She was African

American with flawless features and skin. She could wear any look and be beautiful. And Kensal? She had blonde hair to fit the part. She was a complete airhead, but so funny that it was impossible not to be completely forgiving. She would do anything for anybody and did not have a mean bone in her body.

Maggie watched them, as they all made their way towards hair and makeup. She always tried to put them in the dresses that best went with their personalities, and she thought that was one of the things she loved most about her job.

An hour and a half later, the models came charging out of the back room.

"Do my eyes look okay? I just hate eye shadow. And the lipstick! Not my color," Latasha whined.

"Who cares, we're getting paid," Elle stated while chewing her gum.

"I just wish I could do my own makeup and hair this good," Cassandra commented in her soft tone.

"Don't you all just love the way that toner feels on your face?" Kensal added, lost in thought. "I just close my eyes when they are putting it on and pretend I'm lying on a beach in Mexico, absorbing the sun."

Soon people started pouring through the doors, and Francis announced in his hasty expediting mannerism that the show started in only ten minutes. Matt took a seat back by the sound board attendant, and Sally stayed behind the stage curtain, waiting to assist in any quick clothing changes that the models needed help with.

Maggie sat in the front audience at a round table with Francis who twitched nervously about, while anticipating the presentation of his latest fashion deliveries. The music came on and the lights in the room got dim as they awaited the start of the show.

Latasha came out first, flaunting bright floral turquoise prints on a maxi dress that fell loosely against her hourglass shape. She wore her beautiful wavy hair under a hat, suggesting that she was headed for the Bahamas. Maggie admired her rhythm as she walked, and thought *she must have been born with it.*

Cassandra appeared with her long brown hair curled in a way that projected her youth. She strutted down the runway in an effervescent mannerism. She was adorned in Francis' latest design— one that made all the heads turn—a soft blush organza sheer dress layered over silver metallic fabric. It barely swept the top of her strappy sandals, which glittered in the bright lights.

Kensal strutted out next, as if she knew all eyes were on her, her hair blowing in the breeze of the fan. Maggie admired her stunning appearance, as she sported a tight khaki color-blocked dress that mimicked a sheath from the 1950s, only longer. Francis styled the neckline with exceptionally large colorful stones, and she paced the runway in a high platform shoe, having no problem keeping in step.

Last, but never least, Elle stepped out. She wore a shapely white halter style sundress made of linen, covered in a special designer lace and finishing with a ruffle extending to the bottom of the lace hemline. Her short brown hair wisped about in a messy style around her face as big dangly earrings protruded from her lobes. She looked sassy and sophisticated.

www.lovetheillusion.com/105.htm

The day passed quickly enough, and to Maggie's surprise they even managed to finish up earlier than anticipated. She listened to Francis talk all about how the show had gone exceedingly well, but that he had projected more orders than what they received. He blamed the economy, mentioning that if people would not be so senseless as to pay two to three hundred dollars a ticket to see Antonio DeLuca perform, they would have more money to purchase clothing. She found his comment humorous, but assured him that all sales were down in other venues as well, and promised to stay on top of the accounts when they returned home, and hopefully gain a few more orders.

After the events came to a close, Maggie left to go back to her room, anticipating Antonio's dinner invitation. She could not wait to see him.

As she opened the door to her room, she immediately saw a red rose standing alone in a vase, sitting on the table that sat next to the window. She recalled the last time she held a red rose, standing over her mother's grave. *How did he know?* Her face brightened on her way over to it. She picked up a note card that was situated flat on the table next to the vase:

"Meet Stanley in the front lobby— 8:00."

She looked at her wrist watch, now six. *Why am I supposed to meet Stanley?* She wondered. Wasn't she going out with Antonio? She picked up the note and vase and headed down to Antonio's room.

"Maggie!" He opened the door, surprised to see her. He was dressed in a pair of shorts, and his hair was wet from the shower. She studied his wet hair, thinking that he looked amazing.

"I got done early…and I have this note and flower from Stanley, and…"

"You look gorgeous!" His eyes glazed over her.

Maggie blushed, and continued, "So I'm wondering why I'm supposed to meet—"

"That flower's from me," he interrupted her. "You need to meet Stanley, and he'll show you to my limo that will take you to…I can't say, or it'll wreck your surprise. And you might want to change into something more… uh…dark!"

She gave him a curious smile.

"What are we going to do? Mud wrestle?"

"Trust me. You don't want to wear that dress. But, I will see you later." He seemed in a hurry.

Maggie started back toward her room, wondering what he had up his sleeve. *Why do I need to wear something dark?*

She rummaged through her suitcase. She had gotten beer on the black dress and…she had black jogging pants. *Yuck…probably all sweaty!* She leaned over to delve into her shopping bags. She could not even remember everything that she had bought on her break with Sally. "Perfect," Maggie announced, resorting to her souvenir t-shirt with large letters spelling out "New York" vertically off to one side.

She rode the elevator down to the first floor where she saw Stanley who was on the lookout.

"Hi Stanley!" Maggie smiled wryly. "Antonio said I was supposed to meet you?"

"Yep, I'm in charge of getting you into the right limo. Bradley has the night off."

"Thanks. I appreciate it." Maggie followed him out. "So, you don't have to bartend at Biagio's?" She had fun teasing him.

He smirked as he opened the door of the limo.

"Have fun," he called out.

After a quiet ride, the limo pulled up to a quaint yellow brick house with white shutters. Maggie thought it resembled one she had seen in a children's book when her mother used to read to her. It declared modesty, but overstated in charm and warmth.

"Have a good night," the driver told her as she stepped out of the limo.

Maggie felt strange approaching the house. She walked up the brick pathway, until she got to the door. She reached for the doorbell, and soon after she heard it chime, Antonio opened the door, wearing a big smile.

She stepped inside, noticing his smooth attire—a thin grey cotton sweater that had a zip up collar, khakis, and a pair of black designer casuals. His hair was neatly combed, and she could see the strong outline of his face, covered in a five o'clock shadow.

"I'm cooking dinner for you tonight," he announced.

She was surprised that he could cook.

"Sweet! Are we having macaroni or hot dogs?"

"Are you kidding me?" He looked at her, wearing a grin. "I can cook! I got my mamma's spaghetti recipe down to a science."

"So, why did I have to change for this?"

"Well…" Antonio walked over to the stove. "You got ketchup on your blouse and beer on your dress, so I didn't want you to get spaghetti on that nice dress you were wearing!"

"Is that so?" She gave him a spirited smile, thinking him clever. "So let me guess, you got me a bib?"

"No." Antonio laughed as he stirred the sauce.

She sat down at the kitchen table. Her eyes followed him as he walked over to the table where she was sitting.

"Would you like some of that wine?" He passed her a grin.

Maggie noticed the familiar label. It was the Italian wine that she drank at the bar — the same kind he had delivered to her room.

"Are you still trying to get me drunk?" She watched his eyes immediately attach to hers.

He smirked intuitively.

"Don't you think I could have accomplished that by now, if I had wanted to?"

Maggie bit her bottom lip and decided, "Where's the bottle opener?"

"Here, I'll get it," he offered.

The table was decorated with a red and white plaid tablecloth. A candle sat lit in the center of the table, and linen napkins were folded on top of the plates. Music from *"The Phantom of the Opera"* drifted in from the next room. It was obvious that he put a lot of effort into this night.

While Antonio poured the wine, Maggie inhaled the fresh basil, garlic, and onion that were simmering in the tomato sauce on the stovetop. Next to the stove, she noticed a basket of garlic toast.

Maggie sipped her wine, recalling when she first saw him at Biagio's. She could not believe that he was now cooking dinner for her. She wanted to ask him if he dated anyone else, because she thought for sure he must. She still wondered why he was spending so much time with her. Did he think it was convenient that she left in a day—then he did not have to worry about her chasing after him? She was still fascinated by him, wondering what it would be like to be his girlfriend. *Perhaps just for tonight,* she would pretend.

She watched him stirring the sauce. She could not help but wonder why he had not yet kissed her. Maybe he just liked her as a friend. Or...Was he waiting for her to make the moves on him? *Is that what he was used to?* And should she? *No. It would already be hard to leave.* But the thought of kissing him left her heart beating fast in her chest.

Antonio brought the spaghetti and garlic toast over to the table. She watched as he strategically placed the sauce on top of the noodles. After he finished the preparations, he sat down and placed his napkin on his lap, indicating it was time to eat. He took a sip of the wine with his eyes on her.

"Go ahead, try it."

"So, is this your house?" Maggie disrupted his gaze.

"No. It belongs to Bradley and Rainelle," Antonio explained.

"Really?" Maggie thought back to the lady that she had met in the bathroom at the Night Owl, that later danced with Bradley. "What are they doing tonight?"

"I sent them out to Bouley. Rainelle was ecstatic that she didn't have to cook." Antonio grinned.

"It's a beautiful house." Maggie viewed the open staircase. She looked back to Antonio. She could not keep her eyes off him.

He glanced over to the staircase and passed her an intimate look. "Yeah, Rainelle knows how to add that personal touch." He seemed deep in thought and she wondered what he was thinking. Although they were keeping to small talk, it seemed more serious.

Maggie resolved to keep things "light."

"So, Antonio, why did you decide to make us spaghetti? You're just dying to see if I can eat it without getting any on my clothes?" She started laughing.

Antonio hesitated, his mouth full of spaghetti, but then informed, "I had accounting send me a copy of your bill when you ate at Pappio's Italian Restaurant, next to the hotel. I saw that you had spaghetti. I love my mamma's spaghetti and was wondering if it was better than what you ate at Pappio's?"

"You're a good cook!" she had to admit as she wound another fork full of spaghetti. Antonio raised his brow as the side of his mouth curled into a grin.

"Well, it's a family recipe."

Maggie and Antonio took turns catching each other's stares, and when they got done eating, Antonio said, "Okay, now that I cooked, you have to clean the mess!"

She got up from the table, willing to comply.

"I'm just kidding." He grinned.

They cleaned up the kitchen together, and after everything was put away, Maggie shuddered, feeling a bit chilly.

"Didn't you make us some chocolate mousse for dessert?" She smiled. She was having fun being his girlfriend.

"No, I've never made dessert before. But Rainelle left some chocolate cupcakes for us that she made, and I frosted them." He removed them from a cupboard, setting them down on the counter.

"Really, that's so sweet of her. But, I think I ate too much spaghetti. Can we eat them later?"

"Sure. You look like you're cold."

He started walking over to the chair in the living room.

"Yes, it's not quite the season for short sleeves at night," she said, rubbing her hands up and down her arms to break the chill.

He grabbed an alpaca afghan off the chair and wrapped it around her while peering into her eyes and embracing her in a hug.

She loved the close attention he gave her. She cuddled next to him with her hands against his chest, remembering when they danced at the Night Owl.

Moments later, he guided her with the blanket to sit down on the couch, and he sat next to her, placing his arm around her. Maggie did not want the night to end.

"I think we ought to put on the news and see if this storm is going to get us," Antonio decided, holding the remote to a widescreen.

"Are we going to get snowed in here?" she asked.

He gave her a look of suspense. "Yep, that's the plan. You're going to keep drinking that wine, and then you're going to get stuck here with me."

Maggie sat speechless as she came to the conclusion that she liked the idea. But she did not trust herself alone with him.

"Don't worry," he dismissed her concerns. "It's not supposed to hit until three this morning."

"....WE INTERRUPT THE PROGRAMMING WITH A SPECIAL NEWS BULLETIN, FROM THE WEATHER STATION AT CHANNEL 7 NEWSROOM. JUST WHEN YOU THINK WINTER IS OVER, WE ARE VIEWING THE WINTER STORM TRACKER,

REPORTING THAT A SEVERE ICE STORM WILL BE MOVING INTO OUR VIEWING AREA BY THREE TOMORROW MORNING. IT WILL BRING A HEAVY MIXTURE OF SLEET AND RAIN, MAKING TRAVEL CONDITIONS EXTREMELY RISKY. IF YOU ARE PLANNING TO FLY IN OR OUT OF ANY NEW YORK AIRPORTS, CALL AHEAD FOR FLIGHT CANCELLATIONS. PLEASE STAY TUNED TO CHANNEL 7 NEWSROOM WHERE WE WILL CONTINUE TO KEEP YOU UPDATED ON THE MOVEMENT OF THE STORM. REPORTING LIVE, FROM CHANNEL 7 NEWSROOM IN NEW YORK CITY, THIS IS DAN ROBERTS."

"That does not sound good," she said, wondering how late she should stay.

"Yeah, we're supposed to have another show Saturday night, so hopefully it doesn't impact the turnout. People have already bought the tickets, but I feel bad if they can't get here," Antonio explained.

"Most people probably don't arrive the day of the show," she assured him.

"Exactly." Antonio thought about it. "That means that they would possibly get here Friday, which is bringing bad weather."

Maggie absorbed his concern for his fans.

"Can you postpone the show?" she asked.

"No, we have never done that before, or cancelled either. The only way would be if I was sick or something, and so far I've been lucky."

She sat next to Antonio, feeling lucky to be with him.

He got up and walked over to the fireplace.

"Should we make a fire while we wait for the ice?"

"Sure," she agreed.

Maggie watched as he assembled the logs in the fireplace and lit the match, recalling the ring of fire when she was on stage. Her eyes danced over him as he assembled the logs around the flame. She waited for him to sit back down next to her.

"There!" he stated, his mission accomplished. He stood up and wiped his hands on the sides of his khakis. "So...." Antonio paused, giving her a sweet look. "Now that I've cooked dinner and made a fire, am I redeemed from your first impression?" He gave her a curious smile as he sat back down next to her.

"You are," Maggie decided, "but you're still a liar, *Chad*." She wore a smirk, hoping to hide her true feelings for him.

www.lovetheillusion.com/113.htm

"I'm not a liar! Chad's my nickname. You can't blame me for having a little fun when you didn't recognize me. I just couldn't help myself. And Stanley thought you didn't recognize me because I wasn't wearing my mask. It was so funny," Antonio recalled.

"That would have been less frightening," she teased.

"Really...then I'll no longer be able to cook spaghetti for you!" he threatened.

"Pappio's is pretty good." She enjoyed getting under his skin.

Antonio reached over and grabbed the top of her arms and pushed her down onto the couch. As she stared up at him, he bent over her, his face inches from hers. Maggie felt as if she was going to melt right through the couch when he whispered, "My spaghetti is better!" He held her down, after making his proclamation, as he looked into her eyes, and she looked into his. She studied his lips, wanting his kiss. *What is he waiting for?* He seemed to read her mind, but looked satisfied just knowing he was getting to her.

He got back up and decided, "It's time for cupcakes!"

She followed into the kitchen where Antonio was leaned against the counter eating a cupcake in one hand and holding the paper wrapper in the other. She watched in amusement, wondering why he would stand over the floor making crumbs as opposed to eating over a plate.

"These are really good. Try one," he offered.

The candle was still burning, and she went over to the table to blow it out. He looked at her mysteriously.

"Are you afraid of fire?"

She wondered what he meant to imply.

"Is that a reference to when you had me dragged up onto the stage to run your flaming hoop over me?"

"Maybe." He grinned at her, enjoying his recollection.

"You're just lucky you didn't burn me! But I think I was more frightened when you took off the mask."

He seemed upset that she redirected the conversation, but he played along. "That was the best part of the whole show. You were thinking that I stood you up—and then there I was, standing right next to you!" Antonio appeared proud.

"That was just thrilling for you, I'm sure." She rolled her eyes, realizing his quest for shock.

She watched him, his eyes glued to her. Standing a few feet from him, she recalled being at Biagio's and first perceiving his sweet side. Her first assumption was right. And he knew how to use it to his advantage. He knew just how to balance the intimacy and sweetness as if he held the owner's manual right in front of him. She really wanted to kiss him.

Maggie gathered up her emotions and placed them on a shelf.

"So Antonio, should I call you Antonio, or should I call you Chad?" Maggie considered which she preferred.

"That depends, are you my friend or my fan?" he challenged her. She contemplated his quick wit.

"I would have to say both," she decided, attempting to sweet-talk him. She then broke eye contact with him, aware she felt more for him than simply wishing to be his friend or fan.

He appeared flattered.

"You should call me Chad," he decided. "Antonio is what my fans call me, and since you liked me before you knew who I am, I think you should call me Chad. It's my nickname, from my mamma's maiden name, Chandler. She gave it to me. She used to scream it at me when I would cause trouble." He laughed under his breath as if he never outgrew the pursuit.

She imagined him as a cute little troublemaker.

"Then Chad," Maggie was curious, "do you have your own...place, somewhere in the city or other...place...in the States?" She stumbled for words after once again calling him Chad.

"You saw where I stay. Our company paid money to renovate various sections of the hotel to accommodate our production staff.

And also to ensure security and various means to allow me privacy—like that elevator that we went in to leave and return—that only operates with my key pass. So, since we do all of our rehearsals and most of our shows in New York City, it's easy for me just to stay there. I like it there."

Maggie observed him as she sat down at the kitchen table to finally eat a cupcake. She pondered his lifestyle as he leaned casually against the kitchen counter, sharing more information and opening up to her. "I bought a house in Italy. It's beautiful. It's surrounded by land and a river that runs through the back of the property. Across the river you can see a village. It's a beautiful sight, all lit up at night. We sit out at night and catch fish. It's one of our favorite things to do. My parents stay there and take care of the place while I'm away. My mamma and papa love to spend time on the boat. And I bought them a puppy, Daphne, and now she's two years old. Have you ever seen a Maltese? It's the cutest dog ever."

www.lovetheillusion.com/116.htm

"And we have a garden, where we grow all the vegetables you can imagine. Mamma and Papa sell what they jar up at the local market, but just for fun, you know. They are retired, but very young at heart though, and my mamma says when she misses me, she looks at my papa, and there I am—a spitting image. I love them a lot, and I try to go home as often as I can."

"I noticed during the interview that they asked about your parents moving back to Italy. They didn't like it here or..."

He immediately shifted his eyes to the floor. "Just a bad situation. I don't want to talk about it." He paused and then sounded agitated. "And you know what? *Every* time I do any interview, no matter what, they always bring it up. I have to stay alert, so that I can redirect those reporters back to what they should be asking in the first place! They love to get off track, you know, like with Arianna. They got everyone probably thinking she's having my baby!"

Maggie felt her insides curl. She waited to see if he would say anything else about her.

"So tell me about your family." He seemed embarrassed, as if he had talked too long.

"Well, I'm the only girl out of four siblings," Maggie began, "so I got kicked around pretty good when I was growing up. My brothers always gave my parents the impression that they were looking out for me, but I knew I was the one looking out for myself. They knew how to dish it out. They were all into the sports, and so when they played, they played rough. One time, I decided to be brave and play football with them. What a mistake! It was them against me! After a half hour, I hadn't even touched the ball. I started bawling when Greg, the oldest, yells to me, the youngest, 'Waaaa, waaa, you're such a baby,' and flies the football in my direction at about fifty miles an hour. You know, I caught the ball dead on. And after they recovered from their shock, they all raced over to tackle me. Elliot and Mason grab the ball out of my hands; I'm on the ground, yelling out, 'you cheaters!' And after they steal the ball, they run it into their end zone for a touchdown. When I got up, my arm was out of its sockct. My mom was working, so my dad had to sit with me in emergency for over four hours to get in to a doctor who put my arm back in its socket, and..." She thought of any additional information that she wanted to share. "We never had any pets. My dad has allergies."

"Sounds like a rough childhood." He laughed.

"I survived!" She waved her hand, indicating the insignificance. "You know, now, we all get along great. They're all married, and I'm even Auntie Maggie to Greg's daughter, Kyra. I just love her. She's already a little fashion diva, at the age of five. They live here in the States...so, unfortunately, I don't get to see them very often."

"Where is that?"

"They were in Boston, where I grew up, but now they just moved to Chicago. I kind of feel close to them, being here in New York."

Maggie and Antonio both were aware that their relationship had transcended to a new level after another evening together, but the front door opened and Bradley and Rainelle were home.

Maggie heard them laughing, and Bradley announced, "We just saw the funniest movie ever; it's this action comedy adventure. Things kept blowing up when you least expect it and Rainelle kept jumping in her chair, and I say 'Girl, you better watch out, or you're gonna spill that popcorn all over the place.'"

"Thanks for lending us your house," Maggie said. "It's a great place, very homey."

"No, thank *you* Antonio," Bradley concluded, giving him a light punch in the arm.

Silence lingered on the ride back. Maggie wondered what Antonio was thinking. Without even looking at him, she sensed that he too was in deep thought. The air felt heavy, as if it spelled out an ending to what had begun as an awkward coincidence at Biagio's, several days ago. And now, she never felt so good sitting next to someone.

They got back to the hotel, and they made their usual entry through the secret passage. And Antonio walked her to her room.

Standing in front of the door, he took her hands in his.

"Maggie, I think the storm is going to delay your flight...If so, I can arrange for us to use the pool."

Maggie accepted his offer, but her voice broke. "Call my room when you want to go." She dropped his grip, and turned to go into her room. She knew better than to kiss him; it was already a mistake to be spending so much time with him. Her feelings for him were intense. And she was leaving soon.

His t-shirt, that she wore the night before, was still on the floor near the bed where she had left it that morning. She stared at it until she fell asleep.

Chapter 7

Maggie quickly sat up as an adrenaline rush tore her out of her sleep. She reached for the remote which was still on top of her novel and turned on the flat screen. It was five a.m., and she had only slept a few hours. She immediately found the news channel and read the small print at the bottom of the screen...DUE TO THE HAZARDOUS WEATHER CONDITIONS, ALL FLIGHTS ENTERING AND LEAVING NEW YORK AIRPORTS HAVE BEEN CANCELLED UNTIL FURTHER NOTICE. PLEASE CONTACT YOUR AIRLINE CARRIER FOR NEW FLIGHT SCHEDULE INFORMATION. MANY OF THE RUNWAYS ARE GLAZED OVER WITH ICE AND NO LONGER MEET OUR SAFETY REGULATIONS. WE WILL UPDATE YOU AS WE GET IN NEW INFORMATION, BUT FOR NOW, THE ICE STORM HAS CAUSED FLIGHT CANCELLATIONS. THIS IS A SPECIAL NEWS BULLETIN FROM JD 2 NEWSROOM IN NEW YORK CITY. DUE TO THE HAZARDOUS WEATHER CONDITIONS, ALL FLIGHTS ENTERING AND LEAVING NEW YORK.... Maggie continued reading, until she realized the information kept repeating the same thing.

"Yes!" she exclaimed in a fierce whisper, with her hands clenched into fists under her chin. She got out of bed and picked the t-shirt up off the floor, holding it close while dancing around her room. *Another day with Antonio!* Now she only had to wait for his call. It would be their last day together, but she resolved to be strong and not indicate that she was devastated to be leaving. She thought they had a special connection that maybe in time, somehow would...*What am I thinking?* Her mind brought no conclusion as to how it would ever work out. All she knew was that there was no turning back the clock or removing what she felt in her heart. As quickly as she felt the train on the tracks of destiny, speeding her along to fall in love, she already felt the bumps from the railroad ties slowing things to a screeching halt! She dropped the t-shirt on the floor and crawled back into bed.

Maggie lay wide awake, scrutinizing the situation. An hour passed, and she eventually fell back asleep, but suddenly awoke to the hotel phone ringing on her nightstand. She rolled over, groggy, picked up the phone, and heard Antonio's voice.

"Maggie?"

"Yeah," she answered with a yawn.

"Were you sleeping?"

"Uh, yes..."

"The flights are cancelled."

"Okay," she acknowledged, not wishing to mention that she had been jolted out of her sleep at five a.m. and already checked the news.

"You sound tired. Should I call back later?"

"No...No..." She picked up her voice, sounding more alert. "I'm up."

"Did you pack a swimsuit or should I send Stanley out to get one?" Antonio sounded amused.

"I don't know. Let me check." Maggie deliberated, failing to recall whether or not she had remembered to pack her suit.

Her suitcase was stuffed to capacity. Hopefully, it was in there somewhere. Then she saw it—her one-piece suit that she used for exercise. *Great!* She had been too preoccupied to recall *that* plan. It was made from thick solid navy knit, a retro look from the 1940s. And she even remembered to pack her swim cap! She did not like chlorine to get in her hair. Not the look she wanted to present to Antonio, of all people. He would probably die laughing if she wore her swim cap. She considered telling him that she was without a suit, but thoughts of Stanley purchasing some skanky bikini sent her racing back to the phone.

"Yep, I got one." She spoke reluctantly.

"Come down to the pool at nine."

"Okay, I'll see you then." Maggie hung up the phone. *Sorry, Antonio. No bikini!* And now, *no choice but to humor him*…or shock him…and it was about his turn for that!

Passing the mirror on the way out, she displayed a bald-headed look in her white swim cap. She thought Antonio would absolutely choke on his own laughter, wondering how she ever made a living in the fashion industry.

www.lovetheillusion.com/122.htm

She headed down the hall, deciding at the last minute to make a quick stop by Francis' room to see if he was aware of the news.

She knocked on the door. Moments later, she saw him standing in a black robe. He looked surprised to see her.

"Maggie, what brings you here? Looks like you're going swimming?"

"Well, actually, I just came by to tell you that the flights are cancelled."

"Yes, Maggie, I am aware of that," he said pretentiously, "but they think we can fly out same time tomorrow."

"Oh! Hi Maggie." Elle came out of his bathroom with a towel wrapped around her.

Maggie stood speechless for a moment. Then she turned around and left.

"POOL CLOSED FOR RENOVATION." A white sheet of paper with black letters spelled out the information. It was taped to a grey shade that had been pulled down over the glass door. Maggie turned around to leave when she saw Bradley standing inches in front of her. She jerked back, startled.

"I'm sorry. Did I scare you?" He took a step back.

"Uh, no, Ch...Antonio told me to meet him here."

"I see!" He judged by her ensemble. "Just a minute," he said as he reached into his pocket and pulled out a ring of keys.

"Too bad you had to work today. Are the roads okay?"

"It's a mess out there, but I managed just fine. You know hotel staff can't get 'snow days.'"

She watched as he unlocked the door and motioned for her to go in, while wearing a goofy smile. Then she saw Antonio. He wore navy swim trunks and was seated next to a canopy table, reading the newspaper. Their eyes met, and he put the newspaper down and stood up.

www.lovetheillusion.com/123.htm

Maggie blushed as she approached him, waiting for him to appreciate her humorous ensemble.

"Are we in charge of the renovation?" She made reference to the sign on the door.

"I hope not!" Antonio gave a quick laugh. "But it will probably at least need cleaning after we order our breakfast." A smile came over his face, and she knew his eyes were on her swim cap.

"It's retro. You know, easier to exercise," she explained.

Still smiling, he reached out to touch her swim cap and gave her his assessment. "It's very cute."

Maggie smiled back with her schoolgirl charm and turned to notice his t-shirt that was draped over a chair. She tried to read the writing.

"It's a restaurant in Italy," he explained. "And speaking of restaurants, do you want breakfast?"

"Are you cooking again?" She wore a sweet look.

"Do you see a stove in here?"

Maggie surveyed the pool area. A steam Jacuzzi took up the back wall, and to its right stood a towel rack. The room was well lit from the reflective light of the sun as it hit the ice and shown through the three large windows facing the outdoors.

Antonio's eyes were on Maggie as they both stood in their blue swimwear.

"So, should we eat or swim first?" he asked.

"I would have a bagel," Maggie decided, "and some coffee?" She smiled at him.

He picked up his phone, and while waiting to place their order smiled back at her.

"This is Antonio D. I'm in need of six bagels and a fruit platter, two coffees and orange juice, some whip cream for the fruit...cream and sugar, and don't forget the silverware and napkins...at the pool...Thanks Jolene!"

Maggie listened, amused.

He put his phone away. "It will be a half hour."

She stood still, pondering his living arrangements, when he went over to the edge of the pool and called out, "Time to go swimming!" He jumped into the pool like a cannonball landing in the water. Maggie watched in disbelief, as the water came up in a splash, getting her all wet.

She took off her yoga pants and draped them over his t-shirt on the chair. And when she turned around, she saw him treading water, watching her. She went over to the shallow end. As she hit the water, she arched her upper body into a dive and swam underwater until she arrived where he was. She popped up right in front of him, her face dripping.

"You swim like you were in the Olympics." He sounded surprised.

"High school swim team… three first place medals," she stated proudly.

"Wow!" Antonio grinned.

She grinned back, pleased to impress him.

"Every meet, when it was my turn to race, I would pretend all three of my brothers were after me. It worked every time!"

He laughed.

"Can you dive too?"

"Yeah, but only one medal—fifth," she complained, adjusting her swim cap.

He stared at her in amusement.

"Should we race?" he suggested.

"Sure!"

They made their way to the end of the pool.

"Ready?" Antonio raised his brow while wearing a grin. "Go!" he yelled out, while using his feet to push off the edge of the pool. She saw that he already had a lead.

As they raced across the pool, Maggie tried keeping an eye on him through her goggles, until she made it to the other side. As soon as her hand hit the edge of the pool, she realized they tied. She waited for Antonio to make mention of it, but instead she heard him call out, "Again."

Maggie swam another lap, until her hand reached the edge of the pool again. She saw Antonio's hand landing a second behind hers. "Ha! I won!" Maggie beamed.

"You did not!" he argued. "There's no medal for that! That was a tie!"

"Fine, one more time, there and back!" Maggie challenged, hoping to put him in his place.

"One more time!" he yelled. "Go!"

Maggie swam as fast as she could, and with precision. When she returned to the edge of the pool, she reached her feet for the bottom but did not see Antonio. Now she realized that he had never left, but instead was yelling, "Go, go Maggie White!"

"Oh!" she exclaimed. "You are terrible!"

"Okay," he flirted. "This time I'll go. Ready?"

She watched his lips move until they yelled, "Go!"

Maggie swam her fastest. She reached the end and flipped onto her back, proceeding with a backstroke but did not see him. She stopped. There he was, still standing at the edge of the pool! He started laughing.

"OH, you are such a liar," she blurted.

"I'm just trying to tire you out, so that I can dunk you!"

He smiled.

"You wouldn't!"

"I would!" He dove towards Maggie, but she swam to the edge, grabbed the ladder, and got out of the pool. She stood dripping wet with her arms folded, looking down at him. He followed up the ladder and over to where she was standing. "You're not safe here!" he informed, and pushed her back into the water.

"I'm going to get you, Chad DeLuca!" Maggie yelled at him from the pool.

He laughed as if he had no worries. She made her way up the ladder when she heard a knock on the door. Their food had arrived.

"I called your phone back, but..."

"Sorry, we were in the pool," he said, grabbing the tray. "Thanks."

The door shut and he brought the tray over to the table.

"Here, I just cooked breakfast!" he announced.

They dried off and sat down to eat.

Maggie eyed up the tray of food—six bagels and a big platter of fruit in the middle—decoratively arranged. Surely they would never eat all of that.

She looked at Antonio and then noticed a small tattoo on the left side of his chest. Her eyes fastened on the script, about a half inch in height. *What does that say?* She squinted, trying to make out the inscription, and reaching no conclusion, looked back up at Antonio, who was completely aware of her inquisition. His face turned cold. She immediately stopped chewing. His eyes burned with anger, causing hers to jump away from the intensity.

She sat quietly, waiting to see if he would say anything. It seemed like minutes had passed when he finally uttered, "My brother, Matteo."

Maggie bit the inside corner of her mouth, lost for words.

"I'm sorry," she finally indicated, remorsefully.

Antonio looked deep in thought.

"He died when he was only six...two years ago," he told her.

"That's so sad." She felt his grief.

"I think of him every day. Not a day goes by when I don't think of him. But he's in my heart." Antonio covered the tattoo with his hand over his heart. "Matteo," he said again, as if his thoughts had drifted miles away.

Maggie understood he too felt the pain of losing a loved one. They finished their food in silence, but by the time they were done eating, the mood had slowly shifted out of a depressed state.

"Should we sit in the hot tub?" Antonio passed her his sweet look.

"Sure," she nodded. She thought his eyes, that had been a window into his sadness, were now back to life.

He got up, walked around the table, and reached for her hand. Maggie slowly placed her hand in his, recalling their first handshake in the hotel hallway. She now knew his sweet side—the one that triggered her curiosity, when she met him at the bar.

She sat next to one of the jets, waiting for him to join her.

"I feel so guilty," she admitted.

"For what?"

"Here we are, stuck in an ice storm, spending the day in the pool—probably what the other hotel guests want to do, but they can't because it's closed down for us!"

Antonio laughed it off. "Well, what else are we supposed to do?" He sat down next to her. "Salvador doesn't want to drive us anywhere on the ice! And our dance crew was supposed to go over some parts for the show tomorrow, but I cancelled. Some of them actually left the hotel for a couple days—Amber, for one—and I wouldn't want to see her out in this."

His thoughts quickly shifted as his face lit. "We just got these new lights! They are super cool, and I can't wait to set them up—strobe lights that go off in all different directions and there's a lens that reflects against them, so that it looks like there are these chunks of paper-like confetti floating in the air...like snowflakes...in 3D without glasses!"

"That sounds amazing! Your show is already incredible. I've never seen anything like it, and the choreography is great."

"The dancers are a distraction, so that no one sees what I am doing."

"Yeah, right," she let go of a laugh, "I think you have that down pretty well without them. I did not know how I was floating, and I was right there!" She saw him grin out of the corner of her eye, his arm around her.

Maggie sat silent, thinking she heard a noise.

"Chad?" She grabbed his other arm to get his attention.

"What is it, dear?" He gave her a sweet look and wrapped both his arms around her, holding her in a tight squeeze, her hands resting on his chest. She remembered slow dancing with him at the Night Owl. She loved being in his arms. It was a distraction, until she heard the noise again.

"Do you hear...listen..." Maggie gave concern. "What is that? Do you hear that screeching noise? It sounds like it's coming from–"

"It's just the jets whistling," he interrupted her. He brought his lips to her ear and whispered, "They're whistling at the cute girl in the swim cap!"

She burst into laughter. "Shut up! You're so full of it!" She pushed away from him while reaching around the back of his head, giving his hair a tug.

"You're going to have to pay for that!" He grabbed hold of her, again, proceeding to take her swim cap off.

"STOP!" Maggie screamed, as he managed to manipulate the swim cap off her head. Her hair felt heavy and full of knots as it fell onto her shoulders, when she heard the noise again. "Chad, what is that? There it is—that noise again!"

He stopped and listened, holding her swim cap in his hand. She watched as he went over to the steps and got out of the Jacuzzi. He stood still and listened again.

"Someone's hurt!" he exclaimed, dropping her cap as he made his way over to the door. He disappeared, and she wondered where he had gone. Now she could hear the sound of screaming drifting into the room, louder than before. She proceeded to follow him, but he already returned with a boy, about four in age, screaming his head off.

Antonio squatted down next to him, trying to get him to talk. "Hey buddy. It's okay. Don't cry. Are you lost?"

The boy nodded, continuing to let out sobs intermittently between screams.

Antonio spoke in a quiet tone. "We can find your...mom?" he took a guess. The boy nodded, his screams reduced now to just a sob. Antonio picked up the boy, and carried him over to the table where he left his phone.

"Bradley. It's Antonio. I got a kid here that can't find his mom. He was screaming outside the pool room." Antonio set his phone back down on the table and positioned the boy in a chair. He bent down in front of him and explained, "I just called security, and they'll be right here. They'll get your mom, I promise."

Maggie noticed how easily Antonio calmed the boy. She took a seat next to them.

Antonio put some strawberries on a plate, and then sat down on the other side of him. "Would you like some strawberries while you wait?" he offered.

The boy sniffled and nodded.

"We even got whip cream!" Antonio informed. "Do you want some?"

The boy reached for the can and tipped it upside down, waiting for it to come out.

Antonio laughed. "No, you gotta press it," he explained.

Maggie watched with Antonio as the boy took the can in one hand and pressed the nozzle with the other. Out it came, all over the place! It landed on the boy's arm and on his shirt, and Maggie saw some had even landed on Antonio's chest and arm, while Antonio eyed up the canopy pole that also got hit.

"That was supposed to land on the strawberries," Antonio said, laughing. The boy laughed too and wiped his hands that were full of whip cream onto his pants, forgetting why he was crying.

"What's your name?" Maggie asked him, after he started eating the strawberries.

"Marcos," he said, with his mouth full.

Maggie pointed, indicating to Antonio that he still had whip cream on his arm. He wiped it off as Bradley made an entrance.

"This is Marcos," Antonio told Bradley.

"Marcos, I'm Bradley. And I will help you find your mom."

Marcos looked at Bradley who stood over six feet tall. He became frightened and started bouncing in his chair, shaking his head.

Bradley reached down his hand to the boy.

"Come on. Don't you want to find your mom?"

Marcos started screaming again. Maggie wished that she still had her swim cap on, to fade the noise.

"Do you want to stay here while Bradley tries to find your mom?" Maggie suggested.

Marcos thought about it for a moment and wailed out, "Yeeessss!"

Maggie and Antonio snickered as Bradley concluded, "Looks like you two got yourselves a boy. I will try to hurry back."

Bradley spoke into his security pager on his way out. "We got a boy that lost his mom. I'm headed over to the front desk."

Antonio looked at Maggie while tapping his fingers on the table next to the can of whip cream. Maggie suddenly knew he was up to no good.

"Marcos, did you notice that you missed someone with this whip cream?" Antonio grinned.

Marcos sat quietly.

"Marcos!" Antonio stated his name once again. "Do you think that we should have a bit of fun and get that pretty lady over there with this whip cream?" Antonio had one eyebrow pinned up, waiting for Marcos to respond, while Maggie glared at him. Marcos' face warped into a devilish grin. Soon he was laughing hysterically. Antonio shifted his eyes playfully onto Maggie. "That's a go!"

Maggie tried to make a getaway, but Antonio grabbed her around her waist, while holding the whip cream over her head.

"No, Antonio!" she screamed. She tried to get the whip cream away from him, but he held it high above his head.

"Sorry, dear, we have to entertain the boy," Antonio whispered. And seconds later she heard the sound of the can as it sprayed into her hair.

www.lovetheillusion.com/133.htm

Antonio ran back to the table, he and Marcos grinning wildly at each other.

"You are going to get it now when you least expect it!" Maggie warned Antonio as she quickly headed for the pool.

Marcos was turned around in his chair, watching her in amusement.

Maggie jumped in the pool and swam under the water to get the whip cream out of her hair.

She made a proud exit from the pool.

"Wow! No goggles or swim cap!? How was that?" Antonio teased her when she came out. She passed him a dirty look, but he wore a steady grin, indicating that he loved to start trouble.

The door opened, and Bradley returned with Marcos' mom. Marcos immediately got out of his chair and started running to his mother. She bent down to catch him in her arms. They hugged and she soon recognized Antonio.

"Are, are you...you are the magician...you are Antonio!"

"Nice to meet you." Antonio held out his hand. She broke a hand free to shake his, while holding on to Marcos with the other.

"Marcos! Do you know who that is?" his mother asked. Marcos shook his head. "That's Antonio DeLuca! We are going to his show tomorrow night!"

Antonio smiled. "What room are you in? I will send up a stuffed cheetah."

"Can I go simming?" Marcos asked his mother.

"No, Marcos, they..." She paused.

Maggie stood behind Antonio with her hair in wet strands clumped together.

"He can," Maggie offered, waiting for Antonio to give his approval.

"Yeah, we'll be here for a while. He can hang out with us, if you want," Antonio agreed.

"Well, we can't impose..." she considered.

"It's okay, we would love to have him," Maggie said. "It would be fun."

"Does he have a life jacket?" Bradley asked.

"There's a bunch of them in that maintenance closet over there," Antonio informed. Marcos started jumping up and down.

"Yes. Yes. Yes, I'm going simming!"

Everyone joined in laughter, and Marcos' mother explained, "I'm Adonia! We just flew in last night. Good thing, with the weather—really bad now. We came to see the show and stay for a couple days; I'm with my sister and my nephew."

"Where are you from?" Maggie asked.

"All the way from Puerto Rico and you have cold weather now, so it is cheaper to fly."

"You left all that sunshine?" Antonio teased.

"Yes, but it will be fun... always fun to travel and see something new."

Marcos swayed back and forth holding his mother's hand, as she advised, "Well, I guess he can swim, but only for an hour. I will put him in swim trunks and we will be back."

After everyone left, Antonio passed Maggie an intimate stare. He grabbed her arms, playfully leading her back into the hot tub, and she soon forgot that she was mad at him. Instead, she thought he looked dreamy with his wet hair flowing into waves and his brow accentuated as droplets of water were attached to match those that clung to his face and chest.

Antonio watched Maggie through the Jacuzzi steam that misted between them, as Maggie held back, afraid to get too intimate. She was still leaving tomorrow, and now after seeing yet another side of him—his loving nature with a child—she was even more enamored by him.

The clock clapped forward two hours, and after spending time with the boy, Maggie and Antonio stood at the table gathering their things to leave. Maggie had enjoyed watching Antonio entertain Marcos. Although offstage, Antonio had no problem keeping the spotlight—especially when he arranged for a staff member to drop off a toy cheetah. Marcos had worn his biggest smile, and Maggie had, once again, remembered Cheetos. At one moment, Maggie even felt like they were a family, and she thought for sure, Marcos brought back memories of Matteo.

"Okay, you should leave first and I will leave later," Antonio instructed. She gave him a strange look. "Fine," he reconsidered, "then give me your swim cap."

Maggie handed it to him, wondering what he was up to. She watched as he put it on and pushed all of his hair successfully under the cap, making an additional request, "...and goggles, please."

She met his request, watching as he strapped them around his head and positioned them over his eyes. She started laughing.

"What are you doing, Chad? You look ridiculous!"

"I know Maggie, but now I can walk you back to your room, and no one will bother us. Trust me! You do not want any more attention from those stupid reporters."

"But you look ridiculous! People are going to stare!" she said, as he grabbed her hand on their way out.

"Well, I'm used to it. You have no idea!"

They stood outside Maggie's room.

Antonio handed her the cap and goggles as she reached for the door. She paused. She wished to spend more time with him, but her heart was already in danger.

"We should go to Biagio's, say around ten, after they close. We'll have the place to ourselves." His words cut through her concern, while his eyes drooped into hers. She felt a whirling energy inside her as he stood close to her. She wondered, again, what it would be like to kiss him.

"I have to wash my hair tonight. It probably still has whip cream in it!" She lightened the mood. Her feelings for him frightened her. But he reached out, pulling her close to him.

"Should I have to convince you?" He spoke in a serious tone.

Maggie tried to fight her feelings, but she was barely able to breathe. She heard him finalize the details. "I'll stop by at ten." His eyes focused on her lips, as if he considered kissing her, but instead he left, leaving Maggie with her heart pounding in her chest.

Chapter 8

Maggie slipped on her solid red dress. It was a spare alternative for the fashion show. With a square neckline and a one inch belt made out of the same cotton fabric, it was short and sleeveless, another one of Francis' designs. She stepped into her tan patent heels after she pressed her hair with a flat iron, leaving it to hang longer than usual and finally detangled from the mess it had been in.

A big silver bracelet dangled from her wrist as she reached for her white sweater after hearing a knock on the door. She was filled with excitement to see him again, but it was their last night together. She opened the door to greet him.

www.lovetheillusion.com/137.htm

She took another deep breath, thinking that she was still breathless from spending the afternoon with him. She wondered how long it took him to get ready. He looked polished to a crisp, aside from a slight shadow of whiskers, as he stood in a pair of black pants and shoes to match this time. His tan skin contrasted a white dress shirt that lay under a thin silk black tie that carried a splash of red color in it. She wondered how he knew that she was going to wear red, also. *Red*—the color of the lipstick she wore and the color of the passion she felt for him when she looked into his eyes. She drew in a quick breath and tried to exhale it quietly, wishing to escape the trance he left her in as he let her know in a soft whisper, "You look good, Maggie."

He took her hand and led her to the private elevator. When they stepped inside, Maggie felt his eyes on her. She thought maybe he did want to kiss her, but she froze, fearing her departure the next day.

They arrived at Biagio's without having to pass through any crowded hallways. And they now sat behind closed doors, seated at a table next to the bar where they first met.

"So what should we order?" Antonio asked, holding his phone to place a call.

"Isn't the wait staff gone now?"

"We can just order out from wherever you want and have it delivered. You know, like room service."

Maggie watched his lips as he spoke, still wanting his kiss, but fearing the consequences.

"Pizza is fine," she decided.

"Pizza? Is that really what you want?" He chuckled quietly. "We can get anything! Steak, lobster, calamari, salmon, chicken, duck, lamb, pig, a turkey..."

She laughed as his serious suggestions turned silly, leaving his face with a smile.

"Seriously, pizza's good," she confirmed, and so he phoned in the delivery.

He set his phone down, looked into her eyes, and spoke her name. "Maggie, Maggie, Maggie," her name rang out like church bells. "What shall we talk about tonight?"

She wished he would discuss his intentions. Were they just friends? *OR...Did he realize the impossibility?*

He left her in her thoughts as he got up from the table and walked behind the bar, offering her something to drink. "We have wine, we have beer, soda...or I can mix something with any of those bottles up there," he said, looking up. Maggie decided to get up and follow into the space behind the bar, proceeding to help herself. But he thwarted her attempts. "I'm the bartender tonight. You need to go sit down."

"I will not! I'm picking out what I want!" She stared him up and down, feeling flush.

"I see..." He grinned, reading her inclinations.

Maggie grabbed the soda dispenser that was attached to a hose and started pouring soda into a glass without ice. Now she recalled when Antonio sprayed whip cream into her hair.

"You know...I really ought to spray you with this," she threatened. "I think I still owe you from at the pool!" No sooner had she uttered the words than Antonio disarmed her, holding the sprayer in his one hand while pinning her tightly against himself with the other.

www.lovetheillusion.com/139.htm

He stood inches from her face, turning to lean them against the bar counter as she listened to him announce, "There is no way I would let you spray me with that!" He laughed in amusement. "And don't worry. I do not wish to retaliate and ruin that...dress! I like it too much."

She looked into his eyes, wishing he would hold her forever, when he let go.

"I have to get ready to go to Canada. Have you ever been?" He glanced at her as he finished mixing their drinks, ignoring her glass of soda.

"Yes. When I was a kid, it was our last family trip," Maggie recalled, downcast. "I know what it's like to lose someone. My mom died right before I finished high school. She got cancer, and...it went quick. I will never forget standing so helpless, just watching her die, wishing to turn back the hands of time. It was really tough. I thought when I left for college in London, it would make things better, but it was worse. I was on my own for the first time, and thinking how I missed her advice, and how she would always have faith in me—no matter what. I poured myself into my studies because she taught me to love fashion, but I cried myself to sleep for three months straight." Maggie paused, suddenly realizing how much she still missed her mom.

Antonio looked deep in thought, recalling his brother.

"Yeah, losing someone you love is the worst pain you can feel, and you wait for time to heal, but it never completely does."

A knock on the door interrupted their conversation, and Antonio walked quickly over to answer, returning with a pizza in a thin white paper bag from Gianni's.

Maggie thought that she killed the atmosphere with her life's trauma, but he moved her thoughts forward.

"I ordered us a large, since we did a lot of swimming today!"

"*I* did a lot of swimming today," Maggie corrected. "You stood and watched!"

He laughed at her observation as he removed the pizza from the bag, explaining what he ordered. "This side is everything. The other side is nothing, but cheese of course. You can decide what you want." His eyes looked mysteriously into hers, waiting for her response.

Maggie wondered if for some strange reason he was talking about their relationship, but she wasn't sure what he meant by his comment. She gave him a sweet look, but remained quiet.

She felt sad that she was leaving on the plane tomorrow. Although the icy conditions had bought her more time with him, she was reaching the worst conclusion. She could not help but like him. Each time she had made excuses to see him, hoping to dissolve her feelings for him, she had arrived at quite the contrary...worse than she was before. She should have wised up and stayed away. But that became impossible. She loved being with him. She had only herself to blame for not being stronger. Would he date others after she left? She thought for sure he would. She wondered about his past relationships but was afraid to know.

She took a sip of her drink that Antonio mixed, mulling over their last night together. At times she thought that she could peek into his mind and see sadness, but he masked his emotions quite well.

Maggie felt her guts pour out, while she dared to ask, "Chad, do you date anybody?" She picked up a piece of cheese pizza. "I mean…is there…any special person in your life?" Her insides twisted about as she waited for his reply.

He appeared shocked by her for the first time, raising his brow with a straight face. "Yes, Maggie. I have pretty much a new girl every night."

The way he said it sent her insides reeling, wondering if his words were serious or canard. He glared back at her and she looked away, thinking that her question was an obvious mistake. *If he doesn't date others, why doesn't he just say so? Is his private life just an extension of more mystery, stemming from his profession?* Did he wish to keep her in the dark? She whirled about in indecision. *Drop the subject*, she decided. She waited to see if he would return the question, but he remained callous from her inquiry. Maggie felt frustration pouring into her veins. And the fact that she left tomorrow only made things worse. Why did he play with her emotions like this? After the time they spent together, what did he have in mind? To eventually seduce her? She thought about it, and about the passion she felt for him, regretting how she allowed herself to let him mess with her head.

Typical man, always grinding down her sanity little by little! She knew better than to blow up. She needed self-control. She would never beg him to call or stay in contact. Her insides tightened into a concrete wall as she hated the thought of him with someone else. *Too bad!* After she left *that would be inevitable.*

"Is something wrong?" Antonio asked without a hint of empathy.

Maggie forced a smile.

"No, Chad. I love the pizza. It's delicious." She noticed that she ate the half with cheese, and he was eating the side with everything on it.

"That's good," he said, casting his eyes away from their table.

"Why, is something wrong with you?" she probed, wishing for him to share his thoughts.

"No. I'm good," he responded, dully.

Maggie felt irritated by his pathetic attempts at conversation.

"I should get back early tonight," Maggie announced, hoping to trigger some newfound emotion. *Men! Did they ever have any?* She pushed her pizza away and stood up, waiting for him to do the same.

"Should we meet back here at nine," he asked, "for breakfast? The restaurant isn't open to the public 'til noon on Saturday."

"Sure," she agreed, not knowing what else to say.

He got up quickly, leaving the mess on the table.

As they left the restaurant, a couple fans lingered in an adjacent hallway and waved. He waved back. Maggie was sick of the attention—especially now—as she felt her emotions seeping out of her.

When they got to their floor, Maggie thought about their first handshake, after she told him off, and everything that had transpired since. She only knew him for several days, but it seemed a miniature lifetime.

As they approached her room, he touched her arm and told her, "I have something for you."

She turned towards him and proceeded to follow him back to his room, which they had already passed on the way to hers.

When they stepped inside, Maggie scanned his room again. On a table next to a chair sat a pile of cards and envelopes. She wondered where the letters were from, when she heard him say, "That's my fan mail. I read it in my spare time."

She wanted to pick one up and read, but she knew better than to be nosy. Then, she saw a photo of him taken on his Hollywood star with a teenage girl.

"That's me and my cousin. They were out in California when I was…" He stopped short as if it didn't matter. "Okay ready?" His voice popped back into its playful tone.

"Sure…" She tried to sound enthusiastic.

"Okay, but you have to close your eyes," he suggested.

Maggie eagerly closed her eyes. She imagined his arms wrapping around her and holding her in a tight squeeze. She dared to imagine his lips slowly pressing against hers and…

"You have to hold out your hand," he requested, breaking her daydream.

She held out her hand. She felt something land in her hand that felt like a piece of paper. "OK. Open!" she heard him say. She opened her eyes and saw a bookmark—with a photo of Cheetos. She remembered feeding and petting him, and her face melted into a sweet state, meeting his with a smile.

"Thanks!"

"You can put that in your novel," he explained, "and when you are reading, just like magic, you will think of me."

Maggie stood speechless. She wanted to wrap her arms around him and land the two of them on his bed. But since that would only compound the difficulty of leaving, she went for the door instead.

"See you tomorrow." She stared at him as she closed the door. Antonio stood motionless, watching her leave.

And that was the last time she saw him.

The next morning, Maggie was on her way to Biagio's to meet him for breakfast when she ran into Angie, who was all too anxious to tell her that Antonio was unable to meet her for breakfast because the new lights were not operating correctly.

Now she had stepped out of Antonio's world and onto the plane, feeling her body crammed into a small space while her thoughts of the past week were crammed into her brain. She made her best attempt to distance her emotions that clung to his mysterious way.

The models sat in the rear of the plane, while Francis Louis sat in first class by himself reading the Wall Street Journal's stock information. Sally slept against Matt's shoulder, and he seemed ready to fall asleep himself. Now Maggie wallowed in her thoughts, alone, wishing even to speak to Francis rather than agonize in self-pity.

She really missed her mom. Although her mother never had all the solutions, her voice was always soothing, as if everything would somehow be okay. Maggie was now at the point in life that she knew better. Things were not always going to be "okay."

She noticed the elderly woman, in the seat next to her, who appeared to be in her eighties. Maggie turned the other way and looked out the window.

As the plane took off, she tried her best to dismiss the sick feeling that sat in her stomach. Soon, she managed to be distracted by the woman next to her, admiring her classy appearance and fashion know-how for her age. She sparkled with her perfectly white hair that was twisted up in a bun, glasses to land on the mark of the latest fashion, and a tan designer trench coat. She also had tan patent shoes, square-toed with a rectangular buckle to finish the look. She displayed a diamond wedding band—probably dated to the 1940's, but still dazzling in the new era. She wore no jewelry other than that band, and when Maggie finished her assessment, she felt embarrassed—*a momentary diversion.*

Maggie shifted uncomfortably in her seat with her thoughts still encircling her, failing to reach a point of rest.

After what already felt like an eternity of this torture, she counted yet another three hours before the plane would finally be landing. And although she felt completely exhausted, she found it impossible to sleep. Francis had exhausted her, Chad had exhausted her, Antonio had exhausted her, and now this plane ride exhausted her. She thought the time she spent with him to be so confusing. He seemed nice, but he must have just been out for a good time. *How irritating!* She felt her emotions getting the best of her as she soon started losing control, realizing she needed a tissue from her briefcase, now lost overhead in a crammed compartment.

The sweet elderly lady next to her noticed her condition. She reached into her pocket and pulled out a clean handkerchief and handed it to her.

Maggie gratefully accepted. "Thank you. I'm so sorry. I must look completely ridiculous."

"Oh, no," the woman admitted, "I'm sure I've been there." She spoke her words with certainty, and Maggie felt for a moment like she was sitting next to her mother as a tear followed down her cheek and landed in her lap. "You can talk to me, dear. Really, I don't mind." She heard a soothing voice. "Sometimes you feel better if you talk." The woman spoke her words of wisdom, and Maggie believed she had some. Maggie glanced into her eyes that emanated a warm embrace. Maggie thought about it. *I don't know her, she doesn't know me.* Matt and Sally were sleeping, Francis was clueless. She soon came to her decision. *Why not? There could be no harm done.*

"Well," Maggie began, "I was in New York, on business, when I met what I thought was this really amazing guy. Now I have to go back home, and I will probably never see him again."

There was a moment of silence, until the woman spoke.

"I'm Julia, by the way, Julia Winters."

"I'm Maggie, Maggie White," Maggie returned the introduction. "Nice to meet you."

"You know, I have enough tears myself, lately," Julia began. "I was married to Marvin Winters for 65 years. We were married when we were only twenty years old. We were so young, but so in love. He died just last year of heart failure, and now I think my heart is in worse condition than his was."

"I am so sorry." Maggie sniffled, holding back the tears that were no longer hers. "That must be really hard."

"You can never even imagine until it happens. But, I am traveling to England to see my daughter, Christine. She has five girls. Can you imagine that? Not one boy! Her husband said he will just have to live with being outnumbered. They are my family, and they are my love now. I have two sons also. They both live close by, and they help me out. One was married, and it didn't work out and the other son, Jacob...well, he never got married."

Maggie listened intently as Julia told her, "Every day just goes on by. I have to make the best of it. I cannot feel sorry for myself, because that is the worst. I wake up and look in the mirror and tell myself how lucky I am. I found love and had it for 65 years and will never lose those memories."

"Sounds like you have a good perspective on life," Maggie said.

"Well, if I'm honest," she admitted, "I can't say I always did. Life is tough. It dishes out whatever it wants, and sometimes you don't want to catch it. Love can also be just like that. But love is strong. It pushes through whatever lies as an obstacle in its path. It always survives. The same is true for you. You have to trust that and believe it."

Maggie and Julia spent the rest of the plane ride enjoying conversation, and the remainder of the flight seemed to pass much more quickly.

Their conversation came to a rest while Maggie pondered Julia's words. The plane was now preparing for landing, shifting into new pockets of airspace. She contemplated her recent personal shift into another world of space with Antonio. And it was as if the few days she spent with him created in her mind's eye a photo album, special and unique. Although time would fade those memories, she would never forget him. His confident way meshed into his tough, yet striking appeal only to conceal his sweetness. And his fun, carefree adventurous side that kept him mysterious, and the way he looked at her that made her insides curl into a frenzy of passion. *Being with him was simply magical.*

And she would hold on to his memory...forever.

www.lovetheillusion.com/147.htm

Now her mind quickly steered her back to old memories as the wheels on the plane came in contact with the runway pavement. She was back in London where she met Phillip. She remembered the first time she saw him. He was hired by her father, who was an aircraft engineer, to oversee production at the England plant. He and her father met for several business luncheons, and she happened to drop in, at the end of one of their meetings, with a gift she had picked up for her niece, since her father would be in Chicago the following weekend. That was when her father mentioned that he needed someone to look out for his daughter in London, and Phillip called her the following day, inviting her to a wedding he had to attend.

Now six weeks after their break-up, she recognized in an instant that same familiar feeling of being on top of the world, glistening on the highest mountain top, only to end up torn to bits in the deepest, darkest, valley of despair. Once again, she would have to climb out of another one of life's unpredictable valleys.

As they got up to exit the plane, Maggie hugged Julia, and although they had only conversed for a short while, Maggie felt as if she had been a lifelong friend.

Chapter 9

It felt strange to be back in England. Perhaps a large piece of her was still in New York. Hopefully time would mend the heartache that she now felt, and even though she never kissed him, she thought she may as well have, since it was so difficult to let go.

Maggie struggled with her key until she opened the door to her flat. The lights were out, but she could see that Dana had fallen asleep on the sofa. She quietly headed to her room where she collapsed on her bed. It was the middle of the night.

She soon heard a knock, and Dana's voice followed as she entered the room. "Maggie! I thought you would at least say hello!" She plopped into a chair across from Maggie who was leaned against the headboard of her bed, with her arms wrapped around her legs, canvas shoes still on, as she stared at the wall.

"Maggie!" Dana exclaimed. "You look like you've come from the morgue!"

Maggie refused to make eye contact.

"Seriously Maggie, you look gutted!" Dana pressed.

"Another nothing," Maggie concluded. "I'm just an idiot."

"An idiot? Why? What'd you do, sleep with him?" Dana asked with a look of perplexity.

"Are you joking? That's funny! He never even kissed me! I don't even know what was going on this past week."

"You spent a lot of time together, right? So he must be interested." Dana looked at her with intense curiosity.

"I must be cautious after what I've been through. So when I first saw him, I thought 'Great, the complete player package!' You know, totally hot, acts confident, knows just what to say and how to look at you when he says it—not to mention when he looks at me, it makes me crazy! But then I find he's really sweet and a lot of fun, and all I can do is hope my infatuation will croak in the next couple days when I no longer see him."

"Sounds like you've lost your mind," Dana concluded. "Are you in love with him, or what?"

"Definitely not! No more love for me, but I'm feeling its pain again. And I almost hate him for making me feel this way. This is the last thing I need. I finally land a good paying job, get out of my so-called engagement, and now this!"

"Right…I bet you hear from him! Wait and see, maybe he'll call…"

"No. He never even asked for my phone number! Besides, a long distance affair is nothing but trouble, not to mention the small detail of his celebrity—like I need to add *that* to my plate of complications. I need to move on and find someone to date—just temporarily—so I can forget him! I was thinking Jeff Briggs."

"Jeff Briggs, that photographer you work with?" Dana laughed. "From one dish to another who has never heard the word 'no'? I guarantee he will be nothing but a pain in the arse!"

"Yeah, well he's always flirting with me. He makes his rude eye gestures. You know, the ones where he leaves no doubt that he is checking you out? And then he bumps into me all the time, and makes it as if he didn't see me."

"Sounds like he'll be no good, a senseless beast," Dana offered her opinion.

"Perhaps it can be my next life's challenge—to tame him!" Maggie gave her final conclusion while tossing her hand into the air.

Dana looked puzzled.

"So you're going to completely forget Antonio? I would be chuffed to bits to bum with him all week. Did you even think once, 'I'm going to bonk him?' I think if I was up on stage with him, I would have done it right there!"

Maggie's jaw practically hit her knees as she suddenly broke into laughter.

"You know, Dana, I will never be you. You float through life and never worry about a thing. I, on the other hand, contemplate everything until I arrive at impossibilities! I should probably be more like you, but it's hard to change. I'm doomed to misery." Maggie managed to smile at Dana. Her friendship, longstanding after they met waiting tables at a local diner, supported her as she sifted through her man troubles.

"Did you remember to bring me something?" Dana finally asked in excitement.

"I did!" Maggie reached into her bag and grabbed a black t-shirt with the words "New York" spelled down the front. It still had the tags. "This one's yours," she said, handing it to Dana. "I wore mine when Chad or Antonio—whoever he is—made me spaghetti."

"What? He cooks? He cooked for you?"

"Yeah, his mom's spaghetti recipe and it tasted really good."

"He sounds more like your Prince Charming every time you talk about him. How can you not even kiss him? I don't understand."

"Believe me, I wanted to. But that would have made it even harder to leave. Besides, he was never pushy."

"He is *shy*!?" Dana suggested.

"Antonio? Shy?" Maggie burst into laughter. "He's the most confident, egotistical brat I've ever met!"

Dana laughed at her telling. "Really?"

"Yes, get this! I'm in his room and he says he has something for me. That's after I've seen his 'Arianna interview,' and I'm quite certain that he has more women than he knows what to do with. And I'm thinking, 'how repulsive.' That's when he hands me a t-shirt from his show and has the audacity to ask if I would like him to sign it for me—like I'm one of his fans!"

"Aren't you?"

"Perhaps, for these transitory intervals that keep coming and going." Maggie sounded out her frustration.

"Meeting him was a fluke," Dana pointed out, "...and I'm sure he's a handful!" She laughed. "Why wouldn't he be? He's Antooooniooo DeLuuuuuca!" She paused. "So where is this shirt he gave you?"

Maggie went over to her luggage and unzipped her suitcase. When she found the shirt, she flung it at Dana.

Dana held it up. "This is totally awesome! So will you wear it to work Monday?"

"That would be a mistake. Not a fashion statement for Francis!" Maggie smiled at the thought.

The weeks went by, and Maggie still thought about Antonio. But she tried her best to focus on work. Francis had put her in charge of designing a dress for the Festive Party line. And after she designed it, she decided to design another...and another...and pretty soon she ended up with six instead of one! And now the grey and red satin dress would be featured on the Party Dress promotional flyer. Maggie was very proud.

www.lovetheillusion.com/152.htm

Her job was becoming more rewarding, but she still missed Antonio. And as time passed, she became increasingly convinced that she would never see him again. She tried to keep the memory of him alive, but it was fading fast in her mind, and she wished that she at least had a picture of the two of them together. It was time to move on, however, and she did manage to get a date with Jeff Briggs. And he asked *her* out.

He pulled up in his convertible BMW with the radio blasting, on a somewhat cool evening, to take her to dinner. He came to the door with a dozen red roses, and she left the house in a black pencil skirt cut just above the knee, and a knit top with a lazy floral design, tucked in.

They drove off with the top down and as he pulled up to the White Horse Inn, Maggie tried to gather her hair back to its original position as he opened her door and said, "Let's go, kitten."

He ordered a bottle of wine at dinner, flirted with the waitress, and talked about himself the whole time while casually mentioning the other women he dated. And for each time he made eye contact, he also evened the score by staring down at her chest. *He was so pathetic...A total loser.*

After they left the restaurant, he gave her butt a smack as she got back into his car. They drove home in the dark, while the music blared so loud that it made it impossible to carry on any conversation. When he pulled into her driveway, he leaned over and professed, "I had a great time tonight. You're unlike any girl I've ever met!" And she bet she was, but soon to not be, as he leaned forward to French kiss her—before she even had a chance to kiss him back—while he placed his hand on her knee, slowly moving it up her skirt. She missed Antonio.

After her *first* and *last* date with Jeff, she took the red roses he gave her out of the vase and threw them into the trash. Her hand bled from several wounds she got from grabbing onto the stems in haste, forgetting that roses were full of thorns.

And that same night, she reached the decision that she would never be with the one she wanted, and also threw away Antonio's t-shirt.

Returning from work, a few days later, Maggie found Dana watching a video of Antonio's magic show. Dana spoke quickly to inform her, "Maggie, I'm so sorry to be a nosey parker, but you got this in the post from Antonio, and I just *had* to open it!" Dana laughed at the part where Maggie appeared on stage. "It's brilliant! You look so confused when Antonio repeats your name!"

Maggie recalled her startling discovery of who he was, while recognizing the fame attached to his name. He was *quite the funny one*. She picked up the manila envelope that it came in. She peeked inside for a note. *Nothing?* She wondered how he even got her address. But of course, he was a magician!

Maggie stood, her arms folded, as she watched the video while Dana sat on the couch with a bowl of crisps. She reabsorbed her moment of shock. "Well I've seen enough. Enjoy."

Maggie left the room to read her novel.

Lounging across a chair in her bedroom, she removed the Cheetos bookmark, gathering additional thoughts—*just another egotistical move on his part*—more paraphernalia to signify that she was just a fan of his celebrity. *So irritating!*

Two weeks later, the unthinkable happened. Maggie walked into a food market to buy a few groceries, when she managed to run into Jasmine, the one who stole her fiancé. *Talk about an unfortunate coincidence.* And although Maggie tried to hide behind a fruit display, Jasmine had already spotted her and decided to bask in the moment. "Maggie, what have you been up to lately?"

She's such a skank! Maggie wore a look of contempt, refusing to reply, while Jasmine issued her a condescending stare.

Maggie stiffly walked away, but heard Jasmine's final attempt to get under her skin as she made the comment, "Looks like you've moved on!"

www.lovetheillusion.com/154.htm

Jasmine's comment still rang into Maggie's ears as she left the market, wondering what she possibly meant. Had she heard of her latest tragic attempt to date Jeff, who everyone knew was a total player? *How embarrassing.*

When she returned home, she found Dana on the couch. Only this time, she had her nose dug into her favorite magazine that she subscribed to. Dana peered over the top.

"Maggie, tell me it's not bloody likely that your picture made it into Report News?"

Maggie felt a rush of horror come over her.

"Look!" Dana pointed. "Isn't that you sitting on Antonio's lap?"

"What? That's impossible. I never sat on his lap!"

Maggie stared down at the photo.

"Well, isn't that you?"

Maggie squinted, recalling the beer spill incident when she fell onto Antonio. She grabbed the magazine out of Dana's hands. She gasped at the cover, noticing another photo, directly above that, of the two crazy fans that danced with him. She read the caption: "ANTONIO DELUCA ENTERTAINS HIS FANS AT THE AFTER PARTY, AND THEY ARE EAGER TO ENTERTAIN HIM!"

Before she was able to let out a horrified scream, she saw yet another photo of the two of them, pasted behind the beer spill incident, leaving Night Owls together.

This is SO humiliating!

www.lovetheillusion.com/155.htm

Maggie wanted to rip the magazine to shreds, throw a few things, perhaps disassemble the room to a complete shamble—but instead she wailed in defeat, "That must be what Jasmine was talking about...I HATE REPORT NEWS!"

She retreated to her room, where she suddenly relived Jasmine's comment—"Looks like you've moved on"—her nasally voice echoed, a distasteful memory. Maggie impulsively kicked her foot into the side of her bed, and after realizing she inflicted her own physical pain, lay face down on her bed, wishing it would all go away.

Three weeks passed—a total of six weeks since she last laid eyes on him—when a mysterious event took place. She was on a lunch date with Francis—strictly business, of course—when he dropped the bomb.

"Got a call from Antonio DeLuca this morning; he wants us to make his costumes," Francis declared in his candid piety. "He approached me several years ago on the subject, but I refused because it was much too petty to mess with. But now he's become this huge phenomenon and he has sold out shows...big cast, dancers, meaning more costumes, so it's a huge opportunity."

What!? Maggie thought she was going to slip off her chair and land under the table in a coma. But instead, she tried to bury her emotions as she listened to him continue. "So anyways, we made a bid, and we are waiting to hear back from him. It could be weeks. I think he's in Tampa Bay right now, doing a charity show."

"Sounds..." Maggie searched for the right word, but soon reckoned the English vocabulary simply did not have one.

"Splendid!" Francis finished for her. "And you, Maggie, are my bait! We will fly to New York to meet with him to continue negotiating, but never seal the deal, while putting the pressure on. You start measuring everyone, putting your time and effort into it and flirting with him like crazy, until he accepts my final offer, which will sink his pocket book into the casket!"

Help. Maggie no longer looked discreet.

"Well, I wish to take a few days off very soon, and you are fit to handle it all by yourself," she decided.

"A holiday for you, already? Nonsense Maggie! No! I hired you for a reason. You have the fashion know-how of Queen Elizabeth, and I need your input on the costume designs. Antonio can dangle around your beauty as I move in to dismantle his awareness. You are definitely coming, and I insist! And by the way, skirts are now worn a bit shorter than what you have on today—even in the business world—so I will expect you need to get that skirt and a few others into alterations before we depart. And once the contract is finalized, you can be sure I will add a bonus to your next check!"

"That's just...great. What...an opportunity." She struggled for excitement.

"And not to worry—you will be first to know when it's all finalized!"

Maggie's real thoughts talked back to him in her head. *How can he be so smart and so pig-headed at the same time?* The least of her concerns! Now she *would* see Chad again, or Antonio, if she didn't accidentally call him yet another name! It was all starting to make sense, after all. She remembered first meeting him at the bar, and mentioning that she worked for Francis Louis, when he then said, "That's interesting." Perhaps he connected with her just to build himself an even bigger empire in the world of fame. *What a creep!*

As they left the restaurant, she had to consider whether Antonio or Francis carried the bigger ego, and soon offered a bit of forgiveness to Francis, since he at least paid her a decent salary. Her final thought sent tremendous relief—that at least Francis never saw her photos in the smutty tabloids, since he lingered just one notch above reading anything of that substance.

That night required...*a sleeping pill.*

Another three weeks passed, and Maggie successfully removed her inner desire to ever date a man again as she stepped on a plane with Francis to accomplish the grand business deal in Chicago, rather than New York—just another awesome city to visit, leaving her memory in ruins.

There she stood, on the same floor as Antonio's company once again, in the finest skyscraper hotel that money could build. Looking out of another twentieth story view, she thought if she had any brains at all, she would jump. This time on Antonio's floor, she was graced in addition with the presence of Francis Louis, only two doors down from her. *How convenient!* They had all expenses paid, and she could not help but wonder what the two of them were up to.

She recalled the plane ride with Francis—the first time she flew first class—only to suffer the regurgitating monotony of his three favorite activities—reading the Wall Street Journal while rambling endlessly about his savvy in the business world and crashing out for an occasional snooze.

Tonight, she had to meet the two of them for dinner where they would be discussing the groundbreaking event of the merging empires. Maggie already anticipated her hidden agenda—forming her own opinion on which of them was the bigger male chauvinist oink!

She sat down on the edge of her bed, wondering how her life had turned into such a shamble. She needed to think positive and stay in control. Why should she allow either of them to get under her skin? Perhaps she should try getting under theirs. *Just a bit of karma coming their way, first class, arriving at the meeting...in person.* Maggie thought out her revenge. She gleamed with a smile. First, she decided to be fashionably late. Second, she had already taken the liberty of dismissing Francis' advice on the skirts. And once she got there, she would stir up trouble.

Maggie went over to the mirror, admiring her rebellion. Wearing a pinstriped pants suit that screamed masculinity, she decided to remove all jewelry to seal the delivery. If she had to meet with them she would look the part—tough, shrewd, and not subject to their feminine discriminations. She pulled her hair into a tight bun without a strand out of place. She sat down on the edge of the bed and waited for the clock to say 6:10. And when it did, she left for the restaurant where she knew she would be twenty minutes late.

Time to go!

She stepped off the elevator with a look of vengeance.

www.lovetheillusion.com/157.htm

After exiting the cab, she paced quickly into the restaurant, approaching the table in haste, while fixating on both of their uneasy stares, now completely in view. She refused to flinch with emotion.

"Well, good evening to the two of you." Maggie glared at them as she took a seat. "My apologies for being late, but you know what it's like to catch a cab in the streets of Chicago." With that she motioned for the waiter, and requested, "Water, two lemons." *And no pun intended,* she thought to herself. She decided to ignore Antonio while offering support to Francis.

"So..." Antonio spoke, looking right at Maggie. "I'm glad we can finally meet. I've decided to do my next show in Vegas, and am hoping that you would be able to design for the crew—something extraordinary. And although I contacted you, Francis, say, two months ago, you just now confirmed your interest in my proposal. Now, we are left in a bit of a time pinch, but hopefully we can work it out."

"Right." Maggie extended her water glass to "clank" into Francis' glass of wine. "You know, Antonio, Francis is not only on top in the world of fashion design, but he is also quick in executing his visions to meet the customer's needs in a timely manner. You have nothing to worry about!" She smiled at Francis in a coy, steady mannerism. Francis' face radiated as if he just received the bronze award for his shrewdness.

The waitress came to take their food order, but Maggie just turned her menu over to Francis, indicating she would have the same. She barely had an appetite, and wished to vomit instead of eat! She thought perhaps Antonio felt a bit uncomfortable, and she decided to bask in the moment, recalling the recent tabloids.

"Antonio," Maggie spoke in her sarcastic tone, "I have been spinning my wheels just trying to keep up with all the publicity that you have been receiving as of lately, and I have to hand it to you! You know just how to keep yourself in the spotlight! It's *so* impressive!"

Antonio sat confused when she decided her next compliment belonged to Francis as she polished their egos, hoping to drive them to an even greater self-appreciation. She gave Antonio a quick wink, enjoying his new look of frustration. *Is he really clueless?* She decided to give it a break until after the food came.

Almost finished eating, she conspired to inflate both of their egos just one more time, issuing them each one more compliment. Only this time, they would fall right on top of each other.

"Antonio," she started in on him, "did you know how fortunate I am to be under Francis' wing, as my professional career is just starting to blossom? Just the other day, he says to me, 'Maggie I am so concerned that you always look up to date, since you are my right hand executive. Be ever so sure I mean this with the very best intentions, but your skirts need to come up just a bit to catch up to the latest fashion trends!' I must say how grateful I am to receive advice from such an expert in the industry, and to be on such a personal level to feel completely shameless discussing such a topic!" She observed Antonio, while she took a sip of water, after becoming winded in a tunnel of praise for her boss.

Antonio shot back a "look to kill," but she turned her attention to Francis.

"Did you know," she said, speaking in a cozy mannerism, "that Antonio will be one of the most delightful people to work with? He barely knows who I am, but he graciously gave me..." She glared at Antonio. "...a t-shirt, which I wear to bed *every* night—that he took his own pen to, a bookmark of his cheetah which I left in my *Bible*, and a *video* of his latest show! You really ought to see his performance sometime. He has the sense of humor to kill a funeral. See, he brings up a poor damsel in distress, right onto the stage with him and then! It's just like magic! She has her incredible moment of fame, and I'm sure she's never quite the same." She batted her eyes at Antonio and then over to Francis. "Isn't he just amazing? So many celebrities are so egotistical, but he is nothing but a breath of fresh air!" She tilted her head at Antonio the way he had done on their dates, as he blazed a look to confirm that she stood in the cross-fire of war now begun! His face flushed more color sitting at the table with her than he got in the Tampa Bay sun. Meanwhile, Francis wore a look of confusion, but she discerned it would drain off within seconds.

Then Antonio opened his mouth to speak, and she knew that he was ready to start trouble. "So, Maggie, it's nice you made it! Francis said you were hoping to take some time off from work! So, do you leave behind an exotic love life when you come along on these business excursions?"

Maggie was shocked by his dive into her personal life. *How dare him!* She needed a quick response, but what on earth would it be? She had to think fast. Now she knew! She would broadcast her feminine side, reveal her frustration with men, and mock an admiration for her boss, the exception! Hopefully, the two of them would decide they just could not take the embarrassment and call the meeting adjourned.

"My love life," Maggie began, "is just a bit personal, if I might say. But since you ask, I won't be shy. My love life is *extremely* exotic! I had to end my last first date with our photographer after he tried reaching his hand up my skirt! I did not realize that after a dozen roses and an expensive dinner I should be so in debt! I would have loved to introduce him to my *'friend'* Jasmine because I really think they would hit it off, but she's already banging my ex-fiancé! Now, I should almost give up on the male species altogether, but when I least expect it, I am offered a job with Francis Louis! And even though he is old enough to be my father, he continuously unleashes qualities that make a girl scream for more!"

Maggie sat humored by Antonio. He sat leaned back in his chair, after pushing his food aside, chewing gum in attempt to rid his anger. And just as she predicted, Francis wiped his face with his napkin, stood up, and announced, "Time to go. We can finish discussing things tomorrow."

Maggie absorbed her victory. They barely scratched the surface of finalizing any contract…

The good news…She felt *much better!* The bad news…A productive meeting would need to soon follow…tomorrow!

The three of them uncomfortably rode back to the hotel in Antonio's limo. Francis Louis sat awkwardly in the middle, while resting his arm around Maggie, who felt relieved the night was finally over. She planned to check and see if there were any horror flicks playing on pay per view. She thought Antonio should pick up the tab on that, as well.

As they reached the hotel lobby, the press stood in anxious anticipation, requesting them to stand for a photo shoot. She could already predict the headlines now, and she contemplated...*A new dimension of illness!* She hated the spotlight.

Francis Louis stood center while she put on the biggest fake Hollywood smile she could muster. Fans gathered, going wild, as the camera crew flashed amidst reporters taking their turn, moving in for the kill.

Now on the way up the escalator, Maggie gracefully rode alongside them. She saw that Francis was pleased, while Antonio depicted the true fame that belonged to him, waving to his fans.

Finally, they were free from all the attention and on their way down the hall to their rooms. Francis stopped to the right, entering his room first, as Maggie darted ahead, hoping to soon escape from reality. But no sooner did she arrive at her room she knew Antonio stood right behind her. She opened the door, feeling his hand on her arm, as he guided her into her room.

Seconds later, he had trapped her against the wall while the door slammed behind them. His eyes were filled with anger as he stood inches from her face. She stared back in complete shock. She had never seen this side of him.

"What the devil was that, Maggie?" Antonio's eyes pierced through her as he stood in a fit of rage. She fought with all her might to discard her emotions that came rushing back in an instant, intertwined with his presence. He left her standing against the wall, while he paced the small area in her hotel room. *"How* can you do this to me? I am busy for *weeks* on end trying to haggle out a deal with that filthy boss of yours, who makes it impossible for me to meet with you unless I offer up ridiculous amounts of money up front! He's such a greedy son-of-a-bitch, and don't think I haven't read him like an open book! And for your information, I'm not the pathetic financial delegate that he thinks I am. I thought this would maybe lend us an opportunity to spend more time together, but you have turned it into some cynical joke. I even hoped that you could see your family while you were here, and wanted to give show tickets to all of you. And I don't mean Louis! He's on the next plane back tomorrow and I can't wait!"

She hoped he had finished when she explained, "We are both going back tomorrow night."

"Is that what he told you?" Antonio shouted back at her. "Well, I'm telling you, you're not! Your plane leaves two days from now, and we're spending time together. He thinks you're helping to measure for costumes. I can have someone else handle that!"

Maggie stood speechless as she allowed everything to sink in. She hoped that Francis had partial hearing loss and was unable to hear Antonio belting out his frustration from two doors down. She felt bad, but confusion still lingered.

"Antonio, why did you stand me up the morning that I left?"

He stood, deep in thought.

"When we spent time together, I thought I was losing my mind. I feel for you Maggie, but you have all your walls up, keeping me at a distance." He gave her a look of frustration. She stood in silence as he continued. "I know you want nothing to do with the crazy world I live in and I can't blame you, but I know you feel for me too. I'm not saying that because I'm some egotistical jerk, but because I can feel the chemistry between us. Then, you have to leave. I just could not stand to look at you and think it might be the last time I saw you."

Maggie tried to sort out her thoughts and feelings as he explained, "Obviously, it's complicated. You're in England. I'm here. But after you left, that same day, I left a message for that four-horned boss of yours to contact me. It was *my* plan to get you back to me without compromising your job. Meanwhile, I have to deal with Louis who drags me around like a row of tin cans behind his Lamborghini!"

Maggie stood, overwhelmed with disbelief.

"Antonio," she said cautiously, putting her feelings forward, "I do care. It scares me when I look at you and realize what I feel. But I have been through nothing but bad relationships, and I knew we shouldn't be spending time together because I had to leave. Then, I get back home, and my roommate Dana shows me my photos in Report News, where I'm supposedly just some lucky fan you chose for a random hookup!"

Antonio sat down on the bed as he pulled her in front of him.

"You know, Maggie, you can't let those tabloids upset you. I didn't see what you saw, but I understand your frustration." He sat her down on his lap. "Maybe this will help. It's all about *the illusion*. And I will tell you that things are not always as they seem. When I am up on stage, I create something to look real that is not. I make money doing that. Reporters do the same thing. Do you want to read an article that reads, 'Antonio feeds his cheetah, and then he drinks a glass of water at Biagio's during rehearsal breaks?' No, that story is not interesting enough, so they get busy and artistically creative, like me, going for the shock! You have to make up your mind who you want to believe. Me? Or them?"

Antonio's anger soon melted away, his eyes holding her captive in an intimate bond. Maggie pondered the illusion of love.

How do you ever know if it's real?

Antonio stood up, holding her in his arms. She closed her eyes, wishing she could freeze time. But he stepped away from her and said, "I'll see you tomorrow. There's going to be a real meeting at eight a.m. sharp. I'll be emailing Francis the information tonight." And with that he left her room.

Maggie stood motionless, reacquainting her feelings for him. She was afraid. She had never felt like this before.

Chapter 10

The next morning came.

The three of them now sat in a conference room that Antonio arranged with some bagels, muffins, juice and coffee sitting on a side table. The room was oversized for the three of them, and Maggie wished more people would appear to displace the tension. She felt a fragment of remorse for the way she had acted the other night, but one good thing had come out of it. Antonio let her see his full deck of cards. Or so she thought.

Now overdressed, she wore black pants over heels, with a blouse made from a white organza fabric, accented with a modest ruffle trimmed in black. Francis Louis appeared professional but extremely casual, while Antonio just wore blue jeans with a white fitted undershirt, not even taking the time to shave. She knew neither respected the other, as forwarded by their attire.

Maggie stood at the side table fixing her bagel and pouring her coffee, listening to Francis tell Antonio that he already ate at Charlie Trotter's—notably one of the most expensive places to eat in Chicago. They had managed to prepare breakfast for him, although the restaurant was typically not open until noon.

As she approached the table, she felt Francis' eyes glue to her, and when she sat down to gaze at Antonio, he had his arms folded, glaring at Francis. She could not wait for this to be over.

Francis cleared his throat. "So, we have some numbers put together for what we estimated the cost of costume production, travel expenses, and itemized underneath are various miscellaneous fees, attorney contract fees..." He shuffled his proposal across the table to Antonio.

Antonio unfolded his arms and rested his chin in his hand, reading over the details. He sat for nearly ten minutes reviewing everything.

Maggie sat calmly, next to Francis, as was appropriate for their meeting. She had not touched her bagel while she sat on her hands observing his reaction. And her lips were pressed together, indicating she resolved to stay quiet at this meeting.

"Too much," Antonio challenged, pushing the proposal back at Francis. "Dolce & Gabbana will do it for half that!" he said with his eyebrows jammed up on his forehead as high as they would go, waiting for Francis to make the next move.

Maggie felt herself perspire, waiting for things to continue. She took a sip of coffee and peered over her cup at Antonio. He had her in his eye, letting go of his cute grin, while Francis stayed busy combing the estimate with his pen. She thought another ten minutes would pass, but she welcomed the time to stare at Antonio, engaging her feelings for him once again.

Francis looked up, catching Antonio smiling at Maggie. She blushed into Francis' face after he then looked at her. Francis repositioned himself in his chair.

"Antonio! When I take on a project such as this, I am a visionary! I can make you bigger than you've ever been. You started out with your big debut. Several years pass, and pretty soon, you're doing a show every month, here and there. Now, you have quite a few endorsers, allowing you to perform at a whole new level of excellence! They pour money out of their own pockets because they are confident in a substantial return. Now that they have stepped into the picture, it is like BOOM! Off you go, into some crazy stardom. You're a household name in the U.S. and Canada, and what's next? Sweden! Where will you go from there? That, Antonio, is where I come in!"

www.lovetheillusion.com/165.htm

Maggie thought Francis made a pretty impressive introduction, but Antonio folded his arms, indicating he was bored with his presentation. She listened to Francis continue, as his voiced raised a notch, in excitement. "With just the right image on stage, we can turn you into a worldwide icon. Picture this! It's Vegas! Glitz or bling, however you want to say it. A whole new look. We can iconize your style, unlike any other magician out there. Now, not only are you an icon in the entertainment industry, you are a fashion icon for the way you dress on stage! Whatever it takes! We create that look that will symbolize you and no other. So! Now, instead of souvenir booths, we have souvenir shops, as big as ever. We can sell hats, gloves, jackets, jewelry imitations of what you wear for your shows. Kids, teens! They will all go crazy to wear the DeLuca ring! Stanley emailed me a photo after our first phone conversation."

Maggie watched Antonio digesting Francis' hot-headed spiel.

"So!" Francis continued, "My next question for you is this! Do you see your image better portrayed in the style of Elvis Presley or Michael Jackson?"

Antonio immediately started laughing. "That's crazy!"

"I don't think so! I know how fashion works. It's iconic! So, what do you think?" Francis persisted.

"I'd say neither," Antonio dissed.

"You have to trust me on this! I know what I'm doing and it will be big! So the remaining question is, who do we use to baseline your image, Presley or Jackson?" He shoved the paperwork back at him.

"Both!" Antonio sat, humored.

Maggie ducked into a snicker, and quickly recomposed "serious" as Francis turned to look at her. She watched as he took his pen to his legal pad and wrote: "hot and eccentric."

Maggie felt her eyes widen at Francis who stared back at Antonio. *When will this be over?*

"Still too much," Antonio verified with a smirk.

Francis became edgy. "Antonio! I am your chariot ride to bigger and better!"

Antonio reviewed the proposal again and finally took out his pen and wrote a figure. Maggie tried to see the numbers as she watched the paperwork fly back in Francis' direction once again. Francis peered down on the new proposal and exclaimed, "It's a done deal! I will make you so much money it will make your head spin!"

Francis began to get up and Antonio met him halfway with a handshake. They looked far from friends, and Antonio had not cracked a smile when they shook. Francis smiled, but phony and pretentious.

www.lovetheillusion.com/166.htm

Francis turned to Maggie with his hand extended onto her arm. "We will start on the details over lunch!" He then turned to Antonio. "When do you need her back to take everyone's measurement?"

"I got someone else taking care of that," Antonio informed looking at Maggie.

"No. I can't trust anyone else. Maggie's doing it!" Francis glared at Antonio, refusing to surrender his power trip.

"Okay then Louis, two o'clock." Antonio looked disgusted as if he'd had enough. He stood in a tight stance as he watched them leave.

In the cab ride back, Francis chatted all about their victory, and Maggie watched as his hand occasionally bounced on and off of her leg. She was glad to be in pants.

Maggie was back in her room. She wondered if she had time before lunch to make a quick trip to the Art Institute to pick up one of the Van Gogh prints that she wanted for the lounge in her flat.

She thought she did. But as she made her exit, she bumped into Antonio standing a couple feet from her door.

"Where are you going, Maggie White?" He had his hands on his hips.

"I was...uh...to the Art Institute to...get a print for my..." She stumbled, totally off guard.

"That can wait!" He sounded aggravated, pointing at her to keep her attention. "That Louis boss of yours is up to no good! I see the way he looks at you and it makes me sick. Do me a favor! Don't pay him any more compliments!" He locked her into his stare until he backed off. "When and where is your lunch date?"

"It's not a date! It's business. You should know that! It's all about you!"

"Well I cannot *stand* him! He's a full-blown pain in the ass! He's after my money and now he's after you!"

"That's so untrue. You need to chill out."

"Don't tell me what to do! I'm looking out for you! That's right! And I'm just sick and tired of his slimy operations!"

Antonio looked as if his temper was brewing again.

"Antonio! Francis is right in there! He can probably hear you!" She nodded towards his room.

"Then open your door!" He motioned his order.

Maggie turned around slowly, opening her door to let him in.

"Look Antonio! I know I made a mess of things last night, but I am sorry. I'm not this damsel in distress that you need to rescue! I can take care of myself."

Antonio punched his hand into his fist. "No Maggie! Five minutes with that boss of yours is five minutes too long!"

She blushed, feeling overcome in his presence. "We're meeting at noon, at um...Charlie's...I think."

"Charlie Trotter's *again*?" Antonio clinched his teeth. "I can't wait to get his gigantic food bill," he muttered under his breath, as he turned to leave her room. Maggie wished his temper would subside, but Francis knew just how to keep things brewing.

She waited a few minutes and then left to go to the Art Institute.

Once arrived, she decided to purchase admission to the galleries and see all the famous paintings. She soon lost track of time, now already quarter to noon. It was time to call Francis on her cell phone and make arrangements to just meet him there. She was late, again.

Making her way into Charlie Trotter's, Maggie approached the table where Francis stood with a pulled out chair for her to sit down. He was all about formality, so she did not think much of it. They were seated at a table for two near a window. Maggie felt herself yawn as they were approached by the waiter with menus.

"We'll have a bottle of Chateau Margaux, and the brochette, as an appetizer," Francis made his request.

"Sure, no problem," the waiter answered, filling their water glasses.

Maggie removed the starchy white napkin and laid it on her lap. She watched as an elderly lady sat down to the right, adjacent to them. She scanned the menu, hoping it would be a "quick lunch."

After they placed their order, Francis leaned towards her and started one of his tirades. "Okay, here's what we got... the dancers, all of them in an assortment of colors, all bold and dynamic. One set with them all in black and then...one with everyone in white! They need three changes of clothing, right?" Francis paused to consider.

Maggie nodded, trying to show interest in his latest mental masterpiece when he continued. "And we need that clown character to be a little more glitzy, along with those two sidekicks of his, the ones that remove his cape and swing around the props for entertainment. They need to have a dress but tight and short—not styled like Marilyn Monroe. We'll spice up the look with some platform shoes. Imagine a beaded, sequined bra and hipster set, or maybe a long sleeve body suit with shiny patent boots in red that come just over the knee. Now! Picture all of this! Everything I just mentioned with glitz and sparkle, sequins, you name it, all over every costume. It will reflect off the lights and make people crazy. Oh! And Antonio will be shining like never before. Picture this! Black pants but with a wide silver metallic panel to add that bling going down the front of the pants. And to captivate the Elvis Jackson look, we will incorporate some hot pink! I will make my vision a splendid reality, so soon now, and won't it be grand!?"

Maggie realized that, as he was rambling, she had emptied an entire glass of wine. And the elderly lady was now staring at them. Maggie quickly looked away, feeling embarrassed that Francis' excitement was spilling over on the other patrons. It was time to squeeze in her opinion—if that was even possible!

"Francis! You can't put Antonio in an outfit like that. That's completely crass!"

"Oh, it will be spectacular! Pink, black and silver are for sure his colors. That will be the over-the-top fashion statement that will iconize his look. A man in pink! And the thing is, if he had blonde hair, no way! But he has a strong masculine look, so it will be this fascinating contrast between him and his clothes. Can't you just picture him with a hot pink sash around his waist? We will incorporate that hot pink into every outfit!"

"I am...not sure how you have drawn this conclusion?" Maggie questioned as the food dropped in front of them.

"It's simple! The hot pink color represents Elvis, because everyone knows he was hot with the women. And the silver metallic will add that bling...that's Michael...eccentric!"

Maggie opened her mouth to talk, but found that no words were coming out. He sounded so ridiculous she did not even know where to start. Why was she even along? He had not asked her opinion once, just dictated his! Oh yes, she got to measure everyone like a freaking seamstress! She felt her blood starting to boil, but then remembered that this arrangement would at least allow her and Antonio to spend more time together. She put her fork down, contemplating the arrangements.

"What, no good?" Francis motioned for the waiter to come over, but she grabbed his hand down to the table and objected.

"No, Francis! It's not a big deal. I had a chocolate bar at the Art Institute, and I'm not even that hungry."

Francis took his fork and tried what she ordered.

"That's not bad! Why don't you like that, Maggie?"

She watched as he took a few more bites.

She took a deep breath, assuming their lunch date was almost over, when she thought that she smelled his cologne, a bit thicker than usual. She made a face and reached for her water. And as she was drinking, she caught the stare of the old lady once again, scrunching her brow down over her glasses. Maggie spit out her water. *That's Antonio!* Dressed in a blue vintage knit floral dress with white granny shoes, he also wore a wig and wire glasses, and obnoxious earrings from the fifties. A cane and white purse sat on the floor next to the table. Maggie stared back in a look she didn't know she possessed, while he seemed to know that she finally recognized him. Holding back her laughter, she excused herself to the ladies' room.

www.lovetheillusion.com/171.htm

The next thing she knew, Antonio had followed her into the ladies' room. She turned around, looking at him in a state of shock.

"Yeah Maggie, it's me…checking up on you two while you drink a four hundred and fifty dollar bottle of wine, share food, and I can smell his stench from where I'm sitting! Your date is done, NOW!"

How did he assemble his boobs? She wanted to grab one, but started laughing instead. "What are you doing here? You look hilarious!"

"Don't underestimate me as an old woman. I'm ready to clock that boss of yours if he even thinks of making any moves on you!"

"That's completely unnecessary, Antonio. I promise you have nothing to worry about."

"No Maggie, I will make my own decisions on that. Remember what I said? Your date is done."

"You're jealous of Francis? That is the dumbest piece of reality to hit my brain, ever!"

"Don't make me angry, Maggie, or I am going to kiss you in public right now."

She burst out laughing. "Go ahead, it would make my day." She winked at him before leaving to go back to the table.

"Are you alright?" Francis asked upon her return.

"Yes," Maggie assured him, "just caught a sneeze while I was trying to drink. Sorry!"

Francis remained clueless.

Now in the cab, on their way back to the hotel, Maggie tried to tie things up. "So, your ideas, once again, are mainstream genius, so we are pretty much done except for the measurements. And the sketches need to be drawn up. But you should just do that, since you know just what look you want."

"You have to help with the sketches. We can start tonight."

"That won't work. Cha—Antonio has a show tonight and he invited me and my family to come."

"You know, if I didn't know better, I would think the two of you look like you were in love, or some dumb thing."

"Why would you say that?" She laughed off his suggestion as completely absurd. "What does love look like, anyways?"

"How the bloody hell would I know?" Francis looked like he could care less.

"Well, then, there you go! I have to attend his show! He's our client and he's extended this invitation, and it would be completely rude for me to decline!" Maggie insisted.

"We will quick draw them up tomorrow before I leave. I want to have them ready when I get back since you are staying those two extra days," he concluded.

"That would work," she agreed.

"Eight a.m. sharp. And don't dawdle this time, Maggie."

Maggie stood with a tape measure, about to measure Antonio. He needed to help with the soundboard, so he went first. She held the tape measure at the top of his shoulder and ran it down to his wrist.

"So, on our next date are you going to be Miss Daisy, so we can eat out in public without recognition?" She enjoyed teasing him.

"Not a chance." He did not find the humor.

"How did you make those boobies of yours?" She thought he was funny.

"I will never tell." He passed her a grin.

As she wrapped the tape measure around his waist, a girl came up to him, standing in front of him, resting her hands on his shoulders. "Antonio, what are you going to be wearing? I'm sure whatever it is, you will look yummy!"

He let out a quiet laugh.

Maggie decided to tighten the tape measure three inches tighter than the mark.

"Maggie! Be nice! If you mess up my measurements, Francis is going to fire you. Then you'll have to dance on stage with me as one of my showgirls," Antonio warned.

"Me? Look at that girl with her giraffe legs and big boobs. Give me a break!"

"She's just a fill in for Angie, who sprained her ankle. She's gone after this weekend. Besides, she's not even twenty years old!" Antonio dismissed her concerns.

"Oh! So you picked her?"

"She's a good dancer!"

"Well, she's about a head taller than Amber, so that will completely mess up the horizontal presentation when she stands next to you and Amber on stage," Maggie analyzed.

"You sound jealous." He gave her a wink, returning the one she gave him earlier.

"Funny thing! You are losing your mind over me dating my grandfather. Meanwhile, you are busy watching the cradle."

"You know Maggie, your mouth is just always sassing!" he fussed, attempting to finish the conversation. Maggie held the top of the tape measure at his waist and brought it down to his heel, while he stared down at her, keeping her in check.

That evening, Maggie enjoyed dinner with her family, but Antonio called, unable to attend. Francis insisted that there were three more contract documents that he had to sign. He had not wanted photocopies. That way, everyone owned an original signed copy. Maggie hoped *that* was not cause for alarm.

Now she stood behind the stage with Chad, before he became Antonio. She watched people scurry about, and he took the time to tell her that he was so happy that she came. And right before she left to go to her seat, he whispered into her ear, "I can't wait to bring you up on stage and kiss you in front of everyone!"

"That's when I shall tell *everyone* your nickname is Chad!" she warned.

He never did what he threatened, but she felt a nervous wreck in anticipation. Did she feel stage fright? Or was she thinking about his first kiss? She knew she wanted his kiss.

Chapter 11

While Francis sat on a plane back to England, Maggie was on her way down to Antonio's room, anticipating the latest surprise date that he planned. She wore a thin dress blouse with jeans after suffering from "wardrobe malfunction" since Antonio extended her visit by two days.

"I think you might be cold in that." Antonio gave concern.

"No, it's been warmer, I'll be fine."

"No," he insisted. "You need this."

She watched as he went over to a wooden dresser, and pulled out a sweater, olive green in color, made of thin wool. He handed it to her and when she slipped it on, she saw that it hung way too low. *Fashion hazards, now magnified.*

"Chad! I promise I won't be cold!" she argued.

"Trust me, you will!" he insisted. She knew "Trust me" meant "Case closed, not up for discussion."

"Okay," she finally agreed. "But this sweater is so big, I look ridiculous!"

I hope nobody sees me.

They got into the limo, and Maggie shared additional concerns. "You know Chad, I'm not even sure how to tell you this, and don't be angry, but Francis has styled out a silver metallic outfit with a pink sash for you to wear in Vegas." She looked at him out of the corner of her eye to gauge his reaction.

"What? Me in pink? Who would have thought?" He did not seem worried.

"Yeah, well I told him 'no,' but you know him! He has his own visual agenda and half the time I don't even know why I'm there," Maggie enlightened him.

"Hmm... Well, think of it this way," Antonio informed her. "We have let him do what he does best—fashion. If he makes me look ridiculous up there on stage, his name will be right there with me. Don't you think he knows that? Talent-wise, I completely respect him. Personally? He's a..."

She waited to hear a compound expletive, but he finished with "maggot."

They both started laughing, relieved that Francis had left and was now on a plane heading back home.

Then Maggie expressed, "When Francis rambles, he is the worst! I had to sit by him on the plane, and well, you heard him at the meeting," she recalled. "He thinks everyone is listening and thinking how brilliant he is and all I can think is—pleeease stop! His continuous yakking is worse than any woman's!"

He laughed at her analogy, and then asked, "No chance of him standing on...you know...the other side?"

"Well, I highly doubt *that* after he slept with Elle, one of our models. That would mean he's pretty straight."

"Yeah, and it would mean that I'm pretty right about him." He kept her undivided attention as he explained, "He disgusts me the way he plants his eyes on you in all the wrong places. Seriously, Maggie! And you wonder why I lost my temper!"

"Don't worry. I know his kind, and I can take care of myself. I would not let him touch me with a ten foot pole!" Maggie assured him.

"And I would clobber him with one, if he did!"

Antonio placed his arm around her and Maggie was glad to be over the bumpy ride from when she first arrived.

"So, Chad..." Maggie inquired. "I need to ask you a personal question."

"You sound like a reporter, but shoot." He managed a grin.

"I just can't help but ask." She started laughing. "Were you wearing pantyhose?"

His voice became an imitation of an old woman. "Yeah, and my hearing aid, so I could listen in on his shenanigans. I'll tell you, I was ready to clobber him with my cane, pretending that I was just a helpless senile old lady who had the wrong guy. Then when I got hauled off either to a jail cell or to the psycho ward, I planned to call Bradley, and have Stanley post a check for my bail or release!"

Maggie spilled over in laughter. "Chad, you are so funny!"

"I know," he stated, accepting her praise.

"And you have *such* an ego."

She removed his arm from around her, but he warned, "Now you're going to get it!" He grabbed her hands, brought them over her head, leaned over her in the seat, and started tickling her, and just when she thought she couldn't take it anymore, he pulled from his pocket a set of keys, as if he just performed a magic trick. She stopped laughing as he leaned over her with the set of keys. He gave her a mysterious look, yet somewhat inviting, as if to challenge her to guess what he had planned. Her eyes grew wide as she wondered what he was up to and where they were going. She looked into his eyes and then onto his lips, still wishing he would kiss her and wondering why he hadn't. Now she looked back to the set of keys, waiting for him to announce what he had up his sleeve. But it was apparent that he enjoyed keeping her in the dark.

"Where are we going?" she finally asked, her eyes glazed over, wishing to be alone with him.

"These," he replied, holding up the keys, "are so that I can lock you up in a dark room, and see if you can resist my magical powers."

Maggie stared back at him, lost in his seduction.

"What if I couldn't?"

"That…is good to know," he concluded with the same grin he had on his face when they first met. "Actually," Antonio explained, completely changing the mood and moving off of her to sit back down, "Bob Adams owns the indoor hockey arena, and since it's off season, we're going there. I've got the keys. He's endorsing my Vegas show."

Maggie sat back up, shaking off her disappointment.

"Well don't you have connections!" She raised her brow, indicating she was impressed. "So, that's why I'm wearing your sweater? It will be cold?"

"You're so smart," he teased with a sarcastic look, to mimic hers.

"And you are…" she grabbed for words to put him in his place, "just a notch under what you think about Francis!" She placed her insult, elbowing him.

"That's mean. I have been a complete gentleman," he protested.

"Try your hot-headed temper!" she said, playfully.

"Okay, fine…so I have one weakness," he admitted, "but it's only when I'm trying to protect the people I…care about."

Her face softened at his words, and then she heard the driver announce, "Here we are!"

Antonio had her hand in his as they moved in a slow jog towards the building. It was daylight and she could see that there were no cars in the parking lot.

"This will be so much fun." He grinned as if he had a trick up his sleeve.

"Is this going to be as much fun as swimming?"

"Way better!"

They approached the door, using the keys to make entry. Once they got inside, they walked up to the ice arena. Maggie's eyes got big. "Wow! I can't believe it!" She paused. "But you know what? I have never skated in my entire life!"

"Oh! Then it will be even more fun!" He wore a devilish grin. "You know how you love swimming? Well I love skating!"

He motioned for her to follow him to a room where they kept the skates. Then he told her, "After we moved to the U.S., I got to play with the Blackhawks, here in Chicago. We won our division my second year."

She tried to keep her jaw from dropping, digesting his latest revelation. He stood proud, anticipating her response.

"You must be kidding!" she finally said. "So now we are racing?"

"I'm not that cruel and heartless." He wore a grin. "But you will have to watch me on my skates, and I am good!"

"You know I could almost kill you!"

He returned a gratified look.

"We need skates!" He removed several pairs from their cubbies and disassembled the laces before she had a second thought about how she was going to try skating for the first time.

"So how did you get into skating?" she asked.

"I always wanted to play hockey, ever since I was six years old. My mamma says 'No Antonio, you are going to get hurt!' She signed me up for ballet instead, saying, 'but I do need to keep you busy, because you are always finding trouble!' So, I get to my first ballet lesson and it is my worst nightmare—girls everywhere. I was the only boy. They chased me and I was so glad when the year was finally over, but mortified when I had to dance again the following year!" He let out a huff. "The instructor insisted that I had talent, but *I* figured they wanted a cute group photo and a splash in the choreography at the dance recitals." Maggie watched how quickly Antonio laced up his skates as he recalled, "Finally, Papa says 'Elisabetta! You must let him live out his dreams.' And my papa had the final word, and I was determined to make him proud."

"So when did you start performing magic?"

"That was always one of my hobbies as a kid. So I would get to do small stuff, you know, for elementary schools and the library. Eventually, I performed at the high school theater. I had a lot of gadgets and kits that I collected throughout the years and it became my true passion, even more than skating. My mamma was working for the mayor at the time and he set me up to get my big break. I had to choose—hockey or magic—and I chose magic."

"Are you glad you did?"

"Of course! There's nothing like it!"

"So your family came with you, from Italy, to watch you play hockey?"

"No, my papa...he had his own business making furniture. It never made us a lot of money, but one day, a couple businessmen from Treelines, a company in Chicago that also makes antique-looking furniture, were in my papa's shop in Italy. They stopped in on business, wanting him to be partners and move to Chicago. The money was good, so we got dual citizenship and then we moved. But when we got here, it was so expensive to live, and my mamma had to go to work. The mayor was looking for a part time nanny and happened to be friends with the guy that owned Treelines."

Antonio got up, having finished his story, and headed to the ice area. Maggie followed after him, when he stopped in his tracks and announced, "Wait! We need some music!"

"No, we don't." She laughed. "Now I am picturing myself slammed into the ice while listening to 'Here Comes the Sun!'"

When he returned, she could hear music as he stepped onto the ice. "I'll show you how to skate," he called out.

She waited for him to grab her hand, but he flew out around on the ice without her like there was no tomorrow.

She stood, placing her hands on her hips.

Antonio skated backwards, then forwards, and Maggie brought her hands up to her face as she watched him spin into a flip.

"I ought to trip you!" she yelled at him with her hands cupped to her mouth. "But I guess instead I'll just stand here and observe *the magic!*"

He skated up to her and asked, "What was that?" He poured on thick his endearing grin, but she rolled her eyes and moaned,

"Never mind!"

Then he grabbed her hand to lead her out onto the ice.

"Aren't you glad you have my sweater now?" he reminded her.

"Why? So I'm not cold while I sit on the bleachers and watch another one of your performances?" She frowned.

"No, Maggie! I'm going to teach you how to skate. I had to show off just a bit, so I look qualified." He gave her his sweet look.

"UH! Right! Just what you do best! Show off!"

He took her hands in his as he led her onto the ice. He skated backwards, as she skated forward. He looked into her eyes, revealing that he was fond of her, but she worried about falling and was unable to let him romance her into the moment.

Just about the time that she felt a bit at ease, he seemed to notice. And he decided to have some fun. He reached down and scooped her up, holding her in a cradle, and started to speed skate.

Maggie screamed out in hysteria, "CHAD! Put me down!"

But he did not put her down. Instead, he decided to have even more fun. He flung her over his shoulder and skated around in a circle. "Please, stop, and don't drop me!" She looked onto the ice from upside down, until he lifted her into the air before setting her back down on the ice in front of him, her heart racing in her chest. He held her steady, embracing her tightly against himself. "I'm getting mad at you, Antonio," Maggie informed, but he peered into her eyes, turning all of her fright and anger into a hopeless emotional frenzy of excitement. And he kept her safe on the ice, while keeping her in a steady view so that she did not fall.

"Are you having fun?" he finally asked.

"Yes," she stated meekly, smiling up at him.

"That's good to hear." He grinned, but she lost her smile as she had thoughts of leaving again. He must have read her mind and said, "We will be together again for the Vegas show." He passed her a smile as if everything would be okay, but she had trouble returning his smile.

Now, back in her room the following day, Maggie heard the flat screen blaring, after ordering room service—a late lunch.

"...AND LIVE FROM WLS NEWSROOM, WE HAVE BREAKING NEWS THAT JUST CAME IN A FEW MOMENTS AGO."

"THIS IS KATE BRANSON, LIVE, FROM THE HYATT REGENCY HOTEL, HERE IN CHICAGO. WE JUST RECEIVED INFORMATION THAT FRANCIS LOUIS HAS SIGNED PAPERS, AND EVERYTHING IS SET IN MOTION FOR HIM TO DESIGN FOR ANTONIO DELUCA'S UPCOMING SHOW IN VEGAS. SPECTATORS ARE ANTICIPATING THIS MERGE BETWEEN THE BEST OF THE BEST AS EACH PARTY WILL MOVE UP TO A HIGHER RANK COMMERCIALLY. BUYERS ARE GOING TO WANT TO PURCHASE MORE LINES FROM FRANCIS LOUIS, AND PEOPLE WILL BE LINED UP AS NEVER BEFORE TO SEE THE ALL AMAZING MAGICIAN, ANTONIO DELUCA, WHO NOW HAS PLANS TO EXTEND HIS PERFORMANCES TO EUROPE. ONCE AGAIN, THIS IS KATE BRANSON, FROM WLS NEWSROOM, HERE IN CHICAGO."

"THANK YOU KATE. THAT WAS KATE BRANSON REPORTING LIVE FROM THE CHICAGO HYATT REGENCY HOTEL WHERE THE FINAL PAPERWORK HAS BEEN SIGNED..."

"Make me sick," she whispered under her breath.

A knock on the door interrupted her thoughts. She opened up the door to see Antonio. He stood just outside the entrance and informed, "I just found out I have to be somewhere tonight, but maybe you could come."

"Where?" she asked.

"I have to attend a charity event."

"Oh? For what?"

"Matteo." His voice carried a trace of sadness.

"Okay," she acknowledged with concern.

"Do you have a dress?"

"No. Remember, I was spending the week with you and Francis!?"

Antonio wore a sweet smirk.

"I want you to come. I'll get you a dress."

"I can get one…There's a gift shop here."

"No, Maggie! There will be photographers there, people all dressed up, and I know just what you should wear."

She felt insulted, but suggested, "How 'bout we go together?"

"I think *that* will take too long. And I have to meet with Stanley. He is completely outraged at the contract I signed without him. So, I will pick one out at one of the specialty boutique shops and have it delivered to your room."

Maggie scrunched her brow up at Antonio, unsure of his plan. Antonio wore a look of confidence as if he should have earned her trust by now.

"Okay, fine," she finally agreed, closing the discussion.

"Trust me. I will get you something nice, and I will like to pick it out. All I need is your dress size."

"WHAT!" She gasped. "You can't ask a woman that!"

"Maggie, it's not a big deal."

He stared at her, humored by her embarrassment.

"Okay then. I wear a zero," Maggie announced. She watched Antonio press his lips together and shift his eyes off of her, indicating his doubt. "Fine then—a four," she admitted.

He smiled, captivating her with his invitation. "Meet me out front in the lobby entrance, at five. I will have Stanley show you to the limo."

Great! Maggie sat down on the bed. Now she felt trapped in her own hotel room, like a prisoner, waiting for some dress to arrive that she probably would not like. Why couldn't she go shopping? No, he had offered to shop for her. She turned the TV off, lay down on the bed and stared up at the ceiling. *This could be one of his best pranks yet! Maybe he is upset about wearing pink. How scary. He never even asked what "season" I am. Why did I agree to this?* She wondered what color he would pick for her. But worse than that was her mental picture of the paparazzi just flocking about shooting photos of Maggie White, assistant to none other than one of Europe's most enamored fashion designers, looking like she was hired only for reasons of perhaps being his sex slave.

Maggie watched the clock, letting out groans and grunts mimicking labor pains, extending her body to simulate. She lay on the bed until an hour passed, when she finally heard another knock on her door.

She shot off the bed to get the door, only to find a gentleman she had never seen before.

"Maggie White?"

"Yep, that's me."

"Here you go. This is for you."

Maggie grabbed the dress, and then closed the door. She forgot her usual response, "Thank you." She moved the dress quickly over to a hook sitting outside the bathroom door next to the mirror. Through the clear plastic bag, she saw that the dress was white.

"How appropriate," she spoke in a soft sarcastic tone, "a white dress for Maggie White." She proceeded to take it out of the bag. *This is the dress? It is a long, baggy mess! I may as well be going as a NUN! Why did he buy this ugly thing? Oh, yeah—I almost forgot his endearing sense of humor.* She read the price tag, declaring out loud, "Two thousand, five hundred, and seventy-five dollars for this piece of work? You have got to be joking!"

She took further notice, proclaiming her despair, "A LOUIS label…in big huge letters…from look, his latest line, the Euro Expo line." *Where should I be ill?*

As she touched the fabric, she recalled a recent debate between her and Francis about the stylization of this exact dress. "I think it should be short, just above the knee, but loose," she had suggested.

"No way," he had disagreed. "It's gotta' be long, sleek, classy, sophisticated—sexy, but not sleazy—like you got money dripping from the casino's safe." He had won, and there it was!

In haste, she disassembled the dress off the hanger and unfastened the back strap, attached to a brooch and rhinestones. She was horrified to even have to put it on. After removing the tissue paper that was wrapped around the neckline, she stepped into the dress. She scrunched her brow as she hastily struggled to fasten the back strap, and when it was secured, she shuffled over to the mirror.

Maggie stood in front of the mirror, wearing a frown that slowly disappeared. The dress draped along her curves in all the right places—*slimming, but not too tight.* The hemline finished onto the floor, draping with a slight train. She swallowed away her disappointment. *Francis was right.* The dress was stunning—a creamy white, the knit fabric raised in horizontal lines that followed in the center every three to four inches. The rounded neckline presented a contrast made of thin white feathers that provided straps, as crystals and pearls were streamed into the feathers. She ran her fingers across the details, admitting in a defeated whisper, "I can't believe I actually look good." But what would she do with her hair? She decided she had no choice but to stop at the hotel salon for a quick updo. She would look stunning, and elegant.

Maggie's hair stood atop her head in a ravishing loose curled expose, matching what could present on the cover of Vogue magazine. She picked up some round pearl earrings the size of small grapes to finish the look. Everything stacked up grand, until she went to put on her shoes. *Oh no!* She scoffed at her black loafers, but then saw the clock, realizing she had to go.

"Well," Maggie laughed to herself, "he will just have to drool on me from the ankles on up!"

No sooner did she step into the limo than Antonio noticed her feet and let out a small but serious chuckle. "Ohhh, looks like we need shoes."

Maggie was waiting to see what he would do, when he announced to his driver, "We gotta stop for shoes!"

"Are you going to pick those out too?" she asked sweetly, wishing he would.

"No. You can pick out your own shoes." Antonio gave her a frown. "Just don't let it take too long. And only one pair, we don't have *time* to gather a whole new collection." He reached in his back pocket as he caught her deliberate stare. "What? That boss of yours already has my creditors reaching for their calculators." With that he passed her his credit card and watched her get out of the limo, where the driver had just pulled up.

Maggie viewed the shoes displayed in the window before entering the boutique that specialized in formal strappy sandals. She held onto his credit card, which read "AD Enterprises," as she grabbed onto the long steel handlebar that attached to a glass door.

When she got inside, she soon felt enamored by all the shoe displays. *Another world of fashion!* She picked up an orange satin shoe with a big bow and a shiny gold heel, thinking how glamorous they were. She would love to wear them. Did they match the dress? *Maybe not quite, but..."*

"Can I try these in a six?" she asked a clerk.

www.lovetheillusion.com/187.htm

"Oh, I'm sorry, but I think we only have that one display left, and it's a size five," she heard the clerk announce the bad news. Maggie sighed, placing the shoe back on its display. There were so many choices, it was impossible to narrow it down to just one shoe.

Just when she started to get lost in the fashion world of shoes, she remembered Antonio sat in the limo waiting for her.

He's such a sweetheart.

"Do you have these in a six?" Maggie held up her next selection. The shoes had a five inch heel—a raised stiletto with a rounded open toe and glittery sparkles in flashy tones of silver and gold metallic.

www.lovetheillusion.com/188.htm

"Sure, we should have that one in a six. It just came in." The clerk took the shoe and disappeared into the storage room.

The clerk returned with a shiny pink and grey box. Maggie removed the shoes, slipped them on and stood by the mirror. They were perfect!

When she got back in the limo, Antonio sat, chin propped in hand as she handed him his credit card and receipt, and without looking at it he put it back into his pocket.

He glanced at her shoes.

"Maggie, I want to introduce you to my driver. He asked about you since he keeps driving us around."

Maggie wished she had heard the conversation when Antonio announced, "This is Salvador. He and I go way back. I did a show in Texas, two years ago, and we were driving around after my show and some lunatic on his motor bike is chasing us down. I thought we were going to die in a wreck. But Salvador says, 'Don't worry, I will get rid of him,' and the next thing I know, he's four lanes over, behind us, ten cars away. Such a scary maneuver, but after his turn on a squeal, we never saw him again. After that, we kept in contact, and when I decided to get a limo, I called up Salvador, and here he is now, working for me."

"Nice to meet you Salvador," she said with a smile.

Maggie felt over-the-top, a bit lavish, and somewhat guilty—riding limo-style—sitting in a dress and shoes that cost more than her first car. But she soon admired Antonio wearing a grey suit with a cream shirt the color of her dress, under a vest. She thought he looked amazing, and wondered who picked out his clothes.

When they arrived, several bodyguards assisted them out of the limo. Maggie felt uncomfortable inside their boundaries as they walked up the sidewalk until they stood in front of wooden double doors. She knew people were aware that Antonio had arrived. But once they got inside, the bodyguards disappeared, and she followed Antonio through the elevator doors to where the dinner was taking place. And as they stepped out of the elevator, she realized her hand was once again inside Antonio's.

www.lovetheillusion.com/189.htm

Maggie shined in her apparel as she stood next to a fountain punch bowl that sat on a glass table filled with hors d'oeuvres too numerous to count. She watched Antonio pour punch into two crystal cups. She recalled their escort of bodyguards and two security personnel as she heard the racket of fans when they stepped out of the limo. Some yelled out "Antonio," and others were whistling and simply making noise. She felt proud to accompany him.

When they arrived in the banquet room, it was a breathless sight with its archaic décor. She glanced up and noticed the antique black iron lighting fixtures that hung from the ceiling. The round tables were set with grey tablecloths, and the textured wallpaper stood out with its swirl design, a twenties style in cranberry and grey—antiquated and charming. As she absorbed her surroundings, she felt as though she had just stepped into a historical fairytale event.

Antonio broke her out of her daydream, motioning for her to follow him to the table to sit down and she thought that she could spend the rest of the night just looking at him. Now she thought again about what it would be like to kiss him, but she followed him to the table, feeling lucky just to be with him.

When they sat down at the table, Antonio caught her staring at him. He grinned, passing her a sweet look, staring into her eyes and leaving her wondering what he was thinking.

She leaned over and whispered in his ear, "Thanks for bringing me."

He smiled intimately at her until their attention was directed to the podium, where she saw a gentleman repositioning the microphone.

"I would like to welcome all of you ladies and gentlemen here tonight. I am Dr. Adam Jennings, president of Children's Hospital research, here in the outlying areas of suburban Chicago. We are pleased to announce that we have with us scientist and professor Richard Sterling, who will be talking about his latest research and development. But for now, we are pleased to introduce Antonio DeLuca, whom you all know as one of the best showmen ever. He is here to share some thoughts with us on Menkes, a rare but serious childhood disease."

Maggie watched as he got up from the table and made his way to the front. She contemplated her own stage fright and discomfort speaking in front of groups. But he did not seem a bit nervous in the spotlight.

Antonio stood behind the podium as people were clapping and whistling. He respectfully waited for it to quiet down. He held a serious look as he faced the audience, and Maggie discreetly shifted her eyes to capture those to whom he was about to speak. Once it got quiet, he began to speak. "Menkes disease, MNK, also known as Menkes Syndrome or Copper Transport Disease, is not one that a lot of people have probably heard of. It is a disorder that affects copper levels in the body, leading to copper deficiency. It is an X-linked recessive disorder, and therefore more common in males than females. That's all it is, until this disorder affects someone you know and love. For me, it was my brother, Matteo. He was the brother that I always wanted. And when he was finally born, even though we were so many years apart, we formed a friendship and bond unlike any other. He taught me more than I ever taught him as I watched him suffer like I had never seen anyone suffer before. By the time we found out what was wrong, it was too late. Bills were piled up, but that was the least of our concerns as we traveled from doctor to hospital in search of a positive outcome. He died when he was only six." Antonio looked down as he recalled his brother, while bracing himself on the lectern from which he spoke. Moments passed before he continued. "I am here tonight, once again, to make a difference for families that are going down the same rough road that me and my family once traveled. As for Matteo, he will always be in my heart. Thank you."

Maggie watched as Dr. Adam Jennings came back over to the microphone and Antonio stepped aside. "Thank you, Antonio. Your contribution is an enormous help to all the families that cannot afford a tragedy of illness to affect their loved one. Your generosity is greatly appreciated. And tonight, I would like to present Antonio with a plaque to recognize his donation of 500,000 dollars. We would like to thank him for remembering our cause with continued generosity."

Antonio returned to his position behind the microphone and people started clapping, screaming and whistling. He waited for everyone to quiet down and then spoke into the microphone. "Thank you very much. This, as I have mentioned before, is not about my money, it is about helping these families. They have a lot of expenses, and I think if we can at least alleviate the financial burden of the doctor's bills and hospital stays, they can focus on their children." He gave a quick but warm smile and returned to his seat.

"That was sweet," Maggie whispered.

Antonio's face was somber as he expressed, "I will always be in debt to Matteo."

Maggie thought about his words and then offered, "We are always in debt to the people we love."

He held her hand under the table while a group of five different families began to give an account of their own personal story. Maggie tried holding back the tears, as she understood first-hand what it felt like to lose someone you love. She remembered her mother and the handkerchief Julia shared.

The sit-down dinner arrived, made by a well-known chef. A full course meal—bread, soup, salad, and sirloin tips and gravy sauce with orzo and carrots and asparagus done up in a fancy duo. And French silk pie for dessert. Maggie drank a glass of red wine, Antonio's suggestion, and they ate while listening to Dr. Adam Jennings and Scientist Richard Sterling give a presentation about how they were working together to fight this disease.

Following dinner, the upstairs ballroom called for the attendants to participate in dancing the night away. A wooden staircase followed in a semi-circle up to a balcony hosting a lavish bar preceding the entrance into the ballroom.

Maggie held on to Antonio's arm as she took each step carefully in her sparkly stilettos. She gazed over the open balcony, supported by a thick iron stair rail. The ambiance radiated beautifully and elegantly, and Maggie stood breathless taking in the view.

"Do you want to stay?" Antonio asked.

"Of course," she said, wishing to dance with him again.

"Good, did you want anything from the bar?"

"Sure, you pick," she decided, wearing a flirtatious smile.

"So, that's one kiddy cocktail coming right—"

She elbowed him to dismiss his suggestion.

"Never mind, a Brandy Alexander," she decided.

Maggie stood, holding her drink in hand, when she heard the DJ announce a jazz dance to an old song from a 1930s big band.

"Do you want to dance?" Antonio waited for her response.

"I do," Maggie admitted, realizing there was no longer any strength left in her to fight off her feelings for him. She hoped she would never live with regret. He seemed almost too good to be true, and every time she was with him, it was magical.

www.lovetheillusion.com/193.htm

A slow song played next. Maggie leaned into Antonio as he kept them in rhythm. She wanted to stay in his arms forever. She remembered dancing with him at the Night Owl. Now she knew him better. And the more she knew him, the more he captured her heart. She leaned against his chest, closed her eyes, and dreamed of sleeping next to him.

www.lovetheillusion.com/194.htm

She looked up at him and into his eyes, wanting his kiss. He grinned, able to read her mind, but instead shifted his eyes around the room indicating they were in the eye of the public. Maggie placed her head back onto his shoulder, glad just to be with him. She closed her eyes, treasuring her time with him and hating the thought of leaving again. She dared to imagine his kiss. But then she heard a snap and saw a flash, from beneath her closed eyelids. She immediately looked up at Antonio, who lowered his head to hear what she wanted to say.

"Antonio, I think someone just took a picture of us."

She felt his lips brush against her cheek and then he whispered in her ear, "Don't you want to take pictures with me?"

Her eyes spun around, unable to find the guilty photographer. She hopelessly put her head against his shoulder and closed her eyes again.

It had been a somber event, but nonetheless, she did not want the evening to end. She thought back to her recent trip into the ladies' room, where she received a compliment on her dress. She knew Francis created the show-stopping design, but she felt even more defeated after concerning over Antonio's selection.

Once again, he pulled through, in shining colors.

When they left the event, they were escorted out by three security personnel. Once in the limo, Maggie sat down next to Antonio, glad to be away from the crowd. She leaned against him and he placed his arm around her. And on their way back to the hotel, he shared his thoughts with her. He loved the city of Chicago, but recalled the sad event; Matteo had died there.

Maggie woke up to the gut-wrenching feeling of once again leaving Antonio. Her plane would be leaving that afternoon. She recalled his words the past night when he told her to stop by his room before she left.

Now, nothing compared to the empty space that would be there when she tried to live the next four months without him. Dressed in black pants and a black lace sweater, she picked up her silver heart locket and placed it around her neck. The photos inside held a memory of her mother and father, one on each side. Her father gave her the locket when her mother died. She opened the locket to view them, recalling the one man in her life, longstanding, that was of noble character. However, now remarried, he took care of his new family. Maggie found the situation devastating, but tried not to indicate her feelings when they got together for the holidays. He now lived in Washington State, and she did not see him often. But she loved him, cherishing her fond memories of when he used to chase her around the house just to tickle her and tell her that she was his favorite daughter. His affection would even make her brothers jealous. He would always buy her dresses, and as Maggie put the dress that Antonio bought her into her suitcase, she remembered her father. He would always say, "That's my Maggie!"

Chapter 12

Antonio held onto a red rose as he stood in front of Maggie. They stood in the far end of his room, where the wall displayed a flat screen TV. She hated the fact that she had to leave. She nervously skimmed over a pile of books, precisely placed in a stack, next to the TV. His donation plaque from the charity benefit was next to the books, and she recalled their evening together. And as she did, he held the red rose up to her face. Maggie immediately thought of losing her mother, as she contemplated losing him.

"This is for you," he said gently, "one rose, one love—the most beautiful thing in the whole world—but you have to be careful how you hold on to it, or you can get hurt." He moved closer to her face and she felt herself melting like a stick of butter over a fire. She thought she felt dizzy. "I have something else for you," she heard him say.

Maggie held on to the rose and noticed the thorns were trimmed away. She watched him reach into an end table drawer next to the couch, where a llama hair afghan lay neatly folded over one end. He pulled out a book. It was obvious what it was underneath the professional gift wrap—silver and gold matte paper, sealed with a gold shiny decorative bow to match.

"I hope you like it," he said as she took it from his hands. He held the rose for her while she opened the package. He breathed in its fragrance as he watched her open the gift. "It's the sequel to your novel," he explained.

"Thanks," she said after opening it. "I like it."

"I read the first one and it's pretty good," he told her.

"You did not!"

"I did! It was good. I couldn't stop reading."

"Well, I thought it was kind of depressing. I haven't finished it yet."

"No, Maggie! You have to read it to the end. It has a surprise ending. You will love it."

"Okay. I promise I will finish the first one, and then I will read this one." She held it up in the air to seal her promise.

"One more thing," he warned. "Please don't read the tabloids. Trust me. It won't be good for us."

Maggie observed him, wondering what to think of his latest suggestion, when he reached out and pulled her into a hug. She closed her eyes and wished she did not have to leave, as he held her in a tight grip. She loved how he felt. She breathed him in, thinking she could smell a light trace of his cologne. And she still wondered why he still had not tried to kiss her. Would she leave again without his kiss? Her curiosity grew until she finally gazed into his eyes. And although physically close to him, she felt emotionally distant from him.

"Antonio?"

"Yes?" He gave her a sweet look.

Maggie paused, hesitating, but then she surrendered her will. "Do you ever think...that you..." She suddenly came to her senses. "Never mind."

"What?" Antonio seemed to be able to read her mind.

"Nothing." She let out a breath, feeling frustrated.

"You can say..." Antonio looked curious.

She looked up at him, feeling uncomfortable, wondering why she should even have to ask such a question. But she thought about stepping on the plane and the thought of missing him sent her words rushing to her lips, ready to reveal her mind's desire.

"Why won't you kiss me?"

She swallowed, trying to remove the lump in her throat. Silence followed, all the nerves in her body shifting in disarray.

Finally he spoke. "I thought you'd never ask." He gave her a mysterious look.

"What...?" Maggie questioned him, confused. "Why would you wait for me to ask—don't you know...?"

"I have my secret agenda." He raised his brow.

"What's that...*Chad*...to make me crazy?" Maggie frowned.

"To seal your fate...with my kiss," Antonio said with a serious look. He stared into her eyes and then on her lips, until she blushed.

"And what will my fate be?" Maggie disrupted his gaze.

Antonio, still wearing a serious look, affirmed, "That once I kiss you, you'll never want any other man's kiss."

Maggie considered his suggestion, and worried that he spoke the truth. She realized how quickly she forgot Phillip, but feared she could never get over Antonio should their affair come to an end. She stood wrapped in his arms, his words still trailing an echo in her heart, when he whispered in her ear, "So, what are my chances?"

She felt his lips next to her ear. She bit her bottom lip, daring to look up at him. His eyes were waiting for hers, as he waited for her response. She took a deep breath and then let it out, along with her decision. "I will take the risk."

Antonio wore a slight grin. "Then kiss me, Maggie."

Maggie felt every nerve in her body standing on end as she studied his lips, drawn to his proposal. She knew she had to leave again, and the thought of it made her stomach tighten into a knot. She already missed him. The door stood in view and she thought perhaps she should just leave. But she fell captive to Antonio's eyes pulling her back to his intimate stare. Still in his arms, she felt safe. But soon she would be miles away. She looked at the door again, but his eyes stayed fastened on hers. She looked back up at Antonio, who seemed puzzled by her will power. To her surprise, he grabbed her under her legs, scooping her into a cradle, and carried her over to his bed where he left her laying, looking up at him. She watched as he came down on top of her, his arms on either side of her cushioning his weight. His face close to hers, he stared into her eyes and professed, "Love is worth waiting for." At his words, she closed her eyes. And then she felt his kiss.

www.lovetheillusion.com/198.htm

She reached her hands into his hair. Lost in their passion, she kissed him back realizing that it was sweeter than she ever imagined. And for a moment, she forgot that she was leaving.

She stood at the door, wanting more, but knowing she had to leave, or she would miss her flight. Antonio leaned over, cupping her face in his hands, and kissed her lips one more time. Afterwards, he placed his business card in her hand, but the main number was crossed off, and replaced with his private cell phone number. She turned the card over, and saw that he marked it with an "XO." She placed it into the book he gave her.

"I still have your address. I am sending you something," he told her.

"What is it?"

"Well if I told you, it wouldn't be a surprise." Antonio smiled.

Maggie put her hand on the door, wishing to kiss him one more time. But sanity won out. She knew better and instead simply gazed back at him, hoping to imprint his face in her memory. She heard him speak, slowly, "Goodbye, Maggie," as she stepped outside his door and once again out of his world. Her eyes turned watery, and her vision became misty, but she shook it off, trying to be strong. At least this time, she knew that they would see each other again. And she would take with her, at last, his kiss.

As Maggie sat on the plane, she recalled her last plane ride home, remembering her friend Julia and how they had comforted each other in their sadness. She wondered where Julia was. This time there was no one sitting next to her, and she did not miss Francis. She would never tell him that she felt like a princess in his formal evening dress. Nor would she tell him about her feelings for Antonio. Maggie's mind flipped through the last four days of events, like a photo album of memories she treasured more than any other.

www.lovetheillusion.com/199.htm

Maggie soon fell asleep, and did not awake until she heard the stewardess announce, "Ladies and gentlemen, please fasten your seatbelts, as we are now preparing for landing at the London Heathrow airport. It is half past seven in the morning, London time, and we have temperatures of 20 degrees Celsius. Thank you for joining us on this flight. We hope you have a great day."

She felt the plane drop to the next level of airspace and held onto the rose that Antonio gave her. She brought it to her face, inhaled its fragrance, and wished that she still stood in his arms. She reached into her coat pocket for her passport, and there it was...the handkerchief that Julia had given her.

An hour later, she was home.

"Maggie! How are you? You look good, better than last time." Dana stood in the kitchen, making tea.

"You'll never believe how much fun I had. I'm going back in the fall. Antonio signed the papers, and now we're designing all of their costumes."

"You two are still an item?"

"Yes! And he's amazing."

Dana followed her into the lounge.

"Now you are going to tell me all about it!" Dana sat down, sipping her tea.

"I've never gone out with anyone like him, ever. And I have never felt like this before, either, but now it will be four months until I see him again, and I think I'm going to die."

"You are not serious! Now I'm worried about you. You've never gone out with anyone like him because you've never dated a celebrity before! And now you have a totally fictitious idea."

Maggie sat in disbelief while Dana explained, "He knows just how to play you, and you're going to get hurt. Think about it! How can you not see him for four months? You are better off with Jeff Briggs, the photographer you dated at work. At least you will see him. Of all the people I know, you are the least likely to be overcome by something so...so...fleeting! It's so...infeasible...and...totally delusional."

Maggie was surprised and discouraged by Dana's reaction.

"That's mean Dana. You don't want me to be happy?"

"Happy? Men like him are good only for a one-night stand. You sleep with them, and then you move on. And believe me, so do they. You are headed for complete devastation. Think about it! This is something I would do—have fun and screw a rock star. Did I tell you, you are not like me? You are sensible, cautious, always trying to do the right thing, waiting to go to bed once you are wed. Meanwhile, Phillip can't even stand to wait, and has it going on with your friend, Jasmine!"

"I do not need you to dig up my life's dirt. But since you did, why should I give up hope of finding someone that is not a beastly idiot? I know. I'm here. He's there. He's famous. I'm nobody. We live in two different worlds, geographically and psychologically. He lives for shock and surprise, and I live for consistency and non-adventure. But when I am with him, I completely forget everything I just said. He is like this powerful force, just pulling me in, and I can't resist him if I try."

"Right, you will do as you wish, but now that he has slept with you, he will move on. That's how men are. They entangle you in their web, leaving you stuck in a mess—and not in a good way, like Spiderman. Now I do not want to see you hurt again, alright?"

Maggie just stared at Dana. As much as she loved her, she could hate her too.

"Well thanks, Dana, for all the advice, but for your information, he is a gentleman and I never slept with him!" Maggie proclaimed loudly as she got off the chair to leave their discussion.

"Sorry," Dana apologized with a face of confusion. "I didn't mean to be so negative. And just to prove it, I've been keeping a secret from you."

Maggie stood perplexed, staring at Dana.

Dana reached behind the chair and threw a wad of fabric at her. It was the t-shirt Antonio had given Maggie.

"There you are," Dana said. "See! I took it out of the bin, after you buried it in the rubbish— 'To Maggie, Love Chad.' Who is *Chad*?"

"Dana," Maggie explained, "Chad is his nickname. I liked him before I knew who he was."

"Right, now that you do, you must just want his baby," Dana stated.

"You are such a weirdo. Some days, if it wasn't for your sense of humor, I would just roll over in my mud bath and die. But, seriously, we really need to be talking less about my love life and more about…your wedding! Have you been keeping yourself busy, other than your time spent in the dustbin?"

"I've picked out the flowers, wedding invitations, and centerpieces. I still need small things, like the wedding registry, thank you cards…and my *wedding dress*, Maggie! Did I tell you that you better get busy?"

"I know. Don't worry. I will design you something wonderful, that makes you feel like a princess!"

"Now I do not want anything with lots of lace or beads. And princess? Not me. I want something romantic and flowing but not too much detail…"

Maggie pictured her requests. "We can do that."

They stayed up until two that morning and drew out dress designs for Dana's wedding dress. Eventually, Maggie could barely sit up straight, she was so tired. But before she went to sleep, she put on Antonio's t-shirt.

…She was in the limo with Antonio. They had just left the benefit event, and she was so tired. She was leaned against him, and he had his arm around her while Salvador called out, "It's a chase, hold on tight," and the next thing she knew she was on the floor of the limo, on top of Antonio. They stared into each other's eyes until she proceeded to get up, but he held her down and whispered, "Shh, it's the paparazzi! Stay down!" The next thing she knew, she was face to face with Francis Louis who was screaming at her, "Maggie, what are you doing in that dress?"

Maggie sat up in her bed. *It was just a dream.*

At work the next day, Maggie sat at her desk in her cubicle where she had Francis in perfect view. He was wide awake and alert as always. Feeling on the contrary, she wondered how many cups of coffee she would need to make it through the day. She recalled Francis' first words to her that morning, which were also his greeting: "Late night, Maggie?" *How did he know?*

www.lovetheillusion.com/202.htm

And then he began one of his nightmarish explanations of everything they had to do.

The fabric swatches had already been sent and now shipments of gems, sequins, beading and glitter were all headed their way by tomorrow. Francis put Maggie in charge of organizing the swatches to go with each of their drawings so that everything would be ready for production by no later than—you guessed it—the end of the week!

Maggie eyed up his coffee and cigarette, and slowly stood, bracing herself on her desktop, thinking she needed to drink more coffee herself.

"No cream and sugar, Maggie. We are all out. Grace is out with the flu, so when she gets back, I will have her get some," Francis announced. Grace was the secretary. Theo was the bookkeeper. Jeff was the photographer. Matt was general manager, which included everything under the sun, from helping with the soundboard at the fashion shows to contacts with the buyers. He was account manager for all the buyers, so he traveled a lot. Sally was assistant coordinator, having the most contact with the models—unless Francis decided to sleep with one. He ran a tight ship, and they all just loved the boat rides.

The workday dragged on for Maggie. She had visions of Antonio the entire day, as the rose sat on her desk. She remembered dancing with him, and when he finally kissed her. She closed her eyes, reliving the moment and letting her memory reveal to her heart that surely he had sealed her fate long before his kiss. And she could not wait to kiss him again. But she now feared as he held her heart in his hands. *Hopefully, he does not let go.* She would be devastated if he ever moved on. Now she stood once again in the flames of love, dreading getting burned. Soon Dana's words of warning rushed back, alarming her senses. Her mind reached into her soul to protect her heart, but it was too late. She soon faced the fearful question beckoning the truth to be told, and she felt her heart breaking at the words that calculated into her brain: *Will it last?*

When the day finally came to an end, it did so with a grand entrance from Jeff Briggs, the photographer. Maggie broke free from the prison of her own thoughts when she heard Francis say, "It's about time," after he finally got the photos from the latest fashion show. Jeff was good at what he did, when he did it. She thought he was one of the biggest procrastinators to hit the planet, and that annoyed Francis to an extreme degree.

"Look! It's little Maggie, back from her big weekend in Chicago with her famileeeee!" Jeff sneered as he did a little bump with his hip to hit hers, as she stood next to the coffee pot. "Hey, while you were gone, I was out at Nikki's Night Club, just doing my thing and this total babe comes up to me and she's wearing a see through blouse and a mini skirt and I'm thinking, 'Dang! I want to get my hands on that!' So, we're talking, and next thing I know, we end up at my place and I told her that she could be next on the list if we need a new model. Hear that, Louis?"

"So happy for you, Jeff," Maggie reprimanded, "but you know, it takes more than that to be a model."

"Maggie!" he countered, "You are such a booty call...killer! Lighten up, and don't be such a cynic."

And like a breath of fresh air, an email had arrived in her mailbox to brighten her mood. It was from Antonio. Francis had left Antonio with both of their emails, and Maggie was glad they could now keep in touch even at work. She opened it up to read: **"I miss you already!"** Her face glowed as she emailed back: **"Me too."**

The weeks passed slow enough. Francis invited her to dinner after work one night, but she declined, claiming she had out-of-town company—*a lie, but a white one to avoid Francis.*

Finally, the package that Antonio had promised arrived. She opened it to find a photo of the two of them dancing at the benefit. She recalled the pleasant memory as she placed it in a frame, setting it on her bedroom dresser. She also treasured a small stack of emails from Antonio that she had saved over the past weeks, printed and now kept in her lingerie drawer. They were always short but sweet, anything from... "Sweetheart, how are you?" to "Make sure Francis is behaving!" And the last one said: **"You were beautiful at the benefit."**

Tonight, Maggie and Dana were nestled on the sofa with their jammies and slippers, watching a movie. Maggie felt her head beginning to nod, but Dana's voice cut in.

"I'm sorry, but can I just stop the film for a second?"

"What?" Maggie sat up, turning her attention to Dana, realizing that she had started to fall asleep. "Sure."

"Did I tell you that I am angry at Shane? We are saving for the wedding, right? And I really don't have a problem with that. It's not like I have to go out every night or anything, but tonight there was that concert, you know, Gray Doll was in town. So a month ago, I tell Shane that we should go, but no! We are saving for the wedding! I'm okay with that, because when we had looked for tickets, they were like 125 pounds, and that wasn't even for good seats. Then, there are the processing fees and all that."

Maggie waited patiently for her to get to the point.

"Did I tell you how he spent the day?" Dana complained. "I am at work, changing people's bedpans, and he is out at Green Rivers Golf Course with three of his mates, right, that is over a hundred pounds! And if that is not enough, they are plastered at the pub afterwards! How much did that cost?"

"Sounds like you better handle the finances, once you are married," Maggie teased.

"You are right about that!" Dana said, irritated. "I saved seven thousand pounds, and did he even bother? He has nothing."

"That is not good," Maggie agreed, acknowledging Dana's concerns. But then Dana changed the subject, leading Maggie to a few of her own.

"Did I tell you, what I saw in the Report News? It came in the post with your photo from Antonio, but I did *not* want to ruin your day."

Maggie sat up, completely alert, as Dana revealed, "You're in another photo with Antonio! Only this time, you're having his baby."

"What!!??" Maggie shrieked. "Where is this imported news trash that you always have to read?"

"It's under the bed. I will go to get it." Dana bounced off her chair. Maggie followed behind Dana, who headed off to her bedroom.

Dana reached down, picked up the magazine and handed it to her. "This is what I'm talking about!" she said with her eyebrows curled.

Maggie stared in disbelief. Sure enough, that was a picture of her and Antonio...a picture of them running... "Where in the...world was that taken?" Maggie could not believe what she saw. She looked at the photo again, recognizing Antonio's sweater he lent her. "Oh, my—it's us on the way into the ice skating rink!" She remembered they were holding hands and running in a slow jog. "Oh no," Maggie squawked, as she read the caption.

"ANTONIO DELUCA HAS BEEN REPORTEDLY SEEN ON SEVERAL OCCASIONS WITH MAGGIE WHITE, A PARTNER WITH FRANCIS LOUIS IN FASHION DESIGN. THE COUPLE REPORTEDLY ATTENDED A CHARITY BENEFIT TOGETHER AND SHE CAME TO SEE HIM AT HIS CHICAGO SHOW. SOURCES SAY..."

www.lovetheillusion.com/206.htm

Maggie sank into Dana's bed, speechless.

"Maggie, what's up with that? I mean, you actually look sort of pregnant in that photo!"

"Don't be foolish! Of course I'm not! I knew it was a mistake to wear that...that sweater of his, baggy and loose on me..." Maggie picked up the magazine and read it again, and again.

"Well, you don't have to torture yourself with it, Maggie," Dana commiserated. "If it's not true, then it's not true. Just tell me one thing, and we'll let it go. What in the world is it like to make love to Antonio DeLuca?"

Maggie's jaw dropped in response to Dana.

"Are you joking? I haven't slept with him. I already told you that!" Maggie explained.

Dana looked as if she had just watched the London Bridge collapse. "Right, you do not want to tell me!"

"I am telling you the truth! He is a gentleman."

"Ah, there's no such thing!" Dana alarmed. "You tell him 'No' like you're proud Mary?"

Maggie silently absorbed Dana's assumptions, while Dana shook her head, confused. "I got to sort things out. He lives his life in swarms of women and you come along and he just leaves them behind?"

Maggie was eager to explain. "I have spent a lot of time with him, and I never get the impression that he chases women."

"But they are chasing him, right? What does he do with them all?" Dana lowered her voice to personify Antonio. "Hey, ladies, you look all so irresistible, but I just can't choose, so I must go..." Dana continued, laughing hysterically, "I think I've got it! You know how they got that Viagra stuff?" *What is she talking about?* "Right, instead of *that*, he takes something that, you know, has the opposite effect sort of thing. Being a celebrity, he must have available what we never heard of! Now he does not have to worry about STDs, paying child maintenance, or—"

"I'm tired Dana. I'm going to bed."

Maggie got up and left the room, but Dana followed after her.

"Sorry Maggie, I was completely insensitive. I do hope it works for you, really, I do."

The next few days, Maggie found herself thinking more about the photo in Report News than the rose he had given her. It had died, and it was no longer in view. She tried to busy herself and run an extra mile every couple days to release her frustration that had mounted into negative energy, but the separation was getting to her.

In his last email, he told her not to worry if she did not hear from him in a while, because he would be gone in Sweden and performing there for the first time.

As the weeks passed, Maggie felt less connected to him than she did when she first returned. She had vivid memories of their time together, but it lingered as a past event, and the present was overwhelming. She missed him incredibly, and tried desperately to recall the details of his face—his dark eyes that drew her in and his smile that stopped her world but made her spin.

Dana's latest stunt was placing a fan poster in Maggie's room, after Maggie had returned from dinner with Francis. *Yes, that was a mistake, but he was very persistent.* As for the poster, she did not relate to Antonio that way. Maggie viewed the poster, feeling even more distant from him. *I miss you, Antonio.*

www.lovetheillusion.com/208.htm

Maggie left for work the next morning, and the air was crisp, like an early fall was in the air. She breathed it in, thinking that in only six weeks she would finally see him in Vegas. But that night, something would happen that would make her reconsider.

She already felt disconnected from him, and wished he would at least call during his time away in Sweden. He did not seem like one that would engage in lengthy chit chats over the phone, but even a "Hi, how are you doing?" could sustain her. He had been busy doing his show in Canada, and then Sweden, and now the latest news—in her own England's People's Express—was that he had plans to come to the UK soon. Tickets would be on sale in a week. She thought it strange. Would he try to see her if he came? She did not know how he could consider this, without including her in the excitement. The rumor was that after performing in Sweden, he would then come to the UK to perform before he took a break in Italy with his family, until the Vegas show.

That evening became the worst. Maggie arrived home early because Francis decided to leave the office early for the first time ever. As a result, so did the entire office staff. Dana had left with Shane that night, but one of her Report News issues arrived in the mail. There it was, sitting on the table in the kitchen. It was dated for August and on the cover was the alarming discovery that Antonio had made the news again! This time however, she was not in the picture with him. Instead, it was a blonde with a blue streak in her hair. They stood facing each other, outside a theater. He was smiling, and she was handing him something. *This is the worst nightmare!* Maggie looked down to read the caption: CANADIAN SINGER BRANDI JETTS DOES CONCERT IN CANADA; GIVES ANTONIO...

www.lovetheillusion.com/209.htm

Maggie was beside herself. *How can this be? She* remembered Antonio's warning not to read the tabloids. She looked at the photo once again. He appeared happy. She could not see Brandi's face, but the photo was intimidating enough. *What was he doing with her? Is she another friend? Like Arianna?*

Miles away, Maggie felt frustrated. She had not heard from him in days, and knew he was busy in Sweden now, with his first show there. *If only he wasn't famous, with all the women chasing after him.* But that was just one more of the intriguing pieces of his puzzle. She felt lucky to have his attention for so many reasons, and now her thoughts tried to wrap around why he remained interested in her. She was nobody. What was the fascination? He liked the challenge of her running from his pursuit? Surely he could date a lot of women. Her feelings for him were overwhelming and lingered at no control of her own. But could she trust him? He always spoke the words she wanted to hear, but so had Phillip. Was she being blindsided once again?

Maggie's mind became overcrowded with fearful thoughts that swarmed around, chasing her sanity. Her heart was no longer listening to her head—*problem number one!* Dana had already signaled a warning and perhaps she was just a fool. She reached no resolution other than that she would finally have to call him to announce her latest observation. Up until now, she had chosen to wait for his emails, even though she had his number. She did not want to be on the list of those chasing him. She felt intimidated enough, and preferred that he make all the moves, showing he still cared. Now she hated to call about *this*, but she needed answers, now! And it would be the first time she heard his voice since she had left Chicago.

Maggie had her phone to her ear, while her stomach flooded with anxiety. Then she heard his voice.

"Hi Maggie, you finally decided to call me!"

"Hi…Antonio." She hesitated.

"You know Maggie, you can call me Chad. In fact, I'd prefer it."

"That is the least of my worries," she began. She paused, choosing her words carefully. There would be no easy way. "I hate to ask you about this, but there is some tabloid saying that you went to some Canadian singer's room, and do you want to explain that to me, because the photo just makes me ill!" There was a long pause, and Maggie wondered if he was even on the phone anymore. "Chad!" she yelled into the phone.

"Maggie," he spoke in a completely calm voice, "why would you even ask me that? What have I ever done to you that you would even think that? I told you not to read the tabloids. Don't you trust me?"

Maggie retraced his words, wondering if he satisfied her curiosity. She decided, pretty sure, he had not! She saw the photo and there he was! *A skanky bimbo, right there next to him, looking all fresh.* "Maggie, are you still there?" She heard Antonio question her. "How can we have a relationship if you do not trust me?"

"I should know better and assume you are just as all the other men in my life—a liar!"

"No, Maggie, don't say that."

"Well, I cannot take this distance thing anymore. Next time, in Vegas, strictly business, that's it!"

Maggie heard silence and then the phone went dead. "UUGGH!"

Just then Dana came in the door with Shane.

Maggie brought herself to composure.

"Hey, you two, what's up?"

"You will never believe, I won our last argument," Dana bragged. "So tonight, we are going to see a film. No more golf for a while."

Maggie laughed at their trivial difficulties, which paled in comparison to hers.

"Hey Maggie, you should come with us," Shane offered. "Tyler is coming, one of my co-workers. He just got dumped by his lady friend, so I told him we would stop in and get you!"

Maggie was caught off guard.

"Sure, why not," she decided, as she mentally steamed out her dilemma.

I need to forget Antonio.

When she got in the back of their car, the first thing Maggie noticed was his blonde hair and baby blue eyes. He was cute. They talked on the way to the movie, and she thought he seemed nice.

At the movie, he held her hand after she jumped during a scary part. Dana and Shane were lost in their own relationship, which created a somewhat uncomfortable environment. Halfway through the movie, Maggie felt depressed, remembering her feelings for Antonio.

"Be right back," she whispered to Tyler.

When Dana saw her leave, she decided to follow.

Maggie entered the bathroom, and after keeping steps ahead of Dana, entered a stall. But then she heard Dana's drill.

"Maggie, you do not like him? Shane says he is nice—nicer than Jeff, if you know what I mean!"

"He's fine, Dana. I have a completely different issue."

"Go on then."

"Antonio made the front page of Report News, *again*—only not with me—some slutty Canadian singer that gave him her room key!"

Dana stood in shock outside the stall.

"I am afraid I did not see that one yet. Maggie, you have got to let him go! You will go *nuts* dating a celebrity. Look at Elizabeth Taylor. She had eight, or was it nine, husbands. You will never know for sure if he is committed, right? Listen to me!" Dana spilled out contempt.

"I know. You're right. But I ought to just call him up one last time and tell him off! Who does he think he is, to just string me along like a kite in the air?"

Maggie reached for her cell phone to call him back.

"Alright, Maggie, good luck. I'd better get back. I will tell them that you are picking out sweets, and that there's a big line. Make sure you get some."

Maggie pressed the keypads to return her previous call.

"Yes, Maggie." Antonio sounded like his temper was back. She waited quietly to see if he would say anything, but he did not.

"I just need to know one thing. What are you doing with her room card? It's in your hand, so don't lie to me, *Antonio!*"

"Maggie!" He sounded angry. "What do you want from me? They can make the Brooklyn Bridge look like the Eiffel Tower!"

Maggie tried to collect her thoughts as they raced through her head.

"I'm tired of discussing this!" Antonio finished.

"Tell me then," Maggie drove on, "were you, or were you not standing there with her?"

"Probably! She came to my show! Afterwards, she says, 'Hey, my concert is tomorrow night, same place. Do you and your crew want tickets?' Amber stood right there next to me and also Stanley. There never was a room card, Maggie!"

"Where are they in the photo? Inked out?" Maggie blurted in disgust.

"How should I know? I don't know how they create their illusions, any more than they know how I create mine! I'd be in my grave by now if I spent my time worrying about it!"

Maggie thought about it, deciding if she bought his explanation. Now she saw her phone was no longer connected—dead. *He hung up? He is angry? I should be angry! What am I supposed to think? I can't believe he hung up on me!*

Maggie stood in line to get candy and then headed back into the theater. The movie was almost finished. She was glad it was dark, so that no one could see her, as she wore her emotions on her sleeve.

The next few days were terrible days of closure. Maggie took down his poster and removed the photo of them dancing at the benefit. She placed it face down in her lingerie drawer, removing the emails and shredding them to bits. She told Shane that she would date his friend again. He was nice, and what did she have to lose? *Hopefully, he would be a distraction.* And there was Francis. He continued to press on about her joining him for dinner again. Not to mention, his bad habit of leaning into her face really close when he spoke.

Now the weekend, Maggie returned from her jog, when she heard a loud scream coming from the house. She picked up the pace, even though she was completely mentally and physically exhausted.

"Dana," she expressed upon entering, "I can hear you screaming from down at the stairwell!"

"Maggie, you will not believe when I tell you I just talked to Antonio! Your phone went off, right? It came in private, so I picked it up."

Maggie resented her excitement.

"What does he want?" She let out a huff.

"You are to call him," Dana announced. Maggie's stomach felt like it had staples in it. "But maybe, you should wait. He's on telly tonight, doing an interview about his show in England. Are we going to get tickets?"

"Wait...What? Slow down." Maggie stood confused. "Did he tell us to watch his interview?"

"No, I saw it on after Lady Lana's talk show this afternoon."

"Hmm, well, he can forget it. I'm not calling him!"

Maggie felt lovesick.

"You do want to watch?"

"I shouldn't...but...What time does the tsunami roll in?" Maggie could not quench her curiosity.

"Eight," Dana informed.

Maggie stared at her phone, as she held a sick feeling in her stomach. Even though she had said it was over, forgetting Antonio was the last thing on her mind.

I can't believe this is happening to me, AGAIN!

Chapter 13

The interview would be on in minutes. Maggie and Dana sat in front of the flat screen, waiting. Dana seemed to know better than to start conversation, while Maggie sat biting her nails, anticipating the frustration of seeing Antonio on TV rather than in person.

A pretty dark-haired woman wearing a grey satin blouse and triple-strand pearls appeared on the screen.

"Good Evening. I'm Bianca Beckman, and I'm pleased to announce that I will soon be speaking with Antonio DeLuca, who has agreed to answer some questions about his upcoming show, here in the UK."

Maggie watched as he came out, immediately remembering her initial attraction to him. He was dressed in a black t-shirt with jeans and wore a cap on his head. Now she felt uneasy watching him, thinking that he was in England and never told her. She exchanged glances with Dana, who knew she'd better keep her composure.

www.lovetheillusion.com/215.htm

BIANCA: "Antonio, it is such a privilege to get to meet you in person. I have seen your show, last time I was in New York City, and it is just fabulous! And I can't wait to see it again. Now, you were just in Canada, then in Sweden, and next you will perform for us here in the UK?"

ANTONIO: "Yes, that's correct."

BIANCA: "Now, the latest reports indicate that you have contacted one of Europe's top designers, Francis Louis, and that he has agreed to design your new costumes?"

ANTONIO: "Yes, it should be exciting. I just got word from Francis that one of my costumes is ready for the English show. But the rest of them won't be ready until we perform in Vegas."

BIANCA: "Well, your show is already outstanding, and I can't imagine you looking any better on stage, so I must ask how will Francis improve your costumes?"

ANTONIO: "Well, they have always been pretty basic. And we've had the same look since we started, so it's time for a change."

BIANCA: "So, why Francis Louis? I know he's well-known for his sleek, classic dress designs for women, but why did you choose him to make your stage costumes?"

ANTONIO: "Francis? Hmm... well, he's very creative and I'm hoping that he's able to present us with a look that is flashier than our current designs. He has an eye for detail, so I'm confident it will be impressive."

BIANCA: "Will you be touring other parts of Europe after the UK?"

ANTONIO: "I hope so. We'll see how it goes!"

BIANCA: "I see." (She paused, changing the subject.) "I am curious about your former interest—you used to play professional hockey for the Blackhawks, a team in Chicago, when you had to make a choice between hockey and magic. Tell me about that."

ANTONIO: "I love them both, but I chose magic because it's so creative. I still love to skate. I try to fit it in on the side. I skate back in Italy, and I will be there soon with my family."

BIANCA: "Now your parents moved to Chicago, but not for the hockey team, obviously. Tell me about that, and why did they move back?"

ANTONIO: "It was complicated. And I can't remember exactly when they decided to move back."

BIANCA: "So...they are both in Italy now? And they like it better there?"

ANTONIO: "Of course."

BIANCA: "Now, I hate to bring this up, and we all know how much you loved your brother, but did his death have anything to do with their decision to move back?"

ANTONIO: "Perhaps."

BIANCA: "Antonio, thank you for being so patient with me. I just have a few more questions for you. Now you told us that during this interview, we can't ask you about...the women, and the rumors flying around. But, you know we can't be so nice...so, what are you hiding from your fans? Is there someone special in your life?" (She gave him a playful smirk)

ANTONIO: (laughed) "You know you're not supposed to ask."

BIANCA: "Now why not? We just want to know! All your fans out there can't help but be curious, so please tell me, do you date anybody exclusively, or do you date a lot of women?"

ANTONIO: (laughed again) "So...you just *have* to ask me anyways?"

BIANCA: (laughed) "Well, you know that's my job. Your fans want to know."

ANTONIO: "Sorry." (Antonio grinned.)

BIANCA: "So...there *is* someone special in your life?"

ANTONIO: (looked frustrated) "Yes," he finally offered, with a look of regret.

BIANCA: "Did you hear that everyone? He does have a special person in his life, but don't worry. I won't ask who it is. We'll just let that go...maybe next time." (She laughed again.) "Now the last question...and I promise this is the last question...What is your favorite trick, or magic act, if you prefer to call it that?"

ANTONIO: "Hmm...that's tough...my favorite? I would have to say...probably the one where I put the girl through the ring of fire."

BIANCA: "And why would you say that is your favorite?"

ANTONIO: "I just think that the representation is fascinating. You have this girl, totally trusting you, not to let her fall, or get burned. The fire is blazing hot and dangerous. It signifies power, and refining. The ring which holds the fire symbolizes eternity, just like love."

BIANCA: "Wow! I never knew you were so...philosophical! Well, we are out of time now, but we can't wait to see your show in the UK, and hopefully more to come. We wish the best to you, and good luck with your upcoming show."

Dana and Maggie had exchanged glances repeatedly throughout the interview, and now his latest media engagement was up for discussion. Maggie was looking at Dana out of the corner of her eye, and Dana was doing the same. Finally, Dana spoke cautiously. "So...what did you think...that was not so bad?"

Maggie let out a huff. "What is wrong with you Dana? Of course, it's bad."

"Go on then, how do you see?" Dana repositioned herself in her chair, ready for Maggie's explanation.

"Think about it. He's here in England, and so am I? Why shouldn't that upset me?"

"He admitted that he had someone special. Maybe he will surprise you and visit."

"I doubt it. His last surprise was that he hung up on me, with that temper of his!" Maggie recalled. "And speaking of surprises, I cannot take any more of his tabloid surprises. He told me not to read them. Figures! He must assume that as long as I don't read them, it is as if the rumors don't exist! But everyone else is reading them. And if we are together, I look like a fool to put up with his lifestyle. I just can't take it anymore—his secretive, mysterious way, tied to his profession. It makes me insane!"

Maggie waited for Dana to give advice, but for the first time, she sat silent, unsure what to say. Then Maggie shared additional thoughts. "When I'm with him, everything is perfect. He looks out for me, takes me places, makes sure I am happy, and we have fun. But when it comes to an end... I am just devastated because I miss him... so much. And when we aren't together, how do I know he's not seeing others?" She drew a final conclusion. "I *cannot* continue like this."

Dana was confused by everything Maggie said. Finally, she indicated, "Right, Maggie, you really like him. But it is time to move on and there are plenty of fish in the sea!"

Maggie looked at Dana while she processed the harsh reality.

"I know," she reasoned. "You are right. I have to move on. I will date Shane's friend...ah, what's his name."

Dana laughed out loud. "You will go for someone whose name you can't even remember?"

Maggie laughed too.

"Yeah, why not?" she agreed.

Dana did not seem convinced. "Then I should tell Shane to—"

"Yes! I've got to get Antonio out of my head. And perhaps it will be like trying to remove my brain itself, but I must try." Dana gave a loose smile as Maggie continued, "You know what I wonder?"

"No, Maggie, I can't imagine."

"Don't say that to me!" Maggie spewed.

"Why, what have I said now?" Dana tried to piece together the puzzle.

"You said 'No, Maggie!'" Maggie looked downcast.

Dana leaned back, muddled.

Then Maggie explained, "That's what Antonio would always say to me. Yeah, that's right. He would tell me how it was going to be, as if I wasn't listening to him and he knew what was best!"

"Sorry, I won't say it. Now, go on, tell me what else you wonder?"

"I don't know. Now I forgot...oh...wait...I remember. Why do you suppose every interview they ask about his family moving back to Italy? We talked about it once, but he did not say. He said it was just a bad situation. What does that mean? Why does every reporter ask? Now he has plenty of secrets, and what should I do with all of them?" Maggie waited for Dana to solve the mystery.

"Did I tell you, I'm no rocket scientist when it comes to the media? All I know is they do their job to entertain me." Dana passed Maggie a smile, hoping to lighten the mood.

"Hmmm…" Maggie thought, "Just one more magical mystery. I need to clear my head of all this rubbish. I'm going to go read. I finally finished that stupid romance novel with the stupid perfect ending! You want to know something? Life never happens like that, which must be the reason everyone reads! They love the illusion! Hopefully, the sequel will just send me riveting into a deep sleep!"

Maggie opened her book and stared at Antonio's business card. He seemed to be embedded in everything she did, and she felt trapped, unable to escape. She thought about calling, but decided to leave it at that—just a thought. As much as she wished they could be together, it was highly unlikely that the two of them would ever work out. And the media would be a detestable addition to her life. She could not imagine putting up with that!

I need to let go of all this craziness.

As the summer months came to an end, Maggie still found herself thinking of him, longing to see him in Vegas. The days were now shorter, but seemed longer as she waited.

She dated Tyler once more. They went to dinner, and she found that they had a lot in common. He was also on a swim team in high school. And he was into fashion! Well…perhaps that was a stretch. He was a guy, after all. But at least he knew how to dress. It also turned out, that their mothers had known each other through work.

Maggie also managed to get coerced into having dinner with Francis. He was persistent that they needed to work late, and offered to take her to dinner before they would put in additional hours. Maggie felt powerless to stand up to him, although she knew it could be a mistake mixing business with friendship. But surely nothing would ever come of it. He was not her type. Although, he had a way of making you feel lucky just to be with him. And, he indicated his protective way towards her, reminding her again of Antonio. *Only it felt a bit creepy with Francis.*

Dana wanted to go to Antonio's show, but Maggie was uncertain. It was only a week away now and Maggie felt as if she had a clock counting down in her head, slowly ticking away the hours until she would see him again.

Time just stands still!

And the next day, when Maggie came home from work, Dana approached her car, waiting with news.

"Maggie! Maggie! Quick! You must come inside. I am astonished and it is completely brilliant!"

Maggie got out of her car, and hurried inside.

Her eyes circled around the living space, giving her approval.

"Wow! I like it! Where did you get all these? Did they have a sale or something?" Maggie asked.

"No! They are from Antonio! He sent you beautiful flowers and plants with flowers. Look at all of them! I am shocked! Did I tell you, it looks like a funeral parlor in here now?" Dana said.

Maggie thought perhaps it symbolized their love that had died. She started counting...*one, two, three, four, five, six, seven*...seven huge flower pots, nearly taking up all the floor space in the lounge area of their flat. Maggie admired them all.

"Maggie, you will never believe!" Dana reiterated, "I came to the door and a postman has brought *that* over there. I bring it inside, when he says he will be back, and then again, and again, and there are notecards with each one. So sorry, I am a nosey parker and read them all. This is the first one." She handed it to Maggie.

It said: "**Maggie, why don't you trust me?**"

"The second card is funny." Dana picked it up. "It says: '**I hope you don't have allergies.**'"

Maggie picked up the third card that was tucked into its own unique floral display. She read: "**I will be here in England to see you soon.**"

Maggie admired each plant and floral arrangement and how beautiful they were.

The fourth card said: "**You are more beautiful than these flowers.**"

Maggie felt her doubts, slipping away, as she kept reading in a somber state of shock. Roses, lilies, carnations, hydrangeas, and other flowers she had never seen before, filled the room, leaving a fragrance too pleasurable to take in all at once. She read: "**We will be together soon,**" and inside the envelope were two show tickets. Dana quick grabbed one, to claim that one was hers, and she and Dana were laughing, while Maggie held the next card: "**I can't wait to see you.**" It was attached to a display with a cheetah stuffed animal, and an assortment of daisies, in white and yellow.

The last card was hidden—in a display unlike the others—a single red rose, amidst a huge arrangement of baby's breath and greens, as if it was choked off by its surroundings. She picked up the card and read his last message: "**I love you.**"

Maggie stood in disbelief, holding onto his last message.

"Maggie, I think I was wrong about him," Dana had to confess.

Maggie picked up the rose and brought it to her nose, inhaling the fragrance, once again remembering his dark eyes and their kiss that had sealed his love. She then reached down to disassemble the cheetah from its floral display. "This is Cheetos!" Maggie was overjoyed. "I met him, and I got to pet him and feed him!"

"You got to pet the cheetah?" Dana asked. "Look!" She read her ticket. "Backstage passes to the show. Perhaps I can pet him."

"I can't believe this! I am so excited to see him!" Maggie told Dana. But then she lost all expression in her face. "I can't believe I doubted." She gathered her thoughts. "Dana?"

"What?"

"Do you think he's already here?"

"How should I know?"

"He can't be here now, because..." Maggie tried to reason.

"Call him, Maggie!" Dana gave orders.

"Okay, I will!" she agreed, running to get her phone.

She soon heard his voice on the other line.

"Maggie?"

"Chad? I got the flowers...Thank you...You are so sweet, I should have known." There was a long pause. "Chad?"

"Yes, Maggie, I'm here."

"Are you in England now?"

"No, but I knew you would think that. The interview, it was supposed to be in England—more hype, you know. But we are still in Sweden, and I was not able to get away. So, Bianca flew out here and did the interview on one of my lunch breaks."

"Oh," Maggie said, disappointed. "So you aren't here now?"

"No, Maggie! You would be the first to know. Trust me. Now, after I get done in Sweden, I'm flying straight to the UK. My show is that night but then I leave to go back the next day. You have the show ticket?"

"Yes, and one for Dana?"

"That's fine, whoever you want to take. If I can, I will try to see you before the show, but I can't make any promises."

"I can't wait to see you. I never stop missing you. I should be insane by now," Maggie admitted.

"Me too, Maggie, me too," he said. There was a pause. "So...we are good?"

"Yes," she reported timidly.

"One more thing," he instructed.

"What?" She felt guilty for accusing him.

"No more tabloids!"

"Okay," Maggie agreed, but gave the explanation, "Dana sits here and reads them and then—"

Antonio cut her off. "She needs to read a book. You can tell her I said so."

"Ooohhkaay..." Maggie laughed. "But I don't think she's going to listen to you."

"Typical woman," he grumbled under his breath. "Goodbye, Maggie. I will see you soon—and we need to talk about why you don't trust me."

"Fine," she agreed, feeling defeated.

"I love you," he told her.

"Okay," Maggie said, softly, realizing she was unable to return the words. She was still afraid of love. Then she heard her phone was dead. He had hung up.

"So, do you love him?" Dana asked Maggie one morning, out of the blue, only a day away from the show. They sat in the kitchen, while Maggie ate her oatmeal and bagel, and Dana sipped her tea. Maggie was afraid to admit how deeply she felt for Antonio. "Hello, Maggie?" Dana repeated, hoping to bring her out of her daydream. That is exactly where she had been the last week—in a stupor of daydreams. Francis even yelled at her twice—for misplacing something once and for forgetting to relay one of his messages.

"Huh?" Maggie had a squash of oatmeal in her mouth.

"Hey!" Dana repeated again, "Do you love Antonio?"

"I usually call him Chad!" Maggie corrected.

"Right, but did I tell you he's Antonio to everyone else! Seriously, Maggie, do *not* dodge the question, like I'm some reporter," Dana probed.

"I'm not. I just don't know. My feelings are all over him, and it's exciting, but love? I'm not sure. Last time, with Phillip, I thought it was love, but no—instead— the biggest joke ever!"

"Right, then... I will say that I'm in love with Shane, and you must be in love with Antonio," Dana rationalized.

"It's not the same. Our relationship's so complicated," Maggie insisted.

"I'll give you that. But love is love. It either is, or is not," Dana confessed.

"Well, I strongly like him. It's like this. When I met him, I thought, 'Great, the biggest player I ever met,' yet, I was totally intrigued, but afraid because I always fall for the worst ones. Meanwhile, he is fascinated that I don't recognize him. We spend time together, and pretty soon I'm completely into him—the way he smiles, the way he laughs, how he teases me—he's really funny, and always trying to shock me in some way or another. I knew he could make any girl fall for him, and being aware, I felt like his next victim. But he did seem to have a sweet side, and then I figured out he wasn't the creep I thought he was. And now I *love* being with him, but *in* love, I'm not sure."

"Hmm…" Dana was amused. "Let me just sort everything out into my database fact finder. Is Maggie White in love or not?" Dana chuckled.

"Dana!" Maggie felt intimidated. "I just told you!"

"Right…Maggie…." Dana waved her hand to brush away her explanation, "You're *madly* in love with him."

"Whatever Dana… You'll think what you want!"

Maggie laughed under her breath, changing the subject.

"Antonio told me to tell you not to read the tabloids. You should read a book!"

Maggie's laughter increased as Dana lowered her eyebrows and her mouth dropped open.

"He's so protective of you, Maggie!" Dana paused to think about it. "Nope!" she stated victoriously, while grinning at Maggie. "I'll never cancel my subscription!"

The next day, Maggie stood in her pink bikini as she tied up her hair. The weather now hot as a summer day, she wanted a bit of color to look her best when she saw Antonio at his show that evening.

Maggie picked up her novel, the sequel that Antonio had given her. She thought about the love that existed between the two characters in the book. They had their love tested time and time again. And each time it seemed doubtful that they would stay together, they stuck it out and eventually their love became stronger.

She headed out the back door onto their multi-level deck. She positioned her beach towel, lay down on her stomach, and began to read. Thoughts of Antonio flooded her head with each page that she turned. She pondered love, and doubted whether she could ever be sure it was real. She thought about the characters in the book, and how stubborn they were to get their own way. Eventually, one of them had to give in. Other times, outside forces complicated things, making it seem impossible for their love to survive. Maggie tried to determine what made love last. *Not sure.*

"Dana?" Maggie was peering through an open window, which connected their deck to the kitchen. Dana stood there, loading the dishwasher.

"Can I help you?" Dana laughed.

"Can you grab me my sunglasses? They are by the front door," Maggie told her.

"Sure." Dana left to go get them.

Maggie waited for her to return. She flew back at top speed. "I think I might have a heart attack before I'm even thirty!" Dana screamed in a panic, as she came around to the back door and handed her the sunglasses.

"What now?" Maggie asked, squinting from the sun.

"Antonio's here... I think. There's a limo outside the front!"

Maggie felt her stomach flip as she absorbed the shock. She turned around to grab her towel and come inside, but when she did, there he was, walking over to her. She looked startled. Antonio grinned, chuckling quietly when he realized he had managed to surprise her.

Dana waved at Antonio, calling out to him, "Antonio, I can't wait to see your show. I'm Dana, Maggie's flat mate!"

Antonio waved back at her. Feeling suddenly skittish, Dana quickly ran inside.

Befuddled, Maggie stooped over to pick up her towel, embarrassed to be in her string bikini. But he came right up to her, standing close, as if time had never separated them. She looked up into his eyes. They were still the same.

"Maggie," Antonio spoke her name, as he lost himself in a huge grin, "I'm sorry to show up like this and —"

"How did you get here and sneak up on me?" she whispered, as if the paparazzi were hiding in the bushes, with their cameras. "Did anyone see you?"

Antonio placed his arms around her, in a tight hug.

"No," he grinned, "I see you weren't expecting to see me until the show, but I got here early, and you know how I like to surprise you."

Maggie admired his face up close, realizing why she missed him.

"We only have an hour," Antonio explained. "And then I have to leave. Do you want to drive around with me? Salvador is waiting out front."

"Okay, you can come in. I'll quick change."

"Hurry up, love." He watched her vanish from his sight.

"Do you want something to drink?" Dana asked Antonio.

"No, don't bother. I'm fine."

Dana stood in disbelief, as he stood inside their flat.

Maggie fidgeted through the clothing in her wardrobe, wondering how to get ready in a hurry. *Never done that before.* She reached into the dresser drawer and took out the photo that he had sent her. She recalled dancing with him, as she placed it back on top of the dresser. She slipped on a pair of jean shorts that were frayed, and threw a white blouse over her swim top. She slid into her sandals, and off she went.

As she met up with him, his whole face lit with a smile. "Here you are, more beautiful than I remembered." He grabbed hold of her hand, and after they had left her flat, he said, "It's a nice place you have."

"Thanks. I did most of the decorating. Dana's not that particular, and I love to decorate. It's like a whole new world of fashion!" she explained. He laughed quietly at her analogy, while Salvador opened the door to let them into the limo.

Together at last, and alone, Maggie opened up to Antonio. "I can't stand being away from you," she groaned, leaning against him.

He placed his arms around her and said quietly, "I know. I missed you too, and then you have to make things worse by reading the tabloids. You know I was mad at you!"

"Easy for you to say, you should be me."

"You Maggie, have nothing to worry about. *Why* don't you trust me?" Antonio spoke confidently.

"Look at you! Any girl would be lucky to date you, and I worry that—"

"That's ridiculous. You have no idea what I'm thinking."

"And what's that, *Antonio*?"

"I want you to kiss me, Maggie." Antonio waited, looking into her eyes, until she moved closer to him. She took in a deep breath, letting it out slowly, after watching his lips speak, drawn to his suggestion. As she touched her lips to his, he kissed her back, slowly, whispering in between his kiss, "Don't doubt us." She breathed in and out carefully, feeling the rhythm of his heart as she placed her hand on his chest. "I love you, Maggie. Don't forget it."

Antonio grabbed her waist, pulling her onto his lap as she sat facing him. He sat still, gazing at her, his arms locked around her. She reached her hands into his hair, feeling the waves sliding through her fingers. He leaned forward to kiss her, until she fell on top of him, melting into her last dream where they were together in his limo, now living in its fantasy.

Minutes passed, when she heard him whisper, "I have something for you." She sat up slowly, still on top of him, feeling lightheaded and dizzy, wondering what she could possibly want from him, other than his kiss. Her face was flushed as he reminded her, "I said I have something for you." He reached under the seat and handed her a rectangular box, her eyes still drooping from their intimacy. Antonio's eyes were serious, as he watched her take hold of the box and slowly open it. She saw a silver chain, and with her finger she looped it into her hand, holding a ring that hung at the bottom of the chain. She picked up the ring, holding it between her finger and thumb, taking note of its inscription—*Maggie, love is forever. Antonio.*

Maggie gazed down at him as he held her captive with his dark eyes, reminding her once again of when they first met. He took the necklace out of her hands and placed it around her neck.

www.lovetheillusion.com/230.htm

Seconds later, it was locked in place. She placed her arms around him. It seemed they had been apart for an eternity. She leaned against him, until he fell back in the seat, pulling her on top of him. She listened to the quiet hum of the limo as it drove them around, while he expressed his love and kissed her passionately.

Maggie wanted to tell him that she loved him, but she was afraid. She thought that once she spoke the words, it would finalize any possibility of her ever escaping his spell, should things ever disband. She would enter a prison that she could not escape. She thought about his kiss, and knew there was nothing like it. The feelings she had for him left her paralyzed in fear, as she contemplated losing him. She rolled off of him and sat up alongside him. He sat up, wondering what was wrong.

"Are you excited for the show?" she asked, lending a smile that revealed a perfect row of teeth. "Dana's coming. I gave her the other ticket."

"You're sitting backstage. I want you to be my lady in the ring of fire, and maybe Dana can help with one of my other magic tricks."

"Dana would love that!"

"What about you?" Antonio asked. "Can you try to not get me with your nails this time?"

Maggie pressed her lips together, recalling the first time she was on stage with him. She held back a smile.

He let go of his own smile, saying, "Are you going to be nice this time?"

"That depends. Are you going to embarrass me again in front of all your fans?" Maggie gave concern. "You know I don't like to be on stage. And you better not burn me with that crazy ring of fire!"

Antonio grinned and raised his eyebrows. "Are you afraid?"

"Should I be?"

"That would be 'no' since last time I did not burn you."

"If you do, I will scream!" Maggie batted her eyes at him.

As she continued to send mixed signals, Antonio cut to the chase. "Maggie, be honest with me. Tell me why you don't trust me."

Maggie looked at him, for the first time thinking perhaps she should trust him. She tried to explain her fear.

"It's hard for me to trust after what I've been through."

Antonio spoke carefully. "Do you want to tell me about that?"

She decided to share. "I was engaged, right before we met. His name was Phillip and I caught him in bed with one of my best friends, Jasmine. I think he thought I would never find out. That day...I will never forget. I came to surprise him. I had just gotten done interviewing with Francis and he offered me a job, paying way more than what I was making. I was lost in this excitement and wanted to surprise him with the good news. Instead, he surprised me—when I found the two of them together. It was terrible. Dana swears up and down it was my fault because I never slept with him. Now I'm glad I didn't. It's just like you said in your interview. Dana and I watched it. I liked what you said about putting the girl through the fire and making sure she doesn't get burned. Love is like that. You walk through a ring of fire to get to it, hoping that you don't get burned. And if you get burned, you're never the same."

"Eventually, you have to let go of your fear and fall in love."

"I'm afraid of love." Maggie sat, chin in hand, looking up at him.

"You mean you're afraid to love me?"

"Yes," she admitted, casting her eyes away from him.

Antonio looked upset.

"I would do anything to change that."

He took his hand and gently turned her face towards his.

"I'm sorry." She frowned at him.

"It's not your fault."

"You are sweet," Maggie's face softened to his, "and I like the necklace."

He put his arm around her.

"I have to get back, but do me a favor." His eyes carried concern.

"What?" she asked softly.

"Have faith in us and the future." Antonio made his request while Maggie sat still, pondering their relationship... *I want him in my future, but how will that work?*

Now she watched as he poured them each a glass of champagne. He passed her a glass. "To us," he made a toast. She met her glass with his, accepting his toast, wishing he would kiss her again. It didn't take long for him to read her mind. But their time together passed much too quickly, and when she glanced out the window of the limo, she could see that she was back home. "I'll see you tonight!" Antonio reminded her as he leaned over and kissed her one last time.

www.lovetheillusion.com/232.htm

Chapter 14

Dana held the pendant in her hand.

"Looks like we have a double wedding?"

"Dana! Seriously, I've only known him..." Maggie started counting out the months with her fingers, "May, June, July, August...for four months."

"That's pretty long, for the rich and famous," Dana teased, while Maggie was deep in thought.

"Dana, I want to do something for him, but I need your help. I want to make chocolate mousse, because we ate it at our first dinner together. I remember being in the bathroom, fighting my feelings for him, thinking I would just leave. But, he ordered chocolate mousse, and then I had to stay longer. So, what do you think? Can we make some?"

Dana placed a pasta dish into the oven.

"My granny had a recipe book, and I think it's in there, but I never made it before." She went over to the cabinets and pulled out the cookbook. "Let's see..." She thumbed through the pages. "Here it is. Mmm...looks like it's worth the calories. We definitely have to make this. Get some paper and we will write down the ingredients. You go get the stuff, while I watch the pasta and figure out how to make it."

"Okay," Maggie agreed. "I will hurry, because I need time to change out of this swimwear before the show. You too—Antonio is bringing us up on stage!"

"Really?" Dana's face lit. "That's so awesome. I'm so excited! But, it's such a shame that Shane can't come." She passed Maggie her puppy dog eyes.

"Maybe he can," Maggie decided. "I could call Antonio and ask."

"Alright, maybe see if he has an extra ticket."

Maggie reached for her phone.

"Chad?"

"Yes, Maggie." She could hear a smile behind his words. "Are you going to tell me you love me?"

Maggie paused, considering how he could have insecurities. She froze, unable to admit her feelings.

"Is there any way that Shane can come to the show?"

"Sure. Let me think…" Antonio came up with a plan. "I'll have Salvador pick all of you up, in the limo, and tell security to wait outside. They can get Shane in without a ticket."

"Okay, thanks," Maggie agreed. "What time?"

"How 'bout…seven?" Antonio suggested.

"Sounds good—thanks!" She was delighted.

"No problem, Maggie. See you soon. I have to go." Antonio hung up. Maggie held the phone in her hand for a moment and then raced back to the kitchen.

"The limo will get us at 7:00. It's almost five. We'd better hurry."

Dana handed her the list.

Maggie left for the store, and when she returned they got busy in the kitchen.

"Don't we have any dessert glasses?" Dana asked.

"I don't think so." Maggie held the bowl of the chocolate mousse they had made. "This looks delicious, but it will look funny in a cereal bowl." She started to look through the kitchen cabinets.

"A bowl? No!" Dana started laughing. "How about these cosmo glasses? Did you remember strawberries?"

Maggie opened up the refrigerator and handed them to Dana, recalling when Marcos had his mouth full of strawberries.

"Those are just for garnish," Dana explained. "Now, start pouring it into these." Dana passed Maggie a glass.

Maggie and Dana soon admired the row of fourteen cosmo glasses, each filled with chocolate mousse.

"Dana? I think we are going to be eating this for a while!"

They each let out a cackle, their mission complete.

"Shane will be here in a bit. He can help eat these so we don't have to!" Dana suggested, holding air in her cheeks as she moved them into the fridge.

"I could bring them to work, for all the skinny models," Maggie suggested.

"Maggie, I think instead of worrying about how to get rid of all the chocolate mousse, we should be getting ready. Do you even know what you're wearing?"

"No, but something fun— we'll be on stage. I think I have stage fright already!"

"I was thinking, right..." Dana gave Maggie her infamous grin. "We should wear something out of the costume box downstairs. I have that Dracula mask...or the Cher wig?"

"I don't think so, Dana. We're supposed to be random people from the audience."

"Take away all my fun!" Dana scolded her. "That's what you do best, take away all the fun, but I know what you *could* wear!"

"What?" Maggie stated sarcastically.

"Seriously, it'll look really good on you."

Maggie followed Dana into her room.

"This!" Dana said, as she pulled a sleeveless top off the hanger. Maggie saw the tags, still attached. "My mum gave this to me, and it's just too…frilly, with this obnoxious pink ruffle. It's ugly on me, so you can have it!" Dana held it up to her.

Maggie slipped it on and stood in front of the mirror. "I like it! No more frilly than one of Francis' designs. You ought to see the dress he is designing for me to wear in Vegas! It's purple— the color of Antonio's souvenir t-shirts, with three layers of ruffle at the bottom and wire going through it. Not to mention, the obnoxious slit all the way up the leg. And the whole dress shines in silver sparkles. This shirt's bland in comparison."

"Go ahead, keep it. My mum will never know. I keep looking at it, thinking, when and where will I ever wear *that*!"

"Thanks!" Maggie grabbed the shirt. "Then…help yourself to my wardrobe?"

"Really? Don't mind if I do! I feel like I'm going to the shops!"

The girls walked into Maggie's room.

"Look at these!" Dana said, holding up one of the glittery shoes that Maggie wore to the benefit. "Where did you buy the ankle breakers?"

Maggie started to explain, "Antonio and I went a charity benefit in memory of his brother, Matteo. I didn't have anything to wear, so he bought those shoes with this dress." She pulled the dress out of her closet and held it up. "I know. It's outlandish."

"It looks very rich," Dana analyzed.

"See," Maggie explained, "as nice as it is, it bothers me at the same time."

"Why? You, being into fashion design, ought to love that!"

"Ah, it seems so wasteful. When will I wear it again? It bothers me how he just dumps out money and doesn't think about anything."

"You're such a prude!" Dana teased her. "What girl wouldn't just love that?"

"Right, that and the tabloids, the cameras," Maggie deliberated. "And the limo, body guards, media frenzy, not to mention the paparazzi. Wait 'til you see them tonight. I bet we can't even get in and out of the limo without someone bothering us."

"Really? I could be in one of the papers? That would be brilliant!" Dana lowered her voice to imitate the possibilities. "Antonio DeLuca follows two girls home from his show to eat chocolate mousse." She laughed out loud while Maggie grinned.

"Dana, hurry up and raid my closet, before I—"

"Maggie! Those shoes Antonio bought you go with that top!"

"Since when do you know fashion?" Maggie challenged her. She decided to slip them on to see if she was right while standing in front of the mirror. The hemline on her jeans came and rested just above the top of the shoe. "Hmm, interesting...I think it works," Maggie agreed.

"Good! You can keep that shirt. And for me...I'm taking this!" Dana took off with a navy knit sun dress that Maggie used as a swim cover-up.

That works.

They heard a knock at the door.

"Hello, Shane! Come on in." Maggie opened the door and informed, "Dana's almost ready."

"What's that smell?" Shane asked.

"Oh, we made chocolate mousse. Actually, Dana did. You can have some, but it's not set yet."

Shane went over to the refrigerator and helped himself.

"It's not ready yet!" Maggie tried to clarify as she watched him dig in with a spoon.

"Who cares? It's still good," Shane informed. Maggie shook her head in disbelief. "I'm so excited! We're traveling Hollywood style, in a limo!"

"Yes," Maggie explained, "Antonio made the arrangements, so you could come along. But hopefully we don't get followed, or *die* in an accident while being chased by the paparazzi..."

"Sounds like a good time!" Shane laughed. "I can't wait to party with the paparazzi!"

"Yep..." Maggie agreed, "That's exactly his life!"

"I never saw the show," Shane admitted. "I'm excited to see it. So you got these tickets because you are designing his costumes?"

"That's right. We have to go to the Vegas show in October. Francis is busy with the designs already and in fact, Antonio will be wearing one of our designs tonight!"

"Alright! We're ready." Dana made her entrance.

"It's about time!" Shane teased her. "Good desserts, by the way...Hey, I think the limo's here."

"Hi Salvador, this is my roommate Dana and Shane, her fiancé." Maggie introduced them. "Thanks for driving us."

"No problem," Salvador said, with a grand smile, "keeps me busy."

"Pile in! Party in the limo," Shane announced as he slid towards the liquor shelf. In a commonly practiced flash, he tore open a bottle of brandy and became the bartender. Maggie watched as he proceeded to mix their drinks. "Hey, the man's got money! We can have a few!" Shane stated defensively, now holding a bottle of sherry cast Speyside Scotch.

Moments later, everyone held a drink that he had concocted. "Cheers!" Shane motioned as they tapped their glasses together. Shane had his arm around Dana, and she was soaking it all in.

Maggie felt a bit nervous since she had asked Dana not to tell Shane that she was dating Antonio. So far Dana had kept her word. They had even hidden all the flowers Antonio sent.

"So, this is where he keeps all the ladies? Looks like a good time!" Shane voiced loudly.

Maggie bit her bottom lip, hoping not to display a look of disgust while she exchanged glances with Dana who laughed, entertained with Shane's sense of humor.

"Hey, Shane..." Maggie hoped to change the subject. "This tastes weird. What is this?" she asked, holding up her glass.

"Ah! That's for me to know and you to find out later when you wake up and don't remember where you were, or who you were with!" He opened his eyes wide.

Dana started laughing, as did Maggie.

"I'd be afraid if I were you, Dana."

"I'm not afraid of him," Dana revealed as she started kissing him.

Maggie thought they were a cute couple. Dana wore her blonde hair straight and cut to the shoulder, and Shane also had blonde hair. Seeing them together could only bring Maggie thoughts of Antonio. She thought about the necklace he gave her, thinking now of all the things that reminded her of him...the photo, the dress, the shoes, the book, now the necklace, and Cheetos—who slept in her bed where she wore her t-shirt every other night, in between washings. Maggie thought how she would give it all away, if only they could be together. After tonight, they would be apart again. Their distant relationship bred a prescription for misery. Each time they said good-bye, it was worse than the time before. Maggie finished her drink, feeling the effects—and glad enough, considering the circumstances. Now she recalled that she left the necklace he gave her on her dresser.

Shane dragged Dana on top of himself, kissing her, ignoring the fact that Maggie sat in front of them. Maggie got up after deciding to move to a different spot where they would not be in view. But Shane got up and started to mix another round of drinks.

"Don't be shy, Maggie. What shall we have next? So many options..." Shane chuckled.

Maggie and Dana watched him mix another drink. Soon, he passed out another. "This one's much better than the last!" he bragged. "And...Cheers! To a good night!"

Maggie sat dizzy and sure she was inebriated after finishing the third drink Shane had mixed. The limo came to a stop, and they got out. As Antonio promised, a security guard arrived to assist them, issuing them through a back entrance, locked for security reasons.

He led them down a wide hallway and up a few steps, where several stage crew personnel were standing next to Antonio.

"Maggie! You're here!" Antonio walked towards them.

She made an introduction. "You know Dana," Maggie mumbled, "and this is her fiancé, Shane."

"Nice to meet you, Shane," Antonio said as he shook his hand. "Tessa," Antonio called out, "can you show them to the backstage area? We might need chairs, I don't know."

"This way," Tessa indicated. They followed her as she explained, "Most everyone's in make-up right now, and we're behind in setting up, so hopefully it'll all come together...long flight, long day. Most everyone arrived a couple days early, but I just flew in today, with Antonio."

Now behind stage, watching as Tessa set up some folding chairs for them, Maggie could not remember being so happy to see a chair. "What'd you put in those drinks, Shane?" Maggie asked, as she took a seat, barely able to sit upright in her chair.

Shane started laughing. "I don't remember. A little bit of this...and a little bit of that..."

"Straight booze." Dana laughed.

"I think I need some water, or I may be ill," Maggie concluded. "I hope Antonio didn't notice how plastered we are."

"Don't worry," Shane assured her. "He's much too busy with his own agenda to notice."

Maggie got up to find some water. She wobbled in her shoes, finally landing elbows down onto the concessions counter, after waiting in line.

"Can I get three waters please? Make that four," she mumbled, leaving forty pounds on the counter and feeling too loopy to wait for change.

Maggie was headed back to her seat when she finally decided she was lost. After nearly ten minutes, she stopped. *Which way did I come?* She could not remember. She spotted a bathroom attendant, after managing to drink down one of the water bottles. "Can I bother you to tell me what way is the backstage?"

The woman gave her a strange stare and shrugged. Maggie persisted, speaking slowly and looking confused. "Oh, come on, I'm due back at any minute. I know Antonio, and I need to get back. Here, I'll give you this." She reached in her pocket and gave the lady twenty pounds. The woman took the money and led her to an usher, who assisted her to finding her seat next to Dana and Shane.

"Maggie, you're back! We were afraid you got lost." Shane chuckled, signaling a high five.

The show had already started.

"I'd be better off! Sixty pounds later, I have water and a guided tour back!" Maggie laughed, leaning into Shane. "I can't believe I have to go up on stage like this! It will be a miracle if I can even walk a straight line."

"That's so frightening!" Shane clapped, lost in humor.

"I could smack you, Shane! The whole place is spinning, and now the lights make it even worse," Maggie informed, slouched over.

"He's bringing you on stage—like that? I'm going to pee in my pants!" Shane was bent over in laughter.

"I'm also going on, for a card trick!" Dana chimed in.

"Should I just run out there too?" Shane laughed. "I could save you from his magic spell!"

"Right, Shane," Dana cut him off, laughing, "I don't think so. That would be a bit embarrassing!"

Moments later, security personnel tapped Dana on the shoulder and told her she would be needed in a few minutes. And so she went on stage to assist with a card trick. Maggie watched while listening to Shane remark, "Go Dana, bring me back some of those magic cards, so we can make magic together."

"Shut up, Shane, you're so juvenile!" Maggie laughed, hoping she did not have to go up for a while.

They watched Dana who appeared to do just fine in the spotlight.

"Did you see me up there?" Dana asked, breathlessly, upon returning to her chair. "I'm so excited! I was on stage with Antonio DeLuca! Did you get my picture, so I can show people at work?"

"Hey, did I tell you, there's no flash photography," Shane reminded Dana.

Maggie leaned over Shane and grabbed Dana's arm.

"Dana, I can't go up there. I don't like going on sober, much less in a drunken nightmare! You go for me, please."

"Maggie!" Dana laughed. "Get a hold of yourself, alright. You will be fine. The lights are so bright, you can barely see a thing, so get rid of the stage fright!"

Maggie held her stomach, as she focused on a blurry Antonio, motioning for her to come up. She shook her head no, but he finally came off the stage to get her. She stood up, trying to follow him in a straight line as she wore a fake smile, still feeling Shane's drinks. As far as she could tell, he had no clue as he turned to the audience.

"I'd like to introduce you to Maggie White. She's working with Francis Louis to design costumes for my upcoming show in Vegas. She has volunteered to be my lady in the ring of fire."

Maggie heard the crowd scream as she squinted from the bright lights. Antonio turned towards her, walking backwards facing her and the audience, as he led her to his next stunt, the ring of fire. She followed his lead, barely able to walk forward, when she felt faint and lost her balance, falling towards him. He caught her with his free arm. "Woooh!" he yelled, caught off guard.

She could hear various responses from his fans from screaming to gasping in disbelief. Antonio grinned at the audience and explained, "She is in so much fear to be in the air with that fire, she's passed out!" His words rang in her ears, as one of the dancers assisted by holding the ring of fire. He then picked her up in a cradle and walked over to the table, where he lay her down. Now she could feel being strapped onto the table. Antonio secured her ankles, waist and shoulders.

Floating up in the air, she closed her eyes, and waited for it to be over.

And when it was, Antonio assisted her off the table and back to her chair where Dana and Shane were laughing uncontrollably. "Maggie, you were hysterical!" Dana reeled.

"That was too damn funny!" Shane clapped his hands, and then punched the air to give his approval.

Maggie slumped into her chair.

I'm too embarrassed to even move.

Hours later, Maggie woke up in her bed. She slowly sat up, still in her clothes from the night before. She saw the cheetah stuffed animal sitting on her dresser.

She tried to recall the evenings events, vaguely remembering being in the limo next to Antonio. Dana and Shane were across from them. She remembered trying her hardest to sit upright and not too close to Antonio, since Shane was there. Shane was having a conversation with Antonio and, no sooner did the limo come to a rest, Dana called out in excitement that she could see a journalist parked within view. And the last thing she remembered, Antonio had instructed for Shane and Dana to hold a blanket up to hide them as they got out of the limo. Music had played loudly, and she could still hear the tune playing over and over again in her head.

www.lovetheillusion.com/244.htm

Maggie leaned over. It was 2:30 in the morning. She realized Antonio must have left, and felt bad, wishing she could have said good-bye. Now she yearned for water to quench her thirst.

She strolled into the kitchen. She leaned over the sink, filling a glass with tap water.

"Fun night, Maggie?" Antonio wanted to know. He was seated on the sofa, his arms folded. *Is he angry?* She wondered. She noticed he was still dressed in his show clothes.

"You stayed here?" She yawned in his direction. "Your show was amazing last night," she let him know.

"I don't think so, Maggie!" Antonio's words shot like an arrow at her as he got off the couch, and started walking over to her. She froze in position, facing the sink at the kitchen counter, holding onto her glass of water. She started to take a sip, but then saw his hands on either side of her, locking her into a small space as he stood behind her. "Do you mind telling me," Antonio questioned her in a soft, yet angry tone, "where you were and what you were doing before the show?"

Maggie swallowed. She remained still.

"What, Maggie? Drugs? Booze? What?"

Maggie turned around to challenge him.

"I was *not* on drugs!"

"Oh! Drinking then?" Antonio questioned her, inches from her face. "I am shocked you went up on stage like that. You were completely wasted; how can you mix that with show business, especially with kids!?" He walked away from her, one hand in his pocket, the other pulling at his hair.

"We just had a couple drinks in the limo," she explained.

"So, let me get this straight! You get in *my* limo, drink yourself to oblivion before my show and then parade your antics up there on stage, like a big joke?"

"No!" Maggie shouted. "It's not like that! I didn't want to go on stage. And Shane made those drinks, whatever they were. I still don't know. Dana seemed fine, but I could tell I was bombed, and then it was too late. I tried to warn you, but no! You bring me up on stage anyways! I should be mad at you!"

"What?" he questioned her in a state of shock. "Are you kidding me? I'm thinking that we're going to have a nice evening together, and now this! You're so wasted that I have to carry you into your bed, hoping you will come to so that we can have a decent conversation—which obviously, is not the case. *Then*, I sit in your apartment, next to Dana's tabloid magazines! You accuse me of entertaining the women, and now *you* tell *me* this! Who's Tyler?"

She wondered how he knew. Antonio's face grew angry as he warned, "Don't play dumb with me, Maggie. Is that why you're not wearing the necklace I gave you...because of Tyler?"

She remained silent when he said, "Yeah, I know all I need to know about him after Shane starts talking to Dana about some movie you guys went to, and how he can't wait to see you after your last date! How many times were you out with him, Maggie, and *what* were you doing with him?"

"I don't like him. Quit yelling at me."

She placed her hands over her face.

Antonio stood looking at her, dissecting her latest revelation. Finally, he blurted, "I don't have time for this! My plane leaves at three, and I have to get some sleep. Goodbye. I'll see you in Vegas." He walked away, reaching the back door, attached to the deck.

"WAIT!" Maggie screamed. "Don't go!"

Antonio turned to face her.

"Why? Why should I stay?"

She watched him as he glared back at her, waiting for her response.

"I made us chocolate mousse," she finally reported, begging forgiveness. "Remember when we ate it at Bouley? I really liked you, but I was going to leave dinner because it seemed too impossible and weird for us to be together. It's still like that. But this time, I'm the one wanting *you* to stay."

For moments, Antonio just stared at her and she wondered what he was thinking. But then he walked slowly over to her.

"It's a disgrace that you went on stage like that. Don't you know your limit? What were you thinking?"

"I *wanted* to be drunk! Don't you see? I should be nervous just to be on stage, but now after another perfect moment in your limo with you, you have to leave. I love being together and I hate being apart. I dated Tyler to try to forget you, but I can't! Are you happy now? I'm completely miserable! Do you get that? I should spend every day completely wasted just so that I don't have to deal with the reality. How long will we last? I have no idea…perhaps until my next cocktail, which I will then call up Shane and have him mix for me!"

Antonio stood speechless, absorbing her plate of information. She darted him a stare back, wishing he would speak.

"Are you saying you love me?" Antonio finally asked.

"I'm afraid I don't know," Maggie revealed, and then lightened the mood. "But thanks for catching me on stage. I do appreciate that, you know."

Antonio gave her a look of confusion.

"I had to catch you on stage. *And* carry you out of the limo, after you crashed out first on my shoulder and then in my lap, while we got some reporter on our tail, following us to your place, as I schemed up a plan. We all ran up to the back door under a blanket.

You and I came in, and Dana and Shane ran back to the limo and went to his place. I watched the car drive away after them. It should be a good story, when you see them next."

Maggie felt relief that he seemed to have let go of his anger a bit. She reached into the refrigerator, and pulled out the mousse. She handed him a dish.

"Do we get spoons?" he asked.

She opened the silverware drawer and pulled out spoons, passing one to Antonio. She watched him take a bite, and then approached him with a hug.

"I hate it when you are mad at me," she sulked, casting her eyes into his.

"Then don't make me mad!" Antonio said softly, his brow raised, leaning back to look at her, as he took a bite of the mousse.

"Tyler's nothing," she admitted. "We went out twice. Shane decided I should go. He never kissed me, if that's what you're worried about."

Antonio observed her. He let out an exasperated sigh.

"What am I going to do with you, Maggie?" She leaned up to kiss him, but he said, "No, Maggie." She knew he was still angry. She backed off, her feelings hurt.

"Why?" Maggie dared to ask. "How many girls have you been with?"

"What? Why do you ask me that?" Antonio started laughing. "Trust me. You'd be really disappointed if I actually told you about my love life. You think you know all about me. Just like what the tabloids say! Must be true, right? So, where does that leave you— one of the many? No, I can assure you, I can tell you what you want to hear."

"What's that supposed to mean?" She lowered her eyebrows at him.

"Well, I can be pretty sure that you don't want me to tell you the high numbers, so then you figure it out!"

"Okay, fifty?" Maggie took a guess.

"Fifty what? Fifty women?" Antonio laughed out loud while she stared at him.

"What! I'm just guessing!"

He seemed flattered. "You are kidding, right?"

"I don't know. You tell me?" Maggie shrugged her shoulders. "There must be some reason that you kiss me, but you save all the rest for…I don't know…someone else?"

"Look Maggie…I could date a lot of women, but I'd rather be in love. And I love… *you*," Antonio said softly.

"Well then, there's one thing I have not figured out," Maggie asserted. "Why is it you don't wish to sleep with me, like all the other men I have been with?"

"How do you know that I don't?" He gave her a sweet look. "And it's not that simple. First of all Maggie, you are the only woman in my life. I only date you—anyone else, just friends. I do not kiss my friends or do anything else that may creep about in your imagination. Why don't you trust me, and believe me?"

Maggie considered his words. She looked at Antonio trying to remove her doubt. Then he recalled, "I remember my first love, back in high school. On and off for two years, mostly her idea, but we would date others in between, like she could never make up her mind. It seemed everyone wanted to date her. But finally, she decides she's only going to date me. I like the idea, and after a couple months, she's at my house and we're in the hallway. She has me up against the wall and she's kissing me and my mamma comes around the corner, and says, right in front of me and this girl, 'Antonio, sex is not a game!' Do you know how fast she took off? We dated on and off after that, but things were always uncomfortable—for me, anyways. Then, we had to move to Chicago. But when we came back to Italy, I always tried to see her again. Once I did. But, it was hard to be together and make it work, because we were so far apart. I spent three years of my life, thinking maybe it could work. It never did. She is married now to someone else."

"So you still like her?"

"No! That was not the point. She was my first girlfriend, and I was really hooked. We did not have half the connection that you and I have, but I still waited for her, even though it seemed impossible. And, once we came to Chicago, I started performing, more than I did before. The girls were everywhere. I went out with a lot of women, but it wasn't the same. I never knew if they liked me just for my money and I didn't want to be with just anybody. And, I didn't know who to trust. The tabloids were bad enough the way they were. I wanted to feel that connection. It's hard to find. I can't explain what was going on in my head the day I met you. I thought fate brought us together, because I couldn't stop thinking about you. Don't think I'm going to walk away from you, Maggie, because I won't."

Maggie analyzed him, finishing her mousse while he clarified his intentions. Sincerity emanated from his eyes as she recalculated her feelings for him. For the first time, he seemed trustworthy, and she felt his love. She slowly approached him, placing her arms around his neck. "You're not mad at me anymore?"

"No, Maggie. How can I stay mad at you? The only reason I get mad in the first place is because I care about us. I hope you care, too."

"I do! Remember, I made the chocolate mousse. Otherwise, you would have left."

Maggie leaned against Antonio as he held her in his arms. She peered into his eyes, wishing to resolve to trust him. He held her captive with his serious, romantic air, forgetting they ever fought.

"I can't wait until Vegas," he told her. "Maybe we can get you out there early," Antonio suggested, deep in thought.

"Francis is going to suspect something," Maggie informed him. "Speaking of him, what if he finds out what happened at the show tonight?"

"He could," Antonio enlightened her. "That fall you had. The press will be all over that. It won't be good."

"Oh, no," Maggie stepped away from him, "I can't even stand the thought. Francis is going to kill me...or worse, fire me."

Antonio started laughing.

"The press... Who cares! Louis? He can't fire you. You're under contract to assist him with the costumes for Vegas, per my instruction," Antonio confirmed.

"I hope so, but I don't want to see him Monday, either way." Maggie looked concerned.

"Trust me. It'll be fine." Antonio grabbed her arms, pulling her into a hug. "I have to go now, Maggie. It's going to be daylight in a few hours and I have a plane to catch."

Maggie felt her heart breaking as he spoke those words. He leaned over to kiss her. "Don't go!" she whispered as his lips moved on top of hers.

"I wish I could stay." Then he broke free from their embrace, explaining on his way out, "One more thing. It's best if people don't know about us. Trust me. It will only complicate things... more tabloids, more paparazzi, people coming to your house, invading your privacy. I don't want that for you. It's bad enough for me."

Maggie felt shocked by his latest announcement. She watched him leave, taking note of his every move, realizing they would now be separated again. But when his hand reached the back door, he hesitated. And when he turned back to look at her once more, he found he could not take his eyes off her, as she kept her eyes glued on him, watching as he soon retraced his steps in her direction.

Antonio hugged her again, one last time, acknowledging the pain of letting go until the next time they would see each other. "See what you can't do over the phone?" he whispered. Then he kissed her again, and Maggie knew she would feel empty without him. As she stood between him and the counter, enjoying his physical entrapment, she immediately felt her emotional entrapment. She could not control the feelings she had for him, and it was senseless to try.

"Maggie, I have to go, but I will think about this kiss until I see you next. You should do the same."

Chapter 15

Monday came.

As much as Maggie dreaded Mondays, she dreaded this one the most. She stared down at the newspaper on Francis' desk, reading the thrilling front page headline next to a huge photo of her falling onto Antonio's arm. She began to read the article: "MAGGIE WHITE, CO-DESIGNER OF DELUCA'S UPCOMING VEGAS COSTUMING, PASSES OUT ON STAGE..."

www.lovetheillusion.com/251.htm

The article offered unending speculation as to why she passed out, finally mentioning briefly the glamour to soon hit the stage in Las Vegas— compliments of Francis Louis, the prominent European designer. Maggie thought *it could be worse,* but soon calculated the mortifying truth that she had made the front page news.

Everyone would undoubtedly see it, and now she would have to explain...*stage fright...lack of sleep...lack of food...dehydration from over-consumption of alcohol due to being lovesick once again...*

Still peering over her latest demise, she froze, watching as Francis approached, awaiting his response. She hoped that he was not irate.

"Maggie!" he said with a short laugh. "Good job, bringing all this publicity to the show in Vegas! You are awesome, amazing, and I couldn't be more proud! I ought to give you a bonus. I believe there's an article in the Las Vegas paper as well. This whole production is becoming huge, a grand phenomenon as I'm riding on a rocket ship to fame!" Francis' face radiated his approval, leaving Maggie surprised as she absorbed his disclosure.

She stared at him, and then cleared her throat.

"Actually, that was completely accidental. I must have tripped over something on stage."

Francis passed her a look of disbelief.

"Yeah, right...Hey! It's a good thing he caught you, could have been ugly."

Maggie sat at her desk all day, wishing she could reverse time. While it came as a relief that Francis was overjoyed, she still resented the other comments. Jeff added to her embarrassment when he declared, "Maggie, you party animal! I didn't know you had it in you! Let me in on your next escapade, will you?" Although she did not respond to his comment, it irritated her brain all day as it rang in repetition. Then there were those that poured on condolences. "I'm so glad, Maggie, at least you aren't injured. You could have broken an ankle!" and "That was a terrible fall! How embarrassing, but at least you got to land on Antonio!"

Maggie spent the day hiding out in her cubicle, mulling over which comments were the most disturbing. She finally concluded that at least she and Antonio were okay. But she could not tell anyone other than Dana about their relationship. It seemed to be a crazy fantasy already and even more so after Antonio warned her not to tell anyone. Could they continue to survive the distance, the secrecy, and the tabloid obstacles? She hoped so, but...she was not sure. Then, like a flash of lightning in the darkness, she suddenly remembered Julia's words: "Love is strong." Maybe he did love her, and maybe she did love him. Maggie thought about her love for her mother. *It was strong. Even in death.* Her love for her mother would live on throughout eternity, just like the inscription on the ring Antonio gave her: *Love is forever.* She wondered if the next time she saw him she would be able to speak the words he wanted to hear.

The crisp fall air served as a reminder that their departure to Vegas was only a few weeks away. Maggie sat behind her desk at work, trying to focus, but instead stared at her calendar, counting out the days until she would finally see Antonio. *Thirteen days.* Francis was an ever-present reminder as well, dictating his last-minute concerns and nit-picking over final details. He would say at least five times a day, "I'm so excited! I can't wait to see everything come together."

Maggie felt much more excited to see Antonio than the new costumes on stage. But once again, she felt fortunate to have her job and the opportunities it provided. And Francis had kept his word and increased her salary after Antonio had become their client. But she would need the extra income once Dana moved out.

Now Antonio had emailed Francis about getting seasonal costumes as well, and Maggie thought perhaps it would lend additional opportunities for them to see each other. She could only hope so. Excited to see him in only a few weeks, she already wondered when the next opportunity would be.

She folded her arms on top of her desk and placed her head down. Soon they would be together. *I cannot wait to see him.* She closed her eyes and tried to relive standing in his arms and tasting his kiss. His sweet brown eyes looking into hers left her mesmerized. She could not wait to kiss him again. *I think I love him.*
"Maggie!" Francis killed her mental get-away. "There's no time to slack!" Maggie popped up straight at her desk when she heard Francis issue concern. "Remember Antonio's costume we are remaking? The one he wore for the English show? That got burn holes in it from his stupid ring of fire? After he got too close to the flame? When he had to catch you on stage? Well, now we have a serious problem and I need to see you at my desk, immediately!"

Maggie felt her stomach clench into a knot, wondering what his latest discovery was. Then she gathered her suspicions.

She followed Francis to his desk, where Antonio's costume lay across his paperwork. She stared down at it, waiting for him to tell her what she already knew.

"Now, I am sure," Francis began his spiel, "that taking a quick look, you will notice the problem!"

Maggie's eyes widened as she wished to conceal the truth.

"Didn't this get shipped already?" Maggie stood, nonchalant.

"No! And a good thing it did not! You must realize what's missing?" Francis alarmed. *I do realize, but...*

"Is it...still in production?" She acted confused.

"No!" Francis spoke loudly. "I just stopped in by production this morning to view everything before it got sent to shipping. It's an earth-shattering disaster! They do not even have the pattern—it's missing and it must ship today or it might not arrive in time! Now, you tell me, how can we ship his stage clothes without the pink sash?"

Please don't put him in a pink sash! Maggie pressed her lips together while she contemplated, *I do not want Antonio in a pink sash!* Then she heard Francis' voice continue, drowning her thoughts in his added misery. "It was with the rest of our patterns, but when I went to get it, it was no longer there! I can't imagine what we are going to do! It needs to be made today, before noon! *And* they are out of pink fabric now— you know the hot pink color that we selected? I can't imagine how long it will take to reorder that! It was specially dyed to that unique hue! His other two costumes have that hot pink and now this will not! And, he wants to use *this* costume for his next fan poster!"

Maggie watched as Francis scuttled about the office, expecting her to render a solution. Against her better judgment, she dared to offer her opinion. "This costume looks amazing, Francis, I'm sure it will be fine just as it is! He can wear a black belt!" Maggie smiled while looking at the shiny silver shirt and black pants that had silver panels going down the front. She tried to visualize Antonio's new poster, *with the sash?*

www.lovetheillusion.com/254.htm

"Are you bloody insane? That pink sash is the iconic flash in the costume!" Francis went over to an office storage cabinet and started pulling out fabric samples from a box. Maggie watched as he sifted through them, landing each fabric remnant on the floor. She thought his immaturity veiled his distinguished persona as he let go of his frustration. "This is a god-awful nightmare!" Francis raved. "And you! How can you just stand there? You need to get over to production *now* and scrape the premise for any scrap you can find! Perhaps they have some, but they just don't know! Dig through all the trash bins if you have to!" Maggie stood in disbelief as Francis' face turned red in his fit of rage. *Poor Francis!* "Hurry up! Get over there, now!" he ordered.

She went back to her cubicle, grabbed her purse and left the office. *Can't wait to get away!*

Maggie pushed on the big wooden door and saw the bright sunshine. *A beautiful sunny day.* But no sooner did she skip down the concrete staircase than she noticed a reporter was lingering on the premises. She was definitely not in the mood when he rushed in to question her. *Please leave me alone.*

"Are you Maggie White? Do you mind answering a few questions for me? What happened on stage? Are you and Antonio romantically involved?"

Why does he care? Maggie remained silent but issued him a dirty look and, mindful of Antonio's warning, wondered what calamities could follow if she answered. She got into her car, wishing to escape it all. The reporter stood several feet from her car, looking defeated. *Is it even worth it?*

She wished she could escape somewhere with Antonio—just the two of them. Mindful that would never happen, she turned the key in the ignition to make a trip to the production plant.

She reached into her glove box and removed the pattern for the sash and a yard of *the* hot pink fabric...*Can't wait to make Francis' day!*

That evening, Dana and Maggie were together, sitting on the sofa on opposite ends. Dana was eating ice cream, and Maggie was busy filling in a crossword puzzle. She could only resort to such foolishness to get her mind off of everything.

"I think you're holding a grudge," Dana said, seemingly out of the blue.

"Why would you think that?"

"Ever since the show, you've been quiet." Dana gave her a curious look.

Maggie contemplated her concern and then explained, "I just have a lot on my mind. Don't worry. It's not you." She knew Dana could read her like an open book.

"Is it Shane?" Dana continued to probe. Maggie recalled his childish antics, and that despite them, she still found him loveable.

Maggie laughed, admitting her own guilt. "No, I'm the idiot that drank his violent concoctions."

Dana smiled and then revealed, "Hey, he told me to tell you that he's very sorry." Dana spilled out the truth. "He put more booze in your drinks than in ours." Maggie's jaw dropped as she listened to Dana. "Before you hate his guts, though, did I tell you that he also said that he liked Antonio? He said, 'It sounds strange, but he seems to take care of Maggie like she's his prize possession.' He watched him in the limo with you."

"Really?" Maggie's face brightened.

"Yeah, and then he said Antonio seems really nice, not like he pictured. I wanted to tell him about the two of you, but I kept my mouth shut. Now, are you proud of me?"

Maggie smiled at Dana, thinking that she was lucky to have her friendship. "Sure Dana. We need to stay out of the spotlight as much as possible, but that is a useless endeavor. The media's just vicious! Now those paparazzi pukes have figured out where I work. And they graciously call me by name!" Maggie adjusted her voice to a nasally tone. "Are you Maggie White? Are you and Antonio romantically involved?" She begged Dana for sympathy. "Why can't they just leave us alone?"

"Ah..." Dana looked puzzled, but then informed, "The media's very ambitious! And Antonio wants your relationship undercover, like a mystery. But you must just want to tell everyone, right? Maybe then they would lose interest and go away. This just keeps him in the spotlight as they try to figure everything out! He's smart! It's part of the plan!" Dana hoped to enlighten her.

"You can't be serious!" Maggie felt frustrated. "It's no better if they know! Remember, I was expecting his child before we even kissed! How horrible is that? Try waiting seven, eight, nine months to have your revenge! It's only a matter of time before Francis finds out, if he doesn't already have his suspicions. And he will just croak from a stroke when he finds out about my illicit affair with his most prominent client. I'm sure it won't be long before all of Europe is just dying to know more about the hot magician! The only solution is to move to Nauru!" Maggie landed her crossword puzzle book on the table with a loud smack.

Dana listened intently to her tales of woe, but then informed, "Did I tell you, after the limo drove us back from the show, Antonio told us to get lost? He seemed a bit angry. He took you inside, and we ran back to the limo. It was a riot, and you will never believe, we had so much fun! A car started chasing us. It was a thrill, until we got out at Shane's and they saw us! Then they drove away!"

Maggie was entertained by her telling, but then changed the subject. "Dana, I have the photo of your wedding dress. Do you want to see?" Maggie opened the paper file sitting on the end table. "I hope you like it."

She passed it to Dana.

"Ah, just as I pictured," Dana said. "I love it! When can I try it on?"

"Soon!" Maggie got off the couch to make tea as Dana launched into explaining her plans for the wedding attire.

"Now, did I tell you, for the bridesmaid dresses, I just want you to design whatever you want, but red…with those red patent shoes you picked out…for Christmas."

Maggie thought things through, wondering why anyone would want to get married at Christmas time, adding additional stress to the holidays. She couldn't help but dish out pessimism. "That's going to be really busy, getting married two weeks before Christmas!" she told Dana, passing her a look of regret.

Dana seemed oblivious to her concerns.

"I know, but it's exactly what I wanted. I love Christmas," Dana expressed. "It's the season of love!" She closed her eyes, placing her hands over her heart.

Maggie considered Dana's depiction of being in love as she reviewed her own feelings for Antonio. Then she came to a shocking discovery. "Can you believe it's only a few months away? There's no time to waste! I need to work on the bridesmaid dress design right away." Maggie quickly imagined a possibility. "How about red...but lace...over brown satin to pop the color...a red satin sash...and short and sassy," she gave consideration, "above the knee so we can admire the shoe. Hopefully, they can be done by the end of the month," she concluded.

"That sounds...interesting. I trust you...whatever you think!" Dana sounded pleased. "I just can't wait to try my dress on!" Dana's face was bright as she had an additional thought. "Did I tell you my mum says she's just wearing a suit with a hat?" Dana rolled her eyes. "She does not want the mother of the bride look, but Shane's mum is going all out in an outrageous poufy dress, like a Mary Poppins display! I'm sure she will be unsightly."

"That should make for some interesting prints!" Maggie said, predicting the fashion catastrophe.

Dana thought it over.

"That should be the least of my concerns. Did I tell you that *all* of the bridesmaids, except for you, insist they prefer a different shoe! They want to wear a flat...something comfortable!"

"No! Dana! You cannot allow everyone in a different shoe!" Maggie was certain. "That will be a fashion nightmare! The pictures will be an eternal disgrace!"

"Seriously, I don't care if they all want to be barefoot as long as everyone stays happy!"

Maggie gave her a look of doubt.

"Welcome to Dana's Dreamland, a never-ending journey of optimism!"

Dana brushed off her concerns and pronounced her conclusion. "I can't obsess any longer! I refuse to lose any sleep over this." She chuckled.

"The whole thing sounds exhausting. It would be easier to just elope," Maggie decided. "But someday…I want to wear a wedding dress…an original design of my own, not one that belongs to Francis!"

"I think you should marry Antonio," Dana suggested with a big smile.

Maggie lay on her bed looking up at the ceiling. It was the week before they were due to leave for the Vegas show. Time was passing. She had kept herself busy with the Vegas show costumes, and getting the bridesmaid dresses ready for Dana's wedding. Chloe, one of the bridesmaids, tried on the red dress and it was beautiful…and they *would* all wear the red shoe!

www.lovetheillusion.com/259.htm

Everything was going well at work now. Francis had praised her efforts when she returned to the office with Antonio's pink sash before noon, meeting the deadline.

Certainly, things were intensifying as it was only days before their departure. And although everything was shipped, she and Francis were working late to finalize the details of some of the seasonal costume drawings that Francis wanted to present to Antonio. He was adamant that they have a variety of options. Maggie felt exhausted by his efforts, and then he announced, "I think we need to work late. We are almost done, and we need to finish the details of our third sample grouping so Antonio can see them first-hand. I will order pizza delivery."

Maggie turned her nose up, realizing she would be eating mushrooms and anchovies, the two toppings that she most despised.

She stood in front of Francis, listening while he held his phone to his ear and placed the order. "I will have a large pizza with extra anchovies and mushrooms...and make sure it's still hot when it gets here. Last time it was barely warm...yes, I'd like that delivered as soon as possible. And I have a free coupon from last time when it took them over an hour to get here and then I ended up with the wrong pizza!" He put his phone back into his pocket as he kept her in his eye. "You know, Maggie, I'm glad I hired you. We're a good team!"

She felt flattered to receive his compliment.

"Yes, we are." She voiced her opinion. After all, the costumes were impressive. It would be a visual masterpiece once everything came together. She stood next to Francis who was now sitting on the edge of his desk. She picked up a sample board of all the trims they had chosen to put on the costumes. As she admired the details, Francis grabbed onto her arm and pulled her up to him. She second-guessed his intentions, but before she could step away he leaned into her face and kissed her on the lips. Maggie felt every inch of her body freeze in contempt. She stood speechless while various thoughts dumped into her brain. Now, she was in a compromising position, not only at work, but also with Antonio. She feared being in Vegas with the two of them again, this time for completely different reasons. A love triangle was not an option! There was no love in her heart at all for Francis, other than her gratuity for having a job. She quickly moved away from him, explaining, "Francis! I'm seeing someone."

He seemed surprised, and she hoped that he would not ask who it was. He was too proud to act concerned, but also too proud to apologize.

Maggie ate the pizza after she picked off the mushrooms and anchovies, leaving a distorted topping of cheese. She tried not to make eye contact with him, but then realized he did not squirm in the discomfort one bit.

"So, how's Elle?" Maggie decided to pick his brain.

"Elle? Ha, that's nothing," he surprisingly explained.

She sat disgusted by his latest assumption that she could be on his list of "encounters."

Maggie finally left work, pondering her failed employee-boss relationship. Should she call Antonio? And tell him? Or wait until she was in person? *Does he have to know? Of course he does.* If she kept this secret, it would only cause trouble. Either way she told him, it would be ugly. She quickly remembered his words when she begged for his kiss. He was right about sealing her fate, but she was quite sure Francis' kiss was not in the equation. There was no doubt Antonio would get angry, and she could already hear him yelling.

At nine o'clock that evening, Maggie was wide awake in her bed, unable to sleep. She watched the clock on her dresser, quietly ticking away the time, next to the photo of her and Antonio dancing at the benefit. Her stomach turned like a pancake on a grill, and she thought back to the pizza she ate with Francis. She thought she may as well have eaten a bucket of anchovies. She knew that she would not be able to sleep unless she shared her concerns with Antonio. She reluctantly climbed out of bed in pursuit of his opinion.

She picked up her phone, feeling shaky about the situation. Within seconds, she heard his voice.

"Hi, Maggie! How are you? I can't wait to see you."

Hearing his voice melted her heart. As much as she wanted to delay her news and bask in the excitement that they would see each other soon, she knew she had better get to the point.

"I have to tell you something..." She recalled his temper.

"What? You *finally* love me?" Antonio took a guess. She could hear his smile behind his words. Maggie thought about it, unable to cope with that harsh reality—that yes, she did probably love him. She dodged his question.

"You are going to be mad. I hate when you are mad..." She paused, regretting her decision to tell him.

"What?" His voice indicated alarm.

Maggie knew it was best to get it over with.

"Francis kissed me...yesterday...at work..." she reported. Antonio remained silent, so she continued to explain, "I pulled away, and told him I was seeing someone." She waited for his response, but he was still silent. *Is he still on the phone?* Then his voice sent chills up her spine.

"That… son of a…You tell him if…I'm gonna kill him! You! Tell him I said he's *dead* next time he touches you!"

"You know I can't tell him that. He has no idea we're even seeing each other outside of work. But some reporter approached me as I was leaving work the other day, and I'm sure it is only a matter of time before the media announces our affair to the entire globe! I don't know what to do. It's going to get ugly now that Francis wants to pursue me on a personal level." She finalized her concerns. "I need this job!"

Antonio gave no concern. "Are you kidding, Maggie? You need to call in. Tell him you're sick. Once you get here, I'll take care of it. Meanwhile, say you got the flu or something. I don't care if he has to work until dawn. He needs to keep busy so he can keep his filthy paws off of you."

"Are you sure? It just seems risky. If I lose my job, and then we don't work out, I'll be in a mess!" Maggie couldn't believe that she had just presented her worst fear. Without thinking, she had let it slip.

"No Maggie! We're gonna work. You have to trust me. That Francis is nothing but trouble, and I wish you weren't tangled up in his slimy maneuvers. I am just sick and tired him!"

"Francis is going to be in a fit of rage when I don't show up the next two days, and then make a quick recovery at the last minute to leave. *And* he has already told me that I get to fly first class with him. What a privilege," Maggie said sarcastically. "It will be a long flight."

"Don't worry. We will be together soon. Everything will work out. I love you, Maggie. Trust me."

"Okay, then..." She pondered his favorite words: trust me. "I will call in. I hope I don't regret this, and...I'll see you in a few days."

Maggie breathed a sigh of relief. She was glad that was over, but now she hoped she would not set off Francis.

The following day, Maggie was curled up in a blanket, lying on the couch. She had phoned Francis and bluffed that she had food poisoning.

"Have you got the day off?" Dana glanced at Maggie while pouring her tea into a travel mug, as she was on her way to work.

Maggie peered over at Dana from her cocoon.

"No. Yes. I mean, I should be at work, but Francis tried kissing me last night, and now Antonio ordered me to stay home. I hope I'm not making a mistake," Maggie elaborated in a groan.

"You're not serious, Maggie. I can't believe your life! You have more problems than the crisis hot line," Dana remarked.

"Funny, Dana, but I'm not in the mood. I'm actually feeling kind of sick, while I pretend I am. If I lose this job, it's the best I've ever had. Antonio is the best guy I've ever had, so what do I do? I guess I can't have both...love or career? I hope I'll be happy in love with no money." Maggie's words drained out.

"What are you talking about?" Dana attempted to soothe her concerns. "Antonio's got a ton of money, and he doesn't flinch at spending it on you."

"That's if we make it," Maggie agonized. "If we don't, I'm heartbroken, and broke."

"Well," Dana laughed, light-heartedly, "try to have a good day."

Maggie lay on the sofa until noon, poured into the pity of her latest dilemma. She started having second thoughts. Antonio lived in his own world of dictating commands and getting what he wanted. She lived in the constant state of reality. She could not expect him to intervene in her life, wave his magical wand, and just fix everything. And how did he plan to do that? *Would he approach Francis on the matter? That would create a problem!* Now she realized she had only known Antonio for six months but had poured a lifetime of efforts into her career. If she quit with Francis, who was at the top, she would have to take a huge pay cut. Could she risk her job for Antonio? Realistically, she needed her job and needed to face that reality. She could handle this on her own. If Francis made another move, she would just tell him that she would file a complaint, and it would go through the press. Hopefully, *that* would scare him off!

A half hour later, she waltzed into the office.

"Hi, Francis." Maggie scooted past his desk. "I think I was able to shake it off with a couple Tums and an Advil."

"That's my girl!" Francis looked up from the newspaper. "I'm so excited! Do you know how huge this Vegas show's going to be? Now they've planned a follow-up show a few days after the opening. The first show sold out in a matter of minutes!"

Maggie realized the frightful awkward event of the past night was nothing to him. *What a surprise.*

"Really…" Maggie hoped to mask her contempt. "I can't wait to see…it." She verbalized her hidden agenda.

Francis gave no suspicious concern, but rather spilled out additional specifics. "Our flight leaves Thursday. We stay for both shows, so we'll be there for the week." Francis' voice carried a new wave excitement. "This is just the tip of the iceberg...the start of an entirely fresh venue of business. The possibilities are endless!" Her ears fell wide open as he rendered the details. "You can expect another pay rise this week, since we'll be floating in even more money than we were before. I just love the green stuff coming my way! Antonio's so excited to see our designs for seasonal events. And I'm confident he'll be delighted! I just spoke with him a few minutes ago. We've got the job! I'm sure of it! This one went off without a hitch," he finally concluded, his words spoken like a shovel to her grave.

"That's...nice, really nice," she said with no enthusiasm.

While her hopes of seeing Antonio were near guaranteed, she was stuck in a bottomless boat with Francis! A cyclone of fears came over her as she weighed Antonio's intentions. She went into her office cubicle to escape, trying to mentally calculate Francis' last prediction. *Would Antonio and Francis be eternal business partners? And she caught in the middle?* Antonio did not seem to want to deal with him after this show, or so he had indicated to her. Was it simply just a flaw in Francis' perception of things, or were they "buddies" in some weird way, able to tolerate any personal differences to advance their careers?

Francis disrupted her thoughts.

"Maggie, I told Jeff you'd have that file ready for him. He needs to know who's wearing what in that photo shoot we have for Euro Fashions."

"Yeah, I will get right on that." Maggie propped her head into her hands and stared into space. How would she get anything done today? She thought about the next week. *Another trip with Francis to see Antonio...Who could possibly predict what that would entail?*

Maggie lay in her bed the night before she left for Vegas. It would be a miracle if she could even sleep. She had just gotten an email from Antonio before she left work that said: "**I can't wait to hold you in my arms again.**" Now she thought about that, realizing her emotions were spinning out of control as she wondered if they would even get time alone so that she could sort through his true agenda. Francis was definitely an obstacle, but perhaps he would get distracted in the Vegas high life.

Maggie thought about the last time she saw Antonio. She recalled his warning to keep their relationship under cover. Then Dana's words sharply entered her thoughts, landing like a two-edged sword in her brain. *Why did it have to stay a secret?* If everyone knew the truth, wouldn't the flurry of excitement eventually die off? She wondered if Antonio wished to keep things a mystery for his own gain. Was he using their relationship to stir up media hype? *Was he related to Francis in the pursuit of attention and fame?* How could she know? *He seemed genuine enough, but what if it was all a hoax?* Mentally exhausted, she needed to get some sleep, but it felt as though her mattress was laced with pins and needles. She wanted so badly to believe that she had finally found love, but would she ever be sure? Her feelings fluttered at no control of her own just thinking about being with Antonio. She knew she wanted to spend forever with him, and she finally concluded she must love him. Now did he *really* love her? Perhaps Vegas would bring a final answer to her questions.

Chapter 16

It was just a plane ride away until she would see Antonio. Maggie fastened her seatbelt after sitting down next to Francis. Now that she had worked for him nearly eight months, she realized he wore his inflated ego to mask a multitude of flaws. While he read his favorite newspaper, calculating in detail the latest of Wall Street's stock performances, she stared out the window, waiting for that airborne feeling at takeoff. She was so anxious to see Antonio, she already felt like she was floating on air. But she hoped that this trip would not unleash new battles. And she hoped that Francis would not instigate Antonio's temper. But, according to Francis, all was well. She knew that she needed to see Antonio in person to try to make sense of it all. After having trouble sleeping the night before, she hoped to crash out on the plane ride until the layover in Chicago. Soon there would be more memories. *Chicago had them. New York had them. Now Vegas would have them.*

Maggie sat, impatiently.

Hours later, they arrived at the Chicago airport in layover. After making it through customs, Maggie immediately saw a camera crew set up, and soon learned that they wanted a few minutes with Francis.

"Go ahead…" Maggie folded her arms and leaned against a wall, "I can stand here and wait."

"Oh, no," one of the cameramen insisted, "we want you in this photo as well."

Wonderful. Maggie eyed up the ensemble—two camera men, a reporter, and a couple sidekicks assisting with their fleeting endeavors. She slowly made her way over to the impending circus of media attention.

She already felt irritated standing within their sight, when Francis kindly informed, "I'll do all the talking, Maggie." She welcomed his suggestion and stood by his side as he answered a series of questions in regards to the upcoming event.

Just when she thought the interrogation was over, the reporter turned to her and probed, "Rumor has it that the magician has become quite fond of you and that you two have been seen in public on numerous occasions. Are you two romantically involved?"

Maggie felt the tension mounting inside her. She would never ever get used to the reporters. Regardless, her response rolled off her tongue. "Francis and I work for him. That's it!"

She watched as the nosey reporter disappeared from view while Francis issued her a strange stare.

"What was that about, Maggie? Is there something I should know about? Are you entertaining him on the side?"

"Shut up, Francis! You should know better."

She scrunched her brow.

"Do I? I saw how he looks at you. And you? Why wouldn't you go for him? Complete Shangri-La!"

Maggie took the liberty of walking a few steps ahead of Francis, hoping to brush him out of her audible range. She was sick of him.

<u>www.lovetheillusion.com/268.htm</u>

After another plane ride, Maggie finally sat in her hotel room at the Bellagio, where the show was taking place. It was a small break— *momentary serenity.* But now she wondered when she would see Antonio. The show was Saturday night, and it was still Thursday, only noon. She had to relive this whole day, it seemed, after jumping through the time zones.

Her phone went off. It was Francis.

"Lunch is at one-thirty after we meet with Antonio and Stanley. Come by my room at 1:00, and we'll catch a cab to the MGM."

Maggie hesitated. "Uh…I can take the shuttle."

"Forget it, Maggie. Meet me at 1:00. You don't need an opportunity to be late!" Then he hung up.

Men and their demands.

I wish he would leave me alone.

Now in the cab with Francis, Maggie listened as his words spilled out quickly to inform, "Got some paperwork to go over—last minute contract disputes. Stanley says we double billed them for two different shipments. It's a bunch of crap! My accounting department doesn't make mistakes like that. He's probably going to want a credit because the costumes shipped so late, but I told him it was cutting it close. DeLuca dragged his feet for six weeks prior, wanting to do business with me but acting as if he couldn't afford me. Ha, now he doesn't like his bill. That's too bad!"

Maggie sat still with an occasional change in eye position, trying to imagine the upcoming discomforts as she sat through another meeting with Francis and Antonio. Then, she felt Francis' arm around her, against the dash. The whole situation was unsettling.

They finally arrived.

No sooner did they enter the conference room, she saw Stanley with Antonio, already seated at a conference table. Fortunately, she had not seen anyone from the press— *a small break.*

Maggie sat down, excited to be in the same room with Antonio. He sat across from her, immediately giving her a sweet look while concealing a smile. *He's just as I remember.* She stared back at him, imitating his hidden affection. While her eyes rested in his, she realized that they held the potion to calm all her fears. And, any doubts that he truly loved her vanished instantly. She could not wait to have time alone with him.

www.lovetheillusion.com/269.htm

Stanley sat at the head of the table, between Francis and Antonio, a completely new addition to the equation. He started the meeting. "Francis, I would like to begin by saying that we appreciate wholeheartedly the efforts you have made to produce our costumes with precise detail and in such a timely manner. Everything has arrived, and without a fault. But we have received the invoice, and you will notice several double entries here, on line four, line eight, and also on line twenty-two. Do you want to tell me about that? We need a credit before we can issue the final payment."

Maggie watched as the paperwork shuffled over to Francis. He peered over the numbers while she glanced at Antonio out of the corner of her eye. She felt his foot tap against her leg. He nodded, indicating he wished to pass her a note under the table. Maggie slouched down discreetly, meeting her hand in his under the table as she felt the ridged corners of a piece of paper enter into her hand. She closed her hand around it, and carefully slipped it into the pocket of her trousers, while Francis still had his face buried in the invoice. She took a deep breath, eager for the meeting to adjourn.

"I think we must have double shipped these," Francis gave surprise. "You have more costumes than you need? You ought to keep them as extras!" Francis concluded his explanation. "We always factor in a few extra sizes, in case there's an injury and you need a fill in." He brushed off their concerns.

"That was not in the original contract," Stanley informed. "Antonio and I need to discuss it further, and we'll let you know."

"Nonsense," Francis declared. "They are already made!"

"Yes," Stanley agreed, "but I doubt we need an additional..." He paused as he held his pen to the paperwork, attempting mental multiplication. Antonio gave Francis a sour look, but Francis seemed to care less. Then Stanley declared, "You billed us for thirty-five additional costumes at twenty-five hundred a piece! That's..."

Stanley did the mental math in an instant, "eighty-seven thousand, five hundred dollars!?"

"Yeah, what's up with *that*, Louis?" Antonio questioned.

Francis cleared his throat. "Well, if you would take a moment to sort it out, you must realize that each dancer and stage performer has three costumes...that's a grand total of twelve dancers, which equals thirty-six costumes...two assistants means six more costumes...eight acrobatic performers is twenty four additional costumes, and the goofy clown chara—"

"I think we can all do third grade math!" Stanley threw an insult. "Get to the point!"

Francis sat up straight and then leaned over the table at them. "You have 35 stage crew and 35 extras!"

Antonio suddenly looked disgusted. "That doesn't even make sense, Louis! If someone gets injured, we need a set of their three costumes not a random surplus! This is a joke!"

"It's simple!" Stanley decided. "We're not paying for all those extras!"

Francis grabbed the paperwork. "We can make an adjustment... meet you halfway, perhaps—provided you will be signing us to make additional costumes...the Christmas line. I brought preliminary designs."

"Francis," Maggie dared to speak, "did they ask for those extra costumes? If they aren't in the original contract, then they should not have to pay for them! It's that simple."

"Maggie, I'm in charge here!" Francis ordered her silent.

She glanced over to Antonio, admiring his one eyebrow that was pinned up in Francis' direction. Francis remained oblivious, looking just at Stanley, while making his offer.

"Say we 'give you' those costumes at cost. Then, you'll have them, just in case! And on future orders, if you do not want spare costumes, we won't make any!" Francis' voice carried a grand deliverance, reminding Maggie that she only had three hours of sleep. She had been unable to sleep on the plane. Tired as she was, the moment she started to doze off, he had kept her alert with his various diatribes.

"Just…fine!" Antonio blurted out, completely annoyed. Then he whispered under his breath, "Bastard."

Stanley defended Antonio's outburst, yet tried to ease the mounting tension. He explained to Francis, "Antonio and I are reasonable people. We don't wish to cheat you, but like Maggie said, we did not order all those extras costumes. You need to pay attention to the details of the contract, just like the details of the costumes!" Stanley enlightened, hoping to put him in his place.

Maggie tried not to show her amusement when Antonio came to her defense. "Perhaps while you're guiding Maggie along the ropes of success, she should be tying the ropes of proper business etiquette *around your neck!*" Antonio passed Francis a look of disgust.

Maggie squirmed with discomfort, but Francis inadvertently rushed to her aid by announcing, "Meeting adjourned!" indicating that he was done receiving their insults. He left his nose in the air as he waited for her to get up, and when she did, she caught Stanley passing her a wink. Now she got to go eat lunch with Francis. And she was not looking forward to that.

Hopefully, it will be a quick lunch.

"Whatever happened to email? It's way more peaceful!" Maggie teased Francis on the way out.

He appeared disgruntled and then advised, "Next time, Maggie, I'll do all the talking."

Maggie tried not to laugh because he had *no* idea what people were actually thinking when he talked!

Maggie returned to her room. She had finally escaped Francis after her lunch date with him, following the meeting. Time stood still while she watched him eat. She only ordered soup. The dress he designed for her to wear already felt like a paint job on her body, with a revealing slit up the side to the upper thigh, giving another reason to shed a few pounds. What dress was that? The purple one she would wear on stage in front of everyone before Antonio's show, as Francis acknowledged acclaim for Antonio's new costume designs' "grand presentation." And it was purple, the color of Antonio's show shirts. But for Maggie, purple was the color of the passion she felt in her heart every time she looked at Antonio. She could not wait to spend more time with him. She reached into her pocket anxious to pull out his note.

"Front lobby. Look for Bradley- 3:00."

Bradley is here?

She slipped on a pair of white capris and a beaded teal halter top. She put her necklace from Antonio back on and off she went.

No sooner did she step off the elevator, she was enamored by the glitz that only Vegas could exhibit. The ceiling danced with a variety of colors as she sailed through the lobby.

Bradley stood near the front desk, eagerly expecting her.

"Hi Bradley, how are you? You got to come along?" Maggie was happy to see him, laughing at any former concerns of him being a stalker.

"Yep, Antonio told me I had to keep track of you! But he let Rainelle come along too, and we're having dinner here at the Bellagio after I get you to Antonio." Then he leaned down and whispered in her ear where she was to find Antonio.

"Thanks." Maggie waved at him as she nearly skipped her way past the front lobby doors to the outside entrance.

There it was— a black Jaguar with VEGAS on the plates.

Maggie approached the car and a bellhop opened the passenger door. She got in, glad to finally be alone with Antonio. He had a big grin on his face as she smiled back at him.

"It's good to finally see you, Maggie." He gazed into her eyes.

"I know. It's been a long ten weeks." She thought he maybe wanted to kiss her, but he just said,

"Well, we're out of here."

Antonio stepped on the accelerator and sped away from the curb. For the first time ever, she watched him drive. Classical music played, and the weather gauge read 77 degrees—*a perfect fall day in the Vegas sun.*

"Where are we going?" She wondered.

"Around." He left her in the dark.

"Where, around?" Her face glowed as she tried to uncover their next adventure.

"I'm not telling you." He enjoyed leaving her in suspense.

"I guess I'll just have to distract you until you tell me." Maggie reached for the back of his head and started combing her fingers through his hair.

"Hey, stop that. If I wanted my hair a mess, I would put the top down." His cold response told her immediately that he had something on his mind. And now he seemed agitated.

"Sounds fun," she suggested, keeping the mood light. He followed suit in her attempt.

"Okay, but wait until we're out of the city. I know a place we can eat. It's off the beaten path. No one's out there and we can hang out like normal people!"

"Yeah, right...you, normal? I don't think so!" She laughed. "How long will we be in the car?"

"Just until you get sick of me." Antonio grinned.

"So we're going to be in here for days with no food and water?" She passed him a dreamy gaze, realizing how intoxicating he was.

"Sounds like you missed me?"

"I did." She looped the necklace around her index finger.

"Are you wearing that in front of Francis?"

Now Maggie knew he could not wait to undo the jar of worms. She gave him a dry look and played her best card.

"It's usually tucked in, but he questioned me about you."

"Yeah, I saw your stupid interview." Antonio let out a huff. "See, now we're even. So, has he been keeping his hands off you, or do I get to hurt him?"

Maggie changed the subject, realizing that the cameras facing her and Francis were live.

"You should see the dress he designed for me to wear the night of the show. It's skin tight with sequins, and I had to lose weight just to zip it up!"

"Maggie! I didn't ask about your *dress!*"

Maggie stared out the passenger window.

"I called in, the day after we talked, but by noon I got jolted into reality. I need my job, Antonio. I'm taking a risk by calling in.

Francis is demanding, short tempered, and only sees it his way. He never misses a day in the office, and—"

"Taking a risk?" he interrupted her. "That's what you do when you even *stand* next to him! And you do not need to remind me of his revolting personality traits. I'm unfortunately aware!"

She could tell by the tone in Antonio's voice that the conversation was headed for trouble. Then he confirmed her suspicion. "I knew you wouldn't listen to me. Why, Maggie, do you have to be so stubborn?" Antonio's hands were tight on the steering wheel.

"Are you serious? I'm supporting myself. It's not like I can call up my dad for money. I probably could, but how embarrassing would that be! My mom's insurance money paid for my schooling. I will not jeopardize owning my father's respect, becoming his financial responsibility."

Antonio stared ahead while driving.

"I see," he finally muttered.

"So, it's simple." She made brief eye contact with him. "I need my job, and working for Francis is an opportunity, regardless of the obstacles. Don't you see how this job is a foothold for my career? I can't risk that, Antonio. I just can't!" She hoped he understood.

"Has he been keeping to himself, or not?"

Antonio still seemed agitated.

"Pretty good," Maggie defended Francis.

"That's what I figured." He sounded disgusted. "So, you mean to tell me that I have to put up with this...wondering if he's making his moves on you, and what you're doing to keep him in line. I say we send him to court for sexual misconduct!" Antonio guided his own conclusion.

"No, Antonio! That would be pointless. It would be his word against mine and that's risky for me. I don't want to jeopardize my job. Not to mention if *that* hit the press, it would be an excruciating embarrassment! Why can't you understand? You live in a profession that you love and so do I," Maggie concluded in a pleasant soft voice, hoping to keep things peaceful.

"Hmm, interesting," Antonio said, curtly.

Maggie smiled at him apologetically, but he kept quiet and nonresponsive.

"Look, Antonio, don't be mad at me. I hate it when you're mad," Maggie said with alarm in her voice.

"I'm not mad, Maggie," Antonio stated calmly. "I just wish you could get away from Francis, and his...he is just a walking satchel of trouble. I feel like I can't protect you when you're in England and I'm in New York. My mind drives me crazy, thinking about it...it's not a good situation for you to be in. He is not only money hungry, but he is power hungry as well. Not to mention, the circle of people that he entertains are *all* bad news! I've been uncovering more and more interesting facts about him, almost daily." He glanced at her.

"You hired a private investigator to dig up the dirt on Francis?" Maggie laughed uncontrollably. "That's ridiculous! You're just jealous of him and that's so funny! He's fine as a boss. I just have to keep it professional. You don't need to worry. I can take care of myself. I have lived through three brothers, my mother's death, and a scandalous fiancé. Francis is a small rival in my life of chaos. Don't forget! I managed just fine before I met you!" Maggie spoke with conviction.

"Is that so?" Antonio did not sound convinced.

"Yes! Just let it go," Maggie reiterated, triumphing over the discussion.

He tapped his fingers against the steering wheel as she changed the station to a loud beat of music, tired of the subject.

"Fine, then have it your way," he finally declared.

"Are we fighting again? I hate it when you're mad," Maggie uttered with a flirtatious grin.

"Who said I'm mad?" he snapped.

Then she changed the tone of her voice. "You are, Chad. You are mad because you can't get your way. That's all you know, your way."

"Ouch. That was mean!" He faced her in contempt. "Why are you throwing darts at me, when they should be flying towards Louis?"

"He is *my* boss, *my* problem, *I* will deal with him." Maggie brushed him off. "I am sorry I involved you. You obviously can't deal with it! And I can't believe the rope comment you made. He's going to think that I told you he kissed me!"

"I can't *stand* the thought of him kissing you! He's lucky I didn't punch him! I was *nice!*"

"Well, I think it's best if you let Stanley deal with him."

"Don't tell me what to do! He's hired by me, not Stanley. And I will tell him off if I need to."

"Then don't tell me what to do!" Maggie warned.

Silence followed, neither of them wanting to speak. Maggie folded her arms, proud with her last words, while he shot her occasional glances that were mixed with anger and submission.

After they had been riding in silence for over an hour, Antonio pulled over to the side of the road. Maggie looked around. He had parked the car in a completely deserted place.

What are we doing here?

"Get out!" His face was rigid. Maggie gave him a strange glance after viewing the desert—brown, dusty, and drab—as the wind blew the desert sand and dust particles into the air.

She made her assessment, behind the windows of the Jaguar. "I'm not getting out here, in the middle of nowhere! Besides, I have white pants on. There is sandy dust everywhere," she said. Antonio seemed to enjoy her contempt. "This can't be your idea of a fun afternoon." She watched as he ignored her concerns, got out, and came around to open her door, pulling her arm to guide her out of the vehicle.

"We're putting the top down," he bluffed.

"Why do we have to get out for that?" she asked.

Then he announced his true agenda as he had her pinned between himself and the car. "Are you going to quit sassing me and let me protect you from Francis, or not?"

Maggie stood leaned against the passenger door of the Jaguar while Antonio stood in front of her. The wind blew her hair into her face so she could not see him. He reached over, grabbing her hair, holding it in his hands behind her head. Now, she could see his brown eyes settling into hers. She wanted to kiss him, but knew he wouldn't let her. He had his unfinished agenda.

"Fine," Maggie laughed, as she threw her head back, knowing she wanted his kiss, "you can be my knight in shining armor and save me from the evil step-mother of fashion! Just don't rock the boat too much, okay?"

Antonio bit his bottom lip, giving a victorious smile, his hands still holding back her hair. He leaned forward, and with one hand propped against the car, started kissing her. The wind was blowing sand and other debris into them, but Maggie leaned back against the car, glued to his kiss. She clinched her fingers around the fabric of his shirt, holding him close to her.

Minutes had passed when he finally stepped back, indicating a change of plans. He took her hand, leading her through the desert as she held her hair in place with her other hand. Even with sunglasses on, she kept blinking to keep her eyes free from the particles that sifted through the air. She wondered how much sand clung to their clothing as they walked away from the car.

Now they were quite a distance from the road.

It seemed she could see for miles, and there was nothing in sight other than a repetitiously drab desert. But, the wind had died down considerably.

"Do you like it out here?" Antonio questioned her.

She gave him a strange look.

"No. It's windy and depressing. I suppose you like it?"

She smiled at him.

"No, Maggie, I wanted to show you what my life looks like without you." His eyes followed hers.

"That is sweet..." Maggie stared up at him, "...But now that I've seen it, can we get out of here?"

Antonio still seemed agitated. She knew he was still angry about Francis kissing her.

She hoped to redirect his thoughts. She stooped down, enthralled by the vegetation, touching a round cactus with pink flowers growing right out of the top.

"Look at this—the plant life. I've never seen anything like it."

Antonio bent down next to her as they both admired the various cacti and how they grew through the sandy, rock embedded ground. No cars drove by on the distant highway while they knelt down together, alone.

Maggie tried to read his thoughts.

"So, let me guess!" She enjoyed just looking at him, although she sensed he was still a bit angry. "This is where you escape the paparazzi...and where we live out our happily ever after?" She spoke facetiously, trying to lighten the mood. "I can see the tabloids now— 'Rumor has it they are hiding out in the desert, where they sit in their hot, windy seclusion and sip water all day to alleviate their thirst!'" She couldn't help but laugh.

Antonio passed her a sweet look mixed with frustration.

"We can do better than that, Maggie! No one has to know about us. We can keep it a secret. We just both keep denying that we are anything other than professional." He grabbed her hand and sat down in the sand, bringing her onto his lap.

"I won't tell." Then she recalled, "Dana's magazine had me in a picture...with that sweater of yours. I looked fat, and the caption read that I was expecting your baby! Now how do they do that? And why?"

"I thought you were told not to read the tabloids."

"That was before," Maggie explained, lending him a curious smirk. "But now after the last reporter approached me, I wonder how long it can remain a secret."

Maggie wished he would announce an end to the secrecy and let her in on his plans to protect her from Francis. But Antonio seemed lost in thought.

"Yeah, I'm used to sneaking around. I hated it at first, but now I'm just used to it. It's hard, though. There's no turning back. I have to live out my life like this, and some days are crazy. Problem is I care about you. I don't want to take you away from your life of privacy and everything normal…if you want to be with me, it will be like that…crazy…and that's the honest truth. You know I want you in my life, but only if you are willing."

He removed their sunglasses, placing them into a pocket in his shorts. Now his eyes requested her attention as she pondered his words.

Maggie peered into his eyes, realizing what their relationship had become. She hated everything circling around them, but when it came down to just them, it was perfect. She could not resist him. The time they spent together surpassed any other, and she felt like they belonged together.

"I love being with you," Maggie confessed, her brown eyes admiring his. "I can't stand being away." She gazed into his face, wishing to capture in her memory each detail as he leaned back, bracing them in the sand.

She placed her arms around his neck, wishing to kiss him. He read her intentions and leaned back until his dark hair hit the sand. He wore a grin, but she held a look of surprise and hesitation.

"You can't be serious!" Maggie questioned, looking down at him.

"What…You prefer a king size bed?" His eyes radiated his ability to capture her heart.

She playfully attempted to thwart his efforts, although deep down she knew she could not resist him. "There are cactus plants everywhere, and I'm in white pants, and there are already sand particles in my top and in my hair!"

But as soon as she stopped speaking, she could feel her heart beating in her chest.

"Go ahead, kill the adventure." He looked up at her.

She placed her hands on his chest and leaned forward slowly, hesitating, but then blowing caution to the wind. She fell on top of him, as her hands hit the sand, and he put his arms around her, trapping her in her own decision. And as she brought her lips to his, he kissed her passionately.

Minutes passed, and he reached behind her mane of hair that blew in the wind. He played with her halter strap that was tied behind her neck while she ran her hands through his hair, forgetting the elements surrounding them. She sat up, reaching under his shirt, feeling the contour of his chest. He removed his shirt, tossing it into the wind until it landed, clinging to a cactus. She lay back down on top of him, feeling her chest against his. Her lips found his again as he tucked his fingertips into the back waistband of her white capris.

The wind blowing against them, he rolled on top of her, placing his hands in the sand, kissing her neck and then her chest. Soon she forgot they were lying in the desert sand. Maggie grabbed the front pockets of his shorts as his lips again met hers. Moments later, she heard him whisper, "Hold still. Don't move."

Maggie noticed that he was distracted. She turned to look where his attention was drawn. She sucked in a quick breath, gasping for air, before letting out a scream while Antonio landed with his body weight fully distributed on top of her, one hand in the sand as he grabbed hold of a snake with the other. His hand wrapped tightly right below its head as it hissed uncontrollably. Maggie's eyes widened even further, and she let out another scream. He laughed, still holding it in his hand, while he sat over her, braced with his knees in the sand. Maggie watched the snake slither above her as Antonio enjoyed the spotlight. "What do you think? Could I use this in my show?" he wanted to know.

Maggie contemplated his latest trick, feeling her fright slowly subsiding.

www.lovetheillusion.com/282.htm

"Get off of me, Antonio!" she yelled, reaching for her halter straps, as he sat victoriously on top of her. "And get rid of that, NOW!"

"Come on, don't you want to pet it? It's a California King snake!"

She quivered beneath him, and then watched him fling it into the sand, far off in the distance.

Antonio looked down at her, proud to have saved her, but she slapped her hands against his chest, trying to budge him off.

"You! I can't believe you picked that up and held it over me. You just live to freak me out, or what?"

"Relax! It was headed for your beautiful head of hair! I saved you from its toxic venom!" Antonio laughed, teasing her as he wore a grin. She wrestled underneath him, retying her strap behind her neck, as he sat amused from their adventure.

Maggie then saw him looking into her eyes. She stared back into his, pondering her lack of willpower. Did he know she could not resist him? It seemed as though minutes passed, as he kept her locked in a stare. Maggie could barely breathe as she gazed up at him. He looked deep in thought. She wondered what he was thinking, but he just simply said, "I'm thirsty, should we get something to eat?"

She remained silent, realizing her addiction to him. She wondered what would have happened if the snake did not set off the alarm. She watched as he retrieved his shirt that was still attached to the cacti and pulled it on over his head. He then pulled her up from the sand, holding her hand in his. Maggie tried dusting off the sand from her white pants. She noticed he wore black as she tried to clear her head from the ecstatic fog he left her in.

"I can't believe I came out here with you—you and your adventures. Look at us! We are a mess, and my hair must look like a wig from a Halloween display." Her words rolled off her tongue to mask what she was really thinking. Antonio seemed to read right through her fake concerns and gave her more to think about.

"Chill out Maggie. I would still kiss you like crazy, so why do you care?"

He grabbed her hand in his and walked them back to the car.

Maggie did not know whether she felt dizzy from the heat of the sun or from their passionate roll in the sand. She watched her feet hit the sand, and dared to look into his eyes one more time. She wished they were still kissing, rolling in the hot desert sand. Antonio seemed to read her thoughts and she blushed. Now she tried to remember the exact moment that she let go of her heart, but the truth was, she didn't know. She did know one thing for sure. She loved being with him.

When they arrived back at the car, he kissed her one more time. Then he looked into her eyes, dismissing his anger. "I think I just forgave you for letting Francis kiss you." Antonio opened the door for her, her hair blowing in the wind one last time, as he ran his hand through his own locks, hoping to shake free some of the dust. "Get in. Let's cruise this thing with the top down."

He started the engine, and she watched him, intrigued by his wild adventurous side.

They sat quietly, as the wind beat against them, as Maggie ran her fingers through her hair, hoping to discharge the sand into the wind while she brushed off the inside of the Jaguar. Antonio noticed her attempts, shaking his head as he let out a brief chuckle under his breath, realizing it was pointless.

Maggie leaned back, enjoying the bright Vegas sky, a baby blue cast with white fluffy clouds everywhere. She turned the radio up and placed her feet on the dash. Antonio had one hand on the wheel, the other locked in hers, as they exchanged occasional smiles while they drove around, drenched in the happiness of being with each other again. She didn't want the day to end, and Thursday could be another day long if it were up to her. She replayed his kiss in the desert sand over and over again in her mind, wishing they were still in the sand, realizing her feelings for him were too strong to fight. She was stuck in his crazy seduction, but she no longer wanted to escape. It was time to quit fighting what she felt and trust him.

Her thoughts were interrupted by a noise, overhead. She opened her eyes and looked up.

"Chad! There's a helicopter!" Maggie said, pointing.

"I see it," he acknowledged without looking up. "It's been on our tail for about five minutes now."

"What are we going to do? Is it going to follow us until we get out?"

"Don't worry, I've got us covered." He stepped on the gas and accelerated ten miles over the speed limit.

Maggie screamed out a warning, "No! Chad! Don't drive like that! You're scaring me!"

He immediately let off the accelerator and brought the car down to a normal speed.

"I'm just messing with you!" He started laughing. "I can't outdrive that! But I've got a plan."

What's that? Maggie wondered, figuring she wasn't in on it.

But he surprised her and started to explain, "There's a restaurant not too far from here. We need to eat."

"That doesn't sound good, Chad," Maggie warned.

"Trust me, we'll be fine!" he said candidly.

Maggie doubted, waiting for the next intrusion to take place. *"Oh there you two are, together again! Are you romantically involved? When is your baby due?"*

Maggie's mind completely shifted gears, from a feeling of being overjoyed, just being in his presence, to the potential nightmare at hand. Francis would eventually find them out. *How dreadful.* She couldn't even imagine the ridicule he would dish out. She felt her heart racing as her body pumped full of adrenaline. She glanced at Antonio, who seemed to think he was in control. However, he no longer held her hand or sent her flirtatious looks, and she interpreted that to mean disaster was looming.

Chapter 17

A stop sign sat in the distance, while Maggie flooded with anxiety. Antonio slowed the car, and soon it came to rest. He had put the roof back up, and now she waited to arrive at a diner, somewhere off the beaten path. She could still see the helicopter. Maggie hated people invading their privacy. She wished that she was still rolling in the sand with him, and her stomach filled with fluttery sensations as she recalled his touch and his kiss.

Antonio pulled into the parking lot of Sandie's Bar and Grill. Maggie sat uncomfortably still, waiting for the unknown, while Antonio seemed preoccupied. With one hand still on the steering wheel, he grabbed a bag from the back seat and handed it to her. "Put this on," he instructed her. "The bathrooms are right next to the door."

She held the bag, pondering the next mystery, when she heard his command—"Hurry up!"

She got out in a stupor, but then started moving quickly towards the door of the restaurant, aware of his running up alongside her.

She fled into the bathroom and into a stall where she held the bag open, and reached inside. She pulled out a wig—blonde and short—a Marilyn Monroe style; now she was aware of his plan.

"Great!" Maggie announced under her breath as she tried to digest how she would get all her hair inside the wig. She had never been blonde in her life. Maggie shook her head at the thought. She wrestled it onto her head and tucked her hair inside the best she could. She took out her compact and checked to see if she had it all in place.

She decided to step outside the stall and use the bathroom mirror to apply some makeup— *a bit of red lipstick to finish off the look.*

Maggie broke into laughter when she saw the full view in the mirror above the sink. "This is crazy!" she scoffed, looking at her reflection. Her eyes widened as she wondered what Antonio could be wearing. He was such a nut. Would she even recognize him?

She stepped back into the stall to contemplate her exit. How could she keep a straight face? She heard someone come in. She peeked through the crack to see a mother and her daughter. Maggie waited for them to get inside a stall, and then she wiped her perspiring palms. She observed that the front of her white pants were no longer unblemished, remembering their passionate play in the dusty desert sand. She took a deep breath, let it out, and then made her exit, walking slowly into the restaurant area. But she did not see Antonio anywhere. *Where is he?*

www.lovetheillusion.com/286.htm

Just about the time she thought that he left her there as some practical joke, she saw him nod to her from across the room. He sat in a booth towards the back of the restaurant, still in his shades but now sporting a dark mustache over a clean shave and wearing a cowboy hat.

www.lovetheillusion.com/287.htm

Maggie tried to remain discreet as she made her way over to the table. Nobody seemed to notice that she wore a disguise, and she felt plunged into a whole new world of delusion. No one was talking to Antonio *or* trying to get his signature. She calmly approached the table, feeling her adrenaline rush subside. She viewed his ensemble, thinking he looked amazing as a Texas cowboy.

"Cute, Maggie, real cute!" He smiled at her, behind the dark trim that encompassed his top lip.

"Look at you!" Maggie exclaimed in a whisper. "This is crazy. Did anyone recognize you?"

"Nope," Antonio reported as he flashed his pearly white smile again.

"Is someone following us?"

"Yes," he said, laughing in a whisper. "Don't look! I think they just came in."

Maggie turned to look, and saw a gentleman and a woman that had a luggage bag large enough to hold a camera. "I said DON'T look, Maggie!" Antonio whispered back with his teeth clenched and his brow down.

"Sorry," Maggie stated as she absorbed his strange attire.

The waitress approached the table.

"Howdy!" Antonio said in his newly acquired southern accent. "I would have me two eggs over easy, bacon, toast, and flapjacks, orange juice and a little more coffee. Thank you, ma'am!"

Maggie felt her eyes widen as he carelessly enacted his new charade. She spoke slowly, "The same."

Now she tried to contain a smile as he left her intrigued with his scheme. The waitress left, and Antonio grabbed her hands on top of the table.

"Fun, huh?" He sat proudly, waiting for her approval.

"Sure...so now you are out with Marilyn Monroe...and you are...?"

"One of her fans," he revered.

"Chad!" Maggie laughed in amusement. "You are so funny!"

"No, just living life—trying to survive. Now, check this guy out! He's looking *all* over the restaurant for us and has no clue."

"I hope not," Maggie said with concern, trying to adjust to his new look. "I'm still trying to shake the nightmares of Francis finding out."

"What a shame! Now he's leaving and we can eat in peace!" Antonio locked him in a stare until he was out of sight.

"Did you really need that southern accent?" Maggie asked.

"No, that was just thrown in for a little fun." Antonio smiled back at her, realizing he owned the gift of entertainment.

"As if this is not already fun?" Maggie inquired as she took a sip of juice, enjoying her dive into his spontaneous adventures.

"So, you admit you're having fun?" Antonio queried with a smirk, unwrapping a straw with the tips of his fingers.

"I always have fun when I'm with you," Maggie sheepishly admitted.

"What was our best night out?" He looked on with intrigue.

She thought about it.

"I don't know. That's a tough question. I couldn't answer."

"Okay then, if we could relive any moment together, what would it be?"

Maggie stared back at him, recalling their past adventures in the sand. She knew that made the top of the list, but she was too embarrassed to say. She remained silent as he watched her make up her mind. She lingered in thought, but finally shrugged her shoulders indecisively. Antonio appeared dissatisfied. After a long moment of silence, a smirk spread across his face as he shook his head, still waiting for her decision.

"When you made me spaghetti," she finally dictated with a big smile.

"Really?" He seemed surprised.

"It doesn't matter...as long as we're together...and we have fun most of the time," she explained, still smiling as he kept her in his eye.

"*Most* of the time?" he questioned. "When are you not having fun?" It appeared she damaged his ego. Maggie shifted her eyes and playfully responded,

"When you are mad at me?" She reached into her new head of hair.

Antonio's expression changed to one of amusement.

"I'm never really mad at you," he admitted. "But you have this way of walking yourself into bad situations." He left his eyebrows up, waiting for her response.

"I do not!" She wondered why he always had to start trouble.

"Yes, Maggie, you do!" he clarified. "Like right now. You're sitting here eating breakfast with a complete stranger...with a mustache!"

She started laughing.

"But I know the dork underneath!" She tried to get even.

"That's mean..." Antonio discarded her playful insult, "Now, I should have left you in the desert with the snake." His face lit at his next suggestion. "Should we go back?"

"I would," she said seductively, enticed by his invitation.

Antonio drew a slow breath.

"Then you should know that I'm trying not to lose my gentleman status." Antonio held a serious look while he stared into her eyes.

"Then *you* should know that I'm crazy about you." Maggie let go of her heart, feeling free to love him. She stared back into his eyes, mesmerized by his appeal and their intimate connection.

"We should head back to the Strip," Antonio suggested. "We can walk around in our disguises but act like normal people. It will be fun!"

"Okay," she reluctantly agreed, pondering his first suggestion.

They left the restaurant, feeling elated while caught up in Antonio's latest charade.

www.lovetheillusion.com/290.htm

"We'll have to leave the top up, or we might lose our hair!" Antonio informed with a chuckle as he adjusted his mustache.

Once they arrived on the Strip, Maggie expected to gamble, but Antonio was eager just to observe, enjoy the downtown light show, and dawdle in antique shops. He found an antique rhinestone necklace that he bet would look good with any of Francis' designs and bought it for her. She thought it would distinctively match the silver sequins on her dress that she had to wear for the introduction of the show. However, she tried to discourage him from buying it. The price was outlandish, but Antonio simply bought it anyway. Perhaps the necklace would be a distraction from the sparkly purple dress with the slit that fit too tight.

www.lovetheillusion.com/291.htm

Maggie returned to her room that night to discover her latest email from Francis—*a jolt back to reality.* They would be spending the whole day together tomorrow, overlooking several new proposals and recapping the details of their grand entrance. She already missed Antonio, thinking she would be without him for a whole day, starting with breakfast at seven a.m. with Francis. Maggie knew that she was there on business, so there was no way around it.

She spent the entire next day with Francis. *It was a long one.* He had his mind on work, as usual, but had not made any more attempts to make her feel uncomfortable. Nor did he ask what she had been up to yesterday, which she found to be a relief. Maybe everything would pan out, yet. She could keep her job and Antonio.

The following day was another day apart, as Antonio reported that he would be working all day, preparing for the upcoming show, but he promised he would see her afterwards.

Maggie took the opportunity to spend the day at the Lion Habitat and the Shark Reef. Now it seemed strange as she was walking around, she noticed that a man appeared to be following her. When she left the Lion Habitat, she noticed that he was sitting on a nearby bench watching her. And when she visited the Shark Reef, she saw him there as well. Maggie was glad to get back to her hotel.

Saturday night in Vegas was finally here—the big show-stopping event! Maggie arrived in her dazzling purple and silver plum dress, finished with a ruffle train.

www.lovetheillusion.com/292.htm

Maggie stepped into the theater, escorted by Francis, who stood out in a custom tailored Armani suit with a green tie and a purple vest. She could not wait to see Antonio, even if it was only on stage.

www.lovetheillusion.com/293.htm

Two days had passed since Maggie last saw Antonio, and she already missed him, wishing the week did not pass so quickly. She hoped that they could spend time together between the shows as she felt the time ticking away, almost pulsating through her veins. But for now, she had to concentrate on tonight's show. It was a big night for everyone. Stanley and Bradley were in the front row with them. Rainelle had joined Bradley, and Stanley had a girl he was dating with him. Maggie sat between Francis and Rainelle, hoping to avoid any awkward coziness with Francis.

"Hi, Rainelle, how are you?"

"I'm good!" Rainelle indicated with a big smile. "You look beautiful. I love your dress!"

"Designed by Francis, of course." Maggie laughed.

"He's good!" She admired the dress.

"Don't we all know? I can't wait to see our costumes finally on stage! And the place is packed...how exciting!"

Maggie felt Francis nudge her, alerting her to assist him on stage. She knew that she bore his opportunity to flaunt his evening wear, as she stood in a dress worth several thousand pounds.

Francis grabbed her hand and pulled her through a packed auditorium until they stood next to a staircase beneath the stage. Maggie put on a big smile to offset her nerves. She could feel the weight of the necklace that Antonio bought her as it sat around her neck, and she ran her fingertips across the rhinestones. Her other hand in Francis', Maggie walked up the steps, glad to see that Antonio stood stationed behind the magical curtain.

She heard Francis begin speaking. "Good evening ladies and gentlemen. Welcome to our preliminary Las Vegas show that is seen tonight for the very first time! It's unprecedented. Never before has a magic show displayed as many colors and glitz as it does here tonight. I'm Francis Louis, designer for many of the European formal lines, and now proud to design for AD Magic as well. It's a whole new division for us, and we hope that it's just the beginning of many successful endeavors as the two companies will enjoy doing business together. And I would like to hear a round of applause for my designing assistant, Maggie White!" He paused until people were done clapping. Maggie stood, smiling shyly. Then he passed her credit. "She has played an intricate part in bringing to stage what you see here tonight. Enjoy!"

Maggie let out an internal laugh as she recalled the few choices she made, and then offered a wave as she watched the people in the audience stand and clap as Francis concluded, "Tonight, ladies and gentlemen, like you've never seen him before, Antonioooo DeLuca!"

Then, grabbing her hand again, Francis led Maggie off the stage. She thought his hand was simply a brace to eliminate any more disastrous falls—a constant concern in her silver heels, mounted in a platform.

Maggie sat down, anticipating the show. The theater lights flashed out as she waited to see what would come next.

Red smoke appeared in a haze, coming up under the curtain as it rose. Strobe lights beamed in various directions throughout the audience, and everyone was cheering. Mystical music was playing as the smoke engulfed the stage. She waited to see Chad, who would now be Antonio.

The smoke faded, and she sighted a platform with something on top of it. However, it was not Antonio. Cheetos sat, out of his cage, perched like a cat resting in a window sill. But when the music came to a halt, Antonio popped up behind him as a fan blew his cape into the air. Now he wore all black, and *the* hot pink sash. Yes, Francis persevered on that one, contradicting her better judgment. But Maggie observed the presentation, thinking that perhaps Francis was right, after all.

The lights flashed in blue hues and then green. Two girls suddenly appeared and grabbed the ends of the hot pink sash, running in opposite directions and magically removing it. Maggie thought it was funny. Perhaps Antonio did not approve of the sash after all. Now she was sure *that* was his funny way of making his announcement to the audience and to Francis.

For a moment, Maggie felt like a fan watching him, as he led Cheetos around with glitter that flew out of his hand. He motioned for Cheetos to sit and then gave him a treat. The lights moved onto the audience, creating a hazy fog. Large snowflakes descended in 3D. The dancers came out, moving to the rhythm of the music. Two of the dancers, dressed in pink sequined body suits and shiny black boots, were tugging on Antonio's arms to bring him onto a platform, center stage. They led him up a couple steps and then closed the flaps around him, now presenting a gift box with a bow. The box lit up with silver lights covering its surface and a bow that sparkled with hot pink lights. Then the music stopped, followed by a cymbal crash. All the sides of the box fell down, and he had disappeared. Cheetos was now sitting on the platform, staring at the audience. Maggie sat in amazement as Antonio then came around the side of the stage and up the steps that she and Francis had taken earlier.

Several acts later, Antonio wore a black hat on his head. He was dressed in silver metallic with the pants flaring, containing the hot pink color, along with the collar on his shirt. Maggie thought the costuming looked amazing, as small rubber balls now bounced out of his hat. Then, all of a sudden, four birds flew out of his hat and into the audience, and then back onto the stage, landing in a row on the arms of two of the dancers, who had locked hands horizontally as they were supported in the air by stuntmen.

Maggie watched the show with great fascination, as each stunt had been recreated from the last time she had seen the show.

Then she heard Antonio speaking into a microphone. "I need a little help on this next one." He looked into the audience. "Who thinks we should bring up Francis and Maggie?"

Maggie's stomach flopped at the thought of being on stage again. *Why hadn't he mentioned this?* Shouldn't she know these things ahead of time? Now she sat, observing the crowd in an uproar, when she heard Antonio announce, "That sounds like a 'yes.'" Antonio gave a short laugh, as he pointed right at them.

Francis grabbed Maggie's hand once again, looking pleased to now be part of the show.

Maggie forced another smile as she tagged behind him, up the steps and onto the stage. They were now supposed to step into a structure that represented a phone booth, as Antonio explained, "We need you to step inside and make a phone call to tell people to come to the show on Thursday night. We have five tickets left! Get inside the booth, the old fashioned way! No cell phones! One at a time—Francis, you first," Antonio ordered.

Maggie stood mesmerized by Antonio's stage presence while Francis went first. The lights flickered shades of purple and navy blue. The next thing she knew, Francis appeared upside down in the booth. Maggie watched in amazement, with her hands to her cheeks. Then the lights went dark for a second, and when they came back on he was upright again. Maggie wondered how the lights and mirrors worked to create that effect, but soon Francis stepped out and Antonio shrugged, placing his hands in the air, as if he was clueless. Antonio then shook Francis' hand and motioned for him to go back to where she stood.

Maggie watched Antonio who now pointed to her as he gazed into the audience, requesting approval for her to go next. Maggie shook her head, but when Antonio turned to look at her, she blushed, feeling flush, captivated by his confidence and appeal. Antonio motioned for her to go into the booth while giving her his sweet look. She stepped inside, where she saw lights of various color randomly flickering in a small space.

Once the lights went out, she knew it was time to step out. *That wasn't so bad.* Antonio grabbed her hand to assist her. He appeared all happy that she had survived and hugged her. People cheered and whistled while Maggie returned his hug. She was surprised that he was showing her affection on stage, but before she could get lost in the moment, he let go of her and motioned for them to make their exit off stage.

It was intermission.

"So, what do you think, so far?" Maggie asked Francis.

"Pretty good, everything looks good. Actually, it's spectacular!" He sounded happy.

"You did a good job, Francis, with everything!" Maggie said with sincerity.

Francis sat proud, but then surprisingly, passed her credit. "I couldn't have done it without you!"

Right! Maggie laughed to herself, thinking perhaps he was making reference to the pink sash!

"Maggie, the costumes are fabulous!" Rainelle sounded pleased. "The detail and everything...they just sparkle like nothing I have ever seen."

"It's good for Vegas. That's for sure," Maggie agreed.

"Maggie and I are a good team," Francis interjected.

"I can see that!" Rainelle agreed. "Unbelievable. I almost want to see the show again!"

"Tuesday night!" Francis announced, enthusiastically.

Maggie watched the fans returning to their seats to watch the last half. Then the lights started to dim. Black smoke seeped out from under the curtain, eventually turning a bright white.

And when the curtain rose, a tiger stood in a big round ring that was lit with lights that flashed in a series of colors. The dancers came out and danced around the tiger. She had never seen the tiger before.

Antonio came out wearing the silver metallic outfit that Maggie recalled lying across Francis' desk, along with the pink sash. She watched as he fastened the tiger to a chain rope. He led the tiger through the dancers and into a cage. As the cage closed, the lights went out. Seconds later, when they popped back on, Cheetos stood in the cage instead. Antonio stood off to the side, acting confused. Then the lights went out again, and when they came back on the cheetah was gone, and Antonio was now in the cage, signaling the finale of the stunt. One of the dancers came over with a mission to let him out, but then in fun taunted the audience that she would just as soon leave him in there. The rest of the dancers went on with their routine, ignoring Antonio's sad plight. As they all formed into a dance configuration, moving to the new beat of music, Antonio knelt, inside the cage. Then the lights flashed off and when they came back on, Antonio was standing on top of the cage—the true finale.

www.lovetheillusion.com/296.htm

Amber and Angie snuck out and tiptoed among the Zumba dancers, grabbing Antonio's hands and helping him jump off the top of the cage. They led him to the front center of the stage with his arms up in the air. Maggie clapped and whistled, remembering Amber and Angie from the Night Owls party.

When the show ended, Francis stood, waiting to have a word with Antonio. Maggie watched as the multitudes slowly dispersed. She noticed Bradley and Francis had begun a discussion as to where they could all meet up with Antonio. Maggie wanted to see him, but not in the company of Francis. However, that became the plan. She wondered what cocktail could assist in getting her through that!

Now they were waiting for Antonio to come out of a dressing room. He soon appeared wearing a grey dress shirt with a tie and charcoal grey pants. Francis met him with a handshake, and Maggie listened while Antonio discussed with Francis the visual success of the costumes.

Afterwards, Francis turned to the group and dictated, "We're going to catch a bite to eat at the hotel restaurant, in a back room."

Maggie caught Antonio smiling at her, while Francis was watching her. She quickly glanced away, back to Francis, who then looked at Antonio as if he had missed something.

"Should we take the limo?" Stanley asked, disrupting the secrecy.

"Sure," Bradley approved, motioning for everyone to follow him.

They piled into the limo, and Maggie knew she could not sit by Antonio. She also did not want to be by Francis. She sat down next to Stanley's date, but then Francis sat down next to her.

"Hi! I'm Maggie!" She introduced herself.

"I kind of figured that out!" The woman laughed. "I'm Rachel."

"Nice to meet you, Rachel," Maggie said with a friendly smile.

Francis was busy passing out champagne to everyone and making a toast: "To the future!"

Maggie sat amused, attempting to capture everyone's face as they made the toast. Antonio wore his big white smile, as if he approved, but she wondered what he was really thinking. Then Francis stretched and put his arm around her. Maggie took a deep breath as she waited for Antonio to notice, but she saw he already had Francis locked in a stare—one she interpreted to mean he was already contemplating murder. She quickly got up and sat down next to Rainelle.

"Are you going to the show on Tuesday as well?" Maggie started conversation.

Rainelle shrugged. "Probably—I assume you also?"

"Yes, one more event!" Francis interrupted, holding up his glass. He sat back down next to Maggie, resting his hand on the skin of her leg, which was exposed by the slit.

Rainelle changed the subject. "That spaghetti Antonio made that one night smelled really good. I was so happy when I saw that there were leftovers!"

Maggie's eyes popped open and she made a horrified face. "Francis doesn't know," she whispered fiercely in Rainelle's ear.

"Oops!" Rainelle covered her mouth.

Maggie drank a sip of champagne and stared over at Antonio, who was busy in a conversation with Stanley. Then she noticed Francis looking at her as if he had something to say, but not of business nature. *Help!* She quickly turned back to Rainelle, hoping to arrive at the restaurant soon.

A couple of bodyguards walked in their group as they entered through a back entrance of the restaurant, where they were seated in a private banquet room.

Maggie sat down next to Francis, who had eagerly waited for her with a pulled out chair. She tried to dismiss the fiasco of tension, enjoying her perfect view of Antonio who sat down across from her between Stanley and Bradley. She waited to secretly pass him a smile, but when she did, he rendered a blank stare, appearing agitated. Her eyes shifted to notice that Francis took the liberty of resting his arm on the back of her chair.

Maggie excused herself from the table, secretly nodding at Antonio. She went around the corner and stood next to a set of wooden doors and waited for him to follow her. She peeked around the corner and saw him approaching with his cell phone to his ear, pretending to have a call.

Antonio soon stood in front of her, ready to speak his mind. "Maggie, I cannot tell you how badly I want to kill that boss of yours."

Maggie knew that she needed to keep his temper from heating up. She made light of the situation. "Francis is just overly friendly. He's like that to everyone, and he hasn't tried to kiss me since—"

"He needs to keep his grubby hands off you!" Antonio fumed, but then set aside his temper, while his eyes drooped intimately into hers. "I should tell you that you look *very* good in that dress and I want to kiss you right now."

Standing in public, Maggie remained distracted.

"Do you think Francis knows about us? We keep sneaking around, and it's not long before...I think he heard Rainelle talking about the spaghetti dinner!" Maggie warned him.

"I have to talk to you about something, later," Antonio told her.

"What?" she probed, wishing to shatter the secrecy.

"This!" He leaned over to kiss her cheek as he whispered inches from her face, "Meet you back at the table. You go first."

Maggie sat back down, still blushing from Antonio's kiss. Francis sat unaware, buried in the menu, while everyone else had already made up their minds. The waitress was taking orders, despite Antonio's absence, so Stanley ordered for himself and also for Antonio while Maggie placed her order for a salad. She was still concerned over the tight fit of her dress.

When Antonio returned, a group of fans approached the table, coming into the room unannounced after seeing the two of them in the hall. "Can we bother you for a signature?" They were hovering over Antonio while he gracefully absorbed the untimely disruption.

"Sure, you got a pen?"

Maggie watched as he signed five programs. They were filled with photos of him and the dance crew showing off the new costumes.

"I need one of those!" Maggie teased.

Francis elbowed her and informed dryly, "We've got some. They're in my briefcase. I can give you one."

Antonio signaled Maggie a "look of censure," and then proceeded to sign for another two girls that had found their way to the table as well.

"Antonio, are they going to let you eat?" Bradley laughed.

"Probably not," Stanley answered for him.

They ate in profound silence. Everyone was tired from the day's events, but Maggie remained bound and determined to stay up late, trying to squeeze in as much time as she could with Antonio. The trip was half over, and she could not stand the thought of leaving. She wondered how they would make plans to see each other again. He would fly back to New York, and she would go back to England—*another plane ride, another separation.* Maggie felt her emotions set into concrete as she pondered how long she could exist in her own world, without him.

Chapter 18

The zipper on the purple dress was *stuck?* "UGH!" Maggie was caught in a careless hurry to meet Antonio. She pulled and tugged until—it broke! The sound of it tearing apart signaled alarm as she noticed the fabric at the base of the zipper was now torn as well. She watched as the silver sequins hit the floor.

Not good! Maggie stood in disbelief. She still needed to wear that dress for Tuesday's show.

But her mind quickly scooted past her catastrophe. She was elated to meet up with Antonio.

Now in a black cotton sundress, she passed through the hotel lobby to the valet entrance where Antonio was waiting in the car again. She approached, realizing the time that they had together was passing much too quickly.

"I didn't think I was going to get to see you again," Maggie told him as she got into the car. "Francis has been keeping me busy with work, and it is all stuff that can wait until we get back to London!" she complained.

Antonio passed her a look of regret.

"Yeah, well I have to work tomorrow morning. We have to polish up some of the dance moves by the next show. Some of the dancers were out of position, interfering with one of my tricks."

"I never noticed." She gave him a sweet look.

"That's good, but we still need to fix it. But we can do something after that. You pick," he offered, passing her a playful smile. Maggie thought about it. She did not think any of her ideas could compete with his, but then she thought of something she had always wanted to do.

"Let's drive out to the Grand Canyon!"

"Okay," Antonio agreed, but he seemed deep in thought. "I can arrange that."

She wondered what was on his mind. Then she offered another suggestion. "I know we just ate, but can we get ice cream? I'm still hungry after my salad. I was afraid to eat any more than that since I was sitting in a dress that feels a couple sizes too small! And now the stupid zipper broke. I'm sure Francis will be just peachy when he finds out that his precious design is no longer wearable." Maggie broke out into laughter as it seemed trivial at the moment.

"You want ice cream? We can get ice cream," Antonio agreed.

He drove around until they found a street corner with a custard stand.

"Here, you go get it." He handed her a fifty dollar bill. "Surprise me."

"Does this mean you want to try every flavor?" Maggie teased as she held up the bill. Antonio smiled at her suggestion, watching her as she got out of the car.

She stood in line, wondering what to get. She had to surprise him? *Was he tired out from the show, or what?* Maggie read the menu board, deciding just to get two vanilla cones. That is what she liked, so he would have that too!

With both hands full, Maggie stood in front of the car, hoping he would open the door. But instead of obliging, Antonio drove the car ahead four feet, as if he did not like her selection.

She saw the car door finally fling open as someone called out, "Are you Maggie White?"

She got in quick and shut the door, handing him his ice cream cone.

"Aren't you going to talk to your fan? She's pretty cute," Antonio informed.

Maggie glanced out the window where she saw a small girl, about five years in age, wearing two long ponytails to frame her face. The girl was waving to her as if seeing Maggie was a dramatic event. Maggie rolled down the window and waved back. The girl came running up to the car window, accompanied by her mother.

"Hi!" The girl smiled and waved, showing off the signs that she was just getting her new front teeth. "My mom said that you looked just like the girl on stage with Antonio."

"You're cute!" Maggie told her. "And your mom is right about that. Did you like the show?"

"She loved the magic show." Her mom spoke for her. "We all did. It was fun seeing you." She ducked down to get a view of Antonio before turning around to leave.

"How's that?" Maggie wanted to know. "You don't think she's undercover for Report News?" she asked Antonio. "There could be two cameras, hiding behind those ponytails of hers!" Maggie giggled.

"She's harmless," Antonio ascertained. "But this is such a dull flavor," he complained while licking his ice cream cone, "—vanilla?"

"You said I could pick!" Maggie countered, hitting his arm and causing his ice cream to smear his face. She laughed when she saw the mess.

"Are you starting a fight?" he asked in a tired tone, as he wiped his face with his sleeve.

"Maybe!" she teased. "Why? Are you already mad at me?"

Antonio gave her a devilish grin. Then he took his cone and dabbed it in her face to retaliate, leaving a mess on her check.

"Not anymore!" he said, laughing. "Did you forget napkins?" he questioned in a voice of suspense.

Maggie reached in her purse, grabbed a Kleenex, and wiped off her face, dismissing his childish retaliation. She licked her cone, deciding she knew better than to retaliate. He would come up clean and she would end up wearing both of the cones.

"So...where should we go?" she heard him ask in a nonchalant manner, as if he had no plans.

She was surprised that he had no plans.

"Wherever you want," Maggie decided, recalling their most recent adventures in the desert. She wondered if he really had no plans.

"Hmm, should we gamble?" Antonio finally suggested, with his eyes big.

"Sure. How much are you prepared to lose?" Maggie grinned.

"A lot." He smirked.

"Here!" she said, handing him his change.

"Uh, this would be gone in less than five minutes," he said as he tossed the money carelessly into a cup holder. She watched the money, flapping in the breeze of the car fan.

They drove around for a while, eating their ice cream until Antonio finally pulled up along the curbside.

When they got out of the car, Maggie set her eyes on the casino, all lit up with an abundance of lights, but Antonio grabbed her hand and started walking in the opposite direction. Before she knew it, they stood in front of a wedding chapel.

"Oh, look!" Maggie said, excited. "They are marrying someone right now! Let's stand and watch!" The doors of the chapel were open, and she could see a couple in street clothes saying their vows. Maggie felt her hand locked in Antonio's. "I thought we were going gambling," she reminded him.

Antonio burst out laughing.

"Maggie, why would I want to gamble money? I have plenty of it. I want to gamble something else."

"What are you talking about?" Maggie tried to read his eyes that darted into hers, as if he had a trick up his sleeve.

Then Antonio asked, "Are you going to let me marry you?"

Maggie's jaw dropped, and when she was finally able to close it, she questioned him. "What, now? You are joking, right?"

She started laughing.

"Why not, look!" He nodded. "There's the chapel."

"Look at me, in this black dress! That would be bad luck. I've had enough of that, already! Besides, brides are supposed to be in white!"

"So, you don't want to marry me?"

He looked on her in amusement.

Maggie stood flabbergasted by his latest surprise.

"Are you seriously asking me, or are you going to start laughing if I say 'yes'?" Maggie questioned him, with her face still in shock.

"If?" Antonio asked with a grin. "So you aren't sure?"

"Are you?" Maggie asked, thinking that she could pass out from his latest surprise. "You aren't even down on one knee. So, you can't be serious!" She wrestled his proposal.

Then he took a step closer to her and whispered in her ear, "I mean no disrespect. I'm simply not down on one knee because we do not need the attention! But, *if* you say 'yes,' we can go back to the hotel, and I'll get down on one knee as fast as you want!"

Maggie blushed at his words.

She stood still, in shock, wondering what to do with his latest question.

Finally, she spoke. "I can't believe we are standing here in Vegas, at this...this...wedding chapel and you ask me to marry you, like some strange joke."

Maggie grabbed his arms, playing in amusement. But she took alarm to his suddenly serious presentation.

"It's not a joke. I'm serious! Remember what I said at the restaurant?"

Maggie recalled Antonio kissing her cheek.

"I want you to come back to New York with me," Antonio told her. "You can quit your job with that idiot Francis and work for me. You can take over the costume designs. You should love that! You can hire who you want and kiss Francis good-bye."

Maggie listened to him announce her life's plans with the wrapped up details. As she was considering everything, he added, "And I really want to finish what we started in the desert."

He grinned mysteriously.

"So you're not the gentleman you pretend to be?" Maggie sounded curious.

Antonio started laughing.

"You will have to marry me to find out!"

He still wore a grin.

"Then, I can't wait to marry you," Maggie truthfully admitted, "but I always pictured a white dress."

Antonio appeared lighthearted, adding his additional thought. "And...you should probably meet my parents. My mamma and papa would want to meet you." He offered another invitation. "Come to my home in Italy, at Christmas. We can get married at the little chapel. It's been ours for three generations."

Maggie grinned at Antonio now wearing his sunglasses and a cap, admiring his good disguise.

"We would get married at Christmas?" she asked.

"Sure," Antonio spoke in his carefree tone, "Christmas it is!"

She wanted to marry him that minute, but reason ruled her brain, telling her that they hadn't known each other that long.

"We should get married on the day we met!" Maggie concluded after thinking things through. "Then it would be a year." She instantly grew concerned over the short time they had known each other, and her other failed relationships. Her face went sour.

"When was that again?" Antonio teased.

Maggie made a fist and lightly punched him in the arm. He grabbed her, pretending he was going to tackle her, but instead he flipped her around, holding her close to him. "Let's wait until we are married to add the violence!" he told her.

Maggie looked up at him as she stood, wrapped in his arms. She wished to kiss him while wondering what to do with his latest suggestion. Of course, she wanted to marry him, but... *Was it too soon?*

"So, we are engaged?" Maggie giggled in disbelief.

"Absolutely." He let go of a grin, signaling that he was fond of her. "And I suppose you want a ring now?"

Maggie started feeling his pockets.

"Where is it?"

"Where is what?" He seemed to enjoy her assumption.

"The ring that you probably have hidden somewhere," she said, patting around at his clothing, "just waiting for your next so-called magic trick as you make it appear!"

"Sorry, Maggie, I don't have one. I wasn't sure you would. You never told me you love me…but…it seems like you do, so…I took a gamble that maybe you would," Antonio explained.

Maggie thought on his words.

"I want to be with you too, it's just so soon after the last disaster, and I'm just afraid."

Antonio considered her fear, but decided, "Let's go find your ring. I know a place we can look. They are open 24 hours."

"Now?" Maggie questioned.

"Yeah, why not," Antonio decided.

I can't believe he asked me to marry him.

They got in the car, and Maggie shared additional thoughts. "What will I tell Francis?" She recalled his suspicion.

"Who cares, Maggie? We can't keep it a secret forever. I say after we put that ring on your finger, we walk around and drum up as much media attention as possible. Either that or we have to sneak around for the rest of our lives. It will go down like this. First, it will be crazy. Everyone will want to know everything. We do an interview, donate the money to Matteo's foundation, and pretty soon everyone will mind their own business, because something else will become more exciting."

"How do you know?" Maggie questioned him, realizing his constant battle with the media.

"Trust me. I know." Antonio attempted to dilute her fears.

They pulled up to the jewelers, and everything seemed surreal. Still in shock, she found it hard to believe he asked *and* that she agreed. She thought of him differently now. She pictured him as her husband, and then as a father. It felt strange, but right.

Maggie's smile met his, as they held hands and walked into the jewelers.

But the moment she stepped into the store, Maggie felt ice in her veins as she remembered her last engagement ring that she had flung into the bed, where Jasmine was under the sheets, leaving Phillip with a look of shock. Her mind retraced the events as the jeweler set out several selections for her to try on.

www.lovetheillusion.com/308.htm

"What do you like? Pick whatever," Antonio told her.

Maggie felt bad that Antonio stood stuck in the middle, but she could not shake her frazzled feelings stemming from the last engagement. *What if this one ended?* And could they really love each other already, in such a short time?

Maggie's face displayed a lifetime of apprehension. She hoped that he could not sense her hesitation. She stared down at the rings while her mind froze into a frenzy of the past tragedy—the one that had left a broken engagement.

She scanned the sparkly arrangements with doubts racing through her mind. He smiled sweetly as if perhaps he could read her mind, but then grabbed her hand and started to try them all on. Maggie watched him maneuver the rings on and off of her finger. She found that instead of looking at the rings, she was more enchanted looking into his face, soon thinking how lucky she was.

"We will take the one that gets stuck." Antonio laughed.

Maggie had tried them all on. It seemed as though they had a moment of privacy away from the media, but Maggie still felt overwhelmed, nevertheless.

The jeweler waited patiently, anticipating their selection. "So," the jeweler finally asked, "which one?"

Antonio stood next to Maggie as she made up her mind. She remembered when she first met him, her first impression of him—a total player! Perhaps she had misjudged him, but she had calculated that assumption based on his ability to make anyone fall for him. And her heart was ready to admit that it was unable to fight him off. He was like no one else she had ever met—his fun, playful energy hidden under his steamy guise. And the more time they spent together, the harder it was to be apart. Her mind raced with the details of their short courtship, each memory sweeter than the last. And now they were standing together looking at rings.

"Can I talk to you?" Maggie finally asked, motioning for them to leave. Now she had something on her mind and wanted to speak with him, in private.

"Sure." Antonio gave her a sweet look, but she could tell that she had left him confused.

As they stood outside the shop, Antonio held onto Maggie's arms while he looked intently into her face, reading her concern.

"Something's wrong! What is it Maggie? Are you afraid to be with me?" Antonio presented his worst fear. Maggie tried to absorb her racing concerns. "I'm not like the other guys, Maggie." She wore a serious look on her face, while contemplating his proposal. "What?" Antonio asked. "What's wrong? Tell me."

"I just..." Maggie stopped. "Don't be mad, but...I like all those rings...any of them should be fine, but..."

"What Maggie?" Antonio spoke in a soft, worried whisper.

"I want the one that I wore to get into the party that night. That one's special to me. Remember, when you let me wear it to get into the Night Owl?"

Antonio's face went from worry to amusement. Then it brightened with a smile.

"You are kidding! You want *that* thing? That ring is... I never wear it...it's in the safe. And you know I'll let you have it, but don't you want something else, too?"

Maggie shook her head. "No."

"Okay..." Antonio chuckled, "I'll have Stanley get it out of the safe and we will size it to fit you. Why do I think you are stalling the engagement? You don't want some dainty ten karat diamond? That's odd." He passed her a look of disbelief.

"No, I already said what I wanted." Maggie looked up at him. "That ring reminds me of when we first met." She placed her arms around him, assuring him of her affection. He looked down at her, sold on her delivery.

Back in the car, Maggie counted out on her fingers. "Six! Six months. It doesn't seem we've dated very long." She shared her concerns.

"No," Antonio agreed, "but the time in between is forever. It feels like years. So, does absence make the heart grow fonder?" he asked himself. "I think it makes one crazy."

Maggie slowly moved next to him. She placed her head against his shoulder while he drove.

"Where to next?" he asked in excitement.

Maggie sat in disbelief. As much as she felt for Antonio and did not want to be away from him, she never anticipated his proposal. She knew she wanted to eventually marry him, but was it too soon? She needed time to think everything through. And she knew she could not think clearly with his eyes looking into hers.

"I need to get back. I'm cold. I should have brought a sweater," she reluctantly informed hoping he did not gather strange suspicion.

"You can wear one of mine." He passed out her favorite grin.

"Yeah, if you want to be having twins; I just ate ice cream!" Maggie reiterated the tabloid claiming she was carrying his child while picturing her in his sweater.

But she really wanted to get back to her room where she could think everything through. She knew she loved Antonio, but why couldn't she say it?

"Here, we can get you something over there, at that clothing shop." Antonio rendered a solution while he disrupted her concerns.

Maggie cringed, realizing he had no idea what dreadful thoughts were racing through her head. His spontaneity and adventurous behavior landed like a brick in her head, while she tried to calculate the latest happenings into a factual spreadsheet that made sense. But although she was crazy for him, she could not dispose of her fear. *How could he make everything sound so simple?* She knew better. Things were never simple. Should she really just quit her job with Francis? She noticed that Antonio was looking at her, reading her face, full of concern. She quickly smiled at him, hoping to camouflage her anxiety.

Antonio parked the car, and they got out and walked into the boutique.

Maggie soon grabbed a sweatshirt that read, "Las Vegas," scripted in rhinestones. She held it up against herself and then checked the size.

Antonio shook his head. "No, Maggie. That's ugly. Here, try this," Antonio said as he handed her a white jacket with a three tier ruffle going around the bottom. She folded the sweatshirt and placed it neatly back in its cubby as she held up the coat to admire it.

"I don't know. That's a lot to spend, just because I'm cold. I can get something from my room," she told him, wishing he would drive her back. She could feel her body bouncing in anxiety. "We should go back, anyways," she decided. "It's getting late."

"Try it on," he persisted.

Maggie hesitated, but then slipped it on.

Immediately Antonio gave his approval. "That looks good!"

And in a second, he grabbed the price tags and pulled them off of the coat. He then went over to the register, a few feet away, as Maggie stood in a new coat.

Maggie recognized his ability to make decisions quickly. He decided that they should get married, and just like that, he asked. *No big deal!* Now he had found a solution to keeping them from being apart and from Francis making the moves on her. *How brilliant! It should work, right?*

Maggie caught her reflection in the mirror and had to admit that the coat was a sharp fashion statement. Antonio stood smiling at her and now there was no need to go back. But she still knew that she needed to think out his proposal and wished to be in solitude.

And no sooner did they step out of the shop she heard voices landing on top of her existing concerns:

"Isn't that Antonio DeLuca?"

"And…that ah...Maggie girl?"

"It's them."

"Antonio!" someone called out loudly, in an obnoxious tone.

Antonio waved, placing his sunglasses back on.

Maggie whispered, "Do we need to walk fast?" She reached for his hand.

"No, just fans…if it's a reporter, we take off running." He squeezed her hand in his, as if to say that she had better get used to it.

Maggie and Antonio arrived on the Strip. Maggie grew aware that the people who weren't yelling out or waving were staring. She decided to step into a casino, away from the mainstream crowd, to watch a lady spin a wheel. Antonio followed and stood behind her. Maggie had just turned around to look at him, when she saw Francis, standing alongside her. She wondered how long he had been there and was glad that Antonio had let go of her hand.

"Maggie, what are you up to?" Francis sounded suspicious.

"Hi Francis, how's it going? Are you having fun?" Maggie was sure that her face depicted her disappointment to have accidentally run into him. Then he spoke, revealing one of his annoying traits—*persistence!*

"No, I've been trying to call you on your cell phone for the past three hours, but you don't pick up." He offered a suggestion. "Turn up the volume of the ringtone!"

"Sorry. I think I must need to recharge it," Maggie gave as an excuse, reaching into her purse to look at her cell phone.

"Yeah, right." Francis looked annoyed. "We need to go over a new proposal that just came in, figure out costs."

"Not now! It's the middle of the night!" Maggie laughed off his suggestion.

"No, but bright and early tomorrow," he explained. "I was just going to ride back. You can come along."

Maggie looked at Antonio, sensing the tension.

"I'd better go," she told him.

Antonio stood speechless with an exasperated look on his face.

"I will see you tomorrow?" she indicated.

"Ten, at the lobby," Antonio confirmed, unable to smile at her as he then shifted his eyes onto Francis, locking him in an evil stare.

"We're going to the Grand Canyon!" Maggie informed Francis, hoping to lighten the mood, while still standing in a fiasco of tension.

"Better make it noon," Francis dictated. "Are you coming, Maggie?"

Maggie left with Francis, giving Antonio a quick wave. When he refused to wave back, she knew without a doubt that he was angry. But what was she supposed to do? Quit her job on the spot, right next to the Wheel of Fortune? Now Maggie knew better than to let love trample logic. And Francis had come to her aid, allowing her to have some time to herself to clear her head from the fog that Antonio had left it in. And her head had been in a fog ever since she met him!

Chapter 19

After a night of tossing and turning, Maggie still thought over Antonio's proposal. *What would Dana say?* Had they known each other long enough? She wanted to call Dana and announce the news, but her excitement was stuck in delay. Regardless of what Dana would say, she knew that she needed to figure this out on her own. And one thing was certain; she wanted to marry Antonio. The problem was that Antonio would expect her to quit her job. And it was a job that was just starting to render opportunity. Her dress design would be featured on a fashion ad for the Festival Party line, and Francis had indicated that she would have more opportunities. She knew that Antonio had no patience where Francis was concerned, and that his proposal was also his opportunity to cut her professional ties from Francis once and for all. Undoubtedly, Francis had crossed the line when he kissed her at work that day. But since then, he seemed to be backing off a bit. Sure, she could have reported him and filed suit, and whatever else she *should* be doing, but then she risked losing the big advantage that he was for her career. She couldn't help but feel a thread of loyalty to Francis. He had his annoying traits—everyone did. But she had to admit that he was good for her career, and he paid her decent wages. He knew people, and had connections. Then there was Antonio. Of course, she loved him, but what was love worth? Would it last? Or was it some temporary illusion?

Now she reached a disturbing conclusion. She knew why she could not tell Antonio that she loved him. *It always ended in misery.*

At least it had for her. And that brought her to her next greatest fear. She would never get over him, should it end. But her career, on the other hand, was secure; it was a stronghold, the wind in her sails, even under the direction of Francis. Despite him, she loved her job. It had been her dream since she was just a young girl. *Was love worth letting all of that go?* How could she choose between the two?

She realized that marrying Antonio carried a huge risk. She could not deny reality. She knew already the strain that the media would put on their relationship. Not to mention, Antonio wanted her to work for him? *Did he really?* Surely, that would be nothing but "cushy," but if they failed? Then what? Would they fail? How could she know? Weren't there tell-tale signs of that? *Of course not…It was a gamble, just like Antonio said.* Funny thing, she just happened to be in Vegas where people loved that thrill! But she hated uncertainty with a passion. And she couldn't be sure of anything.

After the meeting with Francis ended, Maggie now knew that he had a secret agenda. He had explained that she should not keep company with Antonio when he wasn't around. It was unprofessional. *Like he would know!* He had told her, "Maggie we need to focus on work when we are here. He's got plenty of other women to keep him busy. Now that we have the account, you don't have to overdo it." She lied and told him that they were going in a big group to the Grand Canyon, and then he reluctantly approved. *Why did he care?*

Now approaching the front lobby, Maggie saw Bradley waiting. She didn't think anything of it, except that Rainelle was standing next to him and Antonio was not.

"Maggie!" Rainelle called to her as she approached them.

"Hey, you two, what are you up to?"

Bradley wore a stern look.

"Maggie, I know that you're supposed to meet Antonio here, but he said he got busy and can't make it."

"What?" Maggie stood in disbelief, trying to make sense of his absence. Her heart sank as she was sure that he was irritated with the situation. *Did he have second thoughts?*

Disappointment ushered in when she heard Bradley announce, "The three of us will go to the Grand Canyon. The car's out front."

"Okay," Maggie agreed, feeling lost without Antonio.

Maggie sat in the cab, staring out the window. Antonio had said that he had to work tomorrow, and now Maggie realized that she would not see him until the day of the show. The following day, she had to leave. *Then what?* They would get married? Who were they kidding? Maggie's heart sank further into despair. She sat in the back seat, Bradley and Rainelle in the front. She wondered what Antonio was doing. Didn't he know that their time together was priceless?

As they rode in the car, Rainelle told Maggie various stories of different vacations they had been on. That is what she needed — *a vacation*. A vacation from her life! Maggie thought about Antonio's marriage offer, wondering how serious he was about her working for him. She silently laughed as she pictured him as her new boss. Then for a moment, she doubted her professional abilities. She did not want to be his liability.

Soon they arrived at their destination and were in the care of the tour guide, but Maggie's mind was on a whole new tour of its own. She knew that she wanted to be with Antonio. And she regretted not marrying him last night. She missed him already. But it seemed a crazy fantasy that they could be together, and that someone like him would offer a marriage proposal so soon. And he was quite the spontaneous, carefree individual. She felt lucky enough just to have his attention, and although she was delighted by his resolution to end their long separations, she felt stuck in a slow gear as she tried to digest everything that marrying him would entail. She did not want to live with regret. She needed time to sort through any thoughts of uncertainty. Not only had they only dated six months, but most of that time was spent apart. Did she *really* know him? What she did know, she liked. But there was the media circus ring that danced around him wherever he went, along with the distasteful tabloids that could appear as easily as a rainy day. She was certain that it would only get worse as he was now starting to tour Europe. And if she was to be his wife, she would now become a subject of interest... as well as one of torment. Could she withstand the stress? *Would it be worse than being apart and missing him?* Nothing was ever easy. She was trading one problem for another. However, they would be together. And when she was with him, all of her worries seemed small.

She gazed into the enormous depth of the canyon, admiring the beauty and vast display of space. "The Grand Canyon is one of the Seven Natural Wonders of the World..." Maggie could hear the tour guide speak. But the information clogged her head, as she remained disengaged. The empty space inside the canyon reminded Maggie of the space that separated her from Antonio. Soon she would be back in London. She hated the idea. She wanted to be with Antonio, wherever he was. She thought back to their time in the desert with the elements against them, wishing to be in the sand with him once again. Where was he? He was supposed to be with her.

How could he bail out?

Maggie took pictures of the scenery, and a few with Bradley and Rainelle to get her mind focused on the activity that she had requested. But she decided that she would rather be with Antonio, just looking at him.

When the tour ended, Maggie stopped to use the restroom, but as she stepped inside, a woman followed in behind her.

"Are you Maggie White?"

Maggie turned around, startled, wishing for a moment that she could just scream, but instead she surrendered. "Uhh...Yes." Maggie gave her a blank stare, realizing that her life was becoming a spectacle.

"I'm supposed to deliver a message to you to stay away from Antonio DeLuca. If you don't, there will be consequences," the woman threatened.

Maggie stared back at her, giving no response.

She knew that if she married Antonio, it would send her into a whole new agitating spotlight.

"I mean it!" the woman finalized, and walked out.

Maggie followed her out, and stood motionless as she watched her meet up with a man. They got into a car and drove away. She did not know what to think. *Was that cause for concern?* She saw Bradley and Rainelle waiting for her, and relief surged through her as she remembered that she was accompanied by security. But when she approached them, Bradley seemed completely unaware.

"How about we get something to eat?" Bradley suggested.

Maggie looked at the two of them, feeling like a third wheel.

"Sure...that sounds good," Maggie agreed, thinking that she had absolutely no appetite.

She walked alongside them, following into a restaurant, recalling when Bradley had first assisted her to her dinner date with Chad. She smiled at the thought, bringing her into a better mood. And although her mind was spinning with quandaries, she tried her best to engage in the activity.

"Thanks for bringing me...this has been on my list for a while...after seeing the Grand Canyon, I am simply amazed," Maggie told Rainelle.

"Yes, it is really something to see," Rainelle agreed.

Maggie recalled being in the bathroom at the Night Owl and seeing Rainelle for the first time. She had to admit, all of Antonio's staff and associates were wonderfully kind and friendly.

"So, it's a shame Antonio could not make it," Rainelle voiced her concerns as Bradley held the door open for the two of them.

"Yeah, I know he is busy though." Maggie decided to excuse his behavior.

They all made their way over to a table, and she sat across from the two of them at a table set for four. It was already apparent that Antonio was missing. She looked at Bradley, wondering if he knew why Antonio didn't show. She decided not to be nosy.

"So is Antonio keeping you busy in Vegas?" Bradley questioned Maggie as she squirmed in the discomfort of Antonio's absence.

She wondered if they knew that he had proposed.

"We were on the Strip last night," Maggie explained. She wondered if she should mention the woman in the bathroom. *What was the point?* It wasn't as if he could track her down and pull out the handcuffs. She decided to try to forget it.

"So..." Rainelle gave Maggie a curious look. "Are you and Antonio engaged?"

Maggie gave her a look of surprise, realizing she still did not wear a ring, but that yes, they did know.

"Yeah, he wanted to get married in Vegas," Maggie explained, "but we are going to be married in Italy...on the day we met."

"Congratulations!" Bradley spoke the confirmation, alarming her senses that her engagement was a reality.

Maggie smiled, thinking back to when she danced with him at the Night Owl and he landed her into Antonio's arms. As her mind drifted back in time, Bradley stirred up new memories in the present.

"Antonio is a good guy, Maggie. Don't be afraid to marry him."

"Where is he today?" Maggie finally voiced her concern, feeling suddenly very comfortable in their company.

"I have my suspicions, he will tell you about that when you see him next," Bradley indicated, leaving her in the dark.

Maggie wondered why he wouldn't say, but his words seemed to at least excuse his absence.

Now the rain came down, and Maggie sat in the car, riding back in silence. She wondered about the lady in the bathroom. *Who was she? Why did she say to stay away from Antonio? Was that a threat... some nut job fan of his? And who was the man she was with?* Should she report it? *To whom? Antonio? Bradley? Francis?* Maggie thought about all the people that could have seen them walking around yesterday. She remembered how Antonio hugged her on stage. *Maybe some fan was upset.* None of it made any sense for sure. Or was someone trying to warn her about Antonio? Surely not—she trusted him, but could it be a past relationship? *Did someone he date become obsessed, a psycho?* She thought it a strange coincidence that he was busy today.

Maggie spun her thoughts around, trying to make sense of everything.

"Maggie!" Bradley called out, looking at her in the rearview mirror, breaking her out of her daydream. She noticed that they were back at the Bellagio. "Antonio called and said that he would meet us at the lobby."

Maggie watched as Rainelle and Bradley got out of the car. She reached for the door handle, but Bradley instructed her, "Wait here!"

She sat still, watching Antonio approach. Bradley stood on one side of him and two hotel security personnel were on the other side. Antonio seemed preoccupied as he walked towards the car.

"Sorry Maggie, I got tied up," Antonio said as he got in and sat behind the wheel. His hair was a mess on top of his head, and the outgrowth of whiskers, thicker than usual, made an announcement that once again he hadn't taken time to shave.

"It's okay. You have a busy life. I know." She excused their loss of time together.

"No, Maggie. It's not like that. We have to talk."

"What? You don't want to marry me anymore?" She worried, hoping he didn't have second thoughts.

"No." Antonio frowned at her, not finding the humor. "I have spent the day..." He paused. "Stanley and I have been..." He paused again. "I'm not sure how to tell you this."

"What?" she asked with concern. "Where were you?"

"This is serious, Maggie," he said. "Francis is bad news. I know you work for the guy, and you think you have this great job, but he's up to no good. Now he's working on sending you threats, so that we don't see each other. Somehow, word got out that I am interested in offering you the contract with my company that would be exclusively yours. He does not want to be cut out of the deal!"

"Chad, I'm afraid. Someone threatened me today. Some woman...I saw her leave with a man."

Antonio listened to her, his face etched with concern.

"What did she say?" he finally asked.

"She told me that I should stay away from you, or there would be consequences. When I just stood there, she said she was serious."

"Okay, Maggie, don't panic. I have to tell you, I got the names of the people that were following you today. That's why I didn't come along. I was busy with that, but I put Bradley in charge of you to keep you safe. He's a good bodyguard."

Maggie suddenly felt even more worried.

"Oh no, Chad, you're telling me I need a bodyguard now? I can't take this anymore. What am I going to do? I work with Francis. He lives in England with me. This is creepy."

"Relax!" Antonio said in a cheery tone. "Francis is definitely creepy, but he does not have murder on his list. I doubt you have to worry. But just in case, I know what we need to do. We need to announce our engagement."

"We can't do that! I just got yelled at by Francis this morning for spending too much time with you. He said we were here on business. I might as well quit, before he fires me!" Maggie winced.

"No, you don't have to quit...yet." Antonio sounded convinced. "And Francis would be a fool to fire you."

Maggie was surprised that Antonio did not expect her to just quit her job immediately. She felt relieved when he went on to explain, "When I say we are engaged, he'll know you are his ticket to this contract. Plus, he'll realize that the whole world knows that if something happens to you, he would be suspect. I returned a phone call from a reporter today. They contacted me, wanting an interview on our relationship status. I said 'yes' since it will lend an opportunity to talk about the new costumes, and I will make sure I interject that you and Francis work as a team." He let out a huff. "That's via email once we are married, but he doesn't need to know." He gave her a wink. "We will put out his fears, and at the same time let him realize that since we are engaged now, he can't do business with me without your involvement."

Maggie had her eyebrows lowered as she digested everything. Antonio seemed to have a handle on the situation, and while that came as a relief, she now felt victim to a whole new adversity. She threw her head into her hands.

"I am *not* doing an interview." She sulked, determined.

Antonio reached out to try to shake her hands away from her head. "Yes, Maggie, you have to be there with me, or it will look strange. People will question it," Antonio said as he reached into his pocket. "Here." He handed her a box. "I bought you an engagement ring. Sorry, but you had your chance. The ring you want—with my name on it—I have to get that sized, and you can't wear that to the interview or people will think I'm cheap." He chuckled quietly to himself. "I hope you like it."

Maggie saw his face covered with a smirk as he explained, "I picked it out with Francis in mind—I would hate for him not to notice! And if he kisses you again with that ring on your finger, I will have to kill him!" Antonio passed her his sweet look, followed by a grin. And after taking one look at him, she knew that he meant for her to worry about his selection. She scrunched her brow as she stared down at the box.

She hesitated, realizing his endearing pursuit for shock. She slowly opened the box, and saw her ring immediately catching the light that came through the window of the limo. "Are you joking?" Maggie sat in disbelief. "It's... over-the-top, don't you think?" Her thoughts poured out in a frenzy of shock and amazement while she stared down at his selection.

Now she knew that he definitely loved to cause trouble, and her very own ring screamed out the proof. She felt tongue tied as she contemplated her ability to love it and hate it at the same time. She slipped it on her finger and continued to study it.

www.lovetheillusion.com/323.htm

"I had it custom made," he told her, "and at the last minute. It was the biggest ruby they had...it was in the safe."

Maggie could not help but think it was unique...*wild...just like him* and just like their love.

"I love it," she finally decided, still thinking it was a bit much. As her mouth hung open, he entertained her with his explanation.

"I chose a ruby because it's red, the color of love, and the diamonds that form a circle around the ruby represent eternity...and it's twenty-five karats, so that Francis knows he had better not kiss you *ever* again!"

383

"Wow," Maggie expressed her amazement as it encompassed her finger. She darted her eyes at him, realizing he was now her fiancé. "It might take me a while to get used to this. It pretty much takes up my whole hand."

She tore her gaze away from the ring, smiling at Antonio.

"So when is our delightful interview?" she asked.

Antonio was quick to return her smile.

"It's tonight! We are going there now." He took his hand through his hair, attempting to straighten it.

Maggie dropped her jaw in disbelief.

"NOW...?" *Please not now!*

She looked down at her clothes, as she sat in jeans and a white summer blouse, a bland fashion statement. She ran her fingers through her own hair, realizing that surely it must be a mess after a day at the Grand Canyon.

"I'm going like this?" Maggie felt frustrated appearing in public in such a casual washed-out look.

"Yeah, and with that ring." He sat amused. "You're fine just as you are," he calculated, reviewing her attire.

Maggie sunk her head back into her hands, and let out a sigh. "What do they want to know?" She predicted the interview, fearing the spotlight. "SO...?" Maggie asked again, thinking Antonio was slow to respond. "WHAT do they want to know? Let me guess!" She sounded disgusted. "When are the twins due? Do I enjoy coffee or tea with the other women you see on the side, and hmm...What were we doing in the desert?" She passed him an ungrateful look. "I can hardly wait!"

"It will be fine, Maggie." Antonio made light of her fears. "They will ask how we met and just keep it that we met on business. Don't tell the Chad story. That's for us. Not them. Then, they will ask when the wedding is." He questioned her, "Well? You want to be married in April?"

"Sure." She passed him a smile, forgetting the issue at hand. "What is the weather like?"

"Venice? We usually have fifty to sixty degrees in April."

"That is cold. I will have to make my dress with sleeves?"

"I will keep you warm." Antonio raised his brow, waiting for her eyes to meet his. And when they did, Maggie flooded with excitement to marry him, as he explained, "We can get married in the morning, and afterwards have an outdoor reception. Our backyard is beautiful. There's plenty of room inside, if people are cold." He paused and then spoke intimately, "And then... we disappear and fly out to a private resort for our honeymoon."

"Where will that be, inside the paparazzi mansion?" Maggie started laughing.

"No, Maggie. I'm not telling you!" He grinned. "But it won't be there. Trust me."

"Figures," Maggie contended, trying to get used to his surprises. She didn't care as long as she was with him. Then she counted out the months. *Another six months?*

Immediately, she had second thoughts, feeling sick to her stomach, lost in another bout of missing him. "Maybe...we should get married at Christmas," she finally suggested.

Antonio started to chuckle.

He gave her a new description. "It's beautiful at Christmas. If we keep it small, we can get married whenever you want. Christmas is good. You can fly in a day before the wedding. So, if my mamma and papa don't like you, I have time to send you back!" Antonio teased. Maggie was caught off guard by his flippant remark. Then he issued her his sweet look, to top it off.

"That's mean. Maybe I will show up a few days late!" she said in a hostile tone, not finding the humor.

Then his words turned serious, and she knew he was sincere. "They will love you, Maggie. I promise," he reassured her.

"Dana's getting married two weeks before Christmas. It will be busy, but I know she would want to come."

"You can invite whoever you want. Keep it small though, and no Francis!" Antonio warned.

"Definitely, no Francis." Maggie thought about it. "I would probably just invite Shane and Dana, and my immediate family. We don't need bridesmaids and groomsmen."

"No, we don't—just us, and…my family is small—maybe fifty, plus the locals, friends of the family."

"Have we known each other long enough?" Maggie shared her concern, letting out a sigh.

"Sure," Antonio sounded confident, "long enough to know that I totally love you. And it will be eight months in December. Besides, it's not how long you know someone. Look at people! They are married twenty years and call it quits. I won't call it quits with you Maggie, I promise." Antonio grabbed her hand. "Look what we have already made it through!" He tried to deplete her insecurities. But she soon felt appalled by their next adventure.

She flung her hand into his arm.

"And now we have a dumb interview! You can do *all* the talking. I am just going to sit there." Maggie folded her arms, and stared out the window.

Antonio laughed. "You will be fine. Just make sure you look happy. Or they will think you don't want to marry me."

"And who would *ever* think that?" She gave him a sarcastic look.

He pulled into a parking lot.

"Here we are!" he announced with no concerns. "We're supposed to go in that building and look for studio five."

"Awesome! Here goes a new disaster," Maggie reflectively stated, displaying her pessimism. Antonio shot her a curt look, as if he was finally getting irritated.

"Maggie! Do you think I like this? No—but I can turn this into a good thing. I always donate the money to Matteo's foundation. You should think of him and those families that you saw at the benefit. That's what I do."

Chapter 20

Maggie held onto her stomach as if she had the flu, while Antonio reached for the steel handle to open the glass door.

He immediately noticed her tenacious pessimism and advised, "Knock it off with that Maggie, unless you want them to think you're pregnant." He gave her an inviting look, trying to lighten the mood. She shot him a rude look, when the woman at the reception desk noticed their arrival. Maggie scanned her short fun hairdo and glasses through which she was now watching them. She quickly grabbed onto Antonio's hand with both of hers, parading her pride to accompany him.

"Well, if it isn't Antonio DeLuca in the flesh! And you must be Maggie? I am so delighted to meet you! I'll let Marissa know that you're here. Meanwhile, have a seat. Can I get you something to drink?" The desk clerk smiled as she eyed up the two of them.

"I think we're fine, but thanks," Antonio answered for both of them.

Maggie turned around, giving him an exasperated frown and whispered, "I'll have a bottle of Everclear with a straw." She sat down next to him, already feeling like a spectacle. And the interview hadn't even started yet. She could not wait for it to be over.

www.lovetheillusion.com/327.htm

Antonio glanced at Maggie and laughed. "Maggie, it's not that bad. You look like you're waiting to have your appendix out. Try to smile and look happy. Or people will think I torture you, which is clearly not the case." He grinned at her, and she managed to grin back.

A new face approached.

"Hi, you two...thanks for meeting with me." A lady shook hands with them both, while she introduced herself. "I'm Marissa Kolmar, and I'll be conducting the interview. I promise this will be completely painless."

Maggie was doubtful as Marissa motioned for them to follow her down the hall.

"I've been trying to get this interview for months, and Antonio finally agreed. People want to know what's up with the two of you."

Antonio beamed a smile at Maggie who managed to smile back at him, proud to finally announce to the world that they belonged together.

No sooner did they sit down, Marissa began instructing them. "I will give a short introduction and say who I am, and that the two of you have agreed to do an interview to the public on your relationship status. Okay, ready?"

Maggie watched as the cameraman focused in on them, realizing she would never be "ready." "Take one," Maggie heard the words that made her stomach tie up in a knot. She put on a smile to front her nervousness.

MARISSA: "Antonio, thank you so much for allowing me this privilege to meet with the two of you. Rumor has it that you two are dating?"

ANTONIO: "We're engaged."

MARISSA: "Engaged, so soon? Is that your engagement ring?" (She nodded at Maggie's hand. Maggie smiled at Antonio, wishing he would speak and explain that *he* was the show-off, not her.)

ANTONIO: "Yeah, I picked it...it's a ruby." (He grinned, realizing the ring was entertaining.)

MARISSA: "Wow! I won't even ask how much *that* cost. The price of a small island and I'm sure it's one of a kind."

(Maggie glanced at Antonio to signal her embarrassment that her ring was a sudden focal point for the camera. As much as she loved fashion, she did not consider herself materialistic. And Marissa still seemed to question the engagement.)

MARISSA: "So you two have been dating for, let's see, about two months? And already, Antonio, you want to marry her?"

(Maggie laughed, and her tongue became unglued.)

MAGGIE: "It's been six months."

MARISSA: "Okay, so...six months? And you've been dating on and off, or...?"

ANTONIO: "Since we met. Our companies do business together. And she is like no other girl I have ever met before."

MARISSA: "I see. Now there was a rumor...and I hate to put you on the spot, but that's my job, and people want to know. So, here it goes." (She focused on Maggie.) "Are you expecting Antonio's baby?"

(Maggie felt her face flinch, wondering how the reporters perceived her to be pregnant. She quickly smiled, getting lost in the humor while recalling Antonio's request that she appear happy. She raised her brow at

Antonio, indicating that he had better come to her defense. He laughed off the absurdity.)

ANTONIO: "No, that's just a stupid rumor. Look at her. She doesn't look pregnant!"

MAGGIE: "Yeah, there seems to be a lot of interesting rumors. They have him chasing women all the time and I can tell you that Antonio's not like that."

(Antonio grinned at Maggie and she grinned back at him, while they enjoyed a moment of reality in front of the camera.)

ANTONIO: "So, anybody out there with a wet pen, you need to find something else to write about. I love Maggie, and there's no one else!"

MARISSA: "Do you hear that, all you girls out there? Antonio's in love. So now what are you going to do with all the girls who chase you?"

ANTONIO: "That's just how fans are. I love my fans, but I don't want to date them!" (Antonio smirked.)

MARISSA: "Maggie, you don't seem worried. Is it hard dating, or being engaged to him?"

MAGGIE: "No, we have a lot of fun together. He's very adventurous, always surprising—"

MARISSA: "What I mean to ask is how you will keep him to yourself?"

How RUDE! (Maggie shot Antonio a look, indicating that he had better redirect the interview to a more kosher topic.)

ANTONIO: "Maggie has nothing to worry about, and that is ridiculous to ask that. You seriously want to know that?"

MARISSA: (grinned) "So, when is the wedding? I assume neither of you have been married before, and this must be a big leap of faith for the both of you."

(Maggie looked at Antonio again, wishing that the interview was over.)

ANTONIO: "April?" he teased.

MAGGIE: "Christmas," she clarified.

MARISSA: "Which is it? Tell us! April or Christmas?"

ANTONIO: "Merry Christmas, I guess." (He grinned.)

MARISSA: "And where do you plan to get married? Here in Vegas?"

MAGGIE: "We are going to go to—"

ANTONIO: (cut her off) "Maybe we'll come back to Vegas." (Maggie quickly nodded, realizing he dodged the question.)

MARISSA: "Is your family going to be there? Or are you going to surprise them and elope?"

(Maggie signaled to Antonio to answer that question.)

ANTONIO: "The final plans aren't made yet."

MARISSA: "Speaking of your family, how are they? Rumor has it that they're still back in Italy?"

ANTONIO: "Yeah, that's right."

MARISSA: "Why did they move back? It must have been a tough decision on their part."

ANTONIO: (frustrated) "They missed it there. Italy is beautiful."

MARISSA: "But you prefer the States?"

ANTONIO: "No, my work is here, but I always spend a lot of time with my family back home. Especially for the holidays, you know."

MARISSA: "It looks like I'm down to just a few questions. Let's see. Now, you got to know each other through work. And Maggie, you work for Francis Louis? What an opportunity that must be. Everyone wants to be seen wearing a dress by Louis, and you must have a few! And although he has expanded his women's formal line, he's also designing costumes now? It must be a wonderful opportunity to work for such an icon in the fashion industry."

MAGGIE: "Of course. I hope that we can work on many future projects together with Antonio's company. He's really a fabulous designer."

MARISSA: "So then there's a future there, Antonio?"

ANTONIO: "Yes, absolutely. As long as Maggie works for him, he has nothing to worry about."

(Antonio grinned, sealing the purpose of the interview.)

MARISSA: "Well, thank you to the both of you, and good luck with the wedding plans."

Maggie and Antonio stood up to shake her hand, before making their exit.

"Chad," Maggie whispered as soon as they had left, "*that* was a *nightmare* and I am so glad it's over!"

"Why? It was one of the better ones. We put it right out there. As long as you are in the picture, Francis has my business. That's protection for you, Maggie. Don't you see that?"

"I guess, but that was such a *stupid* interview. Perhaps the stupidest one yet! Why did I sit through that?" Maggie huffed out her disappointment.

"They're all pretty stupid," he agreed, facing her at the door on the way out. The sun shone in on them, as it had begun to set for the day. "Now, it's all over with!" He puckered his lips to sound out a kiss.

"No," Maggie whispered, "it's not *over*! I am going to keep hearing her obnoxious question about how I will keep you to myself! Why did she ask that, just to irritate me?"

"That's what they do best—ask nosy, stupid questions. We already know the answer to that." He dismissed her worries. He grabbed her into his arms and tried to kiss her but she pushed him back.

"Everyone has you on this pedestal, and I am nobody. I don't like that feeling. Your fans are all probably wondering why you picked me."

"Maggie! That is the most ridiculous thing you've ever said. Do you know who is on my pedestal?" Maggie broke their eye contact.
"You," he eagerly admitted. "I admire you! You are everything I ever wanted. You are sweet, and innocent, and fun to hang out with...not to mention absolutely beautiful. I was in love the first day that I saw you."

"You were not in love the first day that you saw me!" She tried to break free from his hold, but Antonio held onto her securely.

"How do you know what I was thinking? Now let me kiss you!"

Maggie watched him as he closed his eyes. Soon she felt his gentle kiss.

"Don't doubt us, Maggie. I love you." He gave her his sweet look, and Maggie felt her heart melt.

Maggie let go of a smile as they drove away. She was glad to be done with the interview and on their way back to the Bellagio.

"So, when does *that* spectacle air?"

"Soon, my dear," Antonio responded playfully.

"So, you don't think I have to worry about Francis' threats now?"

"Nope, I have that private eye working inside his little circle of friends, if you can even call them that. They all have a list of trouble." Antonio enlightened her.

"Murder?" Maggie asked, concerned.

"No, but they are quite the slime buckets! Try a bit of blackmail, money laundering, fraud...but I will know if there's anything we need to worry about. Once I marry you, he's done. I got enough security people to keep you safe. My home in Italy is protected. It's a big place, and it is overlooking a river with the city in view. You'll love it."

"Thanks for cutting me off before I invited the entire paparazzi to our wedding!" Maggie considered their battle for privacy.

"No problem," Antonio said, pointing his finger at her. "You almost made our small wedding a big one!" He managed a laugh.
But Maggie had a new concern.

"I was wondering why she never asked how I will be working for Francis while in New York with you." Maggie was curious. "Doesn't *that* seem...questionable?" She hoped he would reveal his true feelings—that he wished she would quit her job with Francis.

Antonio brushed it off. "That's of no interest to them. People do business together internationally all the time," he explained. "Reporters only want to dig up the grit. Strange they have little interest in Francis. He should have reporters contacting him left and right! Either way, he should have plenty of coal in his stocking."

Antonio's hostilities towards her dearly beloved boss had left her with her own "shredded string of loyalty."

"I almost feel bad for Francis." She mocked his quest to keep them apart. "I will have my cell phone off *all* the time if I work for you. He will never be able to get ahold of me!" Maggie let go of a devilish grin, thinking that Antonio was rubbing off on her.

Antonio passed her an intimate look, while indicating that she would never be able to keep up to him when it came to causing trouble. "Forget the cell phone," he enlightened. "You can tell him he can't get ahold of you because we are too busy under the sheets!" He let go of a chuckle, assuming he spoke the last, finishing the discussion about Francis.

Maggie remained speechless, recalling his former concern to be a gentleman. She tried to free her mind of his suggestion, but it teased her brain with delight. *The real issue...* She knew he wanted her to dissolve her association with Francis. *And* that Antonio's proclamation during the interview of being business partners with Francis could only be a huge lie. Antonio would never tolerate him, she concluded.

Maggie thought about the entire interview once again.

"Chad? Why do they always ask you about your family...about them moving back to Italy?"

Antonio's face changed in an instant.

"Why?" Maggie pressured him. "Why *did* they move back?"

"Not now, Maggie, not now!"

Maggie's jaw dropped as she remembered previously trying to uncover the secret he kept, that he refused to share.

"How dare you?" Maggie raised her voice. "You have secrets from me, and we're engaged?" She gave him an evil eye, but he refused to make any eye contact. She grabbed his arm, pinching it. "I am not going to like secrets, Antonio DeLuca!"

He kept quiet.

Maggie returned the silence, knowing he negated her concerns. How would she uncover the mysterious deceit? She wondered if she should just let it go, when she heard him speak. "It has nothing to do with us," he promised. "Trust me. Can you just drop it?" He sounded uneasy.

"It's okay." She sulked, still curious. "I guess I should trust you." Her voice carried a trace of sarcasm.

"Good. Then, that's that!" he remarked, in closing out the subject.

Maggie took in a deep breath and let it out, signaling that it wasn't over. But he had no problem challenging her.

"Don't be stubborn, Maggie!"

"Me? You are the stubborn one—you with your little secret!" Maggie reflected. "What! Let me guess! You burned the house down with an explosion from your latest magic trick, so they had to move away?"

Antonio started laughing under his breath and shaking his head. "I am a troublemaker, aren't I?" He appeared a bit proud.

"So, that's it?" Maggie asked. "I guessed it?" She saw that he wore a huge grin.

"No, Maggie, you will never guess it! Now, am I going to have to pull over and kiss you to get you to stop talking?" Antonio suggested. Her eyes studied his thick brow that seemed to dictate his authority.

"I wouldn't let you!" She frowned, playing his game.

"Are you offering ultimatums?" Antonio squinted in her direction. "That's *tempting*," he concluded with a smile.

Maggie sat, her arms crossed, finally irritated by his efforts to keep her in the dark. "I want to go back now. I'm tired, and it's been a long day." She tried to push his buttons. She glared at him, frustrated with his ability to manipulate her emotions.

"Okay." Antonio was fine with her suggestion, not budging in the least.

Maggie stared out the window, and then at her ring, as he drove them back. It felt heavy on her hand, and she wondered if she would ever get used to its weight.

When they arrived at the Bellagio, Antonio handed the keys to a valet, and Maggie took off four feet ahead of him.

As she approached the elevator, she could hear someone yell, "Hey! Antonio."

She ignored the commotion until she heard someone whistle. Now two teenage girls were waving at him. Maggie was sick of the attention he got from the opposite sex. She stepped inside the elevator without him, watching the door close. But he grabbed onto the door, pushed it open, and stepped inside. Antonio was smiling, as if the whole thing was a big joke, but Maggie folded her arms, refusing to look at him. She pressed her lips together, watching the elevator go to the seventh floor.

The door opened, and Antonio followed behind her as she paced quickly to her room, key card in hand. No sooner had she opened the door to her room, he grabbed onto it, following in behind her. He came and stood in front of her, grabbing onto her arm. "Maggie, just let it go."

She frowned at him, wondering why he kept secrets.

"It won't change anything between us," Antonio tried to explain. "You know I love you. Why can't you just let it go?"

www.lovetheillusion.com/336.htm

Maggie pulled away from him and sat down on the edge of the bed. "Leave, Antonio, just leave!" she yelled, offended by his latest surprise. And although she refused to look at him, she knew his eyes were on her as he came and stood in front of her. She let out a huff, exhausted by her failed efforts. "Leave, I said!"

"I'm not going anywhere." His voice was smooth and steady. "I'm staying."

She dared to look up at him, her eyes following along his scruffy after-five shadow that adorned his face, accentuating his lips. And when their eyes met, she knew she was in trouble. She realized she could not fight him off, nor did she want to. She feared he could read her mind. She watched as he unbuttoned his shirt and stood in front of her, his eyes remaining focused on her. She viewed the contour of his chest as he stared down at her. Now she knew that he could read her mind and she could definitely read his. And it was evident that they were *not* going to discuss his secret. She could barely breathe as she sat mesmerized, watching him as he kept her in a mystical trance. She reached up and ran her fingertips across his waist, feeling his fit body. Antonio stared down at her, his lips without words. She remembered his warning, back in the car, that he would kiss her to get her to stop asking about the family secret as she now sensed that reality.

Antonio grabbed onto her hands as they caressed his chest, bringing her up to him. He kissed her gently on her lips and then let go of her hands slowly, taking a few steps away from her... yet, his eyes were still locked in hers. She sat back down on the bed. She felt sedated. Her eyes followed him as he went over to the wall and dimmed the lights. And as she watched him, she wondered what he was up to.

He grabbed her arms and pulled her up next to him. He kissed her, refreshing her memory of how sweet his kiss tasted. Now there was no doubt. She was unable to resist him. She felt her body fall against his until he sat down on the bed and pulled her onto his lap. Now she felt their passion like never before as he brought her down to the bed, resting on top of her. Maggie soon forgot she was angry. She reached her hands into his hair, leaving it disheveled as he kissed her neck, while his hand roamed her upper body under her clothes, until he finally unsnapped her bra. She knew whatever he was keeping from her would never kill the passion that existed between them. She would accept it, regardless. She grabbed onto his belt buckle, pulling him closer to her.

Maggie lay underneath him, thinking that perhaps he was going to finally break down and make love to her. She always wanted to wait until her wedding night, and he seemed to want to be that gentleman. With past relationships, she had been determined, but there was something about Antonio that made him the exception. She found him irresistible. Surely, she had been the only woman to ever run from him, but the harder she had tried to fight him off, the more persistent he was, and she now realized that he had finally broken down all of her walls, leaving her completely helpless—just as he wanted her.

He grabbed her hands and held her down, and she felt trapped beneath him. His secret was the last thing on her mind. She could feel the sweat between them, as her blouse was stuck to his chest. She could feel him nibbling on her ear and then stroking her neck with his tongue as he whispered, "I love you and I can't wait to make love to you."

Maggie thought on his words, wanting to return his words. But surely, he already knew. She closed her eyes, preparing for what she knew they both wanted.

Antonio continued to kiss her as she removed his belt from his pants. She dropped it on the floor at the side of the bed. She heard the clank when it hit the floor, and it seemed to signal an alarm. He sat up, resting on top of her. He took a deep breath in and slowly let it out, while he melted his eyes into hers. "Are we done fighting?" he finally asked, letting go of a grin.

"I think so," Maggie decided with her eyes locked in his.

To her surprise, he stepped off the bed. She kept her eyes on him, wondering what he was doing. She watched as he buttoned his shirt together, leaving it mismatched. What was he thinking? She already knew what she was thinking. Why was he leaving? Now even though she had never told him she loved him, he had to know. Should she speak the words to make him stay? Instead, she sat silent, watching his every move as he walked towards the door. Maggie held her breath as she wanted to beg him to stay. She looked down at the floor to where his belt lay. She could not recall ever being in this situation before. She had no idea what to think or what to do. Was he really leaving after all that?

As he reached for the door, he hesitated, and then slowly turned around to look at her.

She sat speechless, just looking at him, while she contemplated what triggered her curiosity the most—his secret or their passion? She reached down to the floor and grabbed his belt, holding it up in the air, signaling to him that he forgot it. But he just said, "You can keep that. Have a good night."

She stared back at him, realizing she must look completely frustrated. She watched the door close. And it did not take her long to realize, once again, that his secret was the last thing on her mind.

Twenty minutes later, Maggie still sat on the edge of the bed wondering what just happened. "UUGGH! He is such a *brat!*" she concluded, trying to discern if she was still mad about his secret. Now she wondered about his willpower to leave. Was he mad that she still had not told him she loved him? *How could he not know?* She would call Dana. She missed her advice. And she was definitely in need. Maggie stared at the clock. Dana would be getting up for work by now.

"Maggie, how are you? How's life with Antonio?" She could hear Dana's voice echoing with smiles even though she was miles away.

Maggie wondered where to start.

"Guess what. We're engaged," Maggie reported in an aggravated tone.

"Really? That's totally brill! Aren't you over the moon? You sound angry." Dana sensed the tension.

Maggie rambled out the various details. "He's being a jerk. He's got a secret. Oh, first! I should mention that I had to sit through one of his infamous interviews to announce our engagement to the entire world. He wanted to get married here in Vegas, but it felt strange. First, I never expected him to ask, and now things are a mess."

"Wait. What? Slow down, Maggie, I can't even sort everything out. So, when are you getting married?"

"Christmas, in Italy, and you can tell Shane about us, since it will soon be public information. But don't forget, we don't want the paparazzi there, so don't tell anyone *where* we are getting married."

"Maggie, I am so happy for you. I really, at the same time, can't believe this, so…what about a secret?"

"You tell me! These reporters keep asking him about why his family moved back, as if they want to dig up the past and have him talk about it. But he won't talk about it."

"That's strange, but what could it be?"

"Who knows? But, shouldn't he tell *me*? I will be his wife! No, he will not share! He threatens to kiss me to distract me from my concern. I tell him to just leave, but instead he starts making out. Then, he tells me he can't wait to make love and I am thinking the same, but that's when he gets up and leaves!"

Dana laughed. "Hmm…quite the willpower! That's a good thing when it comes to love. I hate to say it, but it sounds like he won that one! The main thing is you love him too, and you trust him, right? Or you wouldn't marry him. Just let it go."

"You think? After all the relationships I have been through, he seems a breath of fresh air, but now this! Not to mention the package deal of his celebrity. Am I still a fool? Is there no decent man left? I'm doomed to misery, why not him! I'm pretty sure whatever he is hiding wouldn't keep me from marrying him. He could be head hit man for the Mafia, and I'd still probably make love to him."

Dana started to laugh again.

"Maggie, you sound ridiculous. Actually, I think you've finally found the gentleman you always wanted! And I bet he knows it."

"Yeah, well he's making me crazy."

"As for the secret, he has a complicated life, more than most people. It's probably nothing."

Maggie wondered how she made sense out of everything so quickly.

"But why won't he say? I go back in two days, and the next time I see him, it will be our wedding. I wonder if I've known him long enough. The time we have together is great, but how do I know I'm doing the right thing? I always thought people should be engaged for...I don't know...years?" Maggie realized his secret was the icing on the cake of her "dating time table" frets.

Dana rushed in with more smoothing attempts to extinguish her concerns. "The two of you are in a different situation. How long do you want to be apart?"

"I don't," Maggie had to admit.

"Well, then you answered your own question!" Dana rang her response like a bell.

Maggie thought about it.

"Yeah, thanks, Dana, I'll see you in a couple days." She still felt discouraged.

"Do me this favor— lighten up! You're always so overstressed about everything." Dana made a last attempt.

"Sure, Dana, I will try. See you later."

Maggie still sat on the edge of her bed. She wondered why Antonio thought he could just kiss away her anger. She suddenly realized that Antonio did not give up his sense of humor in their heated disputes. Maggie felt frustrated, realizing he too carried his share of faults. There was his ego, similar to Francis, assuming he was always right about everything. And if she didn't like it, he would simply kiss her to resolve the conflict. As much as she hated his delusional thinking, she had to admit that she could never refuse his kiss. She remembered waiting so long for him to finally kiss her, and now he used it to his advantage. She hated fighting with him, but soon reached the conclusion that the more they fought, the more they would kiss. She pondered his choice of resolve, unsure what to think.

Now she still thought about his secret, wondering if it would reveal something that she could not live with. Did he have insecurities that she would lose interest in him over a small detail? *Or was it a big one?* Overall, he was pretty straightforward. She tried to imagine what he would be hiding. Her past doubts always left her feeling like a fool—the tabloid of Arianna, her arrival in Chicago when she thought he used the opportunity to get to know her because she worked for Francis, the dress she worried about him picking out that ended up looking great on her, the Canadian singer with the room card...That was only a show ticket. Now she reached the conclusion that while he seemed to find amusement in all of her many concerns, he seemed to have no trouble putting out her worst fears. And he had never done anything that gave her reason to doubt him. So, perhaps this was another one of those "situations." She could only hope so.

She lay back on her bed, feeling tired from the day. She gazed down at her ring, finally having curiosity as to how much it cost. *A ruby, stored in a safe...What was he thinking?* She had to admit, the ring truly depicted his character. It was priceless. And completely unique, just like him. He was like no one she had ever met, and his life revolved around the extravagance, the shock, the mystery...all mixed with his humor...just like the ring. She closed her eyes, wishing Antonio was still next to her. She stretched until she felt his belt, entangled in the covers, underneath her. She picked it up and examined it, thinking he just loved to mess with her head. But she was sure of one thing. He loved her.

Chapter 21

The Vegas sun shone brightly through the crack in the curtain window. Maggie sat up in her bed. It was the last day she would be able to see Antonio before the wedding. The thought was exhausting to her. *Everything happened so fast.* She felt so much happiness in that she thought she found the man of her dreams, the one she wanted to be with forever, but there was also a cloud of uncertainty that lingered with the whole event. She had trouble organizing everything in her mind and figuring out how to make sense of it all. She wished that she could spend more time with him, before the wedding. She also wanted their last day to be a good memory, so she knew that after the show, she would have to try to forget that they were still, technically, in an argument over his secret.

Maggie studied her ring finger and shifted the ruby while it caught the light emanating from the window. It sparkled like nothing she had ever seen. It was evidence that their engagement was not just a dream, and she was glad that he had insisted that she have a ring. The other one, with his name, would have to be worn on her other hand. She still wanted it.

And there was her dress—the one with a broken zipper and missing sequins, unraveled around the seam. She would have to either fix it or get a different dress. Surely, there would not be an alteration shop with same day service. She would have to go shopping while Antonio would spend the day getting ready for the show. She wondered why Francis had not found things for her to do. At ten a.m., she had still not heard from him. But that's when her phone rang.

"Maggie!"

Maggie rolled her eyes at the sound of his voice, as she simultaneously got out of bed.

"Last day, huh," she drudged out the words.

Francis sounded excited. "Yeah, I got tickets to a show here this afternoon, complimentary, from one of my connections. I'll pick you up at 1:00. It's a 2:00 show, and afterwards we will get a bite to eat. We should be done in plenty of time to get ready for tonight. It's not until 7:00—but an hour earlier, I guess, because it's a week night."

Maggie felt her eyelids droop to a near closed position.

"Sounds fun, but I have to spend the day shopping. My dress was so tight that the zipper broke."

There was a pause.

She hoped he wasn't overly upset.

"Is that right?" He did not sound as she expected, but rather friendly on the matter. "Well, I should be along to help find a replacement. We can expense it to the company."

Maggie was puzzled by his disregard.

"That's not necessary," Maggie asserted. "I can just pick up a top to go with these black pants I have."

"Nonsense!" He sounded alarmed. "You need a formal dress. This is a big event for us, Maggie. I insist on coming with you on this one. Trust me."

Trust me? Maggie thought. *Where have I heard those words before?* She had just started trusting Antonio, when she found out that he had a secret. Francis, on the other hand, was more than an arm stretch away from being trustable.

"I can pick out my own dress, really," Maggie insisted.

"Maggie! Let me do you this favor. I will pick you up in a half hour," Francis decided, leaving her no choice.

Now she saw that he had hung up.

"Yep," Maggie accepted, speaking the confirmation that she was defeated. *And if Antonio knew…*But what choice did she have? It was business.

Maggie had just tied her hair up in a wet twist when Francis arrived at her room.

When she saw through the peephole that it was him, she grabbed her purse and opened the door. She moved to step outside, but he walked into her room as if they had something to discuss.

Francis smiled at her.

"Maggie, we have been working together for…what, almost a year now? And we have gotten to know each other on a professional level and I must say you have been everything I expected when I hired you. You are conscientious, hardworking, insightful, and are a great asset to my company. We work well together. Now, I would hate to see anything come along and change that. I hope that we can develop a friendship beyond our professional teamwork."

Maggie stood, unaware of which emotion she wore on display. Was it fear, apathy, confusion, aggravation, embarrassment, or a combination of them all? And did he mean a friendship with benefits? Because she wore a ring on her finger that he could not possibly miss!

"So, Maggie, I look forward to our day together," he concluded.

Maggie moved toward the door, but he grabbed her arm and smiled at her in a way that made her want to choke. She swallowed instead, and let him know, "You really don't have to go to all this trouble."

"It's my responsibility to make sure you look good!" he enlightened, as they proceeded down the hall and to the front lobby, where they grabbed a cab.

Maggie sat on the other end of the backseat. Even with the gap between them, she felt uncomfortably too close. She watched out the window and wished for the day to end.

After visiting several exquisite dress shops, they found a halter style satiny light blue floor length dress. It featured ruffles flowing around the hemline and up the front, which had a faded zebra print around the waist. She stood at the counter in the dress as Francis gave his approval.

www.lovetheillusion.com/345.htm

"Thanks, Francis. I feel really bad about the other one. I know you had a lot of thought into the design and everything..."

"It is fine, Maggie. Don't worry your pretty little head about it. Now, we will run this back to the hotel quick, get some lunch and then go to the show."

Maggie figured the less she said, the better, but she could not overlook his generosity. It *was* a company event, however, so why should she have to fork out a thousand plus dollars for a dress that she probably would never wear again. She tried to set aside her resentment over having to spend the day with Francis. The course of events was only beginning, and she could not help but wonder if he would notice her ring.

An hour later, they arrived at a restaurant.

Maggie listened to Francis as he told the waiter all the specific changes to be made on the menu item he had ordered, after she just ordered a salad. She figured she may as well start counting calories, along with the days that separated her from an eternity with Antonio. She felt her mind continuously drifting back to the last night when he kissed her, as she lay underneath him on the bed. She longed to see him again, her anger subsiding. She just wanted to be with him.

Now Francis spoke loudly, turning his attention to Maggie. "I have to tell you, I'm excited to get back and start working on that new account. It should be a big one! They ordered a small shipment to start, but they want a whole new line of spring dresses to be shipped by February. If the ones we shipped sell out, they agree to buy all the spring line exclusively from us! Now, you can help me with the designs. We need to figure out what colors we want to bring out for spring. Do we want navy, or maybe navy mixed with pink or yellow? The possibilities are endless!" Francis had entered his rambling mode, so her mind drifted back to her hotel room. She could not wait to make love to Antonio. Even when she was mad, she could not refuse his kiss. She got lost in its sensation. Francis paid no attention to her distraction. "I think white and yellow could be a sunny fashion statement for spring, and definitely some that are just plain white. White is a magnificent fashion statement. It is clean, crisp, pure, and fresh, all at the same time. Then! We can add a wide six inch waistband to accent the dress...either in navy, pink—even black! Picture this... sheath style, a couple inches above the knee, maybe even a skinny patent belt to land directly center of the colored waistband. And made from the finest linen fabric and lined in satin!"

Maggie started daydreaming about her wedding dress when she heard "white dress." She mentally designed what she would wear on their wedding day...*A sweetheart neckline, with just a three inch cap sleeve...beads and lace following around the neckline and the upper body, with the bottom portion made of satin...and old fashioned gloves from the forties era that go up the arm...And perhaps a lace train that would attach around the waist that could be taken off for the reception and dancing...The skirt...flared at the hem...and gold rhinestone shoes to match a tiara...no veil.*

It will be beautiful...

www.lovetheillusion.com/347.htm

"Maggie," she heard her name called as Francis pulled her out of her daydream.

"Yeah, that all sounds great, I can't wait to get started on that," Maggie gave a quick response, trying to sound alert, but her mind drifted back to how handsome Antonio would look in his tux while she walked down the aisle towards him.

"Looks like you've been jewelry shopping in Vegas." Francis disrupted her daydream. "It never ceases to amaze me how the faux jewelry these days can look so real! Good deals or what?"

She stared back at him, startled, making no comment as Francis gazed at her ruby rock from Antonio. *Does he have any suspicions? Nope.* He was in the dark. That's where she wished she was with Antonio…on a big king size bed…in the dark…

Their lunch arrived, and Maggie tried to make sure she had enough food in her mouth at one time to stall any kind of serious conversation.

"So, did you do any gambling yet?" Francis chuckled. "Ha! I think I was down about a thousand pounds the day we first arrived, but now I am definitely ahead! I'm thinking at least twice that."

"Seriously?" Maggie questioned Francis in amazement. "People can actually win money gambling? I just always figured the chances were so slim, it wasn't even worth trying."

"No, no, no. That is for beginners," Francis piously explained. "I am hot behind the Wheel. That game, I win every time. You need to know exactly when to start, and when to stop!"

Maggie scrunched her brow, questioning his revelation.

"In fact, I am a pro!" Francis bragged himself up. "I bet you I can win, right over there!" Francis nodded in the direction of the casino while they sat at a restaurant on the Strip, the casinos visibly lined up one after the other. "After lunch, I will show you—real quick—before the show!"

Right, just what I need… a lesson on gambling.

Maggie stood behind Francis as he was playing the Wheel of Fortune. She watched him put in six hundred dollar bills. After his last two spins, he finished down by three hundred. Maggie scrutinized the crowded casino and wondered how long everyone had been in there. Undoubtedly, this was an expensive form of entertainment. Prior to Vegas, she had never spent five minutes in a casino, because she feared losing.

"Damn it!" Francis blurted out as he was down to his last hundred credits. He jittered back and forth on the chair, playing full bets, three dollars each. Maggie stood impatiently, waiting for him to finish. She thought about trying the machine next to him. She reached into her purse to pull out a twenty dollar bill, deciding to stick it into the "Lucky Sevens" machine. She put the bill in the machine, and hit the keypad to place her bet. She hit it again, and again, until the machine lit up! Francis nodded at Maggie, giving a "thumbs up."

"I won!" Maggie cried out with her hands in a tight fist up to her cheeks. She wore a big smile, and Francis cashed out the remainder of his money on a paper receipt.

"Well, look at you Maggie. I am just sending all the luck your way." Francis took credit.

Maggie stood, puzzled, still watching all the credits adding up. The machine was reading $600.00 and was still adding, displaying the triple sevens on her bet. She gave Francis a high five, and they both started laughing. "This is so lucky," she exclaimed. "Beginner's luck—I have never, ever done this before! I cannot believe this! It's such a rush!"

The machine finally stopped, announcing her winnings of $1200.00. A security attendant came to stand alongside her, having her sign for the money she won. He then gave her and Francis each t-shirts that announced the winnings: "CHA-CHING."

Maggie threw her t-shirt on over her tank top and jeans, and Francis did the same. And while standing at the cashier desk to gather her winnings, a photographer asked to take a photo of the two of them decked out in their matching Vegas attire. Francis was thrilled to oblige, as the photographer acknowledged his recognition of who they were, claiming that they made a hit in Vegas.

"See Maggie, what fun that is!" Francis cheered her on. "You got it down. Me? I am down for now, but after the show tonight, I will win it all back. You will see. You should come with me for luck."

"I can't. I'm going to be super tired by then. I need to turn in early—you know our flight is the next day." She watched his face, hoping for his approval. The reality…She would be with Antonio.

Now, it was almost 2:00.

Maggie followed Francis into an auditorium that had plush crimson seats, and a red carpet going down the center aisle. The show had just started, and there was a row of about ten girls dancing topless. Maggie glared at Francis, who was ready to enjoy their next adventure.

After taking a seat next to him, Maggie fanned her fingers over her face. *This is unbelievable.*

Fifteen minutes passed, when she declared in a defeated whisper, "Francis, I'm really not into this show. I know it was free, but…"

"Chill, Maggie, this is Vegas," he whispered under his breath, as he glanced over at her. "You gotta live a little."

Maggie peered up onto the stage through her fingers that laced over her face. How could they all look so happy up there? She found it hard to smile on stage with her clothes *on*!

She leaned into Francis' ear. "Be right back. I have to use the ladies' room." She excused herself and headed for the nearest restroom.

Maggie stood in the stall and glanced at her watch. *How long did this go?* She leaned against the stall door, reading the graffiti: "Michelle and Trent, true love forever," "Rock out in Vegas 2002," "Heidi and Beth were here," "Vegas rules, the fun in the sun." Maggie stared at a cigarette bud floating in the toilet. She stepped on the handle to flush it and watched it disappear.

Her watch revealed only five minutes lost. She could not waste any more time in a stall. She left the bathroom, a glimpse in a mirror revealing that her face was noticeably tan from the sun that day.

She stepped outside into a glistening, bright atmosphere. Nearby, she found a beverage stand where she bought a slushy. She took a seat on a bench outside the theater and watched the people go by. Various fashion statements were expressed, as if there were no guidelines. There were old people, young couples, and kids in strollers. She noticed a group impersonating the Beatles, and people stood lined up taking pictures next to them.

The sun beat down on her, and for a moment Maggie forgot that she was hanging out with Francis for the afternoon. She wondered again about Antonio's secret. What was he keeping from her? Regardless, she found herself anticipating their wedding day and was soon reliving his kiss last night, wishing to kiss him again. She admired his pursuit to convince her that he was a gentleman. Now the bad-boy image that she first perceived at the bar seemed to have vanished, except that he came laced with secrecy. And she would give anything to know what he was hiding, now that she could no longer hide her feelings for him.

She closed her eyes, and dreamed about their wedding.

Maggie heard a loud laugh, breaking her daydream, as a couple of teenagers walked by. They each wore colorful leis from one of the casinos. *The casino! Francis!* She needed to get back before the show ended. He surely wondered where she was by now. She stretched out of her position and headed back to the theater, tossing her cup into the trash as she went inside. The theater was now darker than before, after the sun penetrated her view. She retraced her steps, showed her ticket stub, and made her way back to her seat.

"Sorry, long line," Maggie bluffed as she sat back down. Francis made no response. She sat impatiently until the show ended.

Finally!

"Good show!" Francis recapped, exiting the theater. "I can't believe you missed the whole frickin' thing."

Maggie gave him a cynical stare.

"Come on Maggie, you just need me around to show you how to have fun. Tonight, after the show, we can hit the casino again!" Francis' voice carried excitement.

"No, I am getting some sleep!" Maggie laughed off his persistence, thinking she could not wait to be with Antonio.

"That's a mistake. You might as well have fun now, because when we get back, I will have you busy making up for lost time!" Francis laughed as he smiled at her.

She presented a fake smile back, contemplating his evil authority.

In the cab ride back, Maggie noticed his arm rested behind her. She squirmed in the discomforts of him thinking that they were anything other than business partners. And unfortunately, Antonio's attempt to buy her a ring to signal to Francis that she was taken was a failed effort. It was so outlandish that Francis thought it was costume jewelry!

Now she would see Antonio in only a few hours and she could hardly wait. She wanted more of what he started the other night.

Maggie stood on stage next to Francis while he reiterated his speech from a couple days ago. She wore the biggest smile on her face, gleaming inside, thinking that when the show was over she could finally be alone with Antonio.

When she sat back down, she found herself watching a repeat of the show she had already seen the other night, but it was just as fun to watch the second time around. She glued her eyes onto Antonio, who had no clue what she had been up to all day. She would not tell him either. He had his secret, and now she had hers.

Maggie made plans— *plans of retaliation.* She would dish out in return what he left her with the other night. She could play that game. She would love to continue where they let off! She was certain that she could drive him completely crazy. And she would definitely get him to reveal his top secret. Maggie laughed at her thoughts while she watched him on stage, feeling a bit corrupted after spending the day with Francis.

Maggie and Francis left together after the show. Maggie wanted to wait for Antonio, but Francis did not give her opportunity. She decided to send him a text: **I am in my room.**

Now back in her room, she wondered where he was. Two hours had passed since the show, and she was on the bed, dressed in a red satin push-up bra, red lace boy-cut underwear, a pearl necklace and her gold stilettos. She was waving her hands through the money that she had won—a healthy pile of twenty dollar bills. She watched it fly up in the air and land on the floor. She could not wait for Antonio to arrive. Soon she would get to the bottom of his stupid secret.

Finally, she received a text back: MEET ME OUT FRONT IN YOUR DRESS.

She would have to suspend her plan. *If only he knew.* Where were they going, she wondered, that she had to be dressed up? She thought about making an appearance in her Cha-Ching t-shirt that was draped over the chair. But instead, she put the blue dress back on that Francis had bought her and went down to the front lobby.

"Hi Chad." Maggie smiled at him as she got in the car. "Great show— just as good the second time!"

She appraised his smashing attire—a Hugo Boss suit with a white shirt underneath and a navy tie. "You look really good!" Maggie finalized, thinking she could not wait to get her hands on him.

"So why are we dressed up, *Chad?*"

"We are celebrating our engagement! We're going to the Eiffel Tower. It will be awesome. You can see the whole city from up on top!"

Judging from his excitement, Maggie guessed that he had completely forgotten about her wanting in on his secret. Now she wondered about it the whole way there. Certainly, after he had time to think about it, he would realize that if she was to be his wife, she had the rights to know everything. And if not, she was ready to proceed as planned. But first, the Eiffel Tower…

Seated at an elegant table for two, with a bottle of champagne, Maggie cherished the last moments they would be together before she had to leave. Her spiteful gestures were soon replaced with a more serious agenda. She wanted the evening to go well, since it was their last day together until the wedding. Her eyes danced in his and she knew that she loved him.

"That blue looks pretty on you, Maggie," Antonio started conversation, pouring them each a glass of champagne.

"Thanks." She smiled, receiving his compliment.

"Is that one of Francis' designs?"

"No." Maggie bit her upper lip.

"No?" Antonio questioned her. "It's surprising! That's not like him…to not parade you up on stage in something he designed for such a big occasion. Isn't that what he does best, special occasion women's formal wear?" Antonio looked at her while she gazed out the window, overviewing the extravagant display of the city's lights against the dark sky.

"Yeah, he does that well," she agreed, still casting a gaze out the window.

"So, where did you get that one? Not that I don't like it. It's really hot!" His voice carried suspicion.

Maggie challenged him. "Why are you so curious about this dress? It's just a dress!"

"Where did you get it?" Antonio asked again.

She contemplated his intuition. Now she was wondering…*Did he organize someone to spy on us?*

"At a shop here in Vegas," Maggie finally confessed. "I told you the zipper broke on that other one, so I had to go shopping."

"Oh?" Antonio raised his brow. "So, you spent the day shopping...by yourself?"

"Pretty much," Maggie explained, deciding she'd better change the subject before Francis became the topic of discussion over dinner. "I designed my wedding dress today. I have a complete mental picture of how I want it to look." She made eyes at him.

"How's that...?" Antonio awaited her description, although it seemed his thoughts were still on the blue dress.

"I'm not telling. That is always a *secret*. You can't know about the dress until the day of the wedding!" Maggie announced with her eyebrows pinned up in his direction.

"Don't cause trouble, Maggie!" Antonio warned, realizing he was in over his head. "It's our last night together, until I marry you." He passed her a romantic stare. She returned one to imitate his.

"I know! And after we get married, we can't fight anymore, right?" Maggie flirted in a sarcastic tone. She hoped to give him an opportunity to mention his secret.

"No, Maggie. I am sure we will. And you will keep trying to win our fights, but you never will," he retaliated, giving her a playful look to disregard her concerns.

"You are such a creep...with that ego of yours! If you know what's good for you, you will see to it that I start winning all the arguments," she told him.

He laughed under his breath, a lost cause.

Menus in hand, placing their order for the catch of the day, they could not keep their eyes off each other, regardless of the battles they were disputing on their last night together.

But after their waitress left, Maggie noticed someone in the distance taking their photo, adding to the current tension. The cameraman hid discreetly in a hallway across from them, snapping photo after photo, until they both finally acknowledged his presence, wishing to have some privacy and eat their dinner in peace.

www.lovetheillusion.com/355.htm

Maggie brought her eyes back onto Antonio, wondering how he could look any better. "So nice of someone to take our photo," she announced, realizing their relationship was no longer a secret.

"I hope it's a good one." Antonio gave a smile. "I'm going to miss you, when you leave tomorrow."

"Me too," Maggie agreed, staring into his brown eyes. Her eyes circled around his face, capturing his sweetness. She willed herself to commit every feature to memory for when she left.

Maggie sipped the champagne Antonio had ordered. She leaned across the table and whispered, "I can't wait to marry you!" She poured her comment right on top of the underlying tension.

"To us," Antonio made a toast.

Maggie sat silent, wishing to climb inside his head.

She steered the conversation to a new topic. "So, how are we going to plan our wedding, Chad...over the phone?"

"No Maggie. You can just show up with your dress, and we'll take care of the rest," he assured her. "We can get married a couple days before Christmas, spend Christmas with my family, and then fly out to...our honeymoon."

"Who is 'we'?" Maggie offered concern. "Stanley, Bradley, and the rest of your staff?"

"No, my mamma's promised she would get the chapel ready with the music and flowers, order the cake from her friend's bakery, and we have another friend that owns a restaurant that will cater the reception at our house."

"Your *mom* is planning our wedding?"

"Why not, she loves that. And trust me. She will do a good job. I will take care of the honeymoon, and you just need to make your dress."

"Are you sure she doesn't mind? Maybe I could fly out there some weekend and help her with everything."

"That's not necessary, Maggie. I will be home a few weeks early to tie up loose ends. We can spend a few months in Italy, but in spring I will have to get back to New York. You can come. Or you can stay in Italy, whatever you want."

Maggie contemplated what life would be like married to him as he traveled around to do shows.

"Maggie!" Antonio interrupted her thoughts. "Are you with me on this?"

"Yeah, sure, it's fine," she decided. "I will pick out your ring?"

"Sure." He smiled.

"I can't wait to get that ring on your finger, Antonio DeLuca!" Maggie declared. "So, I should get you a ring as flashy as mine?"

"No, Maggie. Please, keep it simple, nothing like what you are wearing." He seemed concerned.

Maggie took delight in his facial contempt.

"Oh, so you are picky?" She raised her brow. "Now, I cannot wait to pick it out! A big channel set display of...some mysterious gem, representing...eternal bliss!" Maggie teased, quietly chuckling as she sipped her champagne.

"You just can't quit sassing, can you!?" Antonio said with his teeth clinched in a playful manner, pouring them each more champagne.

Maggie smiled back maliciously, but then remembered the clock that ticked away their minutes together. She treasured the moment, wishing when she returned to England, she could close her eyes and remember their time together, just as it was right now. She took a deep breath to dismiss her thoughts of the next separation, when the food arrived.

"When does your plane leave tomorrow?" he asked, reading her mind.

"After lunch."

"You need to come by my room before you leave," he requested while taking a bite of his food.

His suggestion brought silence as they ate their last meal together before the big day. Maggie picked at her food, slowly losing her appetite, feeling like she would leave with an unfinished agenda. She wondered if she should just respect his rights to privacy. But why he had to keep secrets, she did not understand, and she knew her job with Francis left him with concern.

The car ride back to the hotel continued in silence, and Maggie knew he felt the same pain of saying goodbye. And for a moment, she pictured what it would have been like to have married him in her black dress.

"Aren't you walking me to my room, Chad?" Maggie asked, standing outside the car.

"Sure," he agreed, as he got out and handed the keys to the valet.

This time she kept in step with him, unlike last night when she had darted off ahead of him. She grabbed his hand, but he seemed in a hurry and preoccupied to make it through the lobby without any attention. The restaurant had actually been pretty quiet, other than a few stares and the cameraman. Maggie thought she was growing accustomed to hearing the comments from fans as they walked through the lobby area, although she tried to drown it out, pretending they existed in privacy.

"Sorry I was mad last night." Maggie sulked, hoping he would continue the discussion, but he did not.

"It's fine Maggie, I understand." Antonio sounded cold, indicating to her that she should not have brought it up again.

She could feel her emotions getting the best of her as she contemplated his mystery. *Why does he have to be such a brat?* Now, she felt jolted back into action to uncover his secret!

Maggie opened the door to her room, ready to engage in her next plan. "Don't be shy. You can come in," she said softly, making eyes at him. He looked as if he had second thoughts, realizing it was against his better judgment. But she watched as he stepped inside anyway, his eyes melting into hers.

He shut the door behind them and took her in his arms right away, while she removed his suit jacket, letting it fall to the floor. Antonio leaned against the door while kissing her lips, as his hands slid across the satin fabric of her dress, fitted at her hips.

Maggie grabbed him by his shirt and tie, walking him over to the bed and flirting with him, when she noticed the money she left lying all over the bed and floor.

"What is all this, Maggie?" Antonio looked confused, staring down at the pile of money.

Maggie started to explain. "I was gambling today. And I won!"

"Gambling?" Antonio frowned. "When, and with who?" He gave her a suspicious look, but when she looked into his eyes, she had a strange feeling that he already knew. *He did have someone spying on us!*

"Francis and I went, after we got my dress." Maggie let go of her secret after two glasses of champagne. "He was crazy. He lost six hundred dollars, but I won twelve hundred! It was just like magic! I stood and watched the machine just adding up my winnings on the 'Lucky Sevens.' They are lucky, at least for me! It was a blast! We got t-shirts and everything." She went over to the chair and held up the shirt. "Can you imagine walking around Vegas in this shirt? Someone even took our photo and..."

"What!" Antonio looked outraged. "Are you kidding me? What do you think you're doing spending the day with Francis? And gambling? I ought to tie you up!"

"I can't believe you are mad. It's not like you think. He insisted on going with me to get a new dress. The zipper broke on the one and...besides, we are here on business together and in Vegas! People gamble every day here. I did it once!"

Antonio looked caught off guard and aggravated.

"I should have known. Bradley informed me that he saw you leave with Francis, and I can just imagine what your day entailed—in and out of the strip clubs, boozing it up, gambling. Just because you work for him doesn't mean you have to slime into his adventures. Don't you understand? I don't want that image! You are going to be my wife! We have plenty of money. We don't need to be gambling. Kids come to my show, Maggie! I *can't* have that image. You hate the tabloids and press coverage? They eat that stuff up and you never end up looking good! It is always exaggerated." Antonio had his hand covering his forehead to contemplate his disgust.

Maggie looked at him and observed his stance. She let out a quick huff and then came to stand in front of him.

"Are you mad because I was gambling, or because I was with Francis?" The tone in her voice indicated her disregard.

"Don't push my buttons, Maggie. You should know the answer to your own question! Try *both* in case you don't and why do I have to explain myself. Getting drunk and… gambling…going to the strip clubs…it's not my image. Don't you see? You are part of that image now." He walked over to the window and looked out.

Maggie stared at him in disbelief.

"Why do you always have to be right about everything? You are such a brat! Always want it your way!" Maggie steamed out her aggravation. "We are not kids. We are adults, *Antonio*." She looked at him, recalling her first impression. "You know what's hilarious? When I first met you, I thought you were mysterious. Let me tell you what that is about! One look at you and a person guesses that you are a total bad dude—a player with the women, up to no good with your steamy guise…but then! Underneath it all, you shoot a perfect arrow. I still find it shocking that you are such a gentleman. And that just goes with the package! You just love to shock everyone!"

He seemed in complete disarray as he took in her comments.

"And for your information," Maggie stood frustrated, "I did not enjoy the strip club! But I would love to strip you naked right now and get to the bottom of your ridiculous secret, which is probably that there isn't one at all!"

"Maggie, it's our last night, and I don't want to fight. Come here," he initiated. Maggie walked up to him with her hands still on her hips and stood inches from him. She stared into his face as if she was ready for a challenge.

He looked back at her, well aware he had his hands full.

"Trust me on this. I love you, but you have to respect me and my career, and don't compromise my reputation. I don't need people drawing conclusions about you that aren't true. Look at me. I walk a straight line, but they maliciously fabricate anyways and they magnify everything! You are a sweet innocent girl, but looking like some crazed party animal in the public's eye! You show up drunk on stage at my show, and now you are probably front page news as you gamble into winnings, spending the day with Francis at the strip clubs! Think about it!"

Maggie stood speechless, as the effects of the champagne wore off.

"How do you know I was at the strip club?" she asked him, still discerning anger in his face. "Oh! That's right! You keep Bradley employed full time, just to keep track of me, as if I need you *spying* on me. I hope he isn't planning to follow me around for the rest of my life after I'm married to you, because I won't like it, Antonio!"

431

She watched Antonio step away, and walk towards the door to leave. She knew he was angry.

"I am sorry, Chad," Maggie overstated loudly. "I hate it when you're mad at me."

He turned around after picking up his jacket and leaned against the door, as if he was trying to let go of his anger, his eyes gazing in her direction.

"Then *why* can't you just trust me?" Antonio asked. "I would be a *fool* not to have you followed while you spend a day with Francis! Now, I don't want to fight anymore," he told her. But he still sounded angry when he said, "I'll see you tomorrow."

And he let the door slam on his way out.

Maggie lay face down on her bed, silently replaying their discussion, wishing that things did not end this way. She could understand his point of view, but she wished he could understand hers as well.

www.lovetheillusion.com/360.htm

Moments passed, and soon she heard a knock on the door. She jumped off the bed, in a haste to answer the door, and when she opened it she saw Antonio standing, as if they had never fought.

"Can I come in?" he asked.

She stepped aside, letting him in.

Antonio stood quietly at the door, as they both looked at each other. Then he finally spoke. "I forgot to kiss you goodnight."

www.lovetheillusion.com/361.htm

"Are we still getting married?" Maggie asked with his lips still on hers.

"What do you think?"

"Why can't you stay?"

"I want to, Maggie. Why do you think I asked you to marry me? Problem is…I want to prove to you that I am not like all those assholes you dated. I would rather have your trust than make love to you."

Maggie listened to his words, realizing all her walls were down and surely her heart was no longer protected. "I love you," Antonio told her, as if he could read her mind. Maggie looked into his brown eyes. She wanted to say it back, but before she could, he reached for the door as she heard him say, "After I marry you, you will forget that I was ever a gentleman."

She watched the door close.

And although he had not shared the secret, Maggie was sure of one thing. She *did* trust him.

Chapter 22

An hour into the flight home, Maggie stared down at her purse that was lodged beneath the seat in front of her. Francis read the newspaper, and the stewardess announced that they would soon be distributing coffee and juice. Maggie reminisced her time spent with Antonio and once again, her mind flooded with memories. She recalled the way that Antonio looked when he handed her a small white box with a red bow and explained, "It's your Christmas present, early. I want you to wear them for our wedding."

Inside the box was a pair of diamond earrings, which were now in her purse. They would match perfectly with her wedding dress. She wanted to look at them again, but Francis sat right next to her, so instead, she closed her eyes and recalled another handful of memories with Antonio.

www.lovetheillusion.com/362.htm

It would be busy when she got back—not only with Dana's wedding, but now having only ten weeks to get her own dress made. She would call her family and tell them the news, and eventually Francis would find out. She was not looking forward to *that*. If there was one person that she wished she could tell right now, it would be Julia, the woman she had met on the plane. Who would have thought things would have ended up like this? But Julia had told her, "Love is strong." And those words now echoed in her heart, as if for a brief moment in time her mother was whispering them to her. It seemed that Julia had happened to be at just the right place at exactly the right time, when she had needed a shoulder to lean on. And as she recalled the memory of Julia it brought a smile to her face.

The airline stewardess made her way down the narrow isle with coffee and juice. Maggie sat up straight, realizing that she forgot to eat, preoccupied with seeing Antonio before she left.

She yawned when she heard a woman's voice.

"Maggie White!"

Maggie felt herself freeze in her seat as she looked around to see if anyone was responding to the woman's announcement.

"Yes?" Maggie said timidly, looking up at her.

"Glad to meet you. Did you want coffee or juice?"

"Uh...coffee, please." She lowered the tray to position her coffee while Francis nudged her to share a read in his newspaper. She immediately saw a photo of them in their t-shirts from the casino.

She sipped her coffee with her eyes glued to the front page: "MAGGIE WHITE HITS THE STRIP WITH FASHION DESIGN TYCOON FRANCIS LOUIS. THEY MINGLE THROUGH THE CASINOS, ADDING TO THEIR WINNINGS IN VEGAS..."

www.lovetheillusion.com/363.htm

Maggie choked on her coffee as she read the last line.

"Who wrote that B.S.?" Maggie muttered under her breath.

"We're gaining fame, Maggie!" Francis sounded excited, but all Maggie could think of was Antonio's warning—his attempt to protect her from the media. She wondered if Antonio had seen the newspaper. *Hopefully not.* Maggie slouched down into her chair, as if she had just received a citation for misconduct. She frowned at Francis, realizing he was partly to blame. If he had not made her purple dress so tight, none of this would have happened.

Maggie realized that she was entering a whole new world, one where people actually cared what she was doing. It would only continue to get worse once the interview on their engagement aired. She hoped that Antonio was right on that decision, because soon Francis would know everything.

When the plane finally landed, Maggie sent Antonio a text message: I AM SO SORRY.

The easiest way to admit defeat.

The next few weeks became a whirlwind of activities, making it difficult for Maggie to even focus on her work. Her father had decided to pay a quick visit, and over lunch they discussed her engagement. At first, he was skeptical of the situation, but by the end of their meeting he had finally given her his blessing: "Well, Maggie, you are a big girl now, capable of making your own decisions, and if this is what will make you happy, then I am happy too." He offered her money and told her to buy something special.

The interview aired, and Maggie and Dana watched it together at night. It had been taped in the States, but Antonio signed for its release in the UK as well. Since Francis Louis was well recognized in Europe, it was of interest to the general public. And with Antonio having recently performed in England, it created quite the media stir.

Now the waiting was over as Francis shared his opinion the following day. "Wow, Maggie! I should have figured. I'm happy for you, but let's be realistic. I give it three months."

That would have been *enough* to ruin a good day, but that afternoon she received a call at work that the press wanted to put a photo in the newspaper, as an engagement announcement. They wanted her to submit a photo by noon the next day. If not, they had several photos that were taken of her standing next to Antonio and Francis on the big opening night. She was absolutely positive Francis did not belong in the engagement photo.

That evening she made a copy of the one photo she had.

Then there was Dana's wedding. Dana tried her dress on and she looked beautiful.

www.lovetheillusion.com/365.htm

Although all the dresses were finally done, Maggie was still busy planning the wedding shower and bachelorette party. These were two events that ended up being a lot more detailed than she had anticipated. She wanted everything to be perfect, because Dana was such a special friend.

Antonio called several times, but he never mentioned the newspaper article. She figured he already knew he was right about that one. And he had already given her a fair warning—his prediction now a reality. But they were counting down the days, and hearing his voice made it harder to wait. He had said, "I have that photo of us dancing, right next to my bed. Every night, before I go to sleep, I look at it."

Maggie wished that she could give him something special for Christmas. Now she knew just what it would be.

The following week, she visited an antique store that sold beautiful wall clocks, from the early 1900s. She bought one and had a metal plate engraved to place on the back of the clock. It said: "ANTONIO, TIME STANDS STILL WHEN WE ARE APART, MAGGIE." She remembered standing in her hotel room, looking out from several stories up as she adjusted her watch to the new time on the stone clock. That was the day she met him, and time would never be the same.

www.lovetheillusion.com/366.htm

It was the Tuesday, just before December. Dana's shower had gone well, and now Maggie was on her way into work. As she walked through the door, she could hear her desk phone ringing. She ran in quickly, hurrying to pick up the call. It was Amber, and she sounded frantic. "Maggie, I got your number at work from Stanley. There's been a terrible accident, and Antonio's in the hospital."

Maggie feebly dropped into her chair at her desk as she listened to Amber give the details. "Last night, we were rehearsing, and we had Cheetos and Tigger both out together for this new idea that Antonio had, and they started going at each other, and he reached out to separate them. He got Tigger back into his cage, but there was blood everywhere. We called 911, and the paramedics came, and now he's in the hospital, and it's not good. He lost a lot of blood. I think you should come."

Maggie's eyes were filled with tears, and as she tried to speak, she could only swallow.

"Maggie, I know he would want you there."

"Okay," Maggie sniffled as she tried to blink back the tears, "I will get on the next flight. Where do I go?"

"I will give you Stanley's number. When you get here, call him, and he will give you directions to the hospital."

Maggie wrote down the number and put it in her pocket. Two seconds later she was on her way out of her office cubicle. She gave a quick glance at Francis as she flew past his desk.

"I have to leave—now! I am taking a leave of absence, sick pay, holiday, vacation—whatever you want to call it," Maggie dictated.

"Maggie, there is no way you can just up and go like that!" Francis declared.

"Then fire me, Francis—whatever you have to do."

The door closed behind her, and she did not take time to notice the dumbfounded look on his face.

Maggie showed up at the airport and was on the next flight back to the States. Antonio had been in New York, rehearsing new ideas before he was to step on the plane himself and go to Italy. He was supposed to leave the following week.

She could barely sit still on the plane. Thoughts of Antonio were excruciating, flooding her mind as she hoped and prayed that he would be okay. Traumatized by the thought of it all, she had no idea what to expect when she got there.

She stared at her watch. Instead of representing the time they were apart, it seemed to symbolize a moment of tragedy over which she had no control.

Staring out the window, she could feel her insides coming completely unglued. She had not even taken the time to pack. She brought no toothbrush, no comb, or change of clothes—nothing.

She sat on the plane in a black pencil skirt, black shoes, and a black top, with a cross pendant that hung around her neck. Black—the darkest color there was, and if anything happened to him, that is where she would be...*in complete darkness.*

Maggie tried to think positive thoughts. She was sure that the hospital personnel would take good care of him. He would be fine. Even if they had to postpone the wedding, she would gladly wait, as long as it meant he would be okay.

At a time when she least expected it, she heard her mother's famous words of proclamation: "When love is real, Maggie, you will just know!" Perhaps she had tried for a long time to deny it, in fear of getting hurt, but she no longer could. She thought of Julia, and the grief she shared in losing the man that she loved for 65 years. Maggie had not even known Antonio for a year. She wondered at the strength of love that made it through that much time. Love was strong. Julia had said so. She had already been through so much with Antonio; it was hard to imagine that they were still together. Although she finally trusted Antonio, the media was a concern. Unfortunately, she would be in a circus ring *with* him, as they made her life a spectacle, as well. It would be rough, but she had to travel this road. It was the one that had brought her to love.

She sat impatiently on the plane, waiting for it to land.

When Maggie finally arrived, it was still Tuesday afternoon in New York City. She was physically exhausted from the flight, but even more exhausted from her mental agony, unable to handle the thought of anything happening to Antonio. He was always so strong and protective of her, but now he was the one in need of her concern.

Maggie called Stanley, who was now meeting her at the hospital.

She finally stepped inside the main lobby. There were camera men outside, and Maggie had to push her way through.

"Are you going to have to postpone the wedding?"

"Maggie, Maggie White!"

"Can I just ask you a few questions?"

"Has there been any word on his condition?"

"How did this happen?"

Maggie gave no response. *Stupid reporters.* She did not have any answers, so why should they?

Stanley sat on a couch in the front lobby, next to a table with a display of magazines. He was busy on his laptop, but saw her approaching.

"Maggie, you're here!" He got up immediately and walked over to meet her.

"How bad is he?" Maggie followed him into the elevator.

"He's on the third floor in intensive care. Tigger got him right next to the brachial artery in his upper arm. Luckily, we wrapped it right away before the paramedics arrived. They think he will be okay, but he lost a lot of blood. He had to have surgery to repair the muscle damage and infection is a concern since it was an animal bite. The nurse said he's pretty knocked out from all the pain meds, so you probably can't talk to him."

Maggie could barely stand to hear the words.

"What room is he in?" she asked as they exited the elevator on the third floor.

"Okay, Maggie," he said with alarm in his voice, as he grabbed her arm and walked her into a lounge area that was adjacent to the nurses' station. "I don't want to make you even more upset, but there is one problem."

"What?" Maggie burned with anxiety.

"Don't freak out when I tell you this, promise?"

"Fine, what!?" Maggie questioned, fired up by every nerve in her body.

"Okay. I am not even allowed to visit him right now. Security is tight the way it is, because he's a celebrity. In addition to that, he's in ICU, which carries a whole new set of rules. Visiting hours...I'm not even sure when that is, but only family's allowed."

"I am going to be his wife!" Maggie blurted out. "It's public information, now!"

"Shhhh...That might not be good enough Maggie," he whispered. "But, I have an idea."

Maggie watched as he reached into his pocket and pulled out a small envelope.

"Antonio told me to get this sized for you. I just picked it up last week. It has his name on it, and I don't know...Maybe it will work to get you in!"

Maggie held on to the ring that she had worn to get into the Night Owl. She placed it on her right ring finger. There it was, just as she remembered.

She listened to Stanley say, "It's your best shot, Maggie. Tell them that you're already married!"

She quickly switched the rings around, placing the new addition on her left finger while Stanley continued to explain, "They won't know what to think...with that ring on your finger, maybe they'll let you in."

"Do you think?" Maggie stood a nervous wreck.

"Yes, I do," Stanley assured her. "If it doesn't work, his parents are on their way in…hopefully by tomorrow…You can see him then. I can let you know when they arrive."

"I don't even know where I'm staying. I don't even have luggage." Maggie burst into tears mixed with laughter as she tried to break through the trauma.

"Here," Stanley advised, "you can stay in Antonio's room." He handed her a key.

Maggie spoke with hesitation. "Oh, no…I feel funny."

"No, I am sure it's what he would want."

Maggie took a deep breath, as she took the keys from his hand. Her hand was shaking. She placed them into her purse as Stanley informed, "Look, I will wait over there. If you can't get in, I can give you a ride back to the hotel. After ten minutes, I will assume you got in, and I will take off. I hope, maybe in a couple days, I can get in to see him."

Maggie hesitated, walking over to the nurses' station. She could still see Stanley out of the corner of her eye.

"I am here to see Antonio DeLuca," Maggie announced, positioning her arms onto the counter barrier.

"Just a moment," said one of the nurses with her back turned. She noticed she caught the attention of another nurse.

"Excuse me! I'm here to see Antonio DeLuca," Maggie repeated nervously.

"And…you are…?" The woman's voice gave suspicion.

"Maggie White, Maggie DeLuca," she corrected herself, wishing someone would recognize her when needed.

"Are you a reporter?" The lady grinned. "You know we can't let anyone in there. Now, I suggest you wait outside until the hospital releases a statement to the public."

"I am not a reporter!" Maggie announced, disgusted at the thought of it. "I am his wife!" *This is so not fair!*

"Well, I'm sorry, but we don't have any records indicating...you will have to show your I.D."

"Okay, fine," Maggie renegotiated, under her breath, letting them take note of her persistence. "I am not his wife *yet*, but we are engaged, and I have *this!*" Maggie showed the ring to the nurse as she clenched her hand into a fist. *See?*

The nurse reached for her hand to take a look. She let her hand go, and then studied her. Maggie stared into her face, watching her expression slowly change. The nurse stepped around the cubicle to meet up with her.

"I'm Susan. I hope I don't get in trouble for this. My supervisor has left for the day, so follow me."

Maggie let out a deep breath and followed behind the nurse. She was middle-aged and seemed to have a kind heart.

Maggie was left standing at the door that led into Antonio's room. She smiled at Susan, glad to have her cooperation.

"Thanks," Maggie finally stated meekly, embarrassed that she had seen her feisty side.

Maggie opened the door slowly. She stepped inside. She could see him under a layer of white hospital sheets. His bed was slightly raised, and he was out cold. She noticed the two bags of liquid that were hanging on a stand next to the bed on the far left of him. On the other side, there was a heart monitor, and she watched as it made its display.

When Maggie got close to him, she could see his face. She took a chair and moved it as close as she could next to the bed. She sat down. She wanted to touch him, but his arms were under the bedding. She did not know which arm had been injured, and she did not want to risk hurting him.

Maggie stared down at him. His eyes were closed, and he appeared to have lost weight. His face was pale, and his hair was matted to his head in various directions. He did not look like Chad. He did not look like Antonio, either. She tried to picture him the way he looked the day she had left.

Maggie was torn inside. She watched as the liquid in the IV dripped into the tube that disappeared under the sheets. She noticed the clock on the wall, and wondered how long he had been here. Maggie leaned over him. She brushed his hair out of his eyes and felt his forehead. The times they spent together seemed like a fog in her memory, as she missed his brown eyes.

Maggie recalled Julia's words. For the first time, Maggie knew she would gladly endure any hardships as long as they were together. She could not live life without him. At last, she spoke the words he was waiting to hear. "I love you Chad," she whispered, "and I love you, Antonio." She knew he was unable to hear her, but she meant it all the same.

The nurse came in. Maggie watched as she filled out paperwork and checked his vitals.

"Is he going to be okay?" Maggie asked, blinking back tears.

"We think so," the nurse assured her. "He's on an antibiotic now. First, we thought he was going into shock from loss of blood. We stabilized him, did surgery, and now infection is our primary concern. And since he's lost a lot of blood, we have to wait and see whether or not the doctor thinks he needs a transfusion."

The nurse uncovered his left arm, where the injury occurred, and then replaced the bandages. Maggie saw the inflammation around the stitches that made their way along the inside of his upper arm, all the way down to his elbow. Maggie held her breath as she watched the nurse put on the new bandage.

"The doctor will be in shortly," the nurse announced on her way out.

Maggie sat impatiently.

The shade was drawn, not allowing a lot of light into the room. She got up, approaching the window to peek out. She reached up, pushed the curtain aside, and watched the busy streets of New York—the city where they met.

She remembered being at the bar and thinking he was a good-looking, immature waiter, lying about his name. Then he had sent her a bottle of wine. She remembered telling him off in the hotel hallway, but then going to Bouley, where she lost her shoe in the fountain. Then he gave her a show ticket, and little did she know who he was. They danced at the Night Owl, drove around in the limo, and went for ice cream after he showed her Cheetos. She was glad that Cheetos was not responsible for his injury.

She remembered Antonio at the hotel pool, chasing her with the whip cream. And later that evening, they ate pizza at Biagio's. That was New York as she remembered. Now it would hold yet another memory, one that wasn't so great. She closed the curtain and went back over to Antonio, still asleep. Her mind flooded with memories, *all of them sweet.*

www.lovetheillusion.com/373.htm

As she watched him sleep, she thought about how much she really did love him and what she would do if anything happened to him. Tired as she was, she could never sleep until she knew that he would be okay.

Maggie leaned back in the chair when the doctor came in.

"Hi there," he said sympathetically, as he walked in and stood across from her on the other side of the bed. "How are you doing? We just got some good news. The lab results are back. I don't think he'll need a transfusion, and he should be getting transferred out of intensive care tomorrow if everything goes as planned. Right now, he just needs to get some rest. But the surgery went well. We had to sew together muscle tissue that had been severed. Tomorrow, though, you should be able to talk to him."

"Okay," Maggie sounded excited, "I will stay here until then!"

"Oh, I'm sorry, but you have to be out within a half an hour. You can come back at ten tomorrow, if you want."

Maggie wanted to sleep in the chair next to him, but felt lucky just to have gotten in. She watched the doctor leave, and then looked at her watch. She needed to pick up a few things anyways, since she did not pack. She sat in the room until the half hour was up, and then stood over Antonio before she left.

"Get better, okay? I will be back tomorrow. I love you."

On her way out, she noticed that a different staff now attended the nurses' station on the night shift. One of the nurses glanced up and seemed to recognize her, but she scooted past, avoiding any questions.

When Maggie stepped outside, it was dark. She hailed a cab and went to a pharmacy to pick up a toothbrush, hairbrush, and a few make-up items. On the way out, she saw a jewelry store across the street, and remembered she needed to find Antonio's wedding band.

She decided to go in.

A man stood behind the counter showing a woman a watch. Maggie peered into the showcase, wishing to find the perfect wedding band for Antonio. She wanted to pick it out in the city where they had met.

"Can I help you, miss?"

"Sure, can I see that band?" Maggie requested, pointing to a display.

"This one here?" the man asked.

"And that one, too, please."

She watched as he removed them from the tray and placed them on the counter. Maggie looked at them each carefully, and then made her selection. It had a gold ring going around the silver band — *just like the ring of fire.*

www.lovetheillusion.com/374.htm

"This is nice. I will take it!" She handed it to the jeweler.

"That was quick!" he concluded with a smile. "Do you need it sized?"

"Oh! I'm not sure." Maggie wondered, placing the ring on her thumb. It was a bit loose, but it fit pretty close to the one Antonio had sized for her. "No, this will be fine—just a box."

She slipped the box into her purse.

"Thanks!" Maggie waved on her way out of the shop.

Now Antonio's ring would be from New York, where they met, and hers from Vegas, where they got engaged. When they held hands they would recall both cities.

Holding a key in hand, Maggie hesitated in front of the door to Antonio's room. Knowing he was not there, she lost courage, entangled in memories and missing him. She must have stood for five minutes before finally turning the key.

She stepped inside and felt the wall for the switch. When the lights came on, it was just as she remembered—not a thing out of place. She walked over to the couch, set down her things and took off her coat, leaving it on a chair.

She admired the antique dresser with the mahogany wood finish, wondering where he had gotten it.

While Maggie stood amidst his things, she thought about his secret. She felt guilty thinking about it, but she was still curious.

She sat down on the bed, where she noticed the photo of them dancing. It sat on the nightstand, just as he said. She ran her fingers along the zebra faux fur that covered the bed. It was soft, yet seemed almost real. She pulled the cover down and felt the white sheets, wishing that he was there with her.

After putting her make-up on the dresser, she changed out of her work clothes, using the space in the armoire to hang up her current attire. She thumbed through his clothing, recalling familiar pieces he had worn.

She went into the bathroom to put away her toothbrush and hairbrush. The whirlpool tub reminded her of when they sat in the hot tub together at the pool.

She missed him now as she came out and stood in front of the big-screen TV, remembering when he had given her the book. She grabbed the remote off of the coffee table and turned on the TV.

Under the trophy shelf was a collection of music and movies. She viewed his movie collection: *Indiana Jones, Transformers, The Towering Inferno, A Knight's Tale,* and *Gone in 60 Seconds.* Maggie decided to watch *"The Towering Inferno."* She recalled when she was just a young girl. Her brothers had watched that movie and she remembered screaming when she saw the fire. Now she thought about Antonio's ring of fire on stage, until she heard the news report, breaking her out of her daydream.

"...WE HAVE BREAKING NEWS THAT MAGICIAN ANTONIO DELUCA WAS ADMITTED TO THE HOSPITAL

AFTER SUFFERING A WOUND INFLICTED BY HIS SHOW TIGER, 'TIGGER', WHILE HE WAS TRYING TO IMPLEMENT A NEW MAGIC STUNT. THE HOSPITAL HAS ISSUED A STATEMENT THAT HE IS ON THE MEND, AND SHOULD BE RELEASED BY THE END OF THE WEEK."

Maggie switched off the news and put the movie in. She already knew everything there was to know. She had seen him. And she did not want to listen to the hype.

She grabbed the blanket off the chair and wrapped herself in it, breathing in a trace of his scent. She was waiting for the movie to start, when she saw an envelope sitting next to one of the trophies. Her curiosity led her to reach for an envelope postmarked two years ago. She peeked inside, and pulled out a letter, written in big handwriting. It said:

"Dear Antonio, I saw your magic show in New York. It was fun. I want to be a magician just like you someday,

Jonathan."

She smiled, thinking about his love for his little fans.

No sooner did she sit back down, she heard a knock on the door.

She opened the door to see Amber and Angie.

"Hi Maggie, you came!" Amber spoke for the two of them.

"Yeah, come on in."

"We were wondering if you want to get a pizza with us…a little late night snack," she offered with a bubbly smile.

"Sure," Maggie agreed, "I was just entertaining myself with a movie, but let me grab my bag."

"So, how is he?" Amber asked. "We saw on the news that he was okay, but—"

"He will be fine." Maggie recalled seeing him. "I am very grateful. He was sleeping the whole time today, but the doctor thinks he'll be out of intensive care tomorrow morning."

"That's good," Angie said, relieved.

"Congratulations!" Amber grabbed at Maggie's hand to see her ring. "That's so cool! You're going to wear that one too?" She immediately noticed her other hand.

"Yeah," Maggie said, "I kind of wanted it. You know...it's sentimental."

Angie smiled. "It's so exciting you guys are getting married!"

"Yes, it is," Maggie agreed. "I still have to pinch myself sometimes to make sure it's not a dream."

"He's an awesome guy. You are lucky," Amber told her.

And Maggie knew, without a doubt, *she spoke the truth.*

Chapter 23

The following morning, Maggie had no problem getting into Antonio's hospital room. The reporters were no longer there, and Susan worked again, leading her to his new location on the sixth floor and to a nurse who explained that he was sleeping, but recovering quickly.

Maggie sat down next to him, his face shadowed in thick whiskers. She reached under the linens and grabbed his left hand, intertwining her fingers with his. She reached into her purse, removing the ring, wondering if it would fit. She took it out of the box and placed it on his left ring finger. To her surprise, it fit perfectly, a sign that perhaps their luck was on the mend. Maggie laughed quietly. She would leave it on his finger and see if he noticed it when he woke up. She wore both of hers now, and she thought *he, of all people, should definitely have to wear his!*

An hour passed and he still slept.

"Chad!" Maggie called out in a quiet voice. "Chad, it's me, Maggie."

He turned his head at the sound of her voice.

"Chad! It's Maggie! I love you!" She watched as he opened his eyes to a narrow slit. "Chad! It's me! I flew out to see you!"

He opened his eyes wider, and she thought he took time to recognize her.

"I love you!" she said again, as he looked into her eyes. She watched as he started to smile. "You are *finally* up! I sat and watched you for four hours yesterday, until they kicked me out!"

"Maggie," he whispered, "you came?"

"Of course I came!" Maggie sounded excited to finally be engaging in a conversation with him. "Francis didn't want me to, but I told him I was leaving anyways!"

Antonio tried sitting up.

He still had one IV in, the antibiotic.

"How are you? Does your arm hurt?"

"Not bad," he mumbled. "I'm hungry."

Maggie's face brightened.

"That's good! I will go tell them that you want a big plate of spaghetti!" she teased.

She went into the hallway to track down one of the nurses, letting them know he needed something to eat.

And when she returned, it seemed that within those few minutes he had perked up considerably.

Antonio was now looking at Maggie, and she was peering into his big brown eyes.

"I missed you," he said.

"I was so worried about you. I left work in a hurry without even packing. I'm staying in your room. Stanley gave me the key. But it's strange in there without you."

"Did you sleep well?"

"Not bad, once I knew you would be okay. Angie and Amber stopped by. Amber was the one that called me, first thing when I got into work on Tuesday morning."

"So, is Francis mad you left?" Antonio wore a big smile.

"He said I couldn't leave," Maggie explained.

"I see. But you didn't listen to him?" He let go of a laugh. "I'm impressed!"

"Yeah, it's funny now, until I get fired."

"Maggie, I already told you, you can work for me," Antonio reminded her. "I promise to be a better boss than Francis, and *that* should not be a challenge. But you should know if you accept my offer, you can kiss the boss all you want." He grinned.

"So, I will have to take orders from you?" Maggie raised her brow.

"Yeah, right...I think I know better than that." Antonio gave her a look of submission, followed by a grunt. "But if you screw up, I'll have Stanley send you into my conference room." He gave her a mysterious look.

"Oh, really...?" Maggie played along. "And where's *that?*"

"My bedroom!" he teased, grinning back at her.

"Hmm...disciplinary bonus...! I like my new job already." She grinned at Antonio, anxious to start their life together.

Maggie was still grinning when the nurse came in with some food. She set down a tray filled with applesauce, Jell-O, toast, a dish of cottage cheese, a glass of water and a pain pill.

"Yum, huh?" Maggie teased. "I guess they aren't going to bring you spaghetti!"

Antonio picked up his toast, and suddenly noticed his hand. He got a confused look on his face that he finished off with a smile.

"What did I do? Sleep through the wedding?"

"I...um...well...I have this." She flashed the DeLuca ring. She watched his eyes play detective. "Stanley gave it to me so I could get in to see you yesterday."

"It worked?"

"Obviously!" she bragged. "And...I was having so much fun wearing this that I thought I would get yours! And it fits!"

"I see." Antonio viewed his ring.

"I got lucky!" Maggie admitted. "Do you like it?"

"Yeah, it's nice. Thanks." Antonio gave his approval.

"It can keep the girls away, *Antonio!* Don't you dare take it off," Maggie warned him.

"I wouldn't. You know I wouldn't." He reached out and grabbed her hand. "Do you want some of my applesauce?"

"No, that's okay." She scrunched her nose, uninterested in his hospital food.

"Did you eat?"

"Just a bagel. I'm fine."

"So, it's not very fun in here. What are we going to do all day?" Antonio perked up.

"You don't need to entertain me. I'm just glad to sit here. I am glad you're okay. I was worried sick."

She watched Antonio positioning his apple sauce on his spoon with his thumb at the end of the spoon, as if he was going to flick it at her. She quickly shifted her concern. "Chad!" Maggie laughed. "You must be better 'cuz you're already causing trouble!"

They looked up and saw two visitors had arrived.

"Mamma, Papa! You made it!" Antonio motioned, putting his food down.

Maggie smiled, a bit surprised. They were not as she had pictured. His mother looked English—blonde hair, petite, and very pretty but nothing like Antonio. He was a spitting image of his father.

"Antonio!" Papa sounded cheerful. "You're still alive. What's it like to fight the tiger, like a brave hunter?"

Maggie and Antonio laughed and Maggie thought he seemed jolly and fun.

"I brought you some baked goods," Mamma said. "Looks like you need to put some meat on those bones!"

"This is Maggie!" Antonio announced.

Maggie blushed, hoping for their approval.

"Of course, it's Maggie. Who else would it be? She's just as beautiful as you said!" Papa came over to where Maggie was sitting. Mamma followed.

"I am so glad to get to meet you, finally." Mamma smiled at Maggie. "Antonio has told us so much about you—all good, of course."

Maggie felt happy to finally meet his family. She watched as they each got themselves a chair and sat down alongside her.

"Did you have a good flight?" Maggie asked.

Mamma said, "The usual. I always wonder what to do with myself on a plane for so long, but Edmondo always says he will start singing if I need entertainment. That's when I get out my book."

Maggie laughed. "Does he have a good voice?"

"Oh, sure he does, but nobody wants to listen to him sing while they're on the plane! He used to sing in a choir," Mamma told her.

Maggie smiled as she pictured him singing.

"Papa used to sing me to sleep when I was little," Antonio recalled. "I remember once, Mamma sent me to bed early because I had broken one of her new glasses, trying to do a magic trick. I was screaming as loud as I could in my bed, and then Papa came in and sang to me and I was quiet."

"So..." Maggie inquired, "Antonio wasn't always a polished magician?"

"Oh, no." Mamma laughed. "He would always have to show us a new trick. Sometimes Papa and I had to do all we could to keep from laughing!"

"Interesting..." Maggie grinned, "So, when was the turning point? The career potential moment, should I say?"

Antonio interrupted, "I vote to change the subject! We can talk about Maggie now. She's in fashion design, and works for Francis Louis!"

"Antonio!" Papa laughed. "You told us, already."

Antonio looked at Maggie, hoping she would "save the day," but she looked back at him as if she wasn't interested.

"So...Antonio was a troublemaker when he was growing up?" Maggie smiled at Antonio, the ball in her court.

"Oh, yes," Mamma began. "He was always into something. I remember once, I went shopping, and when I returned he had moved all of his furniture out of his bedroom, so he had enough room for his stage, and did we want to see his magic show?"

Maggie glanced at Antonio, who looked guilty as charged.

"But now, he has a great show!" Maggie complimented him. "I suppose you have seen it several times?"

"Oh, yes, we come once a year, usually to New York," Papa explained. "We stay on his floor and keep an eye on him!"

Antonio smirked, and Maggie laughed.

Then Mamma changed the subject, telling Antonio, "I have made all the arrangements for the wedding to take place two days before Christmas."

"It will be wonderful," Edmondo announced. "I'm going to sing, and Elisabetta's baking a cake, and there are a couple tulips in the garden for your bouquet..."

"Stop with your ranting!" Mamma gave Papa her look. "None of that—he is not singing, and we have cake and flowers coming from local shops."

"I hope it hasn't been too much trouble," Maggie questioned Mamma.

"Oh, no dear, I haven't anything better to do…and don't worry, I am planning, not Edmondo. He is only showing up in a tuxedo. That's all. No singing and no trouble!"

Maggie observed Edmondo, who wore a wicked smile as if he enjoyed making her worry.

That evening, Antonio's parents extended an invitation for Maggie to join them for dinner. Edmondo announced that he would not be eating any hospital food. And to Maggie's surprise, they took her to their favorite restaurant in NYC, the same restaurant where Maggie had eaten when the waiter delivered Antonio's note instead of the bill. However, she did not want to tell *that* story, so she sat quietly, waiting for them to start conversation.

"Elisabetta, we cannot order the spaghetti here. It does not taste like yours!" Edmondo said.

"I tried your spaghetti," Maggie informed. "Antonio made it for me one night, when I was here in New York. It was so good!"

"It's very simple," Elisabetta explained. "It's made with all fresh ingredients…everything out of the garden."

"I will have to learn to make it!" Maggie suggested.

"No!" Edmondo laughed. "You let *him* cook for you!"

"Do you cook?" Maggie grinned at Papa.

"No, I don't have to. She's better than me. I always tell her, so she doesn't ever make me cook. She makes my mamma's recipes and they are the best!"

The waitress filled the water glasses. "What can I get everyone to drink?"

Maggie waited to see what they would order, when Edmondo decided, "A bottle of champagne, what do you got?"

"Prosecco?"

"Sure," he agreed, with little thought.

After the waitress left, Edmondo leaned over the table, explaining, "We are celebrating that Antonio finally found a girl to marry him!"

"Ha!" Maggie laughed. "There are a lot of those out there! You should see them chasing him around." She wondered if they knew.

Edmondo found the humor. "We always say, look Antonio, there's a girl for you, but no, he doesn't like her—too this, or too that. We just shake our heads and think he'll be single forever!"

Elisabetta cut in. "Antonio was always picky. It's not a bad thing. You can't just be with anybody." She looked at Edmondo, as if she knew better.

"Yes," Edmondo agreed. "She ended up with me, so now she worries for Antonio!"

Maggie laughed. "You don't seem that bad!"

Elisabetta gave a humorous smile. "Just wait 'til you get to know him a little better. He's trouble, just like his son!"

The waitress came and took their order.

Maggie watched as Edmondo ordered the same as what Elisabetta ordered.

"Make that three," Maggie agreed. She liked fettuccini. It was one of her favorites.

"So, how long are you staying?" Maggie asked.

They both looked at each other until Elisabetta said, "We have a week here. We hoped he would be better by then, and that we could all fly back together. You will be joining us in Italy soon?"

"Yes, a couple days before the wedding," Maggie told them.

"How long will you stay in New York?" Elisabetta asked.

"I'm supposed to go back on Friday," Maggie explained. "I can't have too much time off from work. Francis didn't want me to leave." Maggie thought about calling Francis later that evening.

"Well," Elisabetta told her, "we're so glad you came. I'm sure Antonio is too."

"Look at that, Elisabetta — Antonio's ring!" Edmondo exclaimed pointing to the sparkly DeLuca band that Maggie wore on her right hand. "And look at *that!*" He noticed her engagement ring.

"Let me see!" Elisabetta sounded excited.

Maggie held out her hands, feeling a bit embarrassed. Then she explained, "I did not want an engagement ring. I just wanted to wear this one, with his name. He gave it to me to wear on the night after his show, to get into the party afterwards. Stanley got it sized for the wedding, but now I used it to get in to see him at the hospital. It's funny how everyone is prying into your business like they know you, until you actually wished they recognized you. The nurses' station wasn't going to let me into intensive care. I guess even a reporter or whacky fan wouldn't go to that extent, right? To have a ring made with his name on it?"

Elisabetta laughed. "I remember when he got that a year ago. Stanley had it custom made to mark five years of success. They had an awards banquet to attend. But Antonio thought it was the silliest thing ever. I told him, 'Save that. It's special. It represents five years of doing what you love.' Now somebody he loves is wearing it." Elisabetta smiled at Maggie.

Maggie smiled back. "Actually, he's already wearing his wedding band, too! I found one here in New York, symbolic of where we met. So, while he was sleeping, I slipped it on his finger, and it fit!"

"That's not very romantic!" Edmondo gave his opinion, holding up his glass to make a toast. "Now you got married in the hospital!"

Maggie laughed, meeting his toast. "I guess, but I can't wait to wear my white dress! I designed it myself. "

"I'm sure Antonio will like it." Elisabetta was certain.

The waitress returned with the food. Maggie tried to retain her laughter as she noticed that Papa had his napkin tucked into the collar on his shirt. She remembered all the stains that her clothing took in while she was in the company of Antonio. Now she wondered how he was doing.

"Are you going back to see Antonio, after dinner?" Maggie asked.

"I think visiting hours are over." Papa looked down at his watch. "Yep, six o'clock."

"Are you sure?" Elisabetta asked. "I thought family could stay later? Stanley and Bradley were there when we left, and I know Amber and Angie were on their way."

"We need to get some sleep, Elisabetta," Papa said, as he took a big bite of his fettuccini. "It has been a long day."

"I'm so glad I got to meet you both. Chad —" Maggie corrected herself—"*Antonio* talks about you on occasion, and I always wondered what it would be like to meet you. I know he loves you both so much."

Elisabetta explained, "Chad's the nickname I gave him. It was hard to always say his whole name, when I would have to yell...four syllables, or one? You can't shorten Antonio to 'Ant' and 'Tony' belonged to a boy next door, so I called him Chad—but only when he was in trouble. It's from my maiden name, Chandler. I'm English, and from England, like you!"

"Really?" Maggie thought it strange. "How did you meet Edmondo?"

Elisabetta shared in excitement. "He was on business, in town with his father. His family made wood furniture...the best, and they were in town for the week. They were fishing. I was sunbathing on the pier of my parent's cottage, and he drove the boat by and got me wet. He wanted to know if I knew a good place to fish, and I said, 'Far, far, away from this pier!' Now we are married. It has been 30 years. We were married young. I was only twenty. Edmondo was twenty-four. We had Antonio two years later. We always wanted more children, but we had little money. Then..." Mamma hesitated, her face turning somber.

Maggie watched as Papa got up to leave.

"I will say it," she continued. "We moved to the Chicago area to merge with a woodshop that also made furniture. It was supposed to be a good financial move for us, so I suggested to Edmondo, 'Let's have one more child, now.' He agreed, but the money wasn't that good for us. So, I got a job as a part time nanny for the mayor because I still wanted that baby. And after just a few months, I was expecting Matteo." Elisabetta spoke with pity as she mentioned his name, and Maggie felt herself blinking back tears. "Then, some terrible rumor got started that the mayor and I were having an affair, because people would see us together. I was so much older to have another child, so people were quick to assume the worst. It got out of control and we even ended up with our picture in some local newspaper. Then, when Matteo was born, he was so sick, and we had to have him at the hospital, all the time. The hospitals here are the best, but Edmondo was disgusted with everything and wanted to move back to Italy. I said 'No' that we had to stay so that Matteo would get the best treatment. I thought he was going to move back without me. It was tough. I didn't know if our love was strong enough to make it through everything. There were days we hardly talked. People would talk behind our backs, and it was not good. The mayor felt really bad, and asked if he could do anything. He had a wife and kids too, and so he was just as upset about it. He was a good man." She paused. "So, I asked him to help Antonio...to get his magic show more publicity. He was playing hockey at the time, but he had an injury and was sitting out for the season. He was performing magic, but just for fun—nothing like now. So the mayor got a huge advertising campaign together for a big opening night if you will call it that, and things just took off after that. Antonio had saved quite a bit of money from playing hockey, so he invested to make the show like never before, and his show starting bringing in a lot of money. Antonio was so sweet. He started helping us with the hospital bills that were coming in. As you know, Matteo died two years ago. That's when we finally moved back to Italy. Antonio bought us a house, and we sold out our share of the business and retired."

After listening intently, Maggie finally said, "Thank you for telling me. Antonio's always questioned in interviews, about you moving back to Italy, like it was a big deal."

"Antonio will never talk about it. The media still probes the scandal that never was. It was so hard for Antonio to watch what we went through, with the rumors and all the fighting it caused. It made him bitter. He won't speak a bad word about his family, and it made him mad that they would tell lies, even though he knew that we loved each other. And, when Matteo died, it was even worse, like we had stayed in Chicago for nothing. That, of course, is not true. I think he made it longer than he would have. Antonio was a good brother. Even though there was an age gap, he loved him so much. To make a long story short, Antonio would not be so famous doing magic if it wasn't for Matteo. Even in tragedy, there is always some good. But I know Antonio would give it all up to have Matteo back." Elisabetta pondered. "I'm sorry. I'm done now."

Maggie now knew the secret that he was keeping. It wasn't really a secret after all, just a bad memory. She thought about that night they fought about it. She felt remorse, thinking it still angered him and that she had insisted that he share. Now she noticed that Papa was still gone.

"What happened to Papa?" Maggie asked.

"That's a good question!" Elisabetta looked up but then saw Edmondo. The waitress followed behind him, carrying three desserts.

"I was going to pay the bill, but I got distracted by the desserts!" Edmondo explained with a smile.

"He can never pass up dessert," Elisabetta informed, smiling at Edmondo.

"I couldn't decide, so I picked one of each. Now you two can decide, because they all look good to me!"

Maggie laughed as she remembered Antonio's ice cream ensemble.

"I really don't care," Maggie said, "you pick."

Elisabetta looked at Edmondo to see if it mattered to him. Then she took the one he was looking at.

"I knew she would take that one," Edmondo complained. "That's the one I wanted, and she knows that!"

Maggie listened as he spoke Italian. "Cara mia, ti voglio bene." Elisabetta smiled at him when he said those words, and then he looked at Maggie. "You pick next!"

Maggie laughed. "It doesn't matter."

"Don't be silly," he said, requesting her preference.

Maggie took the piece of cake, feeling lucky to marry into his family.

Chapter 24

Maggie was back in Antonio's room, glad to have spent time with his parents. She would see him tomorrow yet, and then she had to leave. She needed to make her phone call to Francis at some point and see if she still had a job, but it was the middle of the night there. It would have to wait until tomorrow.

As she was about to crawl under the covers, she felt her foot hit something on the side of the bed. She peeked under the bed where she found a large photo album. Maggie's eyes lit up as she pulled it out. She opened it up to read:

"To Antonio, Merry Christmas, Love, Mamma & Papa."

"Wow!" Maggie thought out loud. "This will be all the entertainment I need."

It brought a smile to her face, as she paged through photos from his childhood. There were baby photos, his first day at school, a fishing trip, photos of his dance class, and also photos of him playing hockey. Maggie thought he was cute when he was young. She turned more pages to a family photo taken at Christmas. Next, she saw photos of Antonio in show clothes, holding up some of his props for his magic shows.

Now, she saw Matteo, and photos of them together. Antonio was in his skates and hockey jersey at the ice arena; Antonio held Matteo, who was only a few months old at the time. Another photo showed them sitting in a boat, and Matteo must have been about five. It broke her heart to see him and she wished so badly to have met him.

Then she saw the photo of their home in Italy. It looked beautiful—a river behind it, a city in view, just as Antonio described.

When Maggie got to the end of the photo album, she read what Mamma had written:

"Even when you are far away, you are always at home in our hearts."

www.lovetheillusion.com/390.htm

Maggie arrived the next day at the hospital, in one of Antonio's t-shirts, with a bag of chocolate chip cookies from a local bakery. She held a bag of merchandise she had purchased, including a book to read on the flight back, a deck of cards, and a board game—Carcassonne—that the clerk had suggested for entertainment.

Maggie peeked into his room. Antonio sat up now, his hair wet from the shower.

"Hi! You must be feeling better." She gave him a warm smile.

"Yeah, I might actually get to leave today," he informed. "I told them that they should let me out of here!"

"Well, I thought we would be stuck here for the day, so I brought some cookies and a deck of cards so you can show me some magic tricks."

"What's that?" Antonio asked, looking at the box.

"This?" Maggie shrugged. "The store clerk talked me into it. I told her I was trying to pass time at the hospital, and she recommended this game. I hope it's good."

"Nice. But I'm not sure my arm's able to assist in any card tricks yet."

Maggie took off her coat.

"Sorry, but I borrowed this t-shirt. It was the smallest one I could find. I'm short of clothes. I left in such a hurry that I never packed."

"It's fine, Maggie. You don't have to explain." Antonio enjoyed the sight of her in his t-shirt.

"That reminds me, I should probably call Francis! What do you think are the odds that I still have a job?" Maggie laughed.

"Hmmm, I'm not worried about it." Antonio shared his opinion.

"Right, well I think I need to get this over with. Francis should be winding down for the day, if that's even possible for him, so maybe he'll be too tired to yell at me."

Maggie picked up her phone to make the call.

Antonio grabbed the deck of cards and started to peel the plastic off the deck.

"Francis! It's Maggie. You probably know by now why I took off, and I hope you're not angry, but—"

"Yeah, right Maggie. I know. You're in love. I get it. So, when will you return?"

"I still have a job?"

"Yes, but you just used up all of your holiday pay!"

Figures. "Fine, I will see you on Monday?"

"And it will be a late night. You have a lot to catch up on. Nobody was here doing your job for you, you know."

"Yes...I realize that. Well, thanks for understanding."

"Tell Antonio I say 'hello' and hope he gets better soon."

"Okay, I'll tell him. See you Monday."

Maggie hung up, her eyes on Antonio.

"That wasn't so bad. But I just used up my holiday pay." She started laughing. "But Francis says that he hopes you're better!"

"I bet he does," Antonio griped. "Maggie, you have to quit that job of yours before our wedding. It's not that I don't want you to do what you love to do, but that snake is not going to let you off for the week at Christmas *and* a month for our honeymoon." The mention of their dream honeymoon caused Maggie's mind to float off into fantasy land, but Antonio's reminder of her nightmare boss snapped her back to reality.

"You're probably right. He already said Monday would be a late night, since I had a lot of catching up to do. I will probably have a hundred and twenty hours in next week and it will be like I never had a vacation, if you can even call it that. Don't get me wrong—I want to be here with you, really. But I also can't imagine what he's going to say about another five weeks!"

"You're going to be with me, Maggie, in New York and when I'm on tour. In our spare time, we can be in Italy. We can go to England too, if you want. But, Francis and your job are out of the picture. If you still want to work, then work for me. You can make costumes for Christmas, maybe fall...for Halloween we could have 3D ghosts coming out into the audience!" Antonio laughed. "Then there's Fourth of July, and who knows...You can design some fireworks! You can be completely in charge, and I will love whatever you do." Antonio appeared convinced that he presented a good argument.

"Alright," Maggie finally agreed, unable to refuse his offer. "I will give my two week notice when I get back. I also have Dana's wedding coming up, so I should probably just quit now, but I would hate to give Francis a heart attack! And, I do not wish to be on his bad side, either."

"No, Maggie, you don't." Antonio agreed.

She passed him a grin, while changing the subject.

"I saw your photo album."

"Oh no," he said, covering his face as if he was embarrassed, "my baby pictures?"

"Yes, I saw them all—pretty cute! Hopefully, if we actually do have a baby someday, it will look just like you!" She smiled sweetly at him.

"No, Maggie!" Antonio disagreed. "It should look like you!"

"Well," she laughed, "we probably don't have any control over that, do we?"

"Okay, here goes my first card trick. Wanna see?" Antonio grinned, holding out the deck. "Pick a card, any card..."

Maggie studied the deck.

"Okay, this one!" She held it in between both hands, to keep it hidden. "Now what? You guess which one I have, right?"

"Yep...so, is it the ace of diamonds?" Antonio asked, holding the deck with his good hand.

"Yes! How did you know?"

He laughed. "That's an easy one, but if you don't know, why should I tell you?"

"Hmm..." Maggie thought about it, "I remember, the first time I came to your show. You threw that card deck into the audience. Do you know what? I got the ace of hearts! It landed on the floor next to my boot. I still wonder. How did *that* happen?"

"You got the ace of hearts?" Antonio sounded surprised. "Do you still have it?"

"Of course, along with everything else you gave me...but...I have a confession."

"What. I hope it doesn't have anything to do with Francis."

"No. Promise not to be mad?" She paused, thinking how time had changed things. "I threw the t-shirt you gave me into the trash bin, after reading the tabloids. But Dana rescued it, so I still have it."

He gave her a rude look as the nurse came in.

"We have some lunch here for you...chicken noodle soup."

Maggie watched as the nurse set down the tray while announcing, "Allie, one of our staff members, wants a picture with you, and I said I would see what I could do."

Maggie noticed another nurse loitering in the doorway.

"Come on in!" Antonio waved. "You must be Allie?"

The young nurse tried to contain an ecstatic giggle as she marched into the room.

"I can't believe you're letting me do this! I'm so sorry if Janet pressured you into anything...I just casually mentioned the other day how much my kids adored your show, and—"

"It's fine! You can take my picture, but I'll have to wear a hat to cover my bad hair day and I insist that Maggie's in it too. And she would like a cup of soup also, and another carton of juice. Thank you." Antonio wore a cute smile.

The nurse nodded, returning his smile. "That shouldn't be a problem."

Maggie watched them both leave. She turned to Antonio and gave him a sweet look and then said, "Chad, your mamma told me what happened...that she and the mayor ended up in the newspap—"

"No, Maggie! Do *not* bring that up! You think I want a recap of my worst memory? Guess again. You wonder why I get mad when you read the tabloids and not only do you read them, you accuse me of what they say!" Antonio suddenly looked angry.

Maggie stood up and walked over to the window, crossing her arms as she looked out.

"Maggie, I'm talking to you!" Antonio sounded irritated. "Don't walk away from me!"

She turned around to challenge him, when a nurse brought in the extra soup.

Maggie waited until she left.

"So that's it...your *big* secret?" Maggie questioned him in disbelief. "How can you fire up at me while you are laying there in that...that...hospital bed...and I'm simply repeating what your mamma told me?"

Antonio managed to get out of bed and came and stood next to her by the window. He looked into her eyes, explaining, "That's her business, if she wants to tell. You're part of the family now, so maybe she thought you should know, but you are marrying me and I order you not to talk about it!"

"Fine, but obviously it wasn't true, so what's the big deal?" Maggie stared back at him. "Besides, your parents seem happily married!" She thought she made a good argument, but he still looked angry. "Why are you so upset?" she questioned him. "It's all in the past, so—"

"No Maggie, it's not. It's more than that. Don't you see? I would never have ended up where I am today without my brother's illness. I think about this every day. The fame, the money, my whole life is all because of him."

"I don't understand," Maggie said, confused.

"When Matteo was sick, we could hardly pay the hospital bills. The mayor asked what he could do to help. My mamma was too proud to ask for money but she asked for something else." He let out a sigh. "She had faith in me. She always did. She never wanted me to play hockey, but she loved my magic. So, she asked the mayor to help me turn it into a career. Perhaps, she thought if one son was miserable, she wanted to see the other one happy. And so it was. No sooner did she make her request, the mayor put together a huge advertising campaign and after that everything just took off. Life was never the same. But then Matteo died." Antonio looked deep in thought and then professed, "I'll always be in debt to him."

"Antonio," Maggie chose her words carefully, "you shouldn't think of it that way. Things just happen that are not in our control. I still wonder why Phillip did what he did, but if he hadn't, we would not be together." She gave him a sweet smile and he managed to smile back.

"I should send him a thank you card?" he mused.

"You are funny." Maggie reached out to him. "You know what? I'll always miss my mom and you'll always miss your brother, but we have each other. And that is a whole lot of happiness on top of the sadness." She gave him a sweet look. "We don't have to talk about it again. I promise." She wondered why he always came out smelling like a rose in all of their disputes.

He kissed her cheek and said, "Our soup's getting cold."

Maggie ate her soup, waiting for him to forget their previous discussion. She thought his temper simply stemmed from his affection for those he cared about. She felt lucky to be one of those people. She knew Antonio would always look out for her and have her best interest at heart.

When they were done with their soup, she watched as he took a bite of the cookie on his tray. He set it down. "This cookie tastes like a piece of cardboard."

Maggie smiled, holding up the bag of cookies that she had gotten from the bakery. "If you're nice, I'll share these with you," she said in a flirtatious tone.

Antonio lowered his eyebrows. "What? When am I not nice to you? I treat you like a princess, and you know it!"

Maggie took a deep breath, gazing up at the ceiling, questioning his suggestion.

"Are you going to show me more card tricks and tell me the rest of your secrets?" she finally asked.

He grinned.

"Hmmm, maybe I could show you one or two more card tricks. But I don't have any secrets. You should know better."

For a moment she felt guilty, figuring he was right.

She reached into the bag, grabbed a cookie and took a bite. "Yum, these are really good, but I'm not sure that I want to share them!" she teased. Antonio shrugged as if he could care less.

When she saw that she could not manipulate any begging on his part, she handed him her half-eaten cookie and laughed.

He laughed back. "Oh, I'm supposed to be revolted by your germs? Well, I'm not." He took a big bite and chewed it while watching her.

She tried to hold back a smile, but he grabbed her arm and said, "Kiss me, Maggie."

Maggie started to laugh as he puckered up with crumbs all over his face. She leaned over and kissed him.

"I suppose you aren't mad at me, or you wouldn't kiss me?"

"I was never mad at you, Maggie."

"Yes, you were! You get angry, and then I just have to shut up while you spout off about what has boiled your temper!"

"I just care about the people I love. You should know that. You're one of them."

Maggie looked into his eyes that looked softly at her as he confirmed what she already knew.

"I love you too," she told him.

The words seemed to come easy now. The two of them sat and gazed into each other's eyes, until they saw Mamma and Papa at the door.

"Greetings, we're back!" Papa said. "Sounds like you're checking out of here pretty soon...luckily not in a body bag!"

"Edmondo!" Elisabetta was disgusted by his humor.

Maggie and Antonio laughed quietly as his parents came into the room.

"The nurse said I can leave in a couple hours. They're just waiting for the doctor to give the okay." Antonio sounded excited.

"What's this?" Papa picked up the board game.

"Maggie bought that. She thought we might be bored, so she bought a board game." Antonio chuckled, finding humor.

Maggie gave him a sarcastic smile.

"Well, we are! So, let's play!" Papa said, opening up the packaging.

Mamma leaned over his shoulder, as he read the instructions. "Object of the game..." Papa began.

Maggie listened while he read the directions, ready to spend the morning in a new activity.

They played the game and Papa ended up winning both times, claiming it was his favorite game ever. Antonio laughed, saying, "See where I get that from!"

Maggie watched the doctor as he signed the release papers, turning them over to Antonio who was already prying off his hospital band.

Antonio made a grand appearance after changing out of his hospital gown.

"You were cute in your gown," Maggie said, her eyes darting over his attire, "but now you look even better!"

He grinned at her while holding her hand as they walked out of the room, leaving the hospital.

"Hopefully I won't be back here any time soon—not my idea of a fun time."

"We had fun!"

"No, Maggie, we can have a lot more fun than that," he said as they made their way to the exit.

Just about the time Maggie registered happy thoughts to be leaving, they met up with Bradley and Stanley near the back entrance of the hospital.

Maggie immediately noticed that Bradley was preoccupied.

"Dude, there is—I am just warning you—a nightmare of reporters out there. They're swarming *everywhere*," Bradley informed.

Maggie's jaw dropped as she took in a quick breath.

"Bunch of lunatics," she heard Antonio speak under his breath, as he looked momentarily bewildered by the next chain of events. He stopped and turned towards Maggie, giving instructions. "Listen. Walk out as quickly as possible. Do not trip down the steps. Don't look at anyone, and don't say anything. Just keep going. They want information, but there's nothing to tell. I lived! That's it!"

Antonio kept his good arm around Maggie and his eyes on the limo as they walked through the crowd, amidst the noise of the relentless reporters:

"Are you still able to use your arm?"

"Is there any permanent damage to the nerves?"

"When are you two getting married?"

"Is it true that you are already expecting your first child? And is it a boy?"

When they got inside the limo, Antonio tucked his good hand behind his head and wore a big smile on his face, indicating he was glad that was over.

Maggie laughed. "I can't believe they think we are having a baby. That is so funny!"

"So you like them now, because they are funny?" He squeezed her hand, and Maggie rested her head against his good shoulder.

Maggie followed Antonio into his room.

Her eyes watched his as they circled around the room, betraying evidence of her staying there. She had not meant to leave such a mess.

"Did you like staying here?" Antonio wanted to know.

"Not without you," Maggie confessed.

"So, what did you do in here, besides page through my photo album?"

"I watched a movie, read my book, and...not much."

 She tried to pick up a few things.

"I see." His eyes stayed curious.

"What?" Maggie questioned him. "More secrets?"

Antonio grinned. "What do you think, Maggie?"

"I'm not sure, but there better not be any!" she warned.

"There are secrets, Maggie! Lots of them!" He gave her a look to entice her into further questioning.

"What!" Maggie sounded upset. "What, Chad, what!?"

He looked flattered that he could get to her.

"Just say it! What?" Maggie sulked.

He placed his good arm around her and hugged her tight, while he whispered in her ear, "You will never know what I am thinking about doing to you right now!"

Maggie brought her arms onto his chest and leaned back so that she could see his face in view. She looked into his eyes and watched his lips as they slowly moved onto hers. He kissed her gently, and she kissed him back.

"You can still hug me?" She took notice of his one-armed cuddle.

"What do you want to do?" Antonio asked. "Another movie?"

Maggie bit her bottom lip. "Is that what you want to do?"

"Sure," he agreed, giving her a flirtatious stare.

She went over to the movies that were lined up in a perfect row.

"Don't you have any chick flicks? You know...romance? All you have is action adventure...things blowing up...fires...isn't that too much like your own life?"

"So you are saying I'm not romantic?" He turned on the TV and popped his choice of film into the DVD player. She stood watching as it came on, realizing he was in fact the most romantic guy she had ever met.

He lay down against the arm of the couch, facing the TV and motioning her over to him. Maggie came over and sat on top of him, facing him with a silly grin, waiting for him to read her mind.

Antonio laughed out loud. "You're testing my strength after I just got out of the hospital?" he questioned her. "I'm on pain meds, barely awake, and you want me to meet your challenge?"

"Are you going to fight me off?" She knew he was completely exhausted.

"That would be 'no,' so now I have to worry you're going to take advantage of me? I can hardly wait," Antonio teased as he watched her lay down carefully next to him, against his good arm.

Maggie kissed him softly on the cheek and soon noticed his eyes were starting to drift shut. She grabbed a blanket that was draped across the top of the couch and covered them. She watched him until he fell asleep, and then she kissed him softly on the cheek again and snuggled next to him.

www.lovetheillusion.com/402.htm

Maggie opened the lid as she inhaled the aroma of pancakes and scrambled eggs, the results of Antonio's morning room service order. They sat on top of his bed, enjoying their time together before she had to leave again. Antonio kept his eye on her and offered, "I'm going to ride with you to the airport. Salvador's waiting for us downstairs."

"Are you feeling better today?"

"Still a bit loopy, but I should be good as new by the wedding." He winked at her, leaving her flattered. "So, you think I'm a gentleman now—not the player you thought when we first met?" he asked. Maggie blushed at his remark as she ate her pancakes, wondering why he even asked. "I have something for you and I hope it doesn't change your opinion," he explained.

"What's that, *Antonio*?" She watched as he walked over to the mahogany dresser.

"This," he told her, as he opened the top drawer and pulled out a red slip made from lace, signaling lingerie. He held it up, and then threw it on the bed next to her.

Maggie laughed, realizing his latest purchase.

"That's funny. You think I'm going to wear this for you?"

"Well, it's not for me!" He smirked. "Next time you sleep next to me, you can wear *that!*"

"And you picture us sleeping? ...Yeah, right."

"Think what you want!" He grinned.

She grinned back. "Sorry, you're still a perfect gentleman. As for me, I cannot wait to work on ruining your reputation, *Antonio!*"

Maggie sat in the limo, wishing she did not have to leave. Antonio had his hand resting on her leg as she leaned against him. The radio played, taking up the space of the words that neither one could speak. But now it would only be weeks until the wedding. And when the limo pulled up to the airport, Antonio leaned over and kissed Maggie goodbye.

Chapter 25

It was now time to face Francis, hopefully for the last time.

Francis stood an uncomfortable foot away from Maggie, with a lighter at the end of his cigarette. "Hey Louis," Jeff yelled from across the room. "I got first class for all three of us. She can sit right between us."

Francis turned around to acknowledge Jeff. "It's a short week away," Francis exclaimed, letting out a puff of smoke, "'til the Paris-spectacular showdown. I'm surely going to be nominated for 'Most original designer.' *And* I made sure that we have front row seats! Too bad, Maggie, you're going to miss it."

Before she could respond, Jeff announced, "You ought to see your replacement Maggie...long blonde hair that hits her rear and she's got knockout cleavage in that dress Louis designed for her to wear!"

"Well...sounds like a wonderful time. It's such a shame I will miss the event." Maggie turned around when she bumped into Grace.

"Maggie! I brought you a cake from Saint Sugar of London. Only an hour left in the day and then you leave us all behind. I'm really going to miss you." Grace made a sad face.

"What's it say?" Jeff wanted to know. "Ta, Ta? Or did you get lucky and find a cake that says, 'Good luck swinging from the ball and chain?'"

"Funny, Jeff." Maggie gave him a rude look. "It will be hard not to miss you."

"She won't miss us for long. I give it three months," Francis made his prediction, "and then she'll be back. Antonio's probably riding around in his limo right now with all the sexy ladies!"

"Maggie," Grace came to her defense, "I think that you should leave a sympathy card for your replacement...uh, now, what's her name?"

"Cami," Francis announced, "Lefebvre. And I got to admit, she could give any of us a fever." He smiled wickedly. "Why don't you cut that cake, Maggie, and bring me a piece. I hope it has buttercream icing and not that cool whip kind. That would be a disappointment. It's such a shame when they put that on cake."

Sally and Matt came around the corner.

"Maggie, we got you a going away present. It's my favorite romance trilogy," Sally explained. "—something you can start reading on the plane to Italy."

"She's not going to have time to read," Francis declared. "She's sewing for DeLuca now!"

"That can't take long to sew *him* a few dresses," Jeff sneered.

"That would be costumes, Jeff." Maggie despised his comment. "Not dresses! And I'm designing them, not sewing them!"

"Well, you'll have to make yourself a few," Jeff explained, "so you can attend all his high society events. And soon you'll be parading around in maternity clothes as the paparazzi follow you around so that they can get a picture of Antonio's first-born!"

"Don't worry, Jeff. I'm sure my life with Antonio will be much more pleasant than my date with you." Maggie smiled weakly.

"OOhh...! She's getting mean now!" Jeff looked at Francis for sympathy. "Can't wait for Cami!"

"I feel so sorry for Cami." Maggie frowned. "You'd better pay her a decent salary, Francis, since she has to put up with the two of you!"

"That won't be much," Francis revealed. "She's just a retail manager from Gigi and Jane's. But she's got a spicy wardrobe every time I see her and I only have to pay her half of what I pay you!" Francis told Maggie.

Maggie put a piece of cake onto a plate.

"Sounds like you know just how to have your cake and eat it too." She smiled wryly at him.

"Speaking of," Francis said as he took a seat at his desk, "Baylines just ordered from us! A hundred dresses at a pound a piece! Time to celebrate with a piece of cake and I almost forgot to mention, they'll be at the fashion extravaganza next week and I think we ought to party with them after the show. Get ready for a good time Jeff, but Matt and Sally, don't feel bad if you decide to turn in early. Sorry, I was *not* able to get first class for the two of you by the way, but it's a short flight, so it won't matter much. I really need to get myself a private jet. That would be *so* much more convenient than having to worry about the British Airways' fly times."

"You deserve it, Fran!" Matt chuckled as he took a bite of cake. "I can just picture you now sitting right next to the pilot!"

Maggie glared at Francis as she approached his desk with his piece of cake. She was so sick and tired of him and very happy to be leaving.

But she felt bad for the rest of the staff that she left behind—not to mention, the new girl, Cami, who had no idea the "catastrophe" that awaited her.

"You know, Francis," Maggie stood next to his desk, "I want to thank you for being so kind to employ me for nearly a year! And I just don't think I can put into words exactly what I feel when I walk out of here today. So, I hope this makes things a bit clearer." She held the plate of cake in her hand and landed it face down on top of his latest proposal. "There! You and Jeff can share that!" She grinned wildly while Grace, Matt, and Sally laughed uncontrollably as Francis stood silent for perhaps the first time in his life! Jeff had his hand over his mouth and she thought that was a perfect place for that. She threw her coat over her shoulder and walked out of the office with the one thing she could not leave behind—the photo of her and Antonio that sat on her desk.

A cheery event followed. Dana's wedding was perfect and all the dresses looked amazing. And now Maggie was even more excited to marry Antonio. Dana had moved out now, and Maggie felt strange and somewhat lonely in the flat all by herself at night. Now she really missed Antonio as she anticipated their life together.

It was only two weeks before she was to fly out to Italy, where they would be married. She began packing her things, which were few because she had told Dana and Shane to take everything. Shane had bought a house and surprised Dana, who up until this point thought she had been the saver.

Maggie stood in the empty space. Memories lurked, bittersweet. She remembered the endless conversations that she and Dana had regarding dating and men, and now it seemed a bygone. They each found their perfect someone, and the past struggles would be long forgotten. Maggie absorbed the solitude, and vacancy of their place, now empty. She felt happy to be moving on, but at the same time, a big chapter of her life was coming to a close—as if someone held her life's storybook and slammed it shut, and now she would be living in a sequel. *What was next?* She had no idea. But she knew that she would be with Antonio, and she knew that she loved him.

Lost in her thoughts, she heard a knock at the door. She approached, opening the door, noticing a light snow descending in the background. A delivery man waited, handing her a package.

"Can you please sign?"

"Sure," she said, adding her signature at his request. She wondered who would be sending her certified mail. However, she remembered her lease agreement was ending two months early.

"Thanks," she said, closing the door.

Maggie set the envelope on the table, and returned to finish some packing. Afterwards, she made herself some lunch, and decided to call Dana.

"Dana! It's Maggie." She immediately heard Dana's voice engaged in laugher on the other end, just like old times.

"Hey, did I tell you, just because we don't share the flat anymore, I can still recognize your voice!"

Maggie laughed.

"I hate to bother you, but we seem to have gotten some contract termination in the mail that we both have to sign, since our lease is ending two months early."

"Right," Dana went on to explain, "I took care of that already. Don't be upset, but when you were visiting Antonio in the hospital, I signed your name because you were gone. He said that he would keep our security deposits, and not to worry about it."

"Okay, well, I just got a registered letter, so I thought...never mind then."

Maggie looked at the envelope.

"Did you want to come out with us tonight?" Dana asked. "We're going out to that new Danish restaurant, and then...who knows? Do you want to come?"

"Sure. It's getting so strange and quiet in here—and lonely, all by myself. You're gone, not to mention I'm standing in vacancy with no furniture, no cooler...the only thing left is my bed, and when I'm in it, I'm sleeping!"

Dana laughed. "I miss you too! Come over at six!"

"Okay, see you then!"

Maggie tore open the end of the manila envelope that was the size of a legal document. Her eyes scanned the papers in front of her as she stood in complete shock...*A prenuptial agreement?* Of all the times Antonio had shocked her, this seemed to top it all. She held the documents and read each word carefully. It was unbelievable! There had to be some mistake. But there it was, right in front of her.

She viewed the space requiring her signature. She saw the signatures of Stanley and Chad, or Antonio to be exact. Maggie studied his signature. Confident it was his, she ran her finger along the indentation left in the paper after signing. It left a trace of ink on her finger—no chance it was a photocopy that Stanley possibly forged to cover the company's assets.

Maggie became disgusted. She always thought he was so sure about their relationship. Now, she wondered what to do with his latest surprise. Obviously, it was what it was...no point in calling to renegotiate their terms of marriage. She was not a gold-digger! How dare he? He pursued her! He begged for her trust, and finally she gave it and now this?

How could he?

She thought about how he threw money around like there was no tomorrow. He had never spared spending on her either, but now she was to sign a prenuptial? *What in the world—just one more brick in the wall, because he was a hot celebrity? Unreal!* Maggie knew one thing for sure—that his ego would not tolerate her walking out on him. Maybe this was his way of reinforcing his own concern. Once she got accustomed to the finer things, he would have her trapped, just like the magician that he was. Maggie felt powerless. She was completely under his spell, and it was too late to have second thoughts.

The room was empty. She had quit her job. She had nothing but Chad…or Antonio, whichever she was to think of him now. Maggie stewed over the documents again, and again, until it was time to get ready to go out with Dana and Shane. Maybe their opinion was just what she needed.

"Hi Dana, your place looks great. It's really coming along!"

"Hey," Dana explained, "we have a bit of remodeling to do, but it will be fun. Shane said I can pick out whatever I want, and he will do the work to fix it."

"Maggie!" Shane came around the corner. "Congratulations, by the way! What can I mix you to drink?"

"Ha!" Maggie laughed at the joke that would never die, as long as she lived. "That would be *nothing* Shane, but it's so thoughtful of you to think of me."

Shane and Dana joined in laughter, and soon the three of them were out the door.

At the restaurant, Maggie felt strange thinking that Dana and Shane were now married.

"So you miss me, Maggie?" Dana asked. "You are too quiet. Is something else wrong?"

Maggie cast her eyes away from the table, falling victim to Dana's ability to read her like an open book. She knew, however, that she needed their opinion on what was eating away at her all day.

"I have to ask you something," she finally announced, looking Dana in the eye. "For me, it came as a bit of a shock."

"Did I tell you, Maggie? Nothing will shock me!" Dana teased.

Shane laughed. "What? Go ahead—shock us!" He wore a goofy look. *Why did he come?*

Maggie contemplated her wording.

"Remember when I called and said that I got a registered letter? And I thought it was our lease agreement?"

"Yes, but I told you I took care of that!" Dana reiterated.

"Guess what it was!" Maggie said, clapping her hands together.

Dana and Shane both looked completely clueless.

"Prenuptial agreements...ten pages!" Maggie told them, in an aggravated tone. "Can you believe it?"

Dana made a perplexed face and turned to Shane.

"What?" Shane started laughing. "You want my opinion, since when?"

"Why not, Shane, you are of the male species. How do you define a prenuptial agreement?" Maggie challenged him.

"Uh, well, under the circumstances, and they are unusual... he's a celeeeebrity...so not *that* strange. As for Dana and me, well, we share everything, and I never thought about how we would split things up, if...no, I would never have one. It would be like making a prediction that maybe you weren't going to make it. Why get married, if you're not sure?"

Dana seemed happy with his answer, but wanted to reassure her. "Maggie, I really think Antonio loves you. I only saw you together briefly on the night of his show, but I would not hesitate to just sign the papers. Like Shane said, he lives in a completely different world, right? Maybe his company's making him do it."

"Right," Shane agreed, "that's a good point."

I doubt it. Maggie shared her frustration. "Nobody makes him do *anything*— believe me. And I'm so far into this now…it's too late to turn back." She shook her head in contempt.

"It will be fine, Maggie. You love him, and you know he loves you!" Dana assured her.

"It's just…" Maggie searched for the right words. "I'm not a gold-digger. It makes me feel like one. He's always buying me stuff, and money doesn't seem to matter to him. So, if that's the case, then why this? It makes me second guess who he is. It comes down to trust. I just *finally* decide that I trust him. And only recently, I was able to tell him that I loved him. The walls that were up came down. Now they are all up again! Don't you see? He acts like he's into tradition, and so old-fashioned. You would not believe…" Maggie huffed. "Never mind, I will just shut up now."

"What?" Dana asked. "Don't be all mysterious with us. You can tell us anything."

Maggie scrunched her brow at Shane, and then he said, "What, do you want me to leave?"

"No, you can stay. It's just that…" Maggie paused. "…it's too embarrassing."

"What?" Shane asked. "Now I'm for sure staying."

They all laughed, cutting the tension in half.

"When we are together, you know..." Maggie got to the point. "We've not had sex!"

Shane passed Maggie his inquisitive glare. "What? No way! What shade of white are you wearing, Maggie, because we're all going to need our sunglasses on when you come down the aisle."

Dana laughed and elbowed him, letting him know he was done talking. *Shane was always so helpful.*

"Yeah," Maggie looked at the two of them, "when I first saw Antonio, I had a completely different impression. But underneath it all, he is a true gentleman! And he knows I've been hurt in my other relationships, and I think he's sensitive to that, trying to prove that he's not like the others. He seems determined to wait because it's what I originally wanted. Now it's driving me crazy, but—" Maggie recalled her past relationships, and then professed, "He was worth waiting for."

Shane pushed away his plate, indicating he was done eating. "That was good, and I did *not* mean the food."

Maggie gave him a sarcastic stare.

"And I'm sorry," Shane continued, "but that is one gigantic ring he bought you! What's that worth—half the Sears Tower?" Shane's eyes were glued to her finger in disbelief.

Maggie thought Shane was a distraction as she tried to muddle through Antonio's latest surprise.

"Well, thanks for listening," Maggie told Dana, "but I guess I will have to sort this out on my own. I never want to be divorced from him, ever, but maybe deep down he has doubts about us. And that is troubling to me. He always acts like he doesn't—it's always me! Only recently, when he was in the hospital, I finally told him that I loved him. Did I think it before? Yes! But before I said it, I wanted to make sure it was the real thing! People say it all the time, and then like the weather, it comes and goes."

"Did I tell you," Dana gave out advice, "you have to have faith in your love, and that it's real. Stick to it and it will sort itself out. Honestly, if I was you, I would just sign it and be done with it."

That night Maggie tried to read her latest novel, but kept closing it, pondering the prenuptials. She wondered what Antonio was doing right now, as she held onto her Cheetos bookmark. *Does he know I have the papers? Of course he does.* He always knew everything. He would hover over her in his protective mode, concerned for her best interest, and now this! She knew she loved him, regardless. She would rather be miserable with him than live alone without him. The media and his celebrity would undoubtedly add to their difficulties, but she would have to put up with it all. *Now the prenuptials were on the list as well!* She contemplated, but eventually concluded that every time she doubted him, he gave her more reason to trust him. And the battles they fought seemed to stem around his love and concern for her and those he loved. She thought about it. And she knew what she had to do—*trust him*. Trust him that he knew what he was doing and had their best interest at heart. For whatever reason, she knew he meant it for the best. And she remembered the words Antonio said to her, "Maggie, I will never call it quits with you." She felt the same. Now she would ignore what logic told her—Call it off! Avoid the scandalous possibilities! Instead, she would believe things were not as they appeared, and she would follow her heart.

I will marry him, anyways.

Maggie got out of bed and went to get a pen from her purse. It was a blue ink pen, and she thought about how it could represent the "something blue" on their wedding day. And she was ready to take a leap of faith. She took the cap off the pen. She stared at the document one last time. She held the pen in a tight grip as she brought it to the paper, stamped with a seal, as if Stanley and Antonio's signatures mattered the most.

She took a deep breath and signed her name. There was no turning back.

Chapter 26

Maggie stepped off the plane, excited to finally be in Italy. Soon they would be together.

Antonio met her at the airport in a limo, and in a short time they arrived at his estate. She stood amazed by its beauty and charm—the real life photo, just like the one she had seen. She walked alongside him, up a brick pathway, as she viewed the river that ran behind the property.

He got to the door and turned around as she fell into his arms. He gazed into her face and slowly moved in to kiss her. She felt their lips touch, and she closed her eyes to take it all in. He kissed her again, and then opened the door, inviting her in.

"Your arm is all better?" Maggie asked, after feeling his embrace.

"Good as new, except for the scar." He gave a smile. Maggie smiled back as they entered the house where they were greeted by Daphne, their little white Maltese.

She could smell fresh food…something cooking…

"It smells good in here!" Maggie said, bending down to meet Daphne who showered her with affection.

"Mamma's making spaghetti," Antonio announced, passing her a wink. Now she recalled when he made spaghetti for her—one of her favorite memories.

"Hi Maggie, I am so glad you're finally here." Mamma gave a warm welcome. "Dinner's in an hour, so…perfect timing!" Mamma was pleased to see the two of them together. "Papa is out back getting some wood for the fireplace, just to take the chill out of the air."

"I'll show you where you can put your things." Antonio took the lead, as a gardener assisted bringing in her luggage. She followed Antonio down the hall, and up the steps.

At the top of the steps stood a mahogany wall dresser similar in style to the one he had in New York.

"This is beautiful!" Maggie ran her hand across the top of it.

"Tell Papa, he made that." Antonio smiled.

"And you have one like it," she recalled.

"Wait until you see the guest room. He made the furniture in there too."

They entered the guest room, decorated with bright and cheery colors of light blue and yellow. The furniture was white, and a handmade quilt covered the bed, matching the rest of the decor. There were four windows, all in a row, lined up against the back wall and a bathroom off to the side.

Maggie turned back around to look at Antonio, who seemed pleased to show her around.

"This place you have...it's beautiful!"

"It's our place now, Maggie. I hope you like living here." He placed his arms around her.

"You know, I don't care where I live as long as I'm with you," she told him. It seemed as if he had something on his mind, and then she remembered the prenuptials.

"I almost forgot. I have something for you." She stepped away, proceeding to her luggage. "I signed," Maggie told him, "just in case you were wondering. This *is* what you were waiting for, right? The last detail before we can be married." She passed the envelope to him. Antonio reached out for the documents and as she stood empty handed, he locked her eyes in his.

"Thanks," he finally said, seeming to own a mysterious agenda. Maggie watched him as he stood with the documents in hand. Now she wondered. Would he open up the envelope and check to see if her signature was really there?

Antonio appeared deep in thought, shifting his eyes between her and the envelope. "So, you did not hesitate to sign?" he questioned. "Do you think we need this?"

She stood still, wondering what she could say without offending him.

Finally, she spoke. "I understand that you have a lot to lose if things don't work out, and marriage is always somewhat of a gamble, but I am willing to take that chance. That is what you want to hear, right?" She tried to manage a smile.

Suddenly, he tore the envelope in half and let it fall to the floor. Antonio stood still, his dark eyes looking into hers, the corner of his mouth signaling a grin. Maggie stood in shock as she looked down to the floor where the envelope now laid in two pieces.

"What did you just do, *Antonio?*" she asked. "I signed them. Really, I did!"

"No, Maggie!" He held her hands in his, gazing into her eyes. "We do not need this! There never was a prenuptial agreement. It's a fake."

She tried to erase her look of confusion, opening her mouth to speak, but finding no words when he continued, "But, I do need to know that you trust me though, beyond a shadow of doubt, regardless of 'the illusion' of what appears to be. And despite the illusion, whatever it may be, you always need to believe in the truth, that I love you with all my heart. If you marry me, you need to remember that. When we were apart, you could not feel my love, but it was still there. It's like that."

Maggie felt herself blush. "I guess I did well to follow my heart, instead of my head."

Antonio kept her in a gape, as he told her, "Everything that is mine...is yours." He stepped closer to her, bringing them into an embrace. He kissed her cheek and next her lips. Her doubts now removed, Maggie felt his love. She loved his kiss, and she loved him.

Maggie stood at the back of the chapel, Antonio waiting for her up front. Her father was beside her, ready to walk her down the aisle that was decorated with big white bows attached to the pews and flowers built into each ensemble.

Maggie's dress shimmered, emitting a radiance all of its own when the light hit it. A portrait of what she had foreseen now adorned her, as she knew that she had finally found true love. Her hair stacked into a pile of curls on top of her head, she held a single rose in her hand. Her love for her mother lingered in her heart as she recalled the rose that she left on her mother's grave, symbolizing that love. And the love that she held in her heart for her mother gave birth to a yet another, one that would last forever—the love that she celebrated today.

www.lovetheillusion.com/416.htm

The music started playing, and Maggie waited for her cue—the violin. She peered into the rows of loved ones, all arrived for their big day. And as the violin played Vivaldi, she took her first steps. Her father lent her his arm and a smile, as they walked down the white runner. Maggie recalled the fashion shows, feeling like the queen of the runway. Even Francis came to mind, a bittersweet thought. Had it not been for him, she would not be making her steps towards Antonio to spend the rest of her life with him.

She passed Dana and Shane, and thought about how it seemed just moments ago when they were exchanging their own vows. Maggie smiled into a row filled with her brothers, and her niece, who wore a ballroom style dress all of her own. Maggie winked at her, watching her face light up as she viewed Maggie's gorgeous wedding dress. Amidst familiar faces, there were a few that were not, and Maggie was anxious to meet them.

Finally, she saw in front of her, watching her, the one she loved, unlike any other, waiting for her—Antonio. She melted into his facial expression that words could not depict.

As they faced each other to speak their vows, Maggie returned his smile. They both already wore their rings, deciding to leave that part out. She glanced down at the DeLuca ring that she first wore to the party, after his show, when she had wondered how, in his world of delusion, they would ever find love. Months later, she wore it again, realizing that love is stronger than anything else.

She listened as Antonio spoke his vows, which he wrote specifically for her: "When love is but an illusion, it brings heartache and pain. But when it's real, it's magical. My love for you, Maggie, is real. And with every beat of my heart, I will love you, protect you, and cherish you, until death do us part. And like a hot flame, burning in a ring of eternity, so will be our love. Never forget, I will always love you."

Maggie listened to his words, treasuring his love, realizing she loved him too for all of eternity. She would never doubt their love again, knowing that whatever the future would bring, their love would survive. Then she spoke her own vows: "When I met you, I was afraid of love—like the fire around the ring, I feared getting burned. My walls of protection were stronger than steel, but you shattered my fears, removed my doubt, and melted my insecurities. Now I stand before the person that held the key to my heart and knew how to heal its pain. The words that once I feared to speak, now I will say before all, in front of the world. I want them to know, I not only trust you, I love you."

The preacher smiled as he said, "I now pronounce you husband and wife. You may kiss the bride."

Maggie smiled at Antonio, who looked just as happy to kiss her as he ever had. The music started playing again, and they turned to face their loved ones in the pews. For a moment, Maggie felt like she was on stage, and teased him by digging her nails into his hand. He returned her gesture, as he brought their hands into the air. Her mind flashed back to being on stage, when Antonio passed her through the ring of fire. Now that memory would forever stand as a symbol of their love.

And when they took their first steps to make their exit, she realized Antonio's latest surprise, as if it fell right out of his sleeve. She noticed a friend in the front pew. How could she have missed her? It was Julia.

Julia had seen their photo in the New York Times. After reading the announcement of their engagement, she got ahold of Stanley, who assured Antonio that she did not sound like a reporter. He took the call, and decided to fly her out for their special day.

Maggie's face glowed, radiantly, and she soon ran up to Julia and gave her a big hug. "You are right about love, Julia. It is strong."

The reception followed, and it was time for pictures!

www.lovetheillusion.com/417.htm

www.lovetheillusion.com/418.htm

After the reception, with the paparazzi at bay, Antonio drew his final conclusion: "We are out of here, Mrs. DeLuca."

THE END

www.lovetheillusion.com/420.htm

Post Script

It seemed as if Antonio and Maggie finally reached their fairytale ending. But after three short months, Maggie was sitting in her home studio overlooking the river. Antonio was away on business and he was expected home that evening. Meanwhile, she worked on designing costumes for an upcoming show, when she heard the door buzzer.

She stepped outside to meet up with a delivery man. Once again, she held certified mail. She had been served papers. Her heart sank as she anticipated the worst. Antonio had left in a hurry—unexpectedly on business—and did not say what it was about. Did he have second thoughts about their marriage? Maggie thought not, dismissing her darkest fears. However, Francis Louis was suing her for leaving his company and taking the business with her. The lawsuit was for $3.5 million, and Maggie's heart was breaking as she thought about telling Antonio the news.

That evening, she held the papers up to him, with tears in her eyes, but once again he put her fears to rest. "No, Maggie! He will not get our money. I already hired the best attorney money can buy. Where do you think I've been for the past few days? I was hoping you wouldn't have to know about it."

"I'm so sorry," Maggie said softly, feeling upset to have dragged Francis into their marriage.

"It's okay. It's not your fault." He spoke his words sweetly as he leaned in to kiss her. She felt the touch of his lips and knew in her heart that she would always carry the weight of a pessimist. But he would always shine through her gloom with his optimism, and that would bring a sunny day.

Then, she remembered the words that a wise old woman once told her: "Love is strong. It will push through anything."

It seems like just yesterday when I told Maggie that. And I could not wait to tell the story of how she finally found true love. But now I will tell you this...

The affairs of the heart will always be

A mystery unknown

As we hold on and we let go

And often never know

What reaches for our very soul

To journey far beyond

What we can see

In hopes to find

The magical powers of love

Many people doubt that they will ever find that special person to make their life complete. And while heartache comes and goes, *LOVE is worth waiting for.*

Julia

WHAT'S NEXT??

www.lovetheillusion.com/501.htm

CPSIA information can be obtained at www.ICGtesting.com
Printed in the USA
LVOW100635090713

341812LV00005B/14/P